Suzanne woke abruptly out of the middle of a deep sleep. She couldn't put her finger on what it was, but something had awakened her. She lay there a moment, her heart beating fast as she tried to isolate the source of her unease. The room was engulfed in blackness except for the luminous dial on her bedside clock, which read one A.M.

She shifted, and a slight soreness brought everything flooding back . . . Devin touching her, making love to her, falling asleep beside her. A smile brightened her face. So this was how it felt to let go completely.

Languidly she rolled to her side and reached for him, but found only Bartok, purring in his sleep. She sat up quickly in bed, her heart pounding. Surely Devin hadn't left. Then she heard faint sounds of movement coming from another part of the house. Devin. It had to be.

That must have been what woke me, she thought as she slid out of bed. She switched on a small lamp. Sure enough, Devin's shirt and shoes lay scattered on the floor. Hunting for her robe, she moved quickly around the room.

"Devin," Suzanne called out as she moved through the living room past the piano. He wasn't there.

Then she noticed the light shining from beneath her study door. She opened the door. "Devin, my—" she began as she caught sight of him standing in the middle of the room. The words died on her lips as he lifted his face to hers. He was holding a piece of Valentin's transcribed music in one hand and her notes for it in the other.

And he looked like a boy with his hand caught in the cookie jar. . . .

SOMETHING WAS WRONG ...

PRAISE FOR DEBORAH NICHOLAS'
SILENT SONATA

"*SILENT SONATA* has everything! Passion, romance, danger, and more than a touch of magic. A thoroughly enjoyable read with great characters, plot with enough twists and turns to knit a sweater, and a hero who could save my life any day—this one's a winner."
—Eileen Dreyer

AND FOR HER PREVIOUS NOVEL
NIGHT VISION

"*NIGHT VISION* IS A FIRST-RATE SUSPENSE NOVEL THAT IS TIGHTLY WROUGHT . . . A FAST-PACED, EXCITING STORY. . . . Well-rounded, thoroughly convincing characters, the love scenes are passionate and vivid, and the author has a fine ear for dialogue. . . . Eminently readable and realistic."
—*Gothic Journal*

"The past and present are blended well in this intriguing story. Simone and Mark are fully dimensional characters with a lot of charm and energy. . . . *An entertaining and action-filled read. Don't miss it!*"
—*Rendezvous*

"SIZZLING. . . . An interesting, well-written plot that keeps you in suspense as Ms. Nicholas peels the mystery away page after frightening page."
—*Affaire de Coeur*

"A CRACKERJACK SUSPENSE THRILLER WITH PSYCHIC OVERTONES THAT GIVE IT AN EXTRA SPICY AND UNUSUAL FLAVOR."
—*Rave Reviews*

"*A TRUE SPELLBINDER! NIGHT VISION* has it all—mystery, the supernatural, and breath-taking romance. Don't miss it!
—Meryl Sawyer

Also by Deborah Nicholas
NIGHT VISION

Silent Sonata

DEBORAH NICHOLAS

A DELL BOOK

Published by
Dell Publishing
a division of
Bantam Doubleday Dell Publishing Group, Inc.
1540 Broadway
New York, New York 10036

If you purchased this book without a cover you should be aware that this book is stolen property. It was reported as "unsold and destroyed" to the publisher and neither the author nor the publisher has received any payment for this "stripped book."

Copyright © 1994 by Deborah Martin Gonzales

All rights reserved. No part of this book may be reproduced or transmitted in any form or by any means, electronic or mechanical, including photocopying, recording, or by any information storage and retrieval system, without the written permission of the Publisher, except where permitted by law.

The trademark Dell® is registered in the U.S. Patent and Trademark Office.

ISBN: 0-440-21354-1

Printed in the United States of America

Published simultaneously in Canada

May 1994

10 9 8 7 6 5 4 3 2 1

OPM

To my two wonderful buddies, Suzanne Broussard and Susan Rosenberg, who supported my venture into paranormal suspense from the very beginning.

To Barbara Colley, writer and friend, who knows a great deal about music and a great deal more about writing (and about listening to cranky writers complain).

And to my truly marvelous sister-in-law, Audrey Gonzales, who gave me comfort in a difficult time and made it possible for me to write this book.

ACKNOWLEDGMENTS

This book could not have been written without the help of the following people:

The staff of the University of Chicago, particularly the Music Department, which answered all my questions, even the peculiar ones.

Sheila Weber, who showed me around Chicago and patiently waited while I questioned nearly everyone I met.

Mary Lou Fuenzalida, friend and fellow writer, who read and critiqued the music aspects of this novel.

Gregory R. Redenius, Assistant House Manager of the Chicago Symphony Orchestra, who gave me the most informative tour of Orchestra Hall a writer could ever ask for.

And Maureen Kaucher, who took the time to provide essential research on the music world in Chicago and then graciously critiqued my manuscript for errors.

Thanks to all of you.

# 1
♪

Even the applause of the nearly three thousand people filling New York's Carnegie Hall couldn't drown out the thunderous beat of Devin Bryce's heart as he prepared to play his third piece in the recital.

Damn! he thought, instantly realizing what his heightened pulse meant. Not now. Not tonight. Tonight he wanted to keep charge of his own soul.

As he shifted his position on the piano bench and waited for the applause to die, he recognized all the signs of impending possession. The flood of adrenaline. The tension in every muscle. The cold sweat breaking out on his brow. And his fingers, poised above the piano keys, ignoring his mind's commands as if they had a mind of their own.

Then came the plunge into the abyss, the total loss of control as his fingertips struck a chord with dramatic force.

As usual, he had no idea what the chord would be until it sounded. This time the opening to Chopin's Polonaise in A-flat Major rang out. The recital program didn't list the "Heroic" Polonaise, of course. It listed Rachmaninoff's Prelude in G-sharp Minor. Nonetheless, the stunning power of Chopin filled the hall, silencing a few quick whispers from the audience.

Now came the exhilaration, the rush as fingerings he'd never used became his own. Flashes of Poland clouded his vision—not modern Poland, but Poland in the nineteenth century, when a young Chopin had trod there . . .

through willow-lined fields, mountain lanes, Warsaw streets. Devin's breath came in quick gasps. His fingers pounded, then caressed the keys. Reverberating sound, familiar yet alien too, permeated his blood, his lungs, his heart until he thought he'd explode into oblivion. He fought the foreign presence, not wanting to relinquish his will, not tonight at Carnegie Hall. Yet he fought a losing battle.

Sweat drenched his shirt beneath his tailcoat. The audience's awed silence told him they recognized the subtle difference between the pieces he'd played moments before and the one now played by his auspicious "guest." But the audience didn't know why such a difference existed. Thank God. He'd do everything in his power to keep that secret.

For now, he relinquished his resistance to that other presence, seduced by the polonaise's incredible beauty—supple, rich, intense as Chopin's eyes must have been. In that instant, when the music overwhelmed his will, he could see the ghostly hands covering his long-fingered ones, latched to his like leeches. But instead of sucking life, they infused him with it, with the rush, with vigor. Their appearance signaled the point in the piece where he and the ghost became one.

And then it happened—the explosion he'd come to expect . . . and to cherish. Its searing intensity rocked him; its power stunned him. The force imbuing his body strained his muscles till they ached. Every note sprang forth with unearthly brilliance. A shock of his jet-black hair dropped into his eyes, blinding him. It didn't matter. Only the music mattered, the glorious, tempestuous music.

Time passed, but he didn't know how much, for time now lost all meaning . . . became immeasurable. The chords tumbled forth, jubilant, ecstatic. His fingers danced over the keys while unfamiliar images and emotions—Chopin's—danced through his head.

At last he struck the final chord. The notes hung in the

air, a wave of sound palpable as a stone wall. Then they crumbled into silence.

The ghostly hands withdrew. His fingers returned to mortality, and his mind, his soul, were once more his own.

Applause trickled, then rumbled, then thundered until the hall shook with it.

Devin Bryce had enchanted them again.

It's impossible, Suzanne Winslow thought. *"Endnote" can't possibly be missing. It can't!*

She'd promised to make Cindy Stephens a copy, yet the entire composition seemed to have vanished. Quickly she thumbed through her files again, looking at each folder. *Ressu—Sonata One . . . Ressu—Sonata Two . . .* She flipped through them more slowly, checking to see if a file had been stuffed accidentally within another or had slipped down underneath the files.

Ressu—Sonata Twenty-one. The sequence stopped there. No file for *Sonata Twenty-two—"Endnote,"* no folder, no evidence she'd ever had a copy.

Suzanne closed her eyes in sheer frustration as she slammed the drawer shut. Of course she'd had a copy. She was literary executor of the composer's estate, for Pete's sake. Weeks ago she'd transported Valentin Ressu's manuscripts back to her house from his home, and "Endnote" had definitely been with the other twenty-one. She'd been especially careful with it, since the piece hadn't been published and was to have its premiere at the upcoming Romanian Festival.

Oh, no, the premiere! A cold fear slithered through her. *"Endnote" has got to be here,* she told herself frantically.

She opened the file drawer a third time and removed all the files. Then she sat cross-legged on the floor and systematically sorted through every folder from the drawer, every piece of paper. It took her over an hour, but she turned up nothing.

Panic growing in her, she searched the other file drawers,

wondering if perhaps she'd misfiled "Endnote." But that was highly unlikely, she thought as she ran her fingers through her straight blond hair. She never misfiled anything. Organization was the key to her success as a musicologist, and she never forgot it. Besides, she liked an ordered life, and it disturbed her to think of someone entering her realm to destroy that order.

Or had someone? She glanced around her home office. As usual, labeled file boxes containing magazines and journals were ranged alphabetically along one shelf. Her books were categorized by subject, each shelf marked with a neat placard stating what subjects it contained. Next to the stereo, the CDs were organized by period and style, then alphabetically by composer. Everything seemed untouched. She'd have noticed any deviation, for she always adhered to her system. Still, she couldn't shake the feeling that someone else had been here.

At that moment the phone rang and she jumped. Good Lord, she was really letting this get to her. She sat a moment, hearing the phone ring and considering letting the machine get it. Then she shook her head. No, she'd better answer. It could be Mother, calling from the gallery and needing a ride.

Still uneasy, Suzanne lifted the receiver. Just then, her Siamese cat Bartok padded into the room and jumped up into her lap.

"Hello?" she said into the phone as she stroked his silky light-gray fur, feeling slightly reassured by his presence.

"Suzanne? It's Leon. I need a favor."

Suzanne winced. Leon was entertainment editor of the *Chicago Star*. She occasionally reviewed concerts for him, but he hadn't called in a long while. She certainly couldn't deal with him right now. He had a tendency to keep her on the phone forever, and all she wanted to do was find "Endnote."

"What kind of favor?" she asked curtly.

SILENT SONATA

"I need a reviewer for the Bryce recital tomorrow afternoon."

She didn't bother to hide her groan from him. "Not this weekend, Leon, please? I'm swamped." Not to mention she had a missing manuscript on her hands. "Look, I'm tied up with the Romanian Festival, I'm frantically grading term papers, and Mother's here to visit. Besides, I hate reviewing the kind of concerts Bryce does—the same old Chopin and Beethoven. Call someone else, okay, and let me know when you need someone to review an avant-garde performance or something interesting."

Leon growled out some choice epithets. She felt like joining him. She scanned the office once more nervously, looking for anything that was out of place.

"The same old Chopin and Beethoven?" Leon sputtered. "This is Devin Bryce, Suzanne. You know Devin Bryce . . . who pulls down thousands of dollars a concert . . . who they say 'looks like a devil and plays like an angel.'"

With difficulty she returned her attention to Leon. "Only Gerald says that. You know Gerald . . . your music critic . . . who 'looks like an angel and writes like a bore.'"

"And throws up like a man with the flu. Who knows better than me? He threw up in *my* car. Come on, do this tiny favor for me. I have to get a reviewer for Bryce's recital at Orchestra Hall. After what happened at Carnegie Hall last week, my boss is even holding the page for me so it can go out in Monday's Entertainment section. You've got to help me."

She grimaced at being forced to listen to two hours of Mozart, Haydn, and whatever traditional composers the eccentric pianist chose to interpret. Mother had already gone on and on about a recital in Paris where Bryce had played an "inspired surprise rendition of Chopin's 'Revolutionary Etude.'" Suzanne wasn't in the mood for surprises.

She had one too many surprises to deal with right now,

she thought as she scratched behind one of Bartok's ears, wishing she could ask the cat if he'd seen "Endnote."

"I don't know, Leon—" she began.

"It's not like I won't do you a favor in return." His voice turned sly. "Didn't you say you wanted the paper to cover the upcoming Ressu concert in a big way? Nice spread on the front page of the Entertainment section with pictures?"

She groaned. Leon sure knew how to play dirty. "You *know* I want coverage." And he was perfectly capable of withholding it out of sheer meanness. She paused at his quick chuckle. "Leon, you are a scheming, blackmailing—"

"Yep. So . . . you going to review the recital?"

He hadn't given her much choice, she thought. The Romanian Festival planning committee was counting on the newspaper coverage. "Okay," Suzanne muttered. "Okay, I'll do it."

"Don't sound so glum about it," he said. Then he paused. "Hey, didn't you say your mother is in town?"

"Yes. Why?"

"Why not take her? Doesn't she like that classical stuff?"

She started to retort that the last thing she needed was to squire Mother to a recital, then she stopped short. The recital might be just the thing to appease her temperamental mother so Suzanne could get to the bottom of the missing manuscript in peace. Maybe there was a silver lining to this cloud after all.

"Actually, she loves recitals," Suzanne told him. "And she loves Bryce."

"Great, then it's settled. I'll send two tickets over instead of one." He laughed. "I can't wait to see what you think of Bryce's performance. I bet he'll surprise you."

She made a face at the phone. "I can't promise you'll like what I have to say. You know that."

"It doesn't really matter." She could almost see him smiling on the other end. "Nothing you say would keep music lovers from flocking to hear Bryce. Unless you find some dark skeleton in his past—like he was a Nazi or something."

"It's obvious you were once a reporter, Leon." She smiled at Bartok, who eyed her with his usual skepticism. "Always looking for the dirt. Well, don't come to me for that. I'm more into musical discoveries than personal ones."

"Like this great secret angle on Valentin Ressu's work that you're keeping hush-hush until your book comes out?"

The tension in her chest built again. She had to figure out what had happened to "Endnote." "You got it," she told him, trying to make her voice light. "And speaking of books, I've got to get back to work."

"Sure, sure. I'll send the tickets over right away."

After she hung up, she cradled Bartok in her arms. He purred and snuggled into her sweater. With a twinge of guilt she remembered her annoyance when Valentin had presented her with the kitten after she'd received her Ph.D. in music history and theory from Eastman School of Music and had moved back here to teach at the University of Chicago. He'd jokingly told her she needed a man in the house to look after her.

She'd never had a pet and hadn't known what to do with the kitten. But somehow she and Bartok had muddled through, until the sardonic-faced feline had wormed his way into her heart.

Now his little body warmed her slightly. It wasn't enough, however. She was cold, terribly cold, despite the spring sun streaming through the one window. She couldn't shake the feeling that something was very wrong. How could a file go missing right out of her filing cabinet?

Then again, who would steal an old manuscript by a dead composer? She glanced around the room, worry making her insides go taut. She saw no evidence of other theft or breaking and entering. Her office seemed to be in its usual immaculate order.

Oblivious of her worries, Bartok jumped off her lap,

strolled to the center of the room, and began licking his paws. Suzanne tried to shake off her worry. She must have put the manuscript somewhere. That was the only answer.

"Did I accidentally leave it with Valentin's other papers at Mariela's?" she asked aloud, but she knew the answer. She distinctly remembered bringing the piece back and filing it. She even remembered thinking how ironic it was that Valentin's last masterpiece, never before heard by anyone, should be crammed at the back of her file drawer.

Suzanne hadn't looked at "Endnote" much since Ressu's death because it was the last piece, and she'd been too busy cataloging the others to worry about it. But she'd been planning to remove it soon to make that copy for Cindy Stephens, the pianist for the festival concert.

That's it! Suzanne thought. At the last meeting of the festival concert planning committee, Cindy had asked about the copy and Suzanne had promised to bring it to the next meeting. Perhaps Cindy had grown impatient. Perhaps while Suzanne had been out that morning, Cindy had come by. Mother had been here. It would have been just like Mother to go looking for the piece herself and to have given it to Cindy.

Yes, that's probably what happened, Suzanne thought with relief. Then she frowned. She'd repeatedly told Mother not to fool with her files. Of course, Mother would no doubt ignore that restriction if it was too much of a bother. And Mother knew better than anyone how meticulously Suzanne filed everything. She would have known where to find the copy.

Cindy had probably come by and in her usual manner, had wheedled the copy out of Mother. Still, it disturbed Suzanne to think that Cindy now had the only copy. As soon as Mother came home, Suzanne would ask her about the missing file. Suzanne would get to the bottom of this mess then.

Having now formed a plan of action, she turned her

thoughts to other matters. Like her conversation with Leon.

She groaned as she remembered what she'd agreed to. Devin Bryce's recital. Good Lord, how had she let herself be coerced into attending *that*?

Valentin would never have approved, she thought wryly. Her mentor had enjoyed criticizing pianists like Devin, who stuck to more traditional classical music. He'd always claimed that if pianists with Bryce's technical ability would perform avant-garde pieces, the public could learn to appreciate the fine qualities of experimental music. On the other hand, he'd said, such pianists probably wouldn't know what to do with a "prepared" piano if they saw one.

Devin Bryce certainly wouldn't, Suzanne silently agreed. Suddenly curious about the man, she moved to the file card box that cross-indexed all her CDs by performer. Quickly she thumbed through the cards until she found the name Bryce. It listed one CD in her collection containing a performance by him—Tchaikovsky's Piano Concerto in B-flat Minor. She found it easily, then flipped on the power switch to her sound system, slipped the CD into the CD player, and hit *Play*. After a brief pause, the famous four-note opening filled the room.

Almost in spite of herself, she smiled. She'd forgotten how lovely the "Tchaik One" really was. Even though it sounded conventional compared to Valentin Ressu's semitones and cyclic transpositions, she found its conventionality soothing in light of her scare a few moments before.

Bartok looked up from his grooming, then cocked his head as if listening intently to the music.

She shook her head. "You're such a fool for traditional classical music, you little traitor."

He mewed softly. She laughed. "Oh, great, now you're going to sing along. You must really like Bryce's playing."

Actually, Bartok wasn't alone. She had to acknowledge that Bryce's performance was exquisite. Unlike many recorded renditions, it had a quality she hated to say was truly inspired.

"Wonderful piece, isn't it?" a voice sounded from the doorway. "I thought you didn't listen to 'that overblown, blustering Tchaikovsky.' Isn't that what you call him?"

Suzanne sucked in her breath and turned toward the door. "Hello, Mother." She turned down the volume on the stereo.

Felicia Winslow stood there wearing a knit dress of the brightest orange Suzanne had ever seen. A splash of purple near the hem took some of the edge off the effect, but not much, particularly with Mother's plump figure. She looked like a large orange buoy bobbing in a purple sea. Her close-cropped hair completed the image, for her head could easily double for the light atop the buoy.

Bartok edged closer to Suzanne, torn between fleeing from the feared Felicia Winslow and staying to hear the faint sounds of Tchaikovsky. He stayed, but eyed her mother's dress with skepticism.

Suzanne bit back a smile. "I didn't hear you come in. How were things at the gallery with your exhibit?"

Her mother waved her ring-covered hand dismissively. "Awful. No matter how I insist, they never place my sculptures correctly." She rolled her eyes as she gave a dramatic snort. "And that incompetent idiot who made the sign for the foyer couldn't even get the right effect for my name. The lettering is all froufrou . . . you know what I mean. I wanted 'dramatic,' not 'flowery.' Apparently, he doesn't know the difference."

Suzanne listened impatiently, accustomed to her mother's cynical tirades and mood swings. One minute civilization was a glorious adventure, the next it was doomed to extinction before the twenty-first century. In either case, Suzanne had to hear Mother's assessment. Not that she heard it often. Felicia Winslow generally kept too busy to visit her daughter. Only occasionally did she manage to settle into Suzanne's house for a few weeks, if she had an exhibit that brought her to Chicago.

"I have something to cheer you up," Suzanne offered, to stave off a long discussion. "The *Chicago Star*'s regular music critic is sick, so Leon asked me to review Devin Bryce's recital tomorrow. He offered me two tickets, so we can both go."

Her mother's eyes lit up. "Why, that's wonderful!"

It never ceased to amaze Suzanne that Mother, one of America's foremost avant-garde sculptors, had such traditional tastes in music. Suzanne sighed. "I knew you'd approve. You've been trying to get me to a Bryce recital for ages."

"Oh, you won't regret it, Zanny. He plays like—"

"I know, I know. An angel. Well, he'd better play like an angel tomorrow, because I don't feel like cutting him any slack."

A hint of a knowing smile touched her mother's lips. "He will, I assure you. You'll see. He's a genius, a bona fide genius. He'll knock your socks off."

Privately, Suzanne doubted it, but at the moment, she didn't really care. She had more important matters to attend to.

She shut off the CD player. Tchaikovsky, even at low volume, was beginning to get on her nerves. "Not to change the subject, Mother, but have you been in my Ressu files?"

The minute Mother bristled, Suzanne regretted her bluntness.

"And why should I go into your files?" Mother said, punctuating her words with a loud sniff. "I hate Valentin's ridiculous compositions, and you know it. All that nonsense propagated by Cage and his like . . . 'prepared piano'! Hmph! If pianos were intended to have their strings stuffed with paper clips, they'd be built that way!" She moved farther into the room as Bartok fled past her, now deprived of his music. "Valentin was the worst. His music was like howling monkeys. I have no desire ever to look at another piece of his garbage."

In her outrage, Suzanne forgot her question. "I'd think you'd be interested in your ex-husband's music," she gritted out.

Mother shook her head and moved to the chaise longue, dropping her purse beside it before lowering herself gingerly onto the squeaking springs. "It's precisely because I had to live with the man that I have no interest in his music."

"I lived with him too." The words sounded choked, but Suzanne couldn't help it. Three months had passed, yet it still hurt to think about her stepfather's death of a heart attack at fifty. It was extraordinary of her to allow grief to numb her this way, but then she grieved for a rather extraordinary man.

Mother scrutinized her. "You still mourn him, don't you?" Mother shook her head. "Sometimes I think you've mourned more for Valentin than for your own father."

Michael Winslow, Suzanne's father, had been the first of Mother's four husbands. Suzanne had to admit that her vague memories of a quiet white-haired man who'd been almost twenty years older than Mother left her little to grieve for. He'd died when Suzanne was three, before she could really know him.

Still, she said defensively, "That's not true. It's just that you were married to Valentin—"

"For six years. Yes, I know. You've pointed that out many times. Still . . . Philippe Manon and I were married nearly six years, and you didn't form a morbid attachment to him."

"There's no comparison between Philippe and Valentin." Suzanne's voice was almost as stiff as her expression.

Mother shrugged. "No, I suppose not. But at least Philippe didn't leave us for a little mouse like Mariela."

Leave us! *What a joke,* Suzanne thought. Mother would never understand. Men left *Mother* and only Mother.

SILENT SONATA

Mother settled more comfortably on the chaise longue. "You must admit Philippe was a much nicer man than Valentin."

"It depends on what you define as 'nice,'" Suzanne couldn't help muttering. "He was nice to you because you had the money."

With a sniff Mother pulled out a compact and studied her makeup, tsking over it. "Yes, well, at least he didn't spoil you like Valentin did. I never seemed able to get Valentin to understand that a child shouldn't be dragged on tour. He had this obsession about not leaving you with a baby-sitter."

"Thank heavens."

Valentin Ressu had married her mother at the beginning of his career as a composer, when he'd only been twenty-six and Suzanne six. Valentin had indeed insisted on taking her on the tours they'd made for his concerts or her mother's exhibits. He'd always treated her like a little princess.

No, like a daughter, she thought. Valentin had overseen her piano lessons when Mother had been too self-absorbed even to notice her daughter's interest in music. He'd let Suzanne watch him work, patiently explaining why his pieces sounded different from the music on the records Mother played. And somehow he'd always found time for zoos and playgrounds and even Barbie dolls.

When things between him and Mother had deteriorated, Suzanne had blamed Mother for driving away the only real father she'd had. After the divorce, Suzanne had spent less time with Mother and Mother's next two husbands than with Valentin and his new wife Mariela, a gentle Romanian woman. Valentin and Mariela had essentially become her family, although she knew Mother would never understand her attachment to them and their son Paul.

Mother's voice broke into her thoughts. "It would be easier for you to go on with your life, you know, if you hadn't let sweet young Mariela talk you into doing this festival thing."

Suzanne forced down the angry words rising in her throat. Somehow she made her voice even. "I wanted to do 'this festival thing,' Mother. I owe Valentin a great deal, and I want to pay him back in the only way I know how."

Her mother dabbed some powder on her face. "Good heavens, what could you possibly owe Valentin for?"

It took all Suzanne's effort not to tell Mother the truth—that Valentin had rewarded her inquisitiveness with attention when Mother had been too absorbed in her latest work to do more than acknowledge Suzanne's presence. As a result, Suzanne owed him for her interest in music theory, her ability to express herself, and her diligent exploration of all kinds of knowledge.

And at the moment, she couldn't bear to discuss Valentin with her hypercritical mother, particularly when she still hadn't gotten an answer to her question about the files.

"I just do," Suzanne retorted. "You wouldn't understand."

Her mother snapped the compact shut. "No doubt you're right about that."

Mother's sarcasm bit into Suzanne. "Look, Mother. I don't want to talk about Ressu anymore. We'll end up fighting as usual. But I do need to know about the files."

"The files?" Mother asked, digging in her purse.

"Yes, my Ressu files. In the midst of your outrage, you never actually said whether or not you'd been in them."

Her mother pulled out a lipstick. "Of course I haven't been in your files. You've made it clear many times that you don't want a soul disturbing your domain. The one time I went in your desk looking for a pencil, you noticed immediately and grumbled for days. Believe me, I learned to leave your things alone."

Dread began to trickle through Suzanne, yet she persisted. "Yes, but I couldn't find 'Endnote' when I was looking through the sonatas. I thought perhaps Cindy or even Ion Goma might have come by wanting a copy and you might have given it to them. Mariela doesn't have a copy

SILENT SONATA

either, since Ressu stipulated they be given to me so she . . ."

Suzanne trailed off. Mother was too busy concentrating on redoing her lipstick to listen. "Mother!"

A frown replaced Mother's vague expression. "Dear Lord, Zanny, you don't have to shout. I'm sitting right here. Now what were you saying?"

Suzanne gritted her teeth. "I asked about the files."

Her mother screwed the top back on her lipstick. "I said I haven't touched your precious Ressu files."

The panicky feeling that had assailed Suzanne earlier dug into her stomach once more. Mother sounded awfully certain. That copy of Ressu's 'Endnote' had been the only one. "Are you sure? I know I didn't take it out myself, and I can't seem to—"

"I don't have it! Are you accusing your own mother of stealing?"

"Come on, Mother, you know that's not what I'm saying. But I can't think of anyone who'd be interested in it except the committee members, and I didn't give it to any of them."

Her mother stared at her, only slightly mollified.

With a sigh, Suzanne brushed her hair back from her shoulders. "Perhaps you were caught up in something while you were here alone, and someone came by who said they'd help themselves. One of the committee members. There are six—Professor Kelly, Ion Goma, Cindy Stephens, a new woman named Lydia Chelminscu, and of course, Mariela and Paul."

With a frown, her mother tucked her lipstick back into her purse, then stood. "No one came by and asked to look through your files. I'm not even here half the time when you're out." She shrugged. "Besides, I don't understand why this has you so uptight. Dear Lord, you'd think someone had walked off with your jewelry or something." She started toward the door. "You probably stuck the composition somewhere and forgot about it."

Suzanne shook her head in silence, a frown spreading over her brow. She never "stuck things" anywhere. And if no one had been by to pick it up, then where was it?

Abruptly, her mother stopped in the doorway and half turned toward Suzanne. "By the way, you had no visitors but a man did call, one of those committee members you mentioned. You know . . . Gama . . . Gome . . . the one with the foreign name."

"Goma?"

"Yes. He wanted you to call him back right away."

"Right away? When did he call?" Suzanne asked in a barely controlled voice.

Her mother frowned and tapped her forefinger against her chin. "Let me think. Was it this morning? No, I believe it was early yesterday. Unless—"

Suzanne began counting to ten, but at three, she grumbled, "Mother, why didn't you let the answering machine take it?"

Her mother looked at her as if she'd gone mad. "That noisy thing? It's awful hearing that stupid little message repeated every time the phone rings. Besides, isn't it nicer to have a human take a message?"

Yes, Suzanne thought as her stomach muscles contracted into a hard knot. *If the human would take the message.*

"Anyway," her mother continued, ignoring Suzanne's pained silence, "since you're in such a testy mood, I believe I'll go amuse myself at that student exhibit at the university. I do so enjoy critiquing amateurs."

With that, her mother swept from the room like an opera singer making an exit.

"I swear, Mother, one day . . ." Suzanne muttered the moment she heard the front door slam.

Then she sighed. Why get all worked up about it? She couldn't change Mother. Mother was definitely set in her ways, irritating as they might be.

Ion Goma would undoubtedly be obnoxious about this. Unfortunately, no matter how much he ranted, she'd have

SILENT SONATA

to be nice to him, since the Romanian Society had provided about a third of the funding for the festival concert. It was a shame Ion was the one representing the society. The man couldn't tell an andante from an allegro, yet he insisted on expressing opinions about which pianist should play the sonatas and how the titles should be printed on the program.

Well, at the moment she couldn't concern herself with the petty tyrant and his bias against her. He'd have to wait for his phone call. Let him do as he usually did and chalk her rudeness up to her woeful lack of Romanian blood. He would anyway.

She had to find "Endnote." But where to start? She hadn't thought she'd taken the sonata out of the files, but perhaps she had. Perhaps she'd simply forgotten doing it. After all, she'd looked at more than a hundred of Ressu's compositions over the last few months, including the Sonata Cycle to be performed in its entirety for the first time at the Romanian Festival. Between the cataloging and preparing for the festival concert, it was a wonder she remembered anything anymore.

The festival had been nothing but trouble, especially after Valentin died, leaving her to answer everyone's questions about how to perform his music. Suzanne had thought Mariela might cancel the concert, but instead Mariela had decided to make it a memorial concert and put Suzanne in charge. Of course.

All of that had meant that she'd been forced to abandon her critical analysis of Valentin's work for the time being. She only hoped she could work on it this summer when school was out. Her book would contain startling revelations that would make a significant contribution to music scholarship, and she was eager to finish it.

An unnamed fear struck her again. She'd never complete her book without "Endnote." Good Lord, she had to find the piece. She must have misplaced it. What else could have happened?

Crossing the room to her desk, she hoped she'd indeed taken "Endnote" out to study and had simply forgotten leaving it on her desk. But as she dropped into the chair, frustration warred with a persistent panicky feeling. She stared at the sonatas stacked up before her—the ones she *had* been working on. She'd taken those out of the file folders, leaving the folders in the cabinet. If "Endnote" were among them, why were both "Endnote" and its folder missing as if the piece had never existed?

Lifting the top manuscript, she began systematically sorting through the papers on her desk. The sonatas were all intact in their plastic sleeves. The notes she'd made to them were still attached to the outsides of the sleeves with paper clips.

But after a second she realized that something was wrong, terribly wrong. Her heart began to pound as she flipped back through the sonatas once more.

The sonatas were in the wrong order.

She stared blindly ahead as that fact sank in. She always kept the sonatas she was working on in numerical order so she'd never have trouble finding a particular sonata if she needed it. Yet these were jumbled. No, she corrected herself, they were in reverse order, as if someone had lifted each sonata one at a time and placed it down on the desk, then put the next one on top of it.

Someone. This wasn't a case of a misplaced file or a loaned piece. No, someone had very carefully gone through every sonata on her desk. Someone—some stranger—had been in her office.

Her knees shook, and she clamped them together, fighting down a wave of hysteria. Perhaps she'd gone through the sonatas herself, she thought, grasping at straws. Perhaps when Mariela or Cindy or even Ion had been at her house for a meeting, they'd idly looked . . .

No, she thought as her heart hammered furiously in her chest. She'd looked at the pieces since the last meeting. Someone else had done this—someone who thought he was being careful. Someone who had no idea that she kept her desk in such meticulous order.

What else had that someone taken? she thought instantly. With a cry she jumped up and dashed to her filing cabinet, cross-checking the sonatas there with the ones on her desk. To her relief she found a manuscript for every one. Except "Endnote."

She crossed her arms over her chest protectively and sank to the floor. It did no good to realize that only "Endnote" had been taken. It was the only sonata that hadn't been published. If someone had stolen "Endnote" . . . A wave of despair flooded her. It would mean no Sonata Cycle, no memorial concert . . . no book.

Who would steal a dead composer's last sonata? she wondered again. It made no sense. After the festival in a few weeks, it would be known to the world anyway. Was this someone's wretched way of sabotaging the premiere performance? Did someone think that by stealing the last piece of the Sonata Cycle, he could halt the festival concert? A groan escaped her lips as she stared blankly at the floor, wondering what to do next.

That was when she saw it. Against the pristine whiteness of her carpet lay a dark hair about the length of her finger.

Her pulse madly pounding, she picked up the coarse black hair. Then she laid it across her palm and examined it. It was too dark to be hers or Mother's or even Bartok's. Besides, she'd just vacuumed the rug yesterday. No one had been in her office since then except her and Mother and Bartok.

Rocking back on her heels, she shut her eyes and fought the chill coming over her. Someone had definitely been in her office. Someone had gone through all her things, touched all her files. Someone had stolen her copy of "Endnote." The *only* copy.

She groaned. *Now don't panic,* she told herself, fighting for control over her racing heart. *Think. Maybe there's an-*

other copy. Could Mariela have one? Or maybe even one of the other members of the committee?

Suddenly she remembered the freehand copy she'd made shortly before Ressu's death. He'd uncharacteristically refused to give her a copy himself, so one day while he'd been out of his house, she'd found his original and transcribed her own copy.

Unfortunately, she'd kept that copy in her desk. Her heart rose in her throat as she moved quickly to the bottom drawer and jerked it out, rooting through it until she found a purple folder at the bottom. Her hands trembling, she opened it.

Relief flooded her. The transcription in her own hand lay there intact. Somehow the thief had missed it, probably because he hadn't expected to find another copy buried in a drawer.

Thank God she'd been brave enough to sneak around behind Ressu's back and make a copy. Otherwise his masterpiece would have been lost to the world forever.

Clutching the folder to her chest, she sat back on the floor. What now? Ressu's original had clearly been stolen. Should she call the police?

And tell them what? she thought. *That the order of my manuscripts was altered and I found a black hair on my floor? They'd laugh me into the next county!*

But blast it, she couldn't let the mysterious thief get away with this! She'd call the police and *make* them listen to her! She leapt to her feet and began stalking through the house. Surely there was evidence of a break-in that she could find to convince them—a broken window, a jimmied lock.

To her dismay, her search of the house turned up nothing. It was as if "Endnote" had vanished into thin air. Fear and outrage settled into her bones. To think that someone could enter her home and remove a file without leaving a trace! Good Lord, was it that easy? Had it happened before?

She strode into the living room, her sense of invasion

SILENT SONATA

growing. Bartok rubbed against her leg, and she picked him up, burying her face in his fur. Yet even his warm body couldn't comfort her. It was too terrifying to think of someone freely roaming her house, perhaps even while she'd been asleep.

Bartok protested when she squeezed him a little too tightly. She stared into his heart-shaped face. "Did you see anyone, little buddy?" she asked, wishing he could talk. "Did you see the man who's trying to sabotage your old friend's concert?"

He merely stared at her.

For a moment she allowed the panic to overwhelm her. Then she forced herself to get control. At least the saboteur hadn't succeeded. At least she still had her freehand copy. She'd have to lock it away in her safe to make sure the sabotage wasn't successful, but she had it, despite the mysterious thief's efforts to steal it. And no matter how much the police laughed at her, she'd speak to them about the theft.

Most important, she wouldn't let this incident spoil the festival concert. She'd make sure Ressu had his day. And what a day it would be. The Sonata Cycle would stun them all—the listeners, the critics, the naysayers.

She turned to look at the baby grand bequeathed to her by Valentin in his will. It filled half her small living room, but she didn't care. It was almost as precious to her as the bronze bust of Valentin sitting on top of it.

Her eyes examined the bust. Mother had sculpted it when times were good. One thing Suzanne could say for Mother—when she chose to do representational art, she had an extraordinary ability to capture a person's character. Suzanne loved this sculpture best, for it depicted Valentin's craggy forehead and lopsided smile quite well. Sometimes she felt almost as if the bust would become animate at any moment, and Valentin would talk to her as he used to.

"You know," she told the purring cat, "after this festival,

people will be forced to recognize Valentin's genius." A lump formed in her throat, but she swallowed past it. "I'm going to make sure he's remembered. And not just by me either."

Bartok closed his eyes indifferently. With a sigh, she lifted her gaze back to the bust. "That thief is *not* going to ruin this, Valentin. I'll make certain it's the most unforgettable concert anyone has ever attended. They'll never forget you. I promise you that."

The well-polished bronze face just continued to stare at her with its fixed, benign smile.

2
♪

Devin Bryce paced beside the concert grand that dominated one corner of his spacious Chicago apartment. His hands were thrust in the pockets of old worn jeans, as they had been for the last two hours. He couldn't bring himself to sit down and rest or do finger exercises as he should. This afternoon's recital, only three hours away, had him too keyed up, too full of dread.

"You gonna pull a fast one on them again today?" Jack Warton asked from where he'd made himself at home on Devin's comfortable couch upholstered in a plaid fabric that had seen better days.

Devin glanced at his balding, paunchy business manager. Most solo artists on the concert circuit used one of the big management companies like Columbia Artists in New York. Not Devin. Sure, he had a big agency to book his appearances, but Jack was his business manager. Always had been, always would be.

Jack never ceased to shock concert sponsors the first time they met him. In a world of upscale sophisticates for whom classical music merely served as part of an overall image, Jack presented an anomaly. Those with an ounce of perception recognized the sharp intellect and profound love of music beneath the boorish exterior of the sixty-plus ex-soldier. The ones who didn't, quickly learned that they'd better respect his business acumen if they wanted to deal with Devin regularly.

Devin turned back to his pacing and refused to answer Jack's question. His worn tennis shoes thumped rhythmically on the hardwood floor.

Jack lit a cigarette and propped his spindly legs up on the coffee table. "It always knocks me out to see the ladies eat up your surprises. You should hear the old ones brag about how you changed the program at *their* recital. Like you knew them all and did it for them personally."

Devin remained silent, but wished for one of Jack's cigarettes. He had finally quit smoking six months ago, two years after his mother had been diagnosed as having emphysema, but he still craved the taste of tobacco, particularly right before a recital.

Jack searched for an ashtray among the pile of magazines, sheet music, and empty potato chip cans jumbled together on the coffee table. "It's a great image, Devin. I couldn't have invented a better one for you myself. Inspired artist . . . rebel . . . a musician who truly plays what he pleases and says, 'To hell with the bourgeoisie and their narrow ideas.'"

"If I were saying, 'To hell with the bourgeoisie,' I wouldn't be playing recitals of Chopin and Liszt for conservative Chicago concertgoers," Devin growled. "I'd be experimenting like Xenakis with his 'stochastic distributions' and Cage with his 'prepared' piano."

"I thought you hated avant-garde music."

"I do. As it so happens, my tastes and those of the bourgeoisie coincide. But that certainly doesn't make me a rebel."

Jack took another puff on his cigarette. "Aren't you testy today."

The smell of burning tobacco only increased Devin's irritation. "I'm always testy before a Chicago recital."

"Why?"

Devin shrugged as he speared his fingers through his longish black hair. "Hometown jitters, I guess."

Actually, when he played in Chicago, his home base, he lived in constant fear that somebody would unearth his secret. Okay, so his fear made no sense. His secret probably wasn't any safer in any other city than in Chicago, but a Chicago reporter would definitely have less trouble researching his past.

Lucky for him, no one had ever wanted to do so. Besides, it wasn't as if a reporter would jump up in a recital, point to him, and parade his past before God and country. Yet if reporters ever did turn up some crap on his father, they might leap to some conclusions about Devin's unpredictable, inspired renditions of Chopin and the rest, conclusions that could cost him his career.

He feared that most of all.

He shook off the vague unease settling in his bones. No one would guess his bizarre secret. The ghosts of dead composers playing music through a living pianist? Who'd believe such a wild tale?

"Rogers called from New Orleans last night," Jack said, cutting into Devin's thoughts. He stuffed the end of his cigarette into a half-empty bottle of flat cola sitting on the floor. It sizzled as it hit the liquid. "Said they'd put you up at the Royal Orleans if that's where you wanna stay."

"The suite they usually book for me has a wonderful concert grand. Of course I want to stay there. Rogers knows that."

"I don't think that's really why he called. He's a nervous

Nellie. He heard about last week's polonaise and wanted me to assure him you weren't gonna do something weird in New Orleans. Every time you go off on your own in a recital, it makes the music directors nervous."

Yeah, I can understand why, Devin thought. Aloud he said, "It's not like I've ever done it with an orchestra behind me."

"I don't think that's what worries them. They're afraid you'll up and decide not to perform at all. You know, you being an unpredictable, uncontrollable—"

"—rebel," Devin finished for him.

Thank God the ghosts had never taken him over during a symphony. Hell if he knew why, though. Maybe it was because they were musicians. Oh sure, they wanted to play their music the way they'd meant it to be performed . . . or at least that was his theory for why they took over his hands once in a while. But they knew better than to kill the goose that lay the golden eggs by scotching his career forever. If he'd been scheduled to play Liszt's *Totentanz* with some symphony orchestra the other night when he'd launched into the Chopin polonaise, the conductor would have killed him. And never offered him a return engagement.

The knowledge that his hands weren't his own always put Devin on edge. He hated never being quite sure when he'd lose control. All he could do was pray he could keep on concealing his strange abilities behind the mask of "eccentric artist." If the day ever came when the composers took his hands over while he performed with an orchestra . . .

He shuddered at the thought. The piano was his life. What would he do if his very purpose for living were snatched from him?

"So. Are you gonna shock 'em again today or not?" Jack asked.

Devin shrugged, finally settling his lanky frame in his favorite wing-back chair and picking up the well-marked copy of Schumann's Toccata that sat on the floor next to it.

Aloud he said, "Who knows?" but he thought, *Hell, I hope not.*

Every time it happened, he felt as if another soul eclipsed his for a brief time. It made him uncomfortable, particularly since vestiges of the composer's personality seeped through during and after the possession. As he played, he usually got glimpses of the composer's memories. Then for a few days after the performance, he'd have a few quirky urges that he knew came from the composer.

Last week's round with Chopin had left him with a desire for fine wine and expensive flowers. And an urge to read George Sand's novels. He'd had to resist his impulse to stop at a bookstore on his way back from the hall.

Jack chuckled. "Better watch the 'mysterious artist' act with me, guy. I see right through all that crap. To me, you're a snot-nosed kid from the South Side who made good because I didja a favor and listened to you play."

"Yeah, yeah, you made me what I am today," Devin muttered good-naturedly. He'd heard all this before. It was a kind of game he and Jack played, a comforting reminder of all they'd been through together.

Oddly enough, Jack knew about Devin's father. But if Jack had ever guessed Devin's other secret, he never let on. Besides, it didn't matter if Jack knew or not. Devin could trust Jack with his life.

Jack had first heard Devin play when Devin was nine. Devin's father had been dead for two years. His mother had heard about Jack through other mothers of piano students. Despite his rough manner and his background in the military, Jack had garnered a reputation as a first-rate piano teacher with an uncanny ability to recognize talent. Yet he was so much more than that. Once Jack took a young pianist under his wing, he made sure the pianist took all the right steps, prepared for all the right competitions, and made all the right connections.

But a kid had to have phenomenal talent to get Jack's attention. Devin's mother had tried all the conventional methods of getting Jack to hear Devin, but Jack had insisted he was already supervising the careers of more young pianists than he could handle. He'd ignored all her attempts.

Devin had taken it in stride until he'd found his mother crying after the last rebuff. After his father's death, he'd not been a stranger to his mother's tears. Yet something had snapped in him on that particular occasion. He found out Jack's address from his current piano teacher. Then he took three buses to get to the Wartons' home. Jack's buxom young wife answered the door and Devin asked to see Jack. Amazingly, she went to get her husband.

Devin smiled at the memory of Jack coming to the door. "No one makes my mother cry," Devin said. Then he put all the strength he could into his nine-year-old's fist and slammed it into Jack's stomach.

Devin had made a remarkable impact, considering his age and Jack's rock-hard muscles. Cursing a blue streak, Jack lifted him and nearly threw him into the street. But as he held a squirming, fighting Devin aloft, Devin's words registered. Jack put Devin down, unable to resist dragging the whole story out of the feisty little Irish kid.

After Devin sullenly told Jack why he'd hit him, Jack took him inside and made him sit down at the piano. "You wanna play, big shot?" he said. "Play. Now. And don't let me hear complaints about hurting your hand on my stomach, you hear me? Stupid kid, ruining your hands by hitting people . . ."

Devin endured the grumbling and played for all he was worth, stung by Jack's comments into showing what he could do.

From that point on, he and Jack had been inseparable. Jack had dropped his other students one by one to focus on the career of a musical prodigy. Having seen Devin's amazing talent, he hadn't wanted to risk losing the chance to shape it.

Devin knew he could never have come so far without

Jack and his tough, the-world-can-go-to-hell attitude. In a sense, Jack *had* made him what he was today by expecting the best of him and then teaching him how to be the best. And Devin didn't intend ever to forget it, which was why he put up with Jack's grumbling and obnoxious behavior.

Now the man in question stood to his feet and stretched. "Guess I'd better be going. You need to rest, and I need to check on a few things at the hall. What time you gonna be there?"

"One thirty." Devin began studying a particularly troublesome phrase in the Toccata. He said without looking up, "Are you and I still heading out to Morton's for a steak after the recital? I'm hungry as a bear today."

Jack lit a cigarette for the road. "You're always hungry these days, you Irish bastard. It's because you quit smoking."

Devin glanced up from the sheet music, his cobalt eyes focusing on Jack's hand. "I'd kill for a cigarette."

"Yeah, and you ain't getting one from me. Besides, I'm quitting tomorrow."

With a harsh laugh, Devin went back to studying the music. "Like hell. You'll be sucking on those cancer sticks till your coffin's dropped in the ground. Which will probably be any day now."

Jack merely smiled, slicking back with his free hand his few remaining wisps of red hair. "You know, Bryce, if you weren't so goddamned talented, I wouldn't put up with your crap all the time."

"Yeah, yeah, yeah," Devin mumbled, but his mind was already elsewhere, concentrating on the phrase.

He didn't even notice when Jack shook his head and walked out, closing the door quietly behind him.

Devin Bryce wasn't at all what Suzanne had expected. From her seat in Orchestra Hall's first balcony, she watched him walk to center stage as applause bubbled up around her. He resembled a magician or a hypnotist more than a pianist, thanks to deep-set, light-colored eyes—gray or perhaps blue—that shone almost translucent under the lights. She could nearly imagine him fixing those eyes on some unsuspecting victim in the audience and mesmerizing that person into doing bizarre, embarrassing things.

Although no black cape lay draped over the wide span of his shoulders, his black tails worn over a shirt of startling whiteness made him look as mysterious, as enigmatic as a magician. Rich ebony hair spilled down over the top of his collar in back. In front, a hank of the thick, straight mass slanted from a side part over a clear, broad brow while the rest of his hair was swept behind his ears, accentuating a long, squarish jaw and high cheekbones.

What an interesting, even handsome, face, she thought. Admittedly, the bold eyebrows nearly meeting in the middle made him look as if he wore a permanent scowl. But he smiled in response to the applause, a winning smile guaranteed to charm. No wonder women flocked to hear him perform. He had the tempestuous air of the true musical genius and enough good looks to make even a confirmed man-hater salivate. And Suzanne certainly wasn't a man-hater.

"Do you find him attractive?" her mother whispered as if she'd read Suzanne's thoughts.

"Who wouldn't? The man personifies 'tall, dark, and handsome.'"

Her mother gave a little laugh and turned her attention back to the stage.

Why not be honest? Suzanne thought, nervously fiddling with her notepad. She found Devin Bryce incredibly attractive. Of course that shouldn't surprise her. These days she met few eligible bachelors, so her resistance to good-looking men was at an all-time low. The book commanded most of her time, and the festival concert planning committee took the rest. She simply had little time to meet men. So faced with a particularly handsome member of the species dressed in evening regalia, she was bound to have a few hormonal tugs. But that was all it was.

The man in question bowed deeply, then walked to the piano, not a trace of affectation in his easy walk. He did have surprisingly long legs, however, and she wondered how he'd ever fit them under the piano.

But he managed quite well, sitting down on the piano bench and folding his legs into place. She'd thought they would look gangly and awkward once he sat down. Instead, they fit with the piano, as if the man and the instrument were of a piece, two halves of a whole. It made him even more intriguing. And attractive.

Devin Bryce isn't my type, she reminded herself as he stared at the keyboard, focusing his concentration. She definitely steered clear of tempestuous artists, even compelling and glaringly masculine ones. She hesitated to date artists at all, because she didn't like dealing with their egos. The fleeting thought entered her mind that she ought to settle down with a nice CPA who led an orderly, normal life in the suburbs.

Then she chuckled to herself. Who was she kidding? A CPA would bore her to tears. She might not want an artist, but she knew she wanted someone with a modicum of creativity in his blood.

Of course, men with whom she'd had relationships before had accused her of being too controlled and reserved for real passion. Occasionally she'd believed it might be true, that perhaps her mother's many marriages had put her off intimate relationships.

But in her soul she knew better. Her strong control came from recognizing her potential for violent emotion. After all, she still had her mother's genes. And not wanting to be like her mother, she'd kept any unpredictable feelings under tight restraint. Nonetheless, the desire for passion lay just beneath that restrictive surface, where it would remain until she found a man she could trust enough to gift with her passion.

She feared, however, that the man she wanted didn't exist—someone who fed on the artistic life but who gave as well as took; someone who didn't demand constant attention and had a life of his own, yet would be there in the important times. A sensitive man, who was . . .

The exact opposite of Mother, she finished as she glanced over to where her mother waited for the first note with rapt concentration. Actually, Suzanne realized with a pang, she wanted a man like her stepfather Valentin. She looked back to the stage, to the pianist rumored to be a moody devil, and silently compared him to Valentin. Valentin with his easygoing manner bore no resemblance to this darkly intense pianist.

No, Devin Bryce certainly isn't my type, she thought again, shifting in her seat to find a more comfortable position.

Then Bryce began to play. The soft opening strains of Beethoven's Sonata, Op. 110, filled the packed hall, hushing the low murmurs of the expectant crowd.

A pretty piece, she thought, a nice choice for an opening number, and Devin's treatment of it surprisingly delicate, almost gentle. She made a note to that effect.

The quicker movement coming next shone crisp and bright. No doubt about it, she acknowledged as she scribbled another note in her pad. The man could make the keys dance.

As the recital wore on, she found herself watching Bryce's face as he worked. His expression reflected the nuances of every evocative phrase. Her eyes were riveted on his face most of the recital as she strained forward. She only wished she could stand next to him so she could watch his magical hands at work.

His playing fascinated her, even though the music wasn't her preference. She liked clean, bare simplicity and provoking, jarring notes . . . she liked avant-garde. Romantic pieces like the Liszt Bryce played now evoked too much unrestrained emotion for her tastes. Too much wild emotion could twist a person into an unhealthy creature who drained the life out of those around them. Mother's four husbands attested to that.

A faint smile lifting the corners of her mouth, Suzanne shot her mother a sideways look. Mother was in her element, immersed in the music of past centuries. No doubt each dramatic sweep of notes sent Mother's heart pounding in ecstasy. Unfortunately, that ecstasy would later be transformed into melancholy.

If only Mother weren't always swinging from rapture to depression, Suzanne thought, then chastened herself for the thought. No amount of wishing would change Mother. She would play the role of demanding artist until she died, and Suzanne must learn to accept that role, to find her own place in the scheme of things.

The first skipping notes of Chopin's "Black Key" Etude sounded, drawing Suzanne out of her thoughts. Vivacious and exhibitionistic, it demonstrated Bryce's amazing technical skill. No wonder Chopin was considered his forte.

She scribbled down a few adjectives, then found herself seduced by the piece's sheer brilliance. Her eyelids slid shut of their own accord. Only after several seconds had passed did she shake herself out of her state of enthrallment. Furtively she glanced at the audience around her. Pleasure lit their faces too.

Admit it, she told herself as she jerked her gaze back to the stage. *You're enjoying this as much as they are. You ought to have brought Bartok. He would have loved it.*

Good Lord, she thought with a faint grin, what would Valentin have thought to see her sitting rapt and intent at a Bryce recital?

Just as she began to accept that she actually liked the music, Bryce broke off playing in the middle of a particularly intricate passage.

A low murmur rose throughout the audience. Seats creaked as people moved in them, trying to see what was occurring onstage to cause the interruption. The resumption of the music a scant few seconds later squelched the audience noises . . . until it became apparent that the piece Bryce played was no longer the etude. It was no longer Chopin. It was no longer even melodic.

It was dissonant. Strange arpeggios pierced the air, and beneath them all the insistent, rhythmic ebb and flow of one low note. Suzanne's eyes widened in shock as she recognized all too readily the avant-garde music.

Ressu. Bryce was playing Valentin Ressu. Even more surprising, he was playing "Endnote." Startled by that realization, she glanced at Bryce's face and what she saw there slowed her pulse to a crawl.

She'd never seen such horror in a man's face before. Never. Those odd crystalline eyes were fixed on his hands, which flew over the keys as if of their own accord. His lips moved angrily. Though no sound came from them, she thought they muttered curses. As he continued further into the piece, into a passage with which she was all too familiar, Bryce's face grew pale as chalk. His shoulders tensed, as if he struggled for every note. Or struggled *against* every note.

The way Bryce tore through the sonata gave her shivers. It was brilliant and terrifying all at once. What on earth was going on? What had come over Bryce?

The audience mumbled and murmured until they sounded like the angry buzzing of a beehive. Her mother leaned forward in her seat, fury making two red spots appear on her normally fair cheeks.

Meanwhile "Endnote" sounded forth with insolent bravado, daring the affronted audience to accept its audacious attack on traditional chord structures. Only Suzanne seemed to recognize the style of music.

Then Bryce launched into a passage unfamiliar to her. It was in the style of "Endnote," but she could swear she'd never heard the passage before. It chilled her blood. Her heart pounded, and her stomach roiled as it had when she'd watched Valentin struggle for life in that hospital bed during his final hours.

She tried to concentrate on the notes, but she couldn't draw her gaze from the now ashen face of Devin Bryce. Some growing dread drew her to watch him, to listen to the music he played almost maniacally. She clutched her notepad with clammy fingers, a strange panic growing within her.

Suddenly Bryce jerked his hands back from the keys as if some invisible force had released them. With a snarl, he leapt to his feet, knocking the piano bench over in the process. After staring a moment at his hands, he let out a choked curse and stalked from the stage.

Unleashed by his absence, the audience noise swelled to a roar. The house lights remained dimmed for several minutes, but Bryce didn't return. As the audience waited expectantly though not quietly, Suzanne sat in stunned silence, goosebumps stippling every inch of her skin.

Bryce had played a portion of "Endnote" . . . with brilliance, mastery, and a glimmer of mad genius. Valentin himself couldn't have done better. It had touched her, moved her . . . scared her witless.

She ought to be furiously scrawling notes in her pad, but her fingers trembled too much to hold the pencil. Even the fine hairs on her bare arms were standing on end. The minutes ticked by as she fought down the overwhelming sense of panic tightening her throat. This reaction of hers was absurd. She should be angry at Bryce's bizarre melding of Chopin's music and Valentin's, not sitting here shaking from an inexplicable terror.

Suddenly a harried-looking man, probably the house manager, took the stage and announced that due to a sudden illness, Bryce would be unable to complete the recital.

Her eyes narrowed as the man left the stage. Illness, huh? Devin Bryce was about as ill as she was. Any fool could tell that.

Righteous anger welled up within her, providing her with an escape from the strange panic clawing at her. Ill! What was the eccentric artist up to now? What kind of trick was he playing? Was this some absurd way of showing his contempt for Valentin's music?

The panic receded further as her analytical mind took over. No, that made no sense. If Bryce had planned this disturbing performance, he wouldn't have run off the stage in the middle and had the house manager announce he was ill.

And "Endnote," of all things. Devin Bryce had played "Endnote"! The blood drained from her face as panic overwhelmed her again. Slowly she settled back into her chair, on the edge of which she'd unknowingly been perched. "Endnote." No one but Mariela had ever seen the music to "Endnote," not even the committee. And certainly no one had seen the version Bryce had played, with the extra passage. If that version existed.

Of course it exists, she told herself. *Bryce played it, didn't he? He got the music from somewhere.*

She could see again the files in her office, containing all the original manuscripts of the Sonata Cycle except one vital composition.

"Endnote."

Fear shot through her senses, black and fierce, as she remembered the police investigation. They'd performed a halfhearted search before informing her there was no evidence of criminal activity on the premises.

But someone had taken it. Bryce or someone he knew? Had Bryce somehow gotten his hands on the stolen final version, which she'd apparently never heard? How on earth could he have known the music otherwise, when Valentin had never played it in public and it had never been published?

She remembered the black hair she'd found on the floor of her office. Bryce's hair was black, she thought.

"I suppose I owe you an apology," her mother muttered next to her as she stood and jerked up her purse, her face a mask of fury. "The man isn't a genius. He's insane."

No, not insane, Suzanne thought, but something definitely rang false here, something that involved the missing "Endnote" original. And Devin Bryce was in it up to his neck. She could feel it as deeply as she still felt the strange, lurking terror in her belly.

With a shiver, she knelt to pick up her beaded purse, then glanced once more at the stage. She wanted, no, *needed* to catch a glimpse of the mysterious pianist himself. But Mother's plump body shook with emotion, telling Suzanne they'd better leave before Mother could launch into an embarrassing tirade against Devin Bryce. Besides, Suzanne told herself, she'd never catch a glimpse of him now. He'd probably already escaped the hall through a back door.

So she followed her mother into the aisle quietly, although a lingering uneasiness threatened to eat her up inside. She had to know why Bryce had played "Endnote." She had to find out where he'd gotten his copy. Most of all, she had to know what in the name of heaven the man thought he was doing.

Her gaze darted back to the now-empty stage one last time as she inched along with the grumbling crowd up the side aisle. Then her eyes focused on the concert grand, now silent and innocuous as a piece of furniture. The tiniest shiver of trepidation shook her, reminding her of Bryce's almost manic playing of the missing "Endnote."

In that moment Suzanne made a decision. It was high time she met the enigmatic Devin Bryce.

3

♪

Somehow Devin made it from the elevator down the long hall to his fifth-floor apartment. He paused to lean against the wall as he waited for his stomach to stop lurching. Sweat drenched his no longer spotless white shirt, seeping through to the black jacket he'd never bothered to remove. He thrust one hand into his pocket, past his wadded-up tie, and closed his fingers around his keys.

Glancing at his watch, he groaned. Nine A.M. Hell, had he really been out all this time?

His head pounded as he straightened and pushed away from the wall. Yeah. No doubt about it. He'd been at the Bloomsday Pub all night, then wandered the streets finishing off the bottle he'd taken with him. The Irish whiskey he'd been guzzling still held a wicked grip on his body, which screamed in protest at the unfamiliar assault.

It wasn't as if he didn't know how to hold his liquor. He and Jack usually had a few Guinnesses at the Bloomsday Pub after a performance. But Devin had never had more than one or two shots of the more potent Irish whiskey. Never after a routine recital, anyway.

Yeah, but yesterday afternoon hadn't been a routine recital.

The horror he'd kept smothered all night under the blessed blanket of whiskey threatened once more to leap to life.

Don't think about it, Devin commanded with as much firmness as he could muster, given his present state. Deliberately he stepped forward toward his apartment door. The pounding in his head kept time with his pace, reminding him why he didn't usually drink much. With effort he fitted his key in the lock and turned it, then thrust the door open.

He wasn't surprised to find Jack standing in the middle of the apartment. A certain wry satisfaction crept over Devin when he realized Jack looked as much like hell as he did.

"Goddamn it, where have you been, you son of a bitch!" Jack shouted. His few red tufts of hair were sticking up in all directions, testifying that he'd spent the night on Devin's couch.

"And a very good morning to you, too," Devin grumbled while easing the door shut behind him. He rested for a moment against the door and closed his eyes, rubbing the middle of his forehead in a vain attempt to ease his headache. As he did so, he waited for Jack's tirade, which after all these years he knew to expect.

With jerky motions, Jack shook a cigarette out of the half-empty pack he held in his hand. He lit it and took a deep puff, obviously struggling to control his anger.

Apparently the effort proved too much for him. "For the love of God, I had to tell the Allied Arts people and your own goddamned agent that you were sick! I had to call Dorian Michel and kiss his effete little ass because you decided to play piano in never-never land for a while and then disappear!"

"I'm sure you handled it well." Devin patted his pocket for his own pack of cigarettes, only to realize he didn't smoke anymore.

"Yeah. Easy for you to be calm. Looks like you got enough liquor in you to float a battleship. That's just great, just jim-dandy!" He spoke through gritted teeth. "You go out and get drunk while I try to cover for you. Where'd you go?"

"Bloomsday Pub," Devin muttered before he remembered he'd had Patrick, the bar's owner, head Jack off.

Jack's face flushed with wounded emotions. "Funny. I went there myself but they told me you weren't there." He exploded. "You no-good, two-bit Mick . . . who the devil do you think you are? Somewhere you got it in your head you don't have to play by the rules, and you didn't get it from me, I can tell you that! When I asked yesterday if you were gonna pull any fast ones at the concert, I wasn't giving you a goddamned license to launch into the biggest load of crap I ever heard in my life!"

Jack continued in that vein for a while, but Devin couldn't listen. His head felt like the training ground for the cannons in Tchaikovsky's *1812 Overture,* and his throat had long ago become a parched wasteland. What was more, despite his acute nausea, he had this craving for orange juice that wouldn't quit. He'd wanted it since the concert, but he'd drunk whiskey instead.

Now, however, he couldn't resist the craving anymore. With an effort, he turned his back on Jack and forced his body to move into the kitchen. He made his way to the fridge, opened it, and began rooting around in its chaotic contents. Orange juice. His concert had ended in the biggest fiasco of his entire career, and all he could think about was orange juice. *How the mighty have fallen,* he thought, his lips twisting into a cynical smile.

"Where in the devil did that crap come from anyway?" Jack followed Devin into the kitchen, dripping ashes as he went. "It sounded like some of that modern junk you hate. Did you decide to start experimenting here? You think you're not enough of a big shot now, so you're gonna fool around with avant-garde? Goddamn it, what did you think you were doing?"

Don't ask me, Devin thought. *Ask the insane spirit or ghost or whatever the hell it was that took over my hands yesterday. It wasn't my fault!*

Unfortunately, he couldn't tell Jack that. How could he explain that some ghost had apparently played a horrible trick on him? After hours of thinking—and drinking—Devin had decided that was the only explanation. Hands had taken his over, unfamiliar hands playing unfamiliar music. The effects had been the same as when Chopin or Haydn or Liszt possessed him—the same cold sweat, the same surge of power, the same flitting images in his head. He'd recognized the experience. But not the music.

He paused a second in his search for orange juice, waves of terror washing over him again. Discordant chords flooded his memory, ungodly notes of jarring power. There'd been a perverse sort of beauty in them. But they sure as hell hadn't belonged in the middle of a Chopin etude.

A groan escaped his lips. His hands had never entirely been his own, not since the day of his first piano lesson when Chopin had come to him and he'd first seen a pair of ethereal hands floating over his. Those spirit hands had scared him at first, except that the music he'd made when the hands "helped" him had sounded a lot better than the music he'd made by himself.

With a certain childlike naïveté, he'd assumed that every pianist was occasionally visited by "the spooky hands," as he'd called them. He'd been educated on that point very fast, thanks to his piano teacher's scoffing reaction to his description of the hands. After that, he'd kept quiet, except to tell his parents.

Hell, it had been hard to come to terms with his ability, to learn to understand it. Through the years, he'd noticed patterns—the hands would appear only for certain composer's works, and not all the pairs of hands were the same.

Sometime in his college years he'd figured out that one pair belonged to Chopin, one to Beethoven, and one to Liszt. Others occasionally appeared—Tchaikovsky, Rachmaninoff—but for the most part it had been Chopin, Beethoven, and Liszt. In time he'd learned to deal with their invasion of his performances, even to accept it, for accepting it had been the only alternative to giving up the piano.

But what the hell was he supposed to do now that his ability had run amok?

"You know, Devin," Jack snarled, "I'm getting tired of hearing myself talk here. You wanna explain what was going on yesterday afternoon? You wanna tell me what to do about making it up to the sponsors? There were people at the box office wanting their money back. Nobody's ever wanted their money back before!" He paused, lowering his voice. "The Allied Arts people are gonna expect blood from you next time we sign a contract with them."

"They're welcome to my blood right now. It probably has enough whiskey in it to make anyone happy."

Jack's lips tightened at the quip. "Yeah, but is it making *you* happy, Devin? Look at you. You look like hell. You never drink like this. Is something going on I don't know about? You wanna let me in on the secret?"

Devin remained silent, not certain how he was going to explain this to Jack.

"You wanna put your two cents in here? Or are you gonna retreat behind that rebel image and pretend it never happened?"

If only that were an option, Devin thought. "I can't talk about it now. Give me a few hours, and we'll talk." *You'll have cooled off by then, and I'll be able to give you a reasonable lie.*

"I've already been waiting here all night. Come on, tell me what's going on. I can't help you if I don't know."

The cannons going off in Devin's head boomed louder instead of softer. Hell, he needed that orange juice. His search grew frantic now as he shoved items aside, looking for the juice. At last finding a lone bottle way at the back of the fridge, Devin jerked it out. Without even thinking about what he was doing, he searched for a glass, filled it half with water, then added the juice and a couple of cubes of ice to it.

At last he turned around to face Jack and placed the cold glass against his hot, aching forehead.

Jack's gaze focused first on the glass of juice, but then it shifted to the hand holding the glass, and the cussing started all over again. "What in the devil happened to your hand?" he finally managed to say between curses.

Devin tilted the glass up to his lips and took a big swig before lowering it once more. "I smashed my hand through a window."

Never had he seen Jack's bald pate turn quite that shade of purple. "You did what? You idiot, you bastard, you son of a bitch—"

"You're repeating yourself," Devin muttered before taking another swig. He glanced down at the lacerations on his hand, then shrugged. "Don't get all excited, okay? I didn't break anything. There are just a few surface cuts. I washed them with soap. They'll heal."

For once Jack was speechless.

Devin drained the glass, then closed his eyes. Last night he'd hated his hands for letting themselves be possessed, for turning on him and screwing up his life. In his drunken haze, it had made perfect sense to punish them.

Now he wondered how he'd deal with the pain if last night's debacle meant he couldn't play anymore. "You know, Jack, maybe I wasn't meant to be a pianist. Maybe I was meant to be one of those punks you seem to think I am. Maybe I'd be better off smashing windows and stealing cars." He opened his eyes and leveled his gaze on Jack. "It felt good, putting my hand through that window. It hurt like hell, but it felt good too. You ever felt that way?"

"Yeah." Jack gestured into the air, sending ashes flying everywhere. Fury burned behind his eyes. Devin could see him fighting for control. "Yeah, I've felt that way. What man hasn't? You let go of civilization, you get that fire out of your system, you feel like new. But your goddamned hand is busted so you can't play for a while, and then you start missing the feel of the keys under your fingers. Tell me something, big shot. Did smashing that window feel as good as playing Mozart?"

Devin's face clouded. Mozart. Haydn. Chopin. The notes of the "Black Key" Etude tripped through his head, evoking a piercing ache that surpassed the whiskey-induced pounding. The very poetry of the remembered music wrenched his guts.

Nothing felt as good as the piano. Nothing ever had. But damn it, some force larger than he was seemed determined to wrest his talent from him. Was this the beginning of the end? Would he gradually find himself taken over by that other force, unable to play anything without its interruption?

He had to stop whatever—or whoever—had burst into his etude yesterday. The problem was, he didn't have the vaguest idea how. In the meantime, Jack was standing there, expecting some answers. What on earth was Devin supposed to tell him?

"Look," Devin growled, "what happened yesterday will blow over in a few days. People will have their minds on something other than my eccentricities. They'll probably pay my fee since I performed for most of the recital. Sure, they'll expect a little extra next time, but that's no big deal. So if it's the money you're worried about—"

"It's not the money, and you goddamned well know it." Jack walked out of the kitchen and returned with a folded section of the newspaper. Then he approached Devin and waved it in front of his face. "So you want to pretend it didn't happen, do you? Bury your head in the sand? Well, while you're sifting grit through your teeth, you take a look at this, okay?" He pointed to an article circled in red. "Read that, big shot, and then tell me what you're gonna do."

Devin set down his empty glass and took the paper from Jack. He recognized instantly the music and entertainment section of the *Chicago Star*. His eyes focused on the byline. Suzanne Winslow.

He'd read her reviews before, more out of idle curiosity about what was going on in the world of avant-garde than out of any urge to learn her opinion. She wrote only as a guest reviewer, so her reviews didn't turn up in the paper that often. Apparently she worked for one of the local universities as a musicologist and only occasionally reviewed a performance.

Her reviews were sharp, concise . . . and merciless to performers who tried to hide their incompetence under the cloak of avant-garde. She had a nice style, a bit formal perhaps, but then that was pretty typical for music critics.

He'd read something about her recently . . . something about her and an avant-garde composer. He strained to remember, but in his present state, he drew a blank. One thing he knew for sure, however. She'd always been more interested in John Cage than in Chopin.

Yet she'd apparently reviewed his recital. Why was that? he wondered and continued to read, intrigued. It took him only a few minutes to determine that the woman had blasted him royally. With a deftness bordering on cruelty, she'd dissected his performance into neat pieces, then blown them into oblivion.

And all because of one thing, he realized as he reread the paragraphs containing the most damning lines of her review:

Bryce's genius was evident in his dazzling rendition of Mozart's Sonata No. 10 in C Major, a piece he performed with such sparkling delicacy that it resembled shimmering gold silk. The "Black Key" Etude might have fulfilled the promise of that earlier piece had Bryce not chosen to fuse it with music in the avant-garde style of a well-known composer.

"Style of a well-known composer"? Who the hell was she talking about? He read on, his blood racing.

Is this a new technique Bryce has hit upon in his usual egotistical belief that he can play whatever he wants, regardless of his audience's expectations? Will we now be subjected to compositions mingling Xenakis and

Mendelssohn, Stockhausen and Tchaikovsky? We might even accept that from a pianist who recognizes the possibilities implicit in new fusions, but in an artist who has never shown anything but contempt for the avant-garde, we can view this new aberration only as an extension of that contempt.

Devin lowered the newspaper, his mouth dry as he handed it back to Jack. "Suzanne Winslow didn't pull any punches, did she? The lady must have had it in for me for a long time."

"I wouldn't have said it any different if I'd been writing that review, and you know it. *You* probably would have said the same thing if you'd had to listen to that mess you played yesterday afternoon."

Devin couldn't deny that. Still, if Gerald Loughton, the *Chicago Star*'s regular music critic, had written the review, he'd have softened the blow a little. Devin ran his fingers through his hair and wandered back into the living room distractedly. He had to make some decisions here and figure out a way to get through this whole thing. But how could he think when his body felt like smashed bricks?

Jack followed behind him and tossed the paper section onto the couch. "So what are you gonna do about this mess?"

"When and where's my next engagement?"

"St. Louis, a week from Tuesday. After that, you got New Orleans to deal with."

Devin steeled himself. "Have Dorian Michel cancel them both."

"What?!"

"I want them cancelled. Tell him I'm sick. I have some things I've got to work out before I can play again. Just leave me alone, and let me do it."

Jack's eyes narrowed. "Michel's not gonna be happy about this, you know."

"I don't care. After yesterday, the sponsors in St. Louis

and New Orleans will probably be relieved, especially if they got a look at Winslow's review. In any case, it doesn't matter. I've got to cancel . . . unless you think a repeat of yesterday's performance would be better for my career."

Jack stared at him intently, then pulled out another cigarette. "You still gotta explain to me what happened yesterday. I'm your manager. I deserve to know."

For a moment, an intense urge to confide in Jack struck Devin. "It's kind of complicated," he began hesitantly. "Believe me, you really don't want to know."

"Listen, we've never talked about your daddy before, but maybe we ought to. Does this have anything to do with him?" As Devin stiffened, he rushed on. "I mean, I know he had some sort of problem in his head. I know that what he did has gotta be tough for you to live with, even as an adult. They say when you got something like that in your past, it can simmer in the insides of you and explode years later when no one expects it—"

"This has nothing to do with Dad or his 'problem.' Not a damned thing." At least not in the way Jack thought it did. Jack's mention of Dad, however, had reminded him why he couldn't come clean about his own peculiar situation, not even to Jack.

"I'm tryin' to help you here," Jack muttered.

"Yeah, I know. The best way you can help right now is to get Michel to cancel those concerts, and give me time to sort things out. Alone."

Jack didn't even try to mask the hurt in his eyes. "You know, you can carry this loner bit too far. You might find yourself out on a limb by yourself one of these days."

"Believe me, I know that too," Devin said softly, a lump forming in his throat, but he didn't back down. "Trust me on this one, okay? Have the agency cancel my next two engagements. And call me when you've finished taking care of it."

Jack knew he'd been dismissed. He looked as if he were

SILENT SONATA

about to say something, then turned on his heel and stalked from the room.

As soon as the door had shut behind Jack, Devin moved to the couch and collapsed on it, stretching his long legs out in front of him. He closed his eyes and tried to think through the pain creating havoc in his head.

What now? Somehow he had to get through this. Somehow he had to find out what was going on and take steps to stop it. Maybe he should visit a shrink.

No, he thought. *I know I'm not suffering from any delusions, but that's what they'll say is the problem. This isn't in my head, not the way they'd think it is anyway.*

He'd be better off with a psychic, he told himself wryly, then shuddered. The last thing he wanted was to get pulled into that nebulous world of mediums and stargazers, where you couldn't tell the real mystics from the charlatans. Still, he had to start somewhere. But where?

Something pressed into the small of his back, and he rolled to his side enough to wrangle it out from under him. It was the newspaper section with Winslow's review. He slid into a sitting position and stared blindly at the circled column, then focused on the words, "the avant-garde style of a well-known composer." For a moment he continued to stare, the wheels turning in his mind.

The "style of a well-known composer," he thought again. That's it! This Suzanne Winslow knew whose music he'd been playing . . . or at least she knew whose style the music resembled. That was something. Why not start there? If she would tell him what musician was tormenting him by taking over his hands, then . . .

He groaned and fell back against the couch. Why would Suzanne Winslow tell him anything? First of all, her review made it clear she thought he had an ego the size of Wrigley Field. Secondly, he couldn't explain his reasons for wanting the information. What could he say? "Ms. Winslow, I don't know whose music I was playing the other day. You see, ghosts sometimes possess my hands, and I don't know this one's identity. Could you please enlighten me?"

No, that would go over like a ton of bricks. He could imagine Suzanne Winslow's reaction. He didn't know her personally, but the musicologists he'd met fell into two types: gushing and expressive lovers of music or gaunt and bitter failed musicians. He bet she fell into the latter category. He could almost envision a reedy, fiftyish woman with the look of a schoolteacher and a razor-edged tongue.

No, he couldn't talk to Suzanne Winslow about this. So he was back where he'd started. He stretched out on the comfortable couch, tossing the newspaper section onto the floor. The midmorning sun flooded the couch with light, forcing him to wince and close his eyes. He threw his arm over his face. Maybe if he lay here a few minutes and got control of his body, he could come up with a roundabout way to get the answers he needed, he told himself. Maybe . . .

Devin didn't even realize he'd drifted off to sleep until the phone beside the couch rang, its shrill sound jarring him immediately out of disturbing dreams. He thought about stuffing the offending noisemaker under a couch cushion and going back to sleep.

One look at the afternoon sky outside his window made him decide to answer instead. It was probably Jack anyway, calling to tell him what Dorian Michel had said about canceling St. Louis and New Orleans.

He picked up the phone and muttered, "Hey."

The long pause at the other end of the phone told him he'd guessed wrong. "Ah . . . may I please speak to Mr. Devin Bryce?"

The feminine voice sounded young and hesitant. And unfamiliar, definitely unfamiliar.

"This is Devin Bryce," he said formally to make up for the "hey."

He heard a quick intake of breath before the woman

spoke again. "My name is Suzanne Winslow. But before you hang up, I want you to know that—"

"Why would I hang up?" Then the name registered. Suzanne Winslow of the cutthroat review. His eyebrows arched in disbelief. This young-sounding, throaty voice belonged to Suzanne Winslow?

"You didn't read my review," she said. He couldn't tell if her tone held disappointment or relief.

"Of course I read it. I read all the reviews of my performances." He added with malicious delight, "It feeds my ego, you see, and my colossal ego needs all the nourishment it can get. Your review didn't give it much."

The sarcasm wasn't lost on her. "I didn't call to defend my review, Mr. Bryce."

Her abruptly chilly tone seemed more in character for the woman he'd envisioned earlier. "Then why *did* you call?"

"I need to discuss something with you." She paused.

Devin's interest in this conversation was gaining speed by the minute. "Yes?"

"It's difficult to talk about over the phone. I'd prefer to discuss it in person. This evening."

Earlier he'd thought it might be good to talk to her, but her peremptory tone drove all consideration of that right out of his mind. He gave a short, hollow laugh. "Why on earth would I want to meet you? So you can trash my performance to my face? No, thank you. One disemboweling a day is my limit, lady."

She completely ignored his comment. "I think you'd be interested in what I have to say in private about your performance yesterday. Surely even you understand that I had to write an honest review or risk misleading the paper's readers. But I didn't say as much about the music you . . . ah . . . performed as I might have . . . and perhaps should have."

He sat suddenly bolt upright, remembering the conclusions he'd drawn earlier about her knowledge of the piece he'd played. "Is this about the 'well-known composer'?"

"Of course," she said in her no-nonsense voice, as if he ought to realize exactly what she wished to discuss.

He settled back against the couch, working through all the angles. This could be just what he wanted. He could pry information out of her without having to reveal why he wanted it. Hell, he might not even have to pry. It sounded as if she had a secret she wanted to get off her chest, and he'd certainly like to hear it.

Out of the blue, something clicked in his head and he vaguely remembered what he'd read about her and another composer. "You're the one who's been doing all the work on that guy . . . that Romanian composer . . . uh, what's his name?"

"Ressu. And you know quite well what his name is, Mr. Bryce."

Why on earth would she say that? he wondered. Then it dawned on him. It must have been Ressu's music he'd played yesterday afternoon. And, of course, she'd assumed he knew what he was playing.

She continued, "Will you meet me or not? I promise it will be to our mutual benefit."

I'm not sure how it'll help you, he thought, *but it damned well couldn't hurt me.*

"Okay," he said. "When and where?"

"How about eight or nine tonight? And since I'm the one insisting on this meeting, why don't you choose the place?"

Good idea, he thought. He definitely wanted this particular meeting to take place on his home turf. "Bloomsday Pub. I'll see you there at eight."

She didn't know how to reach the place and said so. He gave her directions, then added offhandedly, "I'll pick you up if you want."

"No need." Her refusal was crisp. "I assure you this is

business, Mr. Bryce, and not some pathetic ploy to get a date with you."

"Oh, I don't doubt that." A grin tugged at his lips in spite of himself. Somehow he couldn't imagine this efficient-sounding woman angling to manipulate a man. If she wanted something, he didn't doubt she'd come right out and ask for it. "How will I know you?"

"I know what you look like, so I'll make sure I find you. I'll see you at eight."

"Wouldn't miss it." He hung up the phone.

What a great development, he thought. If this had to do with Ressu, Devin could use all the info he could get from the woman. Hadn't Ressu died recently? If so, that would explain a few things, although he couldn't imagine why Ressu would be haunting him.

Unless the composer did it out of spite for the way Devin had always disparaged avant-garde. Simply because other dead composers had never played malicious tricks on Devin didn't mean one of them couldn't.

The urge for orange juice shot through him again. Had Ressu liked watered-down orange juice? he wondered as the craving settled into his gut. It wouldn't surprise him one bit.

Of course, nothing would surprise him, since he didn't know a damned thing about the man. Devin thought of the one time he'd met Ressu at a cocktail party. They'd been introduced, talked awkwardly for a few moments, and then quickly sought better companions. He couldn't even remember what they'd talked about, but it hadn't been significant.

What little Devin knew about Ressu, he'd gotten from the newspapers. The Romanian composer had settled in Chicago, written atonal, contemporary music for years, and then died a few months ago. Not much information to go on, Devin thought.

Well, that settled it. Before he met with Winslow, he had to learn more about Ressu. He glanced down at his watch.

It read 2:15. He had to get to a music library. His best bet was probably the one at the University of Chicago. Their programs focused on composition, and they were well known for their emphasis on the avant-garde and ethnic music. They were bound to have stuff on Ressu. He had just enough time to get there and take a look at what they had, so he'd be able to outmaneuver Suzanne Winslow when she started bombarding him with questions. Besides, if he could get the lowdown on Ressu, he'd be a hell of a lot closer to figuring out what had happened yesterday afternoon and why.

While he was at it, he'd better also look into Suzanne Winslow's connection with Ressu, he told himself as he maneuvered his stiff bones into a sitting position. He had a sneaky feeling he'd need all the ammunition he could get in dealing with her.

4

♪

Bloomsday Pub in Chicago's Bridgeport neighborhood represented every James Joyce scholar's dream come true. A huge map of the route Bloom had taken on his journeys in James Joyce's *Ulysses* dominated one end of the dark, smoky room, while replicas of Joyce's walking sticks marched along the walls among framed photos of Joyce and his friends.

Suzanne sat at the polished mahogany bar in full view of the stained-glass entrance door. She'd spent the last half hour cataloging all the items in the pub alluding to *Ulysses,* surprised to discover how many she recognized. Valentin had once commented that he was accomplishing with music what Joyce had done with language in *Finnegans Wake*. After he'd told her that, she'd struggled through all of Joyce's works, even though her strongest subject had never been English literature.

She scanned the filled pub again and her eyes lit upon the ornate clock hanging over the door. Anger surged through her.

That blasted man! she thought. Eight thirty and he still hadn't shown up!

With jerky movements she picked up the half-page menu of Joycean-titled munchies, including such delicacies as Plumtree's Potted Meat Pies and Luscious Goosebosom Pâté. Maybe she should order something to take her mind off the time.

No, she thought, slapping the menu back down on the bar. She didn't intend to wait for Devin Bryce much longer. She sipped her glass of Chardonnay, noting that she'd soon have to order another or sit there conspicuously taking up valuable space at the crowded bar. Shifting around on the barstool, she attempted to get the blood moving in her stiff behind.

Typical musician, she told herself as she tucked one gold lock of hair behind her ear. She should have expected this after yesterday's performance and her peculiar phone conversation with Bryce. Obviously he'd been putting her off when he'd agreed to meet her. He must have thought about the whole thing and decided to skip her "disemboweling," as he'd put it.

Admittedly, her review had flayed him a bit, but not nearly as much as it could have. After dashing home to type up her scribbled notes, then filing them by modem with Leon, she'd spent the night tossing in her bed and replaying the afternoon's recital. She'd concluded Devin Bryce had either stolen Valentin's "Endnote" or bought it from the person who had. No other explanation made sense. And his refusal to meet her clearly proved his guilt.

Remembering Bryce's unholy performance of the work made her ache to fling at him the accusing words that burned in her throat. She wouldn't let him get away with this, she thought as she downed the rest of her Chardonnay. Devin Bryce was in for a surprise if he thought avoiding her would keep her from finding out the truth.

She ordered a second glass of wine and nursed it for fifteen minutes. But Bryce didn't show up, and the sleazy-looking man sitting alone at the other end of the bar was eyeing her as if she were a steak hot off the grill. In a few more minutes he'd no doubt sidle in her direction, then offer to buy her a drink. She didn't intend to stay around for that.

"You haven't seen the last of me, Mr. Bryce," she muttered as she plunked a tip down and slid off the stool. Tucking her purse under her arm and straightening her beret, she strode for the door, her heels clicking on the hardwood floor. As she reached for the brass handle, she glimpsed a man hurrying toward her on the other side of the glass. Seconds later he shoved the door open, right in her face.

She jumped back in time to miss the door, but not him. They collided with enough force to knock her off-balance. Fortunately he caught her before she fell. She drew back, still dazed, and reached up to adjust her beret. Then she looked up into the same eerie eyes she'd seen yesterday. They were a light, clear blue, no doubt about it.

And they belonged to Devin Bryce.

He looked as stunned as she, his mouth partially open and those thick brows of his arched in astonishment. "Hell, I'm really sorry," he said as he knelt to pick up her purse, which had fallen and opened up on the floor, scattering its contents everywhere.

All she seemed able to do was stand and gawk . . . at the shock of coal-black hair hiding his face as he knelt . . . at the sculpted muscles visible beneath the rumpled cotton shirt he wore with glove-tight blue jeans . . . and at the long nimble fingers of his right hand plucking up her compact and wallet, and then reaching for her . . .

Tampons. Good Lord, she thought, her face turning a thousand shades of red as he hesitated a fraction of a second, his fingers hovering over the embarrassing items.

"I'll get them," she mumbled, then knelt quickly beside him, snatched the tampons up, took the purse from him, and began stuffing tampons and other items into it, unable to meet his eyes.

"I'm really sorry," he repeated in a husky voice just inches from her, which only increased her embarrassment. "I didn't mean to cause so much trouble. I'm late for an appointment and I . . ."

His voice trailed off as she lifted her eyes to lock with his. An odd kind of crackling awareness shivered between them, unsettling her completely.

"I—I'm the appointment," she stammered as she snapped the clasp of her purse shut and rose to her feet.

Once standing, she felt a little better, more in control of the situation. He stood also, revealing he was a few inches taller than she, and she wasn't exactly short.

She drew in a steadying breath, then thrust out her hand. "I'm Suzanne Winslow," she said in a brisk, businesslike tone, as if she hadn't just been stuffing personal items into her purse.

He took her hand, his strong, supple fingers wrapping tightly around her slender, manicured ones. The contact of warm flesh to flesh startled her. Her image of him had prepared her to expect skin as cool and hard as the ivories he touched daily, not this living, shaping heat. For one brief moment, she felt as the piano keys must feel under his fingers—expectant, waiting to be brushed by genius.

Then he released her hand, and his gaze left her face to survey her body, from her beret, down past her charcoal wool-blend jacket and her maize silk blouse tucked neatly into a pair of charcoal slacks to her expensive black pumps. Despite the thoroughness with which he did it, his frank appraisal made her glad she'd dressed with more care and pizzazz than normal.

"*You're* Suzanne Winslow?" His tone of voice mirrored his incredulous expression.

Something about that expression shattered the strange languid silence she'd lapsed into and brought a resurgence of all her anger at having been kept waiting for nearly an hour. "What's so amazing about that?"

His eyes glittered darkly for a second. "It's just that you're not at all what I was expecting."

"What do you mean?"

"I expected a bun."

That threw her completely. She stared at him wide-eyed, twisting the thin strap of her purse in her hand. "A—a bun?"

The grin he shot her transformed him from self-absorbed artist to charmer, and she reacted to the transformation with a quickened pulse, despite her determination to resist it.

"Yeah. Your hair." He nodded at her thick, straight mass. "It's all hanging down and long and—" The grin widened as he broke off. "It's very pretty. I kind of expected a tight-assed woman with her hair in a bun . . . or one of those short, trendy cuts."

Was his frankness supposed to throw her off balance? Well, it wouldn't work. Retreating into her guise of self-contained, competent scholar, she said in her most formal voice, "I'm so sorry to disappoint you."

The chilly reception didn't seem to faze him. With a rumbling chuckle, he shook his head. "Now *that* is exactly what I expected."

A couple entering the bar was forced to shoulder past Bryce. But Suzanne scarcely noticed the look of irritation they flashed in the direction of Bryce's broad back, blocking the door. Nor did she move when he shifted his body out of the way.

"You expected me to disappoint you, Mr. Bryce?"

"No. I expected the snooty tone. I was definitely prepared for that."

She bristled immediately, especially since the accusation had such a familiar ring. Her mother had always accused her of being a snob, since Suzanne didn't let it all hang out as Felicia Winslow's friends did. Somehow it didn't surprise her that Bryce shared her mother's opinion.

Her words were sharp. "You'd be snooty too if you'd been kept waiting alone in an unfamiliar bar for the last forty-five minutes." Then she wished she could take back the anger in her tone, for she'd always prided herself on being able to control her emotions better than her mother.

His cocky grin softened. "Yeah, I guess I would. And I am sorry about that. I . . . er . . . was in the middle of a kind of research project and lost track of the time."

His tone told her there was more to it than that, but she didn't ask, determined to go straight to the matter at hand. But first they had to get out of the middle of the path, so the people weaving around them could stop flashing them dirty looks.

"Shall we find a table?" she asked.

"Yeah, sure. I'll take care of it."

He called over one of the barmaids, a plump redhead who appeared to be in her late thirties. All smiles and dimples, the woman approached them, wide hips swinging beneath tight polyester slacks of an outrageous chartreuse. "Well, if it ain't our favorite local boy." She screwed up her heavily lipsticked mouth into an amiable smile. "Devin Bryce, didn't I just throw you out of here in the wee hours of the morning?"

He glanced at Suzanne, his eyes briefly glinting defiance before he bestowed on the barmaid the same charming grin he'd given Suzanne moments before. "Nah, Maggie. Must have been some other guy."

Bryce had been here last night? Suzanne thought. Then he certainly hadn't been "ill" as the house manager had claimed.

"How's the hand?" Maggie asked Bryce.

For the first time, Suzanne noticed the flesh-colored bandage wrapped around his left hand. He lifted it for Maggie's perusal, then shrugged. "It'll heal."

"What happened to your hand?" Suzanne couldn't help asking.

"Oh, last night the fool put it—" Maggie began.

Bryce cut her off. "Hey, Maggie, is that room upstairs still available?"

Maggie grinned at his attempt to keep Suzanne from knowing what had happened, then shook her head as if to say, *What's the use?* She told Bryce dryly, "Sure. It's available. You two go on up. But give me your order first. You want Guinness or you want your own bottle of whiskey again tonight?" Maggie gave him a little wink.

He staggered back with a mock expression of wounded dignity. "Mags, you're going to make my lady friend here think I spend all my time hitting the sauce. Hell, she already thinks I'm an arrogant bastard."

"That's 'cause you are," Maggie retorted, ignoring his expression. "Guinness or whiskey?"

"Guinness," he said, the word suddenly crisp and cool, though a smile glinted in his eyes. "And I'd thank you to make it cold enough."

The dimples on her face deepened. "Oh, yes, sir," she said with exaggerated respect. "It'll be cold as a witch's tit." She scribbled down their orders, now all efficiency. "And what'll the lady be havin'?"

"Ginger ale," Suzanne put in quickly. No more wine for her this evening, not if she wanted to keep her wits about her in the battle with Bryce. Judging from his flippant air, it would be some battle. Idly she wondered if he hit the whiskey very often. Had he called for a bottle last night?

"Anything to eat?" Maggie asked Bryce.

"Just my usual fries," he answered, then turned to Suzanne. "Can I buy you a Plumtree's Potted Meat Pie or something?"

SILENT SONATA

"No, no, I've had dinner."

After Maggie strolled away to the bar, Bryce urged Suzanne forward.

"You must come here often," she commented as she allowed him to steer her toward a wrought-iron spiral staircase tucked away next to a sign with an arrow and the word WASHROOMS.

"My business manager, Jack Warton, and I have been coming here since before I was old enough to drink, so they know me pretty well. Also, Maggie's a friend of my mother's."

She stopped and looked at him, startled. "She doesn't look old enough."

He chuckled. "Maggie? She's fifty-two. Looks good for her age, doesn't she? It's the hair. She dyes it a different color every spring . . . says if the flowers can bloom in spring, so can she."

Suzanne couldn't believe Devin Bryce was actually discussing a waitress's hair color. Talk about not being what one expected, she thought as they climbed up to the second floor. Bryce most definitely ran against type. She'd known hundreds of pianists in her day—charismatic performers, prissy showmen, boorish chauvinists, foreign maestros with thick accents—every variation in existence. But she'd never met a concert pianist whose accent had the faintest trace of Bridgeport Irish and who apparently felt as comfortable chatting with a waitress as with a symphony conductor.

Nor one whose arms seemed built more for hefting girders than for working the keys. Her eyes fell on his unbandaged right hand, which reached to open the door of a secluded room they'd stopped in front of. Well, at least he had a pianist's hands, she admitted, then tried to ignore the wayward memory of how one of those hands had felt touching hers.

As he ushered her into the room, she scanned her surroundings. The walls were of the same mahogany used elsewhere in the bar, but here the dark wood unfortunately accentuated the room's smallness. Nor did it help that the window set in one wall had apparently been broken and was now covered with thick, black tar paper. Still, some would call the tight space cozy. With Devin Bryce in it, Suzanne merely found it claustrophobic.

How to begin this peculiar conversation? she wondered as she watched him shut the door. How could she find out if Bryce had stolen "Endnote" without coming out and actually accusing him? The man had an international reputation. You didn't pounce on a man like that without considering the consequences.

She slid around one end of the scarred wooden table that practically filled the room. Trying to appear nonchalant, she dusted off one of three chairs jammed up close to the table, then sat gingerly on its edge.

"Jack and I like to drink in this room," he explained as he too took a seat, though without bothering to dust anything. "It has character."

Oh, yes, she thought wryly as she looked at the somber photo of James Joyce gracing the wall opposite her. The venerable novelist stared disapprovingly at her through his round glasses, as if keeping watch over the countryman who sat right beneath him. She vaguely remembered something about Joyce's being a great lover of music, but wasn't sure if that was true.

"I suppose we're here to talk about yesterday's recital," Bryce began without preamble.

So he planned to be direct about this, did he? She dropped her gaze from the photo of Joyce and met Bryce's equally unsmiling one.

"Yes," she replied. She said nothing more, wanting him to take the lead in the conversation.

Maybe if she gave him enough rope, he'd hoist himself by his own petard, she thought, then groaned inwardly. He had her so flustered, she was mixing metaphors.

Before he could say more, however, the door at the end of the room swung open and Maggie breezed in with their drinks. "Ginger ale for the lady, and a Guinness for you, Devin." Maggie bestowed a sunny smile on him as she set down the frosted mug and glass of ginger ale. Then she placed a steaming plate of thick french fries and a bottle of ketchup conspicuously next to Bryce's mug. She lifted her hand, and for a second, Suzanne got the distinct impression she was going to ruffle his hair, almost as a mother does with her child.

Then Maggie seemed to catch herself and merely muttered, "We try to take good care of our Devin."

Under the room's one bare bulb, Maggie looked far older than she had in the dim lights of the downstairs, much closer to the fifty-two Bryce claimed she was. "He's the only customer who's got musical talent," Maggie continued. "Most of the men who come here are the scholarly types who go on and on about the Joyce stuff. You ever heard Devin play and sing Irish airs? You'd never guess he could sing, too, would you?" Without waiting for an answer, she went on. "Well, if that's all for now, I'll be going on down. I'll check on you every once in a while."

"Thanks, Mags," Bryce said, "but you needn't bother. We'll call if we need you."

"All righty," she murmured, winking at Suzanne. Suzanne found herself smiling in response, but by then the woman had breezed out as quickly as she'd breezed in.

"Irish airs?" Suzanne couldn't resist saying as Bryce drowned the fries in ketchup. "You really do avoid playing modern music, don't you? No rock and roll . . . blues . . . jazz?"

He didn't answer at first. Instead he ate several fries, then licked his fingers before taking a large gulp of Guinness. She wondered how he could enjoy the food with such gusto, when her stomach roiled at the thought of the confrontation ahead.

Finally he fixed her with his gaze, deep, shuttered, intense. "I appreciate a good melody. And yes, I like jazz, too, and rock and roll, when it isn't all rhythm. But I don't do much with atonal, experimental stuff, if that's what you mean. It's elitist music that doesn't touch the people."

"Does that make me an elitist for liking it?"

He shrugged. "Maybe. Only you can answer that. But I come from the South Side, Ms. Winslow. My parents were low to middle class. Avant-garde wasn't exactly accessible to people from my neighborhood. Your average Joe wants melody, emotion, magic. It's hard to get that out of the experimental stuff being performed today. I guess I prefer that my art feed the masses from which I rose. I don't feel comfortable playing avant-garde when it will touch so few."

"You play Valentin Ressu's music," she put in quietly.

He recoiled as if he'd been struck, dropping the fry he'd been about to lift to his mouth. The faint dark circles under his eyes deepened. Then he dropped his gaze from her face and concentrated on choosing another french fry.

"What makes you say that?" he asked in a deceptively casual tone.

So he wanted to be evasive, did he? "Because you played his music yesterday afternoon."

He remained silent a moment. "Ressu was your mentor, wasn't he?"

The abrupt change of subject surprised her less than his knowledge of her background. "How did you know he was my mentor?"

"Everyone knows you're the Ressu expert."

Yes, but she hadn't expected him to know it. He didn't keep up with avant-garde. Did he?

She regarded him with more caution than she had previously. His very skin seemed alive with rebellion. The dark shadow of whiskers brushed along his sharp jaw gave him a rakish look as he put two french fries in his mouth, then chewed.

"I make no secret of my musical preferences, just as you make no secret of yours," she retorted.

"Why did you choose Ressu?"

Judging from his expression, the question was prompted

by genuine curiosity. She answered without hesitation, a sharp burst of challenge in her voice, "Because I liked that he wasn't bogged down in sentiment. Because he stretched the boundaries of traditional Western tonality. Because he didn't rest until he found a unique expression for what he wanted to say musically."

A speculative gleam lit his eyes. "I see. So it had nothing to do with his being your stepfather for a while."

The statement, with all its personal implications, stunned her. Although many of Valentin's close friends knew about her mother's marriage to Valentin, the general public did not. She struggled to maintain her composure. "How did you know that?"

He shrugged, his eyes not quite meeting hers. "I knew Ressu . . . some."

She thought back to the comments Valentin had made about Bryce. If Bryce had been Valentin's friend, Valentin would have said so, but he hadn't. Ever.

Her suspicion of Bryce increased. Time to play hardball, she decided. Leaning forward, she planted her elbows on the table. "Is that why you played 'Endnote' yesterday?"

" 'Endnote'?"

"That piece you stuck in the middle of the Chopin. You know, the one that made you 'ill.' Incidentally, you're looking very well this evening. I'm glad to see your illness has worn off."

She settled back in her chair with satisfaction, lifting her glass to sip the ginger ale. His gaze on her remained steady.

But apprehension flickered deep in his ice-blue eyes. "Oh, yeah, my illness. Amazing how these viruses can come and go so suddenly."

"Nothing like a hefty dose of whiskey to get rid of a virus, huh?"

Her barb was met by the lowering of those dark brows. Bryce leaned back in his chair until he'd balanced it on the back two legs, like a little boy defying his mother.

But the eyes alive with anger were definitely not those of

a child. "Have you got a reason for being so antagonistic, or are you always this obnoxious?"

"Only when I think Valentin's music isn't being given the respect it deserves."

He seemed to ponder that, then leaned forward, the legs of the chair coming down with a bang. "So we're back to that, are we?" He ate another couple of fries before adding, "Why do you insist I was playing Ressu's music yesterday?"

"Don't you *know* what you were playing?"

"It was just a little improvisation." The evasive uncertainty in his voice made the edges of his mouth tauten.

She shook her head. "Don't play dumb with me, Mr. Bryce. I know the piece you played yesterday quite well. It's Valentin's, all right."

"Is that so? What I played has never appeared among Ressu's piano works."

"What do you know about Valentin's piano works?" she said with contempt. "You hate his music."

He shrugged. "Like any other piano student, I studied him."

"You never studied 'Endnote.' "

"Well, at least we agree on something. After your snide little hints about Ressu on the phone this afternoon, I figured you must have decided I was playing Ressu's stuff." A grim smile settled on his face. "But I knew I couldn't be, so I checked this afternoon to make sure he didn't have a similar piece. That's why I was late. Nothing remotely resembling what I played at the recital appears among his works for piano. I scanned every sonata to be sure."

A disturbing sense that something wasn't quite right skittered down her spine. So Bryce had gone so far as to check into Valentin's published works to see if "Endnote" had been published? She might have more trouble with this than she had thought. And clearly Bryce was also more devious than she'd expected.

"You were playing Valentin's 'Endnote,' and you know it

as well as I do. But you're right. It's not listed among his works." She paused before adding, "That's because it's never been published. But it's his, all right."

His eyes narrowed. "What makes you so sure? If it's never been published, how can you be certain I played this 'Endnote'? Just from hearing Ressu play something similar a time or two?"

"No. From transcribing the unpublished manuscript by hand."

Now she had him, she thought as she glanced at his face. She'd expected him to respond with guilt, with fear, with anger at being outsmarted. Instead, he stared at her, a stunned expression carved in his implacable features and his eyes hollow. He shoved the half-eaten plate of fries away from him.

"I see," he muttered.

A feeling of power rushed through her. She ran her finger lightly through the condensation on her glass of ginger ale, watching the drops trickle off her fingers as she sought for the most effective way to make her accusation.

Calm and aloof, she lifted her gaze slowly back to his. "No, you don't see. Not yet. There's more. A lot more. The original manuscript for 'Endnote' was stolen from my files a few days ago."

He didn't fail to catch her meaning. His fingers clutched the mug of Guinness like a lifeline.

"I have a copy, the one I transcribed," she added, wanting to make clear his little scheme wouldn't work. "So I know the piece as well as you know any Chopin. You played it yesterday. There's no doubt in my mind about that. You took Valentin's last piece, his most brilliant work, and tromped on it publicly. I simply want to know why."

Now he looked decidedly pale, though the intensity in his eyes sent fear slithering through her. "Why do you say I 'tromped on it publicly'?"

"You tacked it on to the end of a Chopin piece and took

it up in the middle as if it were some perverse Chopin variation on a theme!"

"You claim to know the piece. So tell me—did I play well the parts I did play? That's the question. Did I play them with contempt?"

She stared at him blindly, her mind shifting to the recital and the rendition of "Endnote" he'd performed, the one that had roused such a strange panic in her. "It was . . ." She faltered a moment, then opted for honesty. "It was the most perfect performance I could have imagined. Except for the passage you added." Not to mention that it had temporarily stricken her with terror.

He seemed taken aback by her words. He blinked, then jerked his gaze from her. "So how was I showing contempt?" His tone was faraway.

"Oh, for Pete's sake, you know why! You didn't even play the piece in its entirety! You stuck some passages from it in the middle of something else, then stalked off and had the stage manager announce you were ill!"

In her anger, she conveniently thrust from her mind the memory of how horrified he'd looked at the time.

His gaze swung back to her, cold, silent, remote. "I didn't tell them to make that announcement. Jack did. I was too busy hightailing it out of Orchestra Hall."

The odd self-loathing in his tone made her shiver. This whole conversation was growing stranger by the minute. "Why? Why did you play 'Endnote' and then run from the stage?"

He seemed to struggle with himself for a moment. The frown lines in his forehead deepened. He patted his pocket, as if searching for a pack of cigarettes, then jerked his hand back to the table.

He met her gaze with eyes the color of skyscraper windows reflecting a vivid blue sky. "You want the truth?"

"Of course."

"Sometimes when I'm on stage, I . . . I have these odd lapses. Pieces of music I hadn't planned on playing pop into my head, and I feel suddenly compelled to play them. Usually, it happens between pieces. This is the first time it's ever happened while I was actually in the middle of another piece, so you can see why the whole thing upset me."

She looked at him, uncomprehending. "What are you saying?"

His gaze shifted from hers to focus on the broken window. "It's kind of a subconscious thing, you know? An attack of the nerves or something. My mind changes gears and my hands go with it."

For a second, a nameless terror came over her again, surging up in her throat like bile, as it had at the recital. Angry at herself for having these strange bouts of insidious fear, she snapped, "That's the most absurd thing I've ever heard."

"Yeah, well, that's the only explanation I have for you."

His profile revealed nothing of what he was thinking, but her instincts told her he wasn't telling the whole truth. Granted, his explanation did make an odd sort of sense. As she'd reasoned before, if he'd chosen to play the piece, why had he stormed off the stage in the middle, looking as though the devil were after him?

Still, something more than a "subconscious" whim was at work here, something that made him evasive and edgy. She knew it. But what could it be, if it wasn't his guilt over having stolen the manuscript?

Besides, his explanation didn't account for how he knew "Endnote."

"Where do you get these 'pieces of music' that pop into your head while you're playing?" she asked.

He lifted the mug of Guinness to his lips and took a big swig. When he set down the mug, a little foam remained on his upper lip and his tongue darted out to lick it off. The gesture seemed so oddly sensual it sent an unexpected wisp of desire curling up through her.

She dragged her gaze from his mouth, wondering how one man could have this much potent charm. What was it about musicians that made even the most sane women melt?

"It's just music I know," he replied, apparently oblivious of the effect he had on her. "I have an excellent memory. Once I hear a piece, it sort of lodges itself in my head. So when I'm in a recital, I'll get this urge to play a Beethoven sonata instead of a Chopin nocturne. When it happens, the urge is so strong, I don't fight it."

"But I explained to you. 'Endnote' has never been published. What's more, Ressu never played it publicly. You couldn't possibly know the piece. Not unless you *have* the original."

There. Her cards were out on the table now. *Let me see you wriggle out of that,* she thought.

He didn't even try. Instead, he slammed one fist down on the table with such force it made the drink in her nearly full glass slosh out onto the table. "You're crazy, you know that?" he exploded. She heard his chair's legs scrape against the floor as he pushed away from the table and jumped to his feet. "Christ! I unknowingly play a snatch of something you think is a Ressu piece, and you're ready to accuse me of stealing his manuscripts!"

Perhaps she'd gone too far, she thought as his outrage sank in. "No, I—I'm not accusing you of stealing," she hastened to tell him. "But you might have seen the missing manuscript. Maybe someone showed it to you, and it stuck in your mind. Then you remembered bits of it later and played it."

His eyes met hers, full of wariness and suppressed anger. But he seemed to consider her explanation as he leaned back against the wall and crossed his arms over his chest. Something in his defensive stance made her think of a sleek Doberman, at its most menacing when cornered. Funny how the fierce set of his jaw thrilled rather than intimidated her. The man was probably a thief and a liar. But he gave forth an electric hum of danger that enticed her as surely as a Stradivarius drew a master violinist.

"I'd really like to get my hands on that manuscript," she added urgently. "It's a later version than mine, and I need it for the book I'm writing on Ressu. It's important to me to have that version. Please. If you'd think back, you might be able to remember who showed it to you."

Alarm registered in his eyes. He drew himself taut, clenching his unbandaged hand. "No one showed it to me."

"But—"

"I must have heard Ressu play it."

"I told you. Valentin never played it publicly."

"Then I must have heard him play it privately."

"Right." She rolled her eyes. Exasperation sharpened her tone. "Valentin invited you over for a private recital of his music, which you eagerly attended since you couldn't wait to hear 'that atonal, experimental stuff' that elitists like us enjoy."

Bryce winced to hear his words thrown back at him. "Just because I don't enjoy performing experimental music doesn't mean I have no interest in it at all. For all you know, Ressu and I had a zillion discussions about it."

Why was he so determined to convince her he'd known Valentin? What was he hiding? "Look, you couldn't possibly have known Valentin well enough for him to have played 'Endnote' for you."

"Oh? Are you the only person he played for? Were you close enough to Ressu to know exactly who his friends were? I mean, how close were the two of you anyway?"

Her eyes narrowed at the callous sneer in his voice. "I hope you're not insinuating anything disgusting, Mr. Bryce, because that would anger me, and I can be quite nasty when I'm angry."

Eyes alive with challenge locked with hers. He leaned forward and planted his fists squarely on the table between them. "Seems to me you're being quite nasty right now. Let me tell you something, lady. I get pissed off when someone accuses me of stealing. So I want you to explain again why Ressu couldn't have played 'Endnote' for me."

"He never played his pieces in progress in front of casual acquaintances. Only intimate friends."

"Well, I was enough of his intimate friend to know he liked orange juice after every concert. He guzzled it, but he added water to it because he liked it thin."

Her mouth dropped open and an odd chill made her bones tingle. She and Valentin used to joke about the gallons of watered-down orange juice he drank when he was on tour.

Her mouth snapped shut at the smug satisfaction she glimpsed in Bryce's face. "So you know he drank watered-down orange juice. Big deal. You could have seen him add water to his orange juice at a party after a recital. That doesn't mean you were bosom buddies. Valentin and I *were* bosom buddies, and I'd have known if the two of you had been close."

He ran his fingers through his hair distractedly. "This is absurd! I'm standing here trying to prove why I played a piece of music yesterday! Even Jack didn't bug me as much about yesterday's fiasco as you are, and he's my damned manager! What does it take, lady, to get you off my back?"

"Tell me where the original for 'Endnote' is. That's all I want."

He shook his head and looked heavenward as if praying for strength. "If I knew, believe me, I'd tell you. What on earth would I do with a manuscript of Ressu's music? As you said, I don't even like his stuff."

"Yes, but you played it, didn't you? Maybe you planned to claim it as your own. Or maybe you want to sell it to a collector. As Valentin's last known work, the manuscript increases in value daily."

His nostrils flared. He muttered a curse, then made his way to the door, knocking over the one chair that stood in his way. "You're nuts, you know that? You're out of your mind."

She rose in alarm as he reached for the door. "Where are you going?"

He pivoted to face her. "I'm getting out of here before you start accusing me of murdering the poor bastard too."

"I want that manuscript back." She put as much force into her voice as she could muster. It was hard to be firm when he stood there, so convincingly shocked and angry she found it difficult even now to believe he could have anything to do with the missing "Endnote." Still, she managed to add in a shaky voice, "If it's money you want, I can find a way to get it."

The gaze he leveled on her held so much venom and outrage, it brought a flush to her face.

"Listen to me, Ms. Winslow, and listen well. I hope you find your precious manuscript and realize what an ass you've made of yourself by accusing me like this. But if you don't find it and you intend to pursue this, you damned well better trot down to the police station and file a formal charge before you accuse me again. I can't promise they won't laugh you into the next state, but then you probably realize that anyway, which is why you came to me with this insanity."

He jerked open the door, then turned to her for his parting shot. "But if I hear you've made these accusations to anyone else without having a shred of proof, I'll—"

"Sue me for slander," she finished, having heard threats like this before. No one who'd done work for a newspaper could escape them.

"No." A grim smile crossed his face. "I don't gamble on things like our crazy legal system to protect myself. I fight my own battles. I don't play by the rules, and I don't worry about getting caught. Remember, Ms. Winslow, you're not the only person capable of thinking up ingenious lies to destroy someone's career."

He swept her briefly with a contemptuous gaze that made all her righteous anger shrivel into nothing. Then he left, slamming the door behind him.

She sat staring after him, her hands shaking at her sides. "So that's what happens when you take on a pianist with an international reputation," she muttered to herself, trying but failing to smile. A great shuddering breath escaped her lips.

What now? The man was lying about something. Any fool could see that. But was he lying about "Endnote"? How could she find out the truth without risking her career?

She turned toward the door, unable to control the sense of foreboding overtaking her, and not simply because of her concerns about the missing manuscript. Something about this whole thing gave her the willies—the way Bryce had played the piece, his evasive answers, his uncanny knowledge about her and Ressu.

She shrugged off the weird feeling and forced herself to focus on the issue at hand—the possibility that Bryce had the original manuscript for "Endnote" or knew who did. At the moment she didn't know what to believe. But if Bryce was mixed up in the thefts, he could sell the piece or tip off the person who'd actually stolen it before she could do anything about it.

Deep in thought, she left the room. If she didn't attempt to thwart Bryce, the original "Endnote" would be lost forever. She'd never regain it. And she'd have failed Valentin.

That thought made her quicken her steps in determination. She wouldn't fail Valentin in this. She couldn't. He'd given her too much for her to let this opportunity to repay him slip through her fingers.

So Devin Bryce wanted a fight, did he? Then she'd give him one. She'd show the cocky, charming virtuoso exactly whom he was dealing with when he came up against Suzanne Winslow.

And in the process, she'd have to do something about her preposterous attraction to him. Otherwise, she'd never get those astonishing blue eyes of his out of her mind.

5

♪

Devin swung his Ferrari away from the curb near Bloomsday Pub, scarcely pausing to watch for a break in traffic before he slammed the accelerator to the floor.

What a meeting! When Suzanne Winslow had proposed it, he'd thought maybe she wanted to berate him for playing Ressu's music so irreverently, but he hadn't expected this.

She thought he was a thief, for Chrisake! A thief! He could still see the suspicion, the accusation on her face as she'd calmly laid it all out before him.

Deftly maneuvering the wheel, he took a right turn on two wheels. The car skidded slightly until it snapped back into the forward movement, but he paid no attention. All he could think of was the irritating Suzanne Winslow.

Her accusations wouldn't have bothered him nearly as much if she hadn't been so . . . so damned sure of herself. That subtle air of sophisticated confidence must come with the territory for women like her, he thought, women whose lives had been cushioned by both wealth and talent.

Suzanne Winslow fit that description to a *T*. He'd read all about her in newspaper clippings at the University of Chicago's library. Actually he'd read more about her mother than about her, but it had given him enough to paint a picture of the girl who'd had a succession of high-society fathers. Until he'd read those clippings, he hadn't connected Suzanne with Felicia Winslow, a notoriously impetuous sculptor whose reputation increased exponentially with her every showing.

How different Suzanne's background was from his,

Bryce thought. Fine art in his neighborhood had consisted of paintings of dogs playing poker. Fine music had been Irish ditties and Lawrence Welk. Suzanne Winslow, however, had been raised in the rarefied atmosphere of true talent. She'd had Felicia Winslow . . . Valentin Ressu . . . and, of course, their numerous friends in both the art and music worlds. She'd tasted the cream of modern expression. No wonder she acted so protective of Ressu's music. With her background, she probably thought of herself as a kind of caretaker of the avant-garde. Unfortunately, she damned well had the qualifications to be one.

Hell, he thought. Felicia Winslow and Valentin Ressu. With two avant-garde artists of that magnitude raising her, it was a wonder the woman didn't talk in modern riddles.

A grim smile flickered over his face. She sure hadn't talked in riddles. Oh, no. She'd been pretty clear. She wanted his head. She'd made no bones about that, he told himself as he shifted gears. After stringing together a thousand unrelated facts, she'd indicted him for a crime he hadn't committed. Then she'd whopped him over the head with her accusations, but only after her soft hazel eyes had first lulled him into thinking her harmless.

He screeched to a halt in front of a red light. Soft eyes, soft skin, soft hair. He cursed under his breath. How on earth could he be attracted to her after what she'd accused him of? Then the image of her bow-shaped lower lip, quivering ever so slightly when he clasped her hand, sprang into his mind and made him curse again.

No point in thinking this way, he told himself sternly. Suzanne Winslow believed him to be a thief. She wouldn't ever accept an advance from him. Too bad he couldn't put her out of his mind completely. But there was no way. He had to deal with her accusations.

He'd thought he had her when he'd thrown out the bizarre stuff about his "wonderful memory" and the pieces that popped into his head. It was as close to the truth as he could come. He'd have used it on Jack except Jack knew

Devin's memory was his weakest point. Devin had to play a piece a few hundred times before it became fixed in his mind.

Fortunately, Suzanne didn't know that. But she hadn't bought his explanation anyway, because it had required his establishing that he'd been a friend of Ressu's, which had been next to impossible. The blind guess about the orange juice had taken her aback, but it hadn't convinced her. She'd been too intelligent to let that one go.

In fact, she'd been too intelligent by half. Somehow he had to stop her from pursuing this whole matter. If she persisted in believing he'd stolen Ressu's manuscript, she might do something about it. Maybe she wouldn't go to the cops, but she might dig into Devin's past, which he couldn't let her do. Things were bad enough right now without her dredging up stuff he didn't want anyone to know.

He ought to go back to his apartment and figure out what to do. But he'd promised his mother he'd come by today, and he hadn't yet had the chance. He knew she lived for his visits. He couldn't bear to disappoint her.

Glancing down at his watch, he made his decision. It was only ten P.M. Mom would be up watching the news. Even though Dad died years ago, Mom continued to live as if he'd walk in any minute, wanting his late-night supper before he collapsed into bed with her in his arms.

Grief briefly stung the back of Devin's throat. Then the light turned green and he made a right turn in the direction of his mother's instead of heading left toward his apartment. As he pulled up to the red-brick "worker cottage," he noted the bright lights shining from the living room window.

Good old Mom. She never alters her schedule, he thought as he thrust the gear into first and shut off the engine. But he didn't get out right away. Instead he folded his arms over the steering wheel and buried his head in them.

What was he going to do now? One of the most intriguing women he'd ever met was watching his every move, trying to sink him into oblivion, and Jack was on his case about yesterday's recital. He ought to get the two of them together. They could take turns asking him what the hell he was up to.

The problem was, Suzanne Winslow had every right to be suspicious. That's what really scared him. An original manuscript of a pivotal piece had gone missing, a piece Devin had played in public. He wanted to curse Ressu for doing this to him, but what good did it do to curse a dead man? Yeah, maybe Ressu's ghost still hung around, but that didn't do him much good.

He tried to remember what those hands had looked like the afternoon of the recital, but he failed. He'd scarcely been concerned with that during the bizarre episode—he'd been too caught up in the terror of having lost control. Changing pieces in a program was one thing, but being suddenly taken over by a strange force in the middle of a piece over which he'd already established control was quite another.

For a second, the fear he'd held at bay reared up to snap at him once more. It took all his control to keep it from tearing at his insides.

He jerked his head up from the steering wheel, staring aimlessly out into the night. Right now he needed to concentrate on finding out what was happening to him. He sure didn't need this mess with Suzanne Winslow on top of it.

But he was stuck with her and her accusations nonetheless. Worse yet, he couldn't explain any of this to her unless he wanted her to get him fitted for a straitjacket. It was a damned shame the woman had it in for him. Under different circumstances . . .

He shook his head ruefully. No, even under different circumstances he couldn't have anything to do with a woman like her. Years of protecting his career had made him avoid any woman with an inquisitive mind. It wouldn't take an intuitive, sensible woman long to get under his skin enough to hear his secrets, and then she'd run like hell. But probably not before telling every reporter around that Devin Bryce was a crazy pianist who claimed composers possessed him when he played.

Nope, he thought, no intelligent woman would believe him. But for a brief moment he indulged himself in the fantasy of holding a woman like Suzanne Winslow in his arms . . . a woman who could distinguish an adagio from an adagietto . . . a woman crisp and bright as a new penny, who smelled of Chanel No. 5 and shampoo. He thought of Suzanne's curtain of hair, which swung about her shoulders when she moved, like a dancer's silk skirt drifting into place at the end of the dance.

His fists clenched around the steering wheel as he forced the image from his head. He'd have to learn to be satisfied with the party girls and models he dated on occasion when the hunger for feminine companionship overwhelmed him. They might regard him merely as "you know, that famous pianist," and spend more time discussing the latest trends in clothing than anything important, but at least they gave him a few hours' company before they flitted off to find the next party. At least they didn't ask any probing questions. He could never have an intelligent, deep woman like Suzanne in his life. Not now, not ever.

To fight the painful ache rising in his body at that thought, he jerked the car door open and slammed it closed with a bang, then strode up the steps to his mother's door.

He found Nora Bryce lying on the couch, propped up by a bright-yellow cushion. She'd tucked a multicolored, knitted afghan around her legs and feet even though it was spring outside, and she had the heat cranked up high.

"Devin!" she exclaimed, the papery skin of her too-thin face creasing in a smile of sheer pleasure. "I thought maybe you wouldn't come."

"Not come!" he said, pressing his fist to his chest as if he'd been wounded. "Have I ever stood up my best girl?"

"Never. You're a good son." Flashing him an affectionate glance, she swung her legs slowly off the couch and patted the space she'd vacated. Her pale-blue eyes suddenly darkened. "Come sit here by your mother and tell me all about it."

He lowered his lanky frame onto the new couch he'd bought her the year before, then pressed a kiss against her cheek. "Tell you all about what?" he quipped, settling his arm on the back of the couch behind her.

"The recital yesterday. Thank you for sending the car and the tickets, but I . . . I couldn't get these old bones to move yesterday. . . ."

"It's okay," he told her, more aware than he wanted to be of the pain she suffered. In addition to the emphysema, she had terrible bouts with her back. The doctors did all they could, but still she remained in pain a great deal.

"I read that horrible woman's review in the *Chicago Star*. It didn't make sense. I think she must have misunderstood what you were trying to do or something."

"Or something." He stared at the television. "So. Anything interesting on the news tonight?"

"Don't try to change the subject," she muttered with a hint of the firm tone she'd used on him as a child.

He grinned and shook his head. "I never can slip anything past you, can I?"

"That's why I'm your mother. So tell me what happened."

The grin melted from his face. "Same thing that always happens. Some old spirit up and decided to borrow my hands for a while. He just didn't have the courtesy to wait until I was between pieces."

She looked down at her lap, plucking invisible threads off the bunched-up afghan. "That isn't how it usually happens, is it?"

"No." The fear rose up in him again, as persistent as the damned ghosts taking over his life.

"What do you think caused it?"

"I don't know." God, he wished he did know.

"Shouldn't you try to find out? Perhaps—"

"Look, Mom. I'd rather not talk about it right now, okay?"

She sighed. Then she dropped her blue-veined hand onto his knee. It looked so delicate. She'd always been a small, birdlike woman, a wispy collection of finely crafted bones that moved with grace and beauty. But her disease had reduced her to an unnatural thinness. Every time he saw her, her increasing fragility clutched at his heart. If he couldn't continue performing, what would happen to her? Sure, his money would hold out for a while, but then—

"Devin?"

"Yes?" he asked past the thickness in his throat, his eyes still riveted on her bony hand.

"Do you hate your gift so much?"

She wouldn't let it go, would she? he thought. Then again, how could she? She'd lived with it, too, all these years, from when he was six and told her about the "spooky hands." She'd never been able to see them—apparently, no one could—but she'd believed him from the first. She was that kind of woman.

He ruffled the iron-gray hair that fell around her shoulders in wiry curls. "No. I don't hate it. I never have. But sometimes I could do without the trouble it causes."

"Your gift wouldn't cause you so much trouble if you wouldn't try to control it," she wheezed, then paused a moment for breath. "You struggle so hard with it that it absorbs you totally. You should learn to let it be, as your father did."

"Then he should have stuck around to teach me how." He hadn't meant the words to sound so harsh, but his mother's sharp intake of breath told him he'd been too hard.

She stiffened and drew herself off a little from him, coughs wracking her body for a moment. At last she drew a raspy breath. "You mustn't blame him. It was very . . . difficult for him back then."

"No, Mom. It was easy for him. He just cut out. It was difficult for us, the two he left behind. You, of all people, should blame him. You say Dad accepted his gift. Then why did he let it destroy him?"

"He didn't . . . take his own life because he had the second sight," she said, faint reproach in her voice.

"No. He did it because he had no job, no future, no way to feed his family. That's what having the second sight did for him. Well, I won't let it do that to me."

They fell silent, his mother as usual uncertain how to deal with her only son's bitterness. He was surprised she'd brought up the recital at all. They spoke little these days of the strange possessions. And even less of his father.

"Devin, is there something else bothering you that you're not telling me about?" his mother ventured at last, then coughed.

Devin forced a smile to his face. Sometimes he wondered if his mother didn't have a little of the second sight herself, or at least a highly tuned women's intuition. "Nothing important. It's a slight problem, but I can handle it. Don't worry about it, okay?"

She gazed up at him, her sweet, rain-blue eyes filled with love. "I'll never stop worrying about you, not until you find someone else to worry about you, some nice girl. Which reminds me—"

He groaned. "No, Mom, I don't care what 'nice girl' you met in the grocery or at the bingo game. I'm quite capable of finding my own women."

"So I hear."

"What?"

"Maggie called not ten minutes before you arrived. She was on her break and couldn't wait to tell me about the woman you brought to the pub."

He closed his eyes and shook his head, though he couldn't repress the exasperated grin tugging at the edges of his mouth. "You shouldn't listen to Maggie. That woman was a business acquaintance."

"Is she married?"

The question stopped him short. He thought a moment. She hadn't worn a ring, but that didn't necessarily mean anything. Damn, he hadn't even found out. "How should I know?" he muttered.

"She couldn't be married or she wouldn't have met you in a bar at night."

"Times are a little different nowadays, Mom," he said dryly, but she ignored him.

"You should ask her out."

"Even if she isn't married, she wouldn't go out with me." *She'd probably prefer having her tongue torn out by the roots,* he added to himself.

"How do you know if you don't ask?"

"I don't want to go out with her. I *can't* go out with her, so let's drop the subject." His tone held a warning that his mother knew better than to ignore.

She took up the inhaler that sat always within her grasp and breathed in for a few seconds. Then she laid it back in her lap, and turned to face him, her expression resolute.

"One of these days, dear, you're going to have to trust someone." With her chin quavering slightly, she nonetheless stared him down and dared him to disagree.

Odd how she could always cut right through his words to find the truth behind them. She knew why he never brought any "nice girls" home to meet her, why he never told her about any women in his life.

"I trust you," he told her quietly. "I trust Jack. That's enough."

But it wasn't enough, he admitted to himself, a gut-wrenching longing turning his stomach into knots. In his heart he knew it wasn't enough anymore.

Devin's foul mood hadn't improved any the next evening after he'd talked to Jack. His manager had grumbled and complained about the trouble the cancellations had created. They'd parted on less than wonderful terms.

The craving for a cigarette now possessed Devin so fiercely, he found himself tapping the eraser end of his pencil on his knee and lifting it to his lips before he stopped himself. *No cigarettes,* he reminded himself, knowing he wouldn't have one, no matter what happened. All he had to do was remember his mother's fragile hand reaching for that inhaler to find the strength to resist his urges.

Turning his mind deliberately to more important matters, he examined the phone number Jack had given him. Thank God Jack had known better than to ask questions when Devin had asked him to track down the number of Paul, Valentin Ressu's son. Jack had made whatever calls it had taken to get it, then had tossed it to Devin before he'd left.

Since last night, Devin had decided to take action. Okay, so he had a composer wreaking havoc on his career. He couldn't do much about that, except wait until the ghost struck again and try to discern a pattern.

But he might have a shot at halting Suzanne Winslow's attack. If he could discover why she was so damned obsessed with finding the original manuscript to that "Endnote" piece, it would simplify matters. It would also help to have a copy of the manuscript, and he sure couldn't ask her for one.

The key to what was going on with Ressu obviously lay in that piece. It seemed too much of a coincidence that Ressu would have him play the same piece that interested Suzanne, on the day that Suzanne happened to be in his audience. Maybe with a copy in front of him, he could figure out what Ressu was up to. It was a long shot, but he couldn't just lie down and play dead. *No pun intended,* he thought wryly.

Devin dialed Paul's number for the third time that day, once more preparing his little speech in his head. This time he got an answer. Within minutes after he'd reached some

SILENT SONATA

young guy with a laughing voice who'd yelled for Paul, Paul came to the phone. From the noise in the background, Devin could tell that Paul's companions in his college dorm room at Roosevelt University were preparing for a wild night ahead. He could scarcely hear Paul's soft hello over the background din.

"Paul Ressu?" Devin said loudly into the phone.

"Yes?"

"My name is Devin Bryce. I wonder if I could speak with you a moment."

The pause was so long that for a second Devin thought the kid might hang up. Then Paul said, "Just a second," and Devin could hear him telling everyone to clear out of his room.

When Paul came back to the phone, he sounded breathless. "Did you say this was Devin Bryce?" he asked, the barest hint of awe in his voice.

"Yeah."

"The pianist?"

"Yeah."

"No shit!" He caught himself. "I—I mean, this is really an honor. I've followed your career since I was a kid. You're the best there is."

"I'm sure your father would have loved to hear you say that," Devin couldn't resist retorting.

Pause. "Father and I didn't like the same kind of stuff." The belligerent tone then faded. "But you and I sure do. I mean, I'm not a pianist—I'm a cellist—but I've heard you play one of the Beethoven sonatas for cello and piano with David Soyer, and you just knocked me out. It was stunning, man, stunning."

Devin felt a little stunned himself. He hadn't expected to find a fan in Ressu's son. "Thanks."

"I wanted to hear you this past Sunday, but I had to go out of town to a competition."

Devin took the opening Paul had unwittingly offered. "You didn't miss much, according to Suzanne Winslow."

"Listen, Mr. Bryce," he blurted out, "don't pay any attention to her. I read that review, but I knew she was way off the mark. Besides, Suzanne isn't into Chopin. She was just bitching because she doesn't like the kind of stuff you play."

"Do you know her well?"

"Hey, is that why you're calling? Because of Suzanne? Did you find out my father used to be married to her mother?"

"I knew that, but it wasn't why I called you. Not exactly."

"Good." Relief was evident in his voice. "Suzanne and I don't exactly get along, but I don't want to say anything bad about her. I mean, I can see why you'd be mad about her review and want to get back at her some kind of way, but—"

"No, no," he interrupted. "I wasn't calling to drum up gossip on Suzanne Winslow. Actually, I wanted to ask you for some information about your father."

"Oh."

"I'm thinking about adding a Ressu piece to my repertoire, and I had some questions."

An awkward pause ensued before Paul stammered, "I—I'm honored and everything, but wouldn't you rather ask Mother?"

No, Devin thought. *Your mother might ask more penetrating questions.* He figured he was better off dealing with the son.

He took a shot in the dark. "My questions concern your father's notations, and I heard you were more familiar with his music than your mom." He paused, and when Paul didn't contradict him, went on. "I got the impression your mom isn't musically inclined. I didn't know if she could tell me much."

A young, relaxed laugh sounded in his ear. At least Paul wasn't observant enough to detect the strain in Devin's voice or find Devin's questions odd.

"Father's notations, huh? You're right. Mother couldn't

help you. She had trouble with Father's English, not to mention his notations. He met her shortly after Grandpa defected to America, taking her with him. Mother's a Romanian girl at heart. Even after twenty years in the States, she has a little trouble with English. And she never was into music." His voice softened the barest fraction. "She was into Father, that's all."

"So I did the right thing by calling you."

"I guess. Actually, you should have called Suzanne." He paused, then chuckled. "But I guess I can see why you didn't, after that review and all. She must have woken up on the wrong side of the bed the day she went to your recital."

"You've got a point there. Anyway, why should I have called Suzanne? Because she's writing a book on your father?"

"And because she's literary executor of Father's estate. She knows the pieces of his music backward and forward. She'd be able to tell you in a minute what his notations mean."

Literary executor. *Ah, hell,* Devin thought, clenching the receiver tightly in his hand. No wonder she was so defensive about Ressu's music. "I didn't know she was literary executor."

"Oh, yeah, sure. Mother didn't know enough about that stuff to do it, and I guess Father thought I was too young to handle it." The edge of resentment in Paul's voice was unmistakable.

Devin's eyes narrowed. "So Suzanne got elected."

"Sure. She was always the most into his music anyway, even after her mother and my father split up. Suzanne and I practically grew up together, she spent so much time at our house. She stayed with us for weeks sometimes when her mother went off to Europe."

"But you don't like her," he probed.

"It's not that. Not exactly." He seemed to consider his next words, then said in a cautious tone, "Suzanne's so rigid. She's got rules and regulations for practically everything she does. If anybody fooled with any of her stuff, she fussed about it. She always loosened up a little around Father, but even he used to call her 'Little Miss Priss' because she kept her room so neat. She doesn't go with the flow, you know what I mean?"

Devin imagined it got pretty hard to "go with the flow" when the flow in your life changed so fast. It sounded as if Suzanne Winslow had reacted to her mother's erratic lifestyle and string of husbands by creating her own sense of order in her world.

Hell, he thought, *now I'm trying to psychoanalyze the woman.* Still, there was one thing he wanted to find out about her.

"She sounds like a dried-up old maid," he commented.

"Nah . . . well, not really. I mean, she's not married, but I wouldn't call her 'dried-up.' "

Odd how relief surged through him at hearing she was single. He chastised himself for being interested. "Let's get back to your father's music," he said firmly, as much for his own benefit as Paul's. "I'm considering adding a couple of the sonatas from his Sonata Cycle to my repertoire, and some of the notations have me stumped."

He paused, allowing that to sink in. He was about to take a chance here, but if Paul and Suzanne didn't get along, maybe he'd be safe doing this. "Also, there's another Ressu piece I'm interested in. But I can't find a published copy. I heard Ressu play it privately once. I've never been able to get it out of my head, so I really want to do it, but I can't find it in the published collections of his work. It's a piece I think he called 'Endnote.' "

The moment of silence on the other end of the phone was almost deafening. " 'Endnote.' Well, that's interesting."

Tension made the muscles in Devin's neck knot like twisted piano strings. "Why?" he asked, struggling to maintain a nonchalant tone.

"Father only finished it a few weeks before he died. I never heard him play it anywhere except at home. He played it for Suzanne and me a few times, but . . ."

"Maybe he played it for me because he knew I was interested in his music."

"I—I didn't realize you and Father were friends. I mean, he . . . he said some things about you once that weren't exactly . . . well . . ."

"Complimentary?"

The silence on the other end was his answer.

"Yeah." Devin's mind spun through possible answers. "We had different tastes, of course. But he knew I respected his work, and he occasionally tried to change my mind. That's how I heard 'Endnote.'"

Not exactly a lie, Devin reasoned, since there was no way of telling why Ressu had chosen to play "Endnote" through him. As for respecting Ressu's work . . . he tried not to think about the place in hell that untruth would earn him.

"Yes, but I thought you didn't like avant-garde," Paul persisted.

Although Paul's statement sounded like only a polite comment, the pressure built in Devin's chest. After years of hiding his secret, Devin figured he ought to be good at this kind of deception, but this was different. He didn't like lying to a kid who thought he walked on water. But if ever such a thing as a necessary lie existed, it was now.

"Uh . . . yeah," Devin finally said, "that's what most people think, but just because I don't play it in concert doesn't mean I don't like it. I do play it for myself occasionally. That's why I recently decided to make a stab at adding some pieces to my repertoire."

"Like 'Endnote.'"

"Like 'Endnote,'" he echoed.

Paul sighed. "Oh, boy, we got a problem here."

"How's that?"

"Well, 'Endnote' isn't published yet. Suzanne and Mother plan to have it played at this Romanian Festival coming up in a few months. The whole cycle will be performed for the first time ever. 'Endnote' was the final work of the cycle, you see. And this festival is the premiere. It's going to be a big deal. Even the Romanian government's helping to sponsor it."

Devin closed his eyes, forcibly holding back the curses running through his head. Right now, he wished Ressu weren't dead, so he could kill him all over again. How could this be happening? Why had Ressu made him play the one piece Suzanne would feel as protective as a mother hen about?

At his silence, Paul continued, "So you see, I couldn't get you a copy or anything until after the festival. If I snuck one to you and Suzanne found out, she'd chop my ears off. And Mother would probably help her do it. They're keeping it real hush-hush. They want it to make an impact."

Hell, it's already made an impact, Devin thought. *If it makes much more of an impact, I'll be sitting in a jail cell.*

Now it was even more imperative that none of this got back to Suzanne, but he couldn't put Paul on his guard. "Look, man, I understand what you're saying. I wouldn't want you to get in trouble, so don't worry about trying to get me a copy of 'Endnote.' But why don't we two get together to go over these notations for the other sonatas? That's all I really need. The other isn't worth your trouble, so don't bother Suzanne or your mom with it, okay?"

Paul chuckled. "I can see you don't like Suzanne a bit. Well, I guess I can understand that. Don't worry. I won't tell her you're going to play Ressu. She'd probably have a heart attack. But it'd be great to meet you, and I know I can help you with Father's notations."

"Great, great." Even if Paul couldn't produce a copy of "Endnote," at least Devin could pump him for more information about it. And if Devin could get on Paul's good side, maybe then the kid would break down enough to get Devin a copy. "Let me check to see when we could do it."

Devin cradled the cordless handset between his chin and

his shoulder, then went in search of his calendar. He found it under a beer bottle on the dining room table. He and Paul set up a time and place to meet and Devin jotted it down in his calendar. He also penciled a note to himself to get some of Ressu's published pieces, so he wouldn't look like a total fool when he met with Paul.

"Listen, Mr. Bryce—" Paul said.

"Devin."

"Devin." A tinge of awe still lingered in Paul's voice. "I want you to know I'll do whatever I can to help, even if it means standing up to Suzanne."

Devin suppressed a groan. "Thanks, but please don't take her on for my sake. I'd hate to think of your Miss Priss chewing you out for talking to me. Meet with me Thursday. That'll be good enough. See you then, okay?"

"Sure thing," Paul said, then hung up.

Devin stood there holding the receiver long after the line had gone dead. Had he made a huge mistake in contacting Paul? If Paul said a word to Suzanne about all this, she'd construe it in the worst possible way. Well, he couldn't let it worry him. He had to do something, and if it resulted in another head-on collision, he'd deal with it. Suzanne seemed determined to collide with him anyway. He might as well make the first move.

He dropped the phone onto the couch, then strode to the piano. He'd had enough of Suzanne Winslow for one day. Time to put her out of his head.

Then he settled onto the piano bench and immersed his problems in the dark, slumberous third movement of Beethoven's Sonata in A-flat Major.

6

♪

A rumble of thunder sounded as soon as Suzanne reached the outskirts of the University of Chicago. She stopped on the sidewalk and withdrew a raincoat from her briefcase, congratulating herself on her foresight.

Above her, thunderclouds shifted and rolled, jockeying for position. After removing her beret and stuffing it into her briefcase, she pulled the raincoat on and cast a pleading look at the sky. With any luck the rain would wait until she reached Goodspeed Hall, the music building, where the planning committee meeting for the festival concert was being held.

She adjusted the strap of her purse on her shoulder and shifted her hard-side leather briefcase to her other hand. She'd better get inside before she got drenched. Unfortunately, four long blocks still lay between her and Goodspeed Hall.

Nothing she could do about it but hurry, she told herself. Low heels clicking along the cement sidewalk, she increased her pace.

Thunder sounded in timpani notes around her, but she no longer paid much attention. Her plans for the festival meeting preoccupied her. As with any major public function, the festival concert had run into its share of snags—scheduling problems, difficulties with the Romanian Society, a participant backing out for personal reasons—but for the most part, things were running smoothly.

But not smoothly enough to suit her. She wanted the festival concert to be perfect. So what if it cost $700 to rent the Steinway she wanted? Valentin's pieces deserved the best, and she'd make sure they got it.

If only the committee hadn't been stuck with Cindy Stephens to play. Cindy had talent, no doubt about that, but she didn't have the seasoned skills of an older performer. Besides that, something about the young piano student bothered Suzanne. Suzanne didn't know Cindy very well, but sensed that the girl wasn't all she appeared to be. Beneath that cheery smile lay a hint of calculating bitchiness —Suzanne saw it in Cindy's snide comments about other performers and her arrogant statements about her own ability.

Suzanne sighed. There wasn't a thing she could do about Cindy. For sentimental reasons, Mariela had insisted on using one of Valentin's private students, and Cindy was certainly the best known and most talented.

Suzanne's concern had been to solidify Valentin's reputation as a composer; Mariela's had been to memorialize his life as a father, husband, and teacher. Somehow they'd managed to fashion a program that would do both. Cindy Stephens had been the compromise.

Of course, Ion Goma hadn't liked the choice of Cindy one bit, for he'd wanted a famous Romanian pianist to perform the cycle. Suzanne shook her head. For once, she was on Ion's side. Too bad he couldn't convince Mariela.

Suzanne's steps grew more determined. Could she truthfully say Cindy was any different from some other snooty undergraduates she'd known? She was probably reading far too much into Cindy's comments. The young woman was talented, after all.

Well, Suzanne would ensure that Cindy's talent shone at the festival. Somehow she'd wrest perfection from Cindy Stephens and get her to play the sonatas with the same verve and vigor Valentin had intended, even "Endnote," the most difficult piece. Too bad Cindy could never play it as well as . . .

Suzanne fought the traitorous thought that darted into

her mind. Okay, so Devin Bryce had played "Endnote" superbly, with as much subtlety and power as Valentin himself. So Devin Bryce could play circles around Cindy. It didn't change anything. Bryce wasn't performing at the festival, and she had to stop thinking about him. She should focus on the meeting she'd be leading in about fifteen minutes.

But she couldn't. Now that he'd entered her thoughts, she couldn't evict him. Two days had passed since their evening at the Bloomsday Pub. She still had no answers, nor could she decide if he was guilty. She'd had time to think and to consider that Bryce's rendition of Valentin's work had perfectly resembled Valentin's style. Surely he couldn't have performed it like that unless he'd known Valentin well enough to consult him about the piece.

On the other hand, she knew, absolutely *knew*, he hadn't known Valentin. So what on earth was going on? He must have a copy stashed away somewhere . . . he *must*. And the only copy in existence—aside from the one she carried in her briefcase now and the one tucked in her safe at home—was the stolen original.

A jagged crack of lightning lit the sky, followed by an earsplitting thunderclap. It jerked her out of her thoughts. Without warning, the thunderclouds she'd been ignoring for the past five minutes suddenly began dumping rain on her.

"Oh, great! Just great!" she muttered as she hurried along the sidewalk, half blinded by sheets of rain. Her rain hood barely protected her face from the drops blowing practically at a 90-degree angle. She held her briefcase over her head, glad it was wide enough to shield her face.

She quickened her walk, but refused to break into a run. Better to have her makeup ruined than to break her neck on wet pavement in these pumps.

Perhaps if rain hadn't been bombarding her with the force of a million tiny needles, she'd have noticed the motorcycle coming up slowly on the street to her left. But she didn't, not until she was shoved to the ground at the same time her briefcase was jerked from her hand.

Pain shot through her arm as she hit the pavement. Hard. For a moment, she sat stunned by the impact, dimly noticing the rider of the motorcycle roar off, clutching her briefcase under one arm.

"Hey!" she shouted as she caught a glimpse of a body completely encased in a black rain slicker, two jean-clad calves sticking out from beneath it with spotless white tennis shoes on the feet. Then the rain swallowed her attacker up.

Rain streamed down her face. Rain pooled into a dark lake in her lap. And all she could do was sit there in horrified amazement, her body shaking and her shoulder throbbing from having the briefcase handle wrenched from her grasp. Even her hands hurt. She looked at them, shocked to find them red and raw. Apparently she'd hit the pavement hard enough to scrape them badly, and the rain was making them hurt.

Gingerly pressing her palms against the pavement, she rose unsteadily to her knees. Her hose caught on the rough sidewalk, but she didn't care. She groped for her purse, wondering why the guy . . . or girl . . . on the motorbike hadn't stolen it too. Why her briefcase? What could anyone want with an ancient briefcase filled with someone else's papers?

Her breath came quickly as she shook her head over the senselessness of the violence. Her briefcase was practically worthless. It wasn't even a designer briefcase. All it contained were her notes for the meeting and . . . "Endnote."

She groaned and stumbled to her feet, rage pouring through her and driving off the rain's chill. "How dare you?" she shouted futilely, the words sounding choked against the wind.

Crossing her arms over her chest, she bent her head and fought back tears. Someone had stolen a copy of

"Endnote" again. Whether or not they'd meant to, the copy was gone.

Then a frightening thought made fear clutch at her insides. Had it been intentional? Could someone have known she'd be carrying a copy, someone who didn't realize she kept another in her safe? If it hadn't been intentional, why hadn't the thief taken her purse too?

Her pulse raced madly. She'd never been mugged before, not in all her years in Chicago. What if the rider came back? If the mugger had truly been after "Endnote," would he or she return or, worse yet, go to her home to search for her other copy?

Recognizing that her thoughts were veering toward hysteria, she bent over and planted her hands on her knees, then took a couple of deep breaths. Good Lord, she couldn't believe this had happened to her. She simply couldn't believe it!

It took her several minutes, and several more deep breaths, to calm down. Finally, when she had her pulse rate under marginal control and her limbs weren't shaking quite so badly, she straightened and looked around her.

She had to do something about this. She couldn't just stand here looking like Bartok after a bath. Still shuddering with both fear and rage, she scanned the sidewalk for one of the campus white phones, direct lines to campus police.

The mugger wouldn't get away with this, not if she could help it. But how could she help it? She hadn't gotten a good look at the motorcyclist or even at the bike itself. Besides, she wasn't sure if the person had actually wanted "Endnote" or if it had been a random attack.

A random attack. She couldn't believe it was only that. Her attacker could easily have taken her purse, and it certainly had more value. No, he must have been after "Endnote."

But how in heaven had anyone known about the copy she'd carried in her briefcase? A chilling thought struck her. Could someone she knew actually have been behind this? Everyone on the committee had heard her promise Cindy at the last meeting that she'd bring a copy to the next meeting. And when Cindy had called yesterday to remind her, Suzanne had promised again to bring the copy. Cindy could have told someone. . . .

Stop it! Suzanne told herself. *Get control of yourself, for Pete's sake, and stop seeing suspicious characters where there are none.*

Still, the incessant questions plagued her. What was going on? Why "Endnote"? Who was behind this madness?

As she finally located a white phone, one person's name sprang to mind. Bryce. Good Lord, surely he had nothing to do with this. She could hardly see him sneaking up in a torrential rain and snatching her briefcase out of her hands.

Okay, so maybe he hadn't personally stolen this copy, a more suspicious part of her whispered, but he could have arranged for someone else to steal it after the conversation between them two nights ago. He knew she had another copy. And he definitely had something to do with the missing original.

What if he *was* behind the mugging? Should she mention her suspicions about him to the police?

Oh, of course, she told herself in disgust. That would go over real well with the authorities. As Bryce had said, they'd laugh at her if she accused him of stealing based on such flimsy evidence, particularly since she'd already called them once about the theft from her office and they'd found nothing.

A determined set to her mouth, she lifted the receiver of the white phone off the hook. Maybe it was a farfetched idea, but she trusted her instincts and her instincts told her Bryce was hiding something. He knew more than he was saying about the missing "Endnote."

She didn't have enough proof yet to mention anything to the police, but somehow she'd get it, and then she'd enjoy seeing him wriggle out of her accusations. Bryce was not going to get away with this . . . this artistic thievery. She wouldn't let him.

Paul scanned the meeting room as he entered, surprised to find Suzanne hadn't yet arrived. Roger Kelly, the university's representative, was there and sat off by himself, grading a stack of papers. Lydia Chelminscu, the representative from the Romanian government, whose blunt features and thinning hair never failed to elicit a touch of sympathy in Paul, had also shown up. Her wide brow furrowed, she pored over some documents, while that weasely little Ion Goma sat beside her, explaining some detail in Romanian.

The two of them suited each other well, Paul thought. Both were insanely patriotic. Hardly a conversation between them went by without some mention of Romania, the now defunct security organization Securitate, or the executed Nicolae Ceauşescu and Romania's new government. Paul might be of Romanian descent himself, but he didn't have their crazy obsession with heritage. He was an American first, as far as he was concerned, and even that mattered little. In a competition, it made no difference to the judges what nationality he was, so he certainly didn't care.

Cindy had also arrived. She sat with her back to him, her fine, light-red hair hanging down her back like a curtain of fire. As usual, she'd dressed with nonchalant casualness in jeans so tight they made his throat raw with desire. His own jeans tightened as he stood there. Shit, but Cindy really knew how to give him a hard-on, even when she wasn't touching him.

Trying to regain some control over his wayward body, he took the seat next to her. Now he was sitting across the table from the one person in the room whom he'd avoided looking at.

Mother. They hadn't been on the best of terms lately, not since he'd moved into the dorm. Mother wanted him to live at home while he attended the Chicago Musical College at Roosevelt University. How could he explain he couldn't breathe in that tomb, not with Father's likeness staring down at him from every mantel, every wall? It was like living in a stupid museum. He couldn't do it.

But he felt bad about letting her down. He knew she needed him right now, although he couldn't give her what she wanted. He studied her closely. Generally Mother's delicate, almost porcelain features mirrored either stubborn resistance or complete bewilderment throughout these meetings. She couldn't always follow the rapid flow of ideas. When it came to running a household, she was efficiency incarnate, but when it came to understanding Father's genius, she was completely in the dark.

That was why she'd always depended on Suzanne, he reminded himself, even before Father's death. Besides, Suzanne had always made allowances for her problems with the language. Suzanne had repeated more slowly for Mother's benefit the staccato phrases with which Father had peppered his conversation. It was Suzanne who'd explained the musical terms, even though it was almost a waste of breath, since Mother's musical sense had remained oddly stunted throughout her marriage. Father had always said he liked Mother that way, that he enjoyed not having to "talk shop" with his wife. After all, Father had mainly been concerned that Mother believe in his abilities no matter what. She'd been more than happy to oblige him.

Today, however, Mariela Ressu looked as if she didn't believe in anything or anybody. Dark circles ringed her almond-shaped eyes, and her normally pale skin seemed bleached out, faded to an unearthly brightness. She looked shell-shocked and distrustful, and he didn't think he could be the cause of the despair in her face.

But who or what was? He glanced furtively at Cindy, wondering if she knew what had upset Mother, but Cindy merely lifted her eyes to him and smiled.

When his gaze returned to his mother, she grew even paler, then rose abruptly from the table. "I go to call Suzanne," she announced. "She is too late. Something must have happened."

"She probably got caught in the rain, Mother," Paul said.

"I call," his mother repeated, and he got the feeling she needed to leave the room to compose herself before she broke down completely in front of all of them.

As soon as his mother had left, he cast a quick glance at the other end of the table where Lydia and Goma remained deep in conversation and Roger continued to grade papers. Then he edged close enough to Cindy to whisper, "What's got into Mother? Do you know? Did she say anything to you?"

Cindy shook her head. "You know your mother. She never says much of anything."

"You don't think she's found out about us, do you?"

With a shrug, Cindy asked, "Would it matter if she had?"

"Of course it would matter! I told you before—the only reason she went against Suzanne's wishes in getting you to play was because I pressured her to. I mean, she didn't have anything against you personally, but—"

"But she bows to our dear Ms. Winslow's opinion every time," Cindy finished with a snippy edge to her voice. "Yes, I know."

"Look. This situation isn't my fault. Don't be upset with *me*."

She sighed, then laid her hand on his arm to give him a brief, surreptitious caress before she removed it. "I'm not upset with you. Believe me, I understand exactly where I stand. Suzanne thinks the pieces are too sophisticated for me. As if that weren't bad enough, Ion agrees with her and would absolutely love to bring someone else in. But Suzanne's gone along with everything up to now—"

"Because of Mother."

With a smile, she added, "And because of you."

"I won't be able to do a thing if Mother figures out how involved we are. If Mother or Suzanne guess the truth, you're out of the festival entirely."

Her face hardened a fraction. "Even though I'm the obvious choice."

For some reason, her self-confidence, which occasionally bordered on conceit, bugged him today. "Yeah, yeah, we all know you were Father's best student," he muttered, unable to resist putting an edge of sarcasm in his voice.

Her eyes narrowed. "You must be terribly upset about your mother. It's not like you to be snide."

He stared at her, wondering briefly why he liked her so much. But he knew why. She made him feel important, at least most of the time. Besides, she had one hell of a body. He thought of the last time they'd kissed, when he'd pressed her up against the door to her dorm room and felt her quiver against him from head to toe.

With a wary eye on the door, he slid his olive-skinned hand to cover her delicate, pale one. Their eyes met for a moment and understanding passed between them.

Then she squeezed his hand tightly, before dropping it with a glance back at Goma and Lydia who still seemed engrossed in their discussion.

"If she does know about us, what are we going to do?" he whispered.

"We'll deal with that when it happens. Pretty soon, it'll be too late for either your mother or Suzanne to keep me from playing at the festival. They'll need me too much." She flashed him a brilliant smile. "And after it's over and I've shown how talented I am, they'll see how smart you were to champion me."

God, how that smile turned his insides to butter. He started to smooth back a tendril of the strawberry-washed hair that had fallen over her eye, but stopped himself in time. He clenched his fist instead. He couldn't wait until after the festival, when he could show everyone how he felt about Cindy, when he could strut around campus with her on his arm.

He could still hardly believe an ugly guy like him had snagged a gorgeous, talented girl like her. He resembled his father, whose craggy features and swarthy skin reflected the Gypsy blood he'd claimed to have. Unfortunately, Paul's hair was neither his mother's pale blond nor his father's rich black, but a nondescript brown that made him look even more unappealing than his wiry body did. He wore his hair long, hoping to look more like the artistic type Cindy went for, but he couldn't do anything about its limpness. Nonetheless, Cindy inexplicably liked him, so he wasn't complaining.

At that moment his mother returned, halting all opportunity for conversation between them, but Cindy winked before she buried her head over the piece of music in front of her.

Mother looked no better now that she'd made her phone call. She told them she'd only reached Suzanne's answering machine, so Suzanne was probably on her way.

They waited a while. Sure enough, a few minutes later, Suzanne burst through the door, water dripping off her raincoat.

"Sorry I'm late," she said as she slammed the door shut behind her. She looked oddly shaken, not at all the cool, collected Suzanne he was used to.

"The rain," his mother said sympathetically.

"Not exactly." She sucked in a deep breath, then released it. Her hands shook as she removed her raincoat. "I was mugged."

"Mugged?" his mother asked quizzically.

The others echoed the word in slightly more outraged tones. As appalled as the rest, Paul grew angry at the thought of someone robbing Suzanne.

"Yes. Mugged. Robbed," Suzanne explained for his mother's benefit. "Someone rode up on a motorbike while I was walking here and snatched my briefcase from my hand."

Now that his mother understood the meaning of the word, alarm drew her mouth taut. "That is appalling," she said in a shaky voice. "Terrible!"

"You called campus security, I trust," Roger said.

"Of course."

"Did they hurt you?" Cindy asked, her voice concerned.

With an expression of bravado, Suzanne shook her head and managed a reassuring smile. "No. Not really. But they got the copy of 'Endnote' I had in my briefcase."

As a murmur rose in the room at that, Goma slammed his fist on the table. "You let them take it from you? A national treasure? You didn't try to stop the thieves or—"

"Calm down," Lydia said in clipped tones with the barest trace of an accent.

Mariela's tone was stronger. "You mustn't shout, Ion. This is very terrible for Suzanne. A criminal has hurt her. You should be concerned for that."

"Hurt her!" Goma pounded the table again. "She is not hurt. She said so. But 'Endnote' is gone—the masterwork, the final piece!"

"I have another copy," Suzanne put in, her face stiff. "The one in my briefcase was simply a copy, so don't worry about it."

Goma settled back in his chair, vestiges of his anger marking a scowl across his brow.

What a jerk! Paul thought. Goma didn't need to jump all over Suzanne like that. Shit, the woman had just been mugged!

"But we *must* worry," his mother put in, her eyes bright with concern. When she spoke, all eyes turned to her. She spoke seldom during these meetings, but when she did, she had something important to say. "Is not this the second copy to be stolen?"

Suzanne nodded, a distracted expression on her face.

"What?" Goma asked. "What are you saying?"

"Valentin's original recently disappeared out of my files," Suzanne explained with a sigh. "Mariela and I don't know for certain that it was stolen, but—"

Paul's mother shook her head emphatically. "Suzanne believes it was stolen, and I am certain she would know."

She turned to Suzanne. "This has gone far enough. Crazy people 'mugging' you for a copy . . . a stolen original . . . we are foolish to continue to plan for this concert. I think we should cancel it."

All eyes swung to his mother. Paul felt a sickening lurch in the pit of his stomach. He glanced at Cindy, who had paled. "Mother. Don't be so hasty."

For once, his mother's voice was steeled with determination. "This is not hasty. This is for the best."

Paul wanted to throw up; he wanted to scream. Cindy's dreams . . . and by extension his . . . were shattering right before his very eyes.

One glance at Suzanne reminded him he wasn't the only person whose dreams were at stake. He watched her fight to maintain her equilibrium.

"Mariela," she said in a controlled voice, "if I'd been concerned about the mugging, I'd have suggested canceling the festival concert myself. But I'm not concerned. It was a freak incident, nothing more. It would be premature to cancel the concert based on something so minor."

"Yes, yes!" Goma added. "A minor thing, nothing more. We have the copy, so there is no need to worry. The concert must go on. It is a crucial part of the festival. So many people have put in their efforts and their time to this end. It must go on. Don't you agree, Lydia?"

Lydia flashed her usual reassuring smile. "Of course, Ion. The festival concert has tremendous importance, not only for American Romanians, but for my country. Ressu was a great Romanian, even if he was not a native. We wish to honor him."

Paul's mother's face looked drawn, anxious. He could tell she felt trapped. He could almost see the wheels turning in her mind as she sought for some other reason to cancel the concert. He had a sneaking suspicion his mother was hiding the real reason.

"But don't you see? It will be ruined," his mother said. "These unscrupulous persons who have stolen 'Endnote'

SILENT SONATA

may present it on their own. You know how these things happen. A quick publication . . . a concert somewhere else . . . a hurried recording. The festival is in six weeks. There's plenty of time for the piece to be heard. Then our premiere will be laughed at. It will be ruined, I tell you, ruined!"

It wasn't like his mother to be concerned about such things as the premature publication of a manuscript. Something was wrong, terribly wrong. But what?

Suzanne looked uncomfortable, even ill. So did his mother. As Paul watched his mother's futile attempts to hide her agitation, his stomach twisted. He couldn't let all of their dreams—Cindy's, his, even Suzanne's—slip through their fingers just because of some inexplicable fear of Mother's. He couldn't!

"Don't be absurd, Mother," he said. "If someone were going to perform or publish the piece, they could do it without stealing it and risking arrest. Father played it for friends. Any one of them could have recorded it."

His mother paled. "He only played it for family."

"That's not true. Devin Bryce heard it," Paul protested in his haste to change her mind.

She stared at him in wide-eyed alarm. Suzanne blanched. The others merely looked confused.

Silently he cursed himself. God, Devin would kill him for this. Well, he had to do something to keep his mother from canceling the concert and ruining Cindy's chance.

"What do you mean?" Suzanne whispered.

Paul glanced from his mother to her to Cindy. Too late to back out now. "I, uh, I talked to Devin Bryce yesterday, and, uh, he said Father had played it for him. He . . . was interested in the piece." At Suzanne's growing expression of alarm, he continued to babble. "I'm sure there are others around who've heard it. That's not the point, is it? This will be the premiere of all the pieces together, the big shebang. Nobody'll care if a few people have heard a version or two here and there."

"Paul is right," Roger put in, nodding kindly in Mariela's direction. "If anything, an early presentation might increase interest and bring more people to the festival. I think we shouldn't let the thefts worry us."

"Yes, yes," Goma said. With an expression of fervency, he turned to Paul's mother. He laid his hands palm up on the table. "Please, Mariela. Remember your countrymen. I left Romania when I was small, but you grew up there. You know what it was like under the Ceauşescus, when the Securitate ruled by terror and intimidation, when there was no artistic freedom. Ressu symbolizes the boundless creative talent latent in all Romanians. You mustn't deprive us of our symbol because of some thievery. You mustn't. This is too important."

Paul bit back a smile. Goma knew how to hit his mother where it hurt. She'd come to America and married Ressu, but part of her had always remained at home in Bucharest. An appeal to her patriotism was the best way to manipulate her.

"I don't know," she muttered, obviously uncertain. Then her tone grew more bold. "Valentin would not have wanted me to put Suzanne in such danger." His father's name on her lips suddenly sounded stiff and unnatural. Normally she spoke the name with reverence, but there was no reverence in her tone today.

Suzanne's gaze locked with his mother's. "I can take care of myself, Mariela. Valentin knew that. Please, don't let his music just die without a hearing. This concert will make his reputation. And that is far more important to me than some foolish fears about my safety."

His mother's lower lip trembled. She stared at Suzanne for a long time with a tormented gaze. He watched his mother's face crumble into submission like a cookie dipped in coffee. The bleak sadness there startled him, making a deep hurt settle in his gut. He wanted to take back all he'd said, to support her decision.

But he couldn't. He just couldn't. Cindy deserved to have her chance.

"I—I will think about it," his mother said.

He relaxed, because he knew what that meant. She wanted to preserve her dignity, but she would eventually come around. She'd spend a few days pretending to consider, and then she'd come around. Thank God.

His gaze shifted to Suzanne, expecting to see her looking triumphant. Instead, she stood at the head of the table, her eyes distant, her mouth tight and grim.

"Yes, think about it," she told his mother, as if in a trance. "And while you're doing that, we'll continue with the meeting, if that's all right with you."

His mother stood. "Yes, do continue, please. But I—I cannot stay. You understand."

With those words, she swept from the room. An awkward silence ensued after the door closed behind her. Suzanne covered it by saying, "She'll change her mind. Things upset Mariela easily, but it will be all right." She managed a smile, though he could see the worry reflected in her face. "Shall we begin?"

Her gaze expanded to take in everyone in the room. Goma looked unhappy, but he nodded, casting a concerned glance at the door through which Mariela had left. The others nodded as well.

With a tight voice, Suzanne began the meeting. Everyone was more subdued than usual. Paul could see the anxiety on their faces and feel the tension in the room. He wanted to reassure them. He knew he could bring his mother around, if Goma's little speech hadn't already done so.

Still, her departure had cast a pall over the entire proceedings that Suzanne's forced, cheery voice didn't help to dispel. They discussed all the issues in record time, and for the first time ever, they were done in an hour.

"Well, that's it then," Suzanne said briskly. "I'll see all of you next week at the same time and place."

One by one, the others stood and said their good-byes until only Paul, Cindy, and Suzanne remained. Since Cindy hesitated, Paul too waited, hoping to have a chance to talk with her alone after she finished with Suzanne.

Suzanne looked at Cindy. "Uh, Cindy . . . I—I need to discuss something with Paul . . . alone, if you don't mind."

A speculative light glinted in Cindy's bright green eyes, but she kept her thoughts to herself. "Oh, sure. I just wanted to know about 'Endnote.' Was the stolen copy the one you were bringing to me?"

"Yes. I'll get you another, don't worry. I know you need to spend most of your time from now until the festival working on it. I'll get it to you, okay?"

"Sure. I do need it, though, so if you could drop it by my dorm room as soon as possible—"

Suzanne stiffened imperceptibly. "I'll get it to you."

"Thanks." Cindy stood and gathered up her music. "Uh, see you later, Paul," she added, flashing him a coy smile before she slipped out of the room.

Now that Paul was alone with Suzanne, his pulse quickened in alarm. This concerned Devin Bryce. He felt sure of it.

And he wasn't wrong. Suzanne stared at him solemnly, then said, "I want to know exactly what Devin Bryce told you yesterday."

He groaned. "Ah, Suzanne, why? Look, I know you don't like the guy, but just because he's interested in 'Endnote' is no reason to—"

"You don't know the situation, Paul," she said in a remote tone, "so don't interfere."

Typical Suzanne, always treating him as if he were still in training pants. "Why don't you explain it to me then?"

"And why don't you tell me when you and Bryce got so chummy?"

"Shit, Suzanne, it's none of your business, is it?"

Her face turned rigid, and he felt instantly contrite. She

sat down slowly, her back ramrod straight. Her gaze looked haunted, her expression suddenly very fragile.

"I'm sorry, Suzanne," he muttered. "I didn't mean to be such a jerk. But I'd rather not talk about it."

She shrugged, her face still as impassive as stone. But beneath the grim expression, she looked as if she'd crumble any minute. With a pang, he wondered if she were still reacting to the mugging.

"You . . ." she began, then paused, her brow furrowing. "You missed Bryce's recital Sunday afternoon, didn't you?"

"Yeah," he said warily.

"He played 'Endnote.'"

Paul went cold. His mind raced over the conversation he'd had with Devin. "He couldn't have. I mean, he was asking me for a copy. If he'd had a copy, why . . ." He trailed off at the stricken expression on Suzanne's face.

"He *asked* you for a copy?"

With a shrug, he nodded. He was beginning to feel like a complete fool. Now he remembered all the information Devin had gotten out of him without even having to ask. But why? Was it as Devin had said, that he was interested in Father's work? Or was there another reason?

"Paul," she began, then faltered. She tossed back a lock of still-damp hair that had fallen in her face. "Look. I know you and I haven't always gotten along, but this festival is very important to me. And to you too, I think." She ventured a smile. "Can't we . . . can't we work together on this? Can't you simply tell me what Devin said? I really need to know."

Her pleading expression told him she was dead serious about this. It made no sense to him, any of it . . . the stolen copies of "Endnote," Devin Bryce calling him up out of the blue, his mother's sudden decision to back out.

"Devin said—"

"Devin?" Her mouth twisted in a faint smile.

"I *am* a musician in my own right, you know," he told

her with a haughty air. "I have as much right to call him Devin as anybody. Musicians don't stand on formalities."

She sighed and dropped her eyes to the table. "I'm being bitchy. Sorry."

He acknowledged her apology with a curt nod. "Devin said he'd gotten interested in Father's work recently and wanted to add some pieces to his repertoire." He ignored the loud snort Suzanne gave at that. "He wanted me to help him go over some notations on Father's pieces, and he wanted a copy of 'Endnote.' "

"Why did he say he wanted it?"

He shrugged. "He said Father had played it for him once, and he liked it and wanted to play it in his own concerts."

"And you believed him?"

Paul tried not to look sheepish. "We-ell. Honestly, I didn't know what to believe. When a guy like Devin Bryce calls you up and says he's a friend of your father's, it's kind of hard to believe he's a liar."

"But to your knowledge, was he ever a friend of Valentin's?"

"*I* never saw them together. But that doesn't mean Father didn't play 'Endnote' for him sometime when I wasn't around."

"He told me the same thing. About Valentin playing 'Endnote' for him, I mean."

He looked at her, startled. Somehow he'd gotten the impression from Devin that he'd never met Suzanne. "You talked to Devin?"

The distracted expression left her face, replaced by a wary one. "Yes." She didn't seem to want to say more.

"He didn't tell me that."

"He wouldn't," she replied, bitterness in her tone.

Something about the sheer anger lighting up her face gave him pause. "Is there something going on between the two of you?"

An expression of surprise crossed her face. "What do you mean?"

"Some kind of personal battle or something?"

Her self-deprecating smile made her look suddenly a little forlorn. "Or something." She seemed deep in thought.

"You know, Suzanne, I told him he should talk to you first. But he . . . well, after that review and all . . . he said he'd rather talk to me."

"I'll bet he did."

No mistaking the anger in her voice now, Paul thought. Her hazel eyes smoldered with barely hidden antagonism.

"What did you tell him about the copy and the notations?" she asked.

"I told him I couldn't get him a copy because you'd have a fit if I did. But I agreed to help him with the notations."

She pondered that a moment. Then she looked at him, a calculating smile playing around her lips. "Did you set up any specific time to do this?"

Something about her expression alarmed him. He hesitated before nodding.

She took his hand, as she used to when he was a kid and she'd wanted to explain something to him. "Paul. I know you don't always approve of the way I do things, but have I ever done anything to hurt you, I mean, really hurt you?"

"No." It was true, actually. He resented her sometimes for her place in his family, but she'd never abused her position, never tried to turn his parents against him or anything like that. She'd often made overtures of friendship to him. He simply hadn't responded, mainly because it irked his Father so much to see him and Suzanne at odds. And Paul had enjoyed irking his father in recent years.

"I'd like you to trust me on this one, okay?" she said. She paused, formulating her next sentence. "Paul, would you let me meet with Bryce in your place?"

At first the meaning behind her words didn't register. When it did he jerked his hand out of hers, shaking his head furiously. "No way. No damned way. He talked to *me*, not you. He trusted me not to get him in more trouble with you. He's nice, Suzanne, whatever you think about him. Besides, a friendship with Devin Bryce could help me. I'm not going to piss him off and ruin my chances."

"Do you want the concert to go on or not?"

"Of course I want the concert to go on—"

"Well, if Bryce has his way, it won't. He can't be trusted, Paul. He's already played 'Endnote' once publicly. I think he's trying to pass it off as his own work."

Paul stared at her in stunned disbelief. "You think he stole the other copies?"

She shrugged and brushed a lock of hair back out of her face. "I don't know. That's what I have to find out."

He considered what she'd said. He could hardly believe someone like Devin Bryce could be a thief. Something occurred to him suddenly. "If he stole a copy, why ask me for one?"

"To make sure he's got all of them, so he can claim the work as his without fear of contradiction."

"That's crazy!"

"Maybe. But people steal each other's works all the time."

"Devin Bryce?" He raised both eyebrows in acute skepticism.

"I know, I know. It doesn't make sense. Nonetheless, I have to check it out."

He could understand that. Still . . . "Why not let me do it?"

"Because he's not scared of you. He's scared of me. I'm the one who heard him play it at his recital and recognized it."

Paul sucked in his breath, then released it in a long drawn-out sigh. What a choice! Lose an association with Bryce or risk the festival concert.

He thought of Cindy, the sensuous way she tossed her hair back before kissing him. There wasn't any choice at all.

For all he knew, Bryce might really be using him, as Suzanne had implied. But Cindy was depending on Paul. He couldn't let her down.

"Okay," he muttered. "You win. Tomorrow afternoon, three P.M., at Olive Park, where it meets the lake. You know where Olive Park is, don't you?"

She nodded. "Thanks, Paul. And thanks for supporting me on the concert. Right now I can use all the support I can get."

She smiled then, one of those silky smiles she had when she was pleased. Funny, but if it hadn't been for Father, he might have liked her better. She was prissy and all, but she'd always been sweet to him. Could she help it that his father had always held her up as an example to be followed? She'd never flaunted her abilities or tried to lord it over him. She'd always had a nice, soft way of showing him she cared, even while she was irritating the shit out of him. If anything awful ever happened, he could rely on Suzanne no matter what. Knowing that gave him an odd sort of comfort.

He watched her gather her things together, her eyes bright, almost happy. Funny, but he got the feeling she was eagerly anticipating this. Was it because she wanted to nail Devin Bryce? Or was there another reason? A thought struck him suddenly that was too humorous to be believed. From all accounts, Devin was a pretty good-looking guy. Could Suzanne actually be . . .

Nah, he thought as he too rose to his feet, ready to walk out with her. Suzanne wasn't like other women. She wouldn't let a man turn her head just because he was handsome. And she hated Devin anyway.

Besides, she was old, at least thirty. By that age, you didn't care about the opposite sex anymore, did you? Nah, Suzanne would end up an old maid, surrounded by her books and her CDs. That was what she wanted, wasn't it?

Or was it? he wondered as he followed her from the room, noting that the smile still clung to her lips.

7
♪

After yesterday's thunderstorm, the sun had decided to take its rightful place in the heavens again. Suzanne hesitated before entering Olive Park and stared up into the sweet blue sky.

It reminded her of a certain pianist's eyes.

Stop it! she told herself as a crystal-clear image of Devin Bryce lodged itself in her head. *You've got to stop thinking of him as a . . . as a man. He's not to be trusted.*

Intellectually, she knew it, but something about him had enticed her from the beginning. It was his talent, she told herself, but knew she lied. There were connections between them—hidden, mysterious connections she didn't understand. For some reason she felt he held the secret to her life and future in his hands.

Boy, are you ever letting your imagination run amok, she lectured herself. *The man has convinced you he's got some sort of special power that puts him above the law. You have to stop this morbid obsession with an amoral egotist.*

Unfortunately, she couldn't stop it. She felt like a train headed into one of those cartoon mountains with a tunnel painted on the side. In the cartoons, the painted black entrance sometimes became a real entrance, but that was in cartoons. In real life, people who headed for painted black tunnels ended up smashed into a million pieces.

With a sigh she strode through the park. In no time she found him standing directly in front of her facing the lake. From the back, he looked as intriguing as he had from the front. A beat-up denim jacket fit tightly across his wide shoulders, and the same faded blue jeans he'd had on when

SILENT SONATA

she first met him cupped a firm behind that would have made a nun lust.

He stood with his long legs wide apart and his hands stuffed into his front pockets. His weight rested on his right leg as he tapped his foot with the left, apparently hearing some music that escaped her. His head nodded in time to the same soundless tempo. It reminded her of Valentin, when he'd been thinking through a piece.

Were all true musicians like that, living obliviously on an invisible plane of silent music and only stepping down occasionally to regale the mortals with a few moments of genius? He certainly seemed oblivious . . . of the lake wind lifting the ends of his thick, raven hair off the collar of his jacket . . . of the spray the occasional wave scattered over him . . . of everything.

Oblivious. And confident. Even from behind she could see it in his easy stance, the set of his shoulders, the nonchalant, rhythmic nodding of his head. Of course he was confident. He thought he was about to deal with Paul, who had as much discretion as a schoolroom tattletale.

Bryce wasn't dealing with Paul anymore, she reminded herself, but a sickening lurch in her stomach threatened to make her lose her nerve anyway. The same lurch had hit her yesterday when Paul had told her of Bryce's call. It had kept her from sleeping and killed her appetite.

She didn't want to take Bryce on, but she had to know what was happening. She'd hoped to scare him off at their first meeting, but obviously she hadn't succeeded. He was coming on like gangbusters, apparently determined to play "Endnote" in public.

Why? She was an analytical person . . . she ought to be able to figure this out. Why couldn't she?

Because it made absolutely no sense. If he wanted to claim "Endnote" as his own, why had he called Paul, thereby involving another witness? If he had the original or knew who did, why ask Paul for a copy? Could he really have been a friend of Valentin's? Could he really have played the piece from memory?

No. She and Paul agreed on that at least. "Endnote" was too complex for someone unfamiliar with avant-garde to master from one hearing. Bryce was a genius, but he wasn't God.

So why did he play it exactly as Valentin would have? some tiny inner voice whispered.

She thrust that errant thought from her mind. Somehow, somewhere, Bryce had studied a written copy of that piece before. It was the only explanation.

Besides, there was the whole issue of the blood-chilling new passage he'd added. She jerked herself up straight. Time to get some answers, some real answers. She hadn't gotten much out of him the other night, but she'd get something out of him today if it killed her.

As she drew closer, the chill wind off the lake buffeted her playfully, making her glad she'd worn one of her berets. But not her favorite. A scowl crossed her face. That blasted thief had stolen the briefcase containing her favorite.

Thoughts of the thief and the mugging sent her striding forward to confront her nemesis.

"Mr. Bryce," she said coolly as she neared him.

He spun around at the sound of her voice. Surprise at seeing her instead of Paul flickered in his eyes, then faded. "You're late."

Nothing fazes him, she thought. "I was afraid if you got here after me and saw me, you'd run before I could see you."

"I never run," he said, not smiling.

"You ran the afternoon of the recital."

A long sigh escaped him, and he looked away from her, the muscles in his jaw tightening. "Yeah, I guess I did. But that was different."

"Oh?"

He gave her a searching look, eyes glinting with silent

meaning, before he changed the subject. "I guess your showing up here means that Paul ratted on me."

"Did you really think he wouldn't tell me about your phone call?"

A grin split his face. In a flash, it transformed him from brooding artist into a sexy, prowling hunk of male. She had to force herself not to respond to the seduction it promised.

"Actually, I did think he'd keep it a secret. Stupid, huh? But he said you two didn't get along. He thinks you're a bit of a tight-ass."

There was no mistaking the amusement glinting in his eyes now.

"Paul thinks everyone over the age of twenty-five is a bit of a tight-ass," she retorted, attempting a laugh.

The grin widened. "Maybe. He seemed pretty comfortable with me though. Paul's a nice guy. I was looking forward to chatting with him today."

I bet you were, she thought. Aloud she said, with considerable sarcasm, "I seem destined always to disappoint you."

His smile faded as he let his gaze trail downward, over her neat-as-a-pin sweater and longish wool skirt to her booted feet. Now she knew what was meant by the phrase, "he undressed her with his eyes."

"I'm not disappointed," he said, his voice deep, husky, imbued with a world of meaning.

Then he brought his gaze back to her face with such sensual directness, it made her blood trill like a flute gone mad. The blatant invitation in his eyes brought a blush to her face when nothing else had.

Suddenly, as she stood silent—speechless, in fact—a shutter seemed to go down over his sensual look, cutting it off as quickly as it had come.

"So," he clipped out. "I guess you aren't here to help me with the notations on Ressu's pieces." He gestured behind him to a satchel resting against a bench.

"What's in that?"

"Ressu's 'Variations on Light' and 'Timescape.'"

She eyed him with acute skepticism. "Are you really interested in playing Ressu's sonatas?"

His gaze met hers. "You know the answer to that."

"So the sonatas in your satchel were supposed to be camouflage for Paul's benefit."

He shrugged.

A quick stab of disappointment hit her. Part of her had hoped he wasn't quite that deceptive, that maybe he'd actually wanted to play Ressu's music.

She grimaced at her own stupidity. For Pete's sake, she should have known better than to believe he might have noble motives for all this.

He turned and picked up the satchel, then inclined his head toward the nearest path into the park. "Come on. Let's find a quiet place to discuss this. I know you're dying to lay into me again, so let's get it over with."

They headed up the path in silence, conscious of the people passing around them. At last they found a secluded park bench set off from the path and surrounded by trees. He dusted it off with his forearm, apparently unconcerned that he dirtied his jacket doing so.

The considerate gesture made something go limp within her. He never ceased to amaze her.

They sat down facing each other on the bench, a good foot of space between them. He set his satchel on the ground, then stretched his arm out along the back of the bench with his fingers stopping just short of her sleeve.

"Paul tells me you wanted a copy of 'Endnote,'" she began, trying to remain calm.

"You'd want a copy too if someone accused you of stealing it. I thought I'd see if it really was the piece I played Sunday. If so, then I must have heard it when Ressu played it somewhere. If not, then you and I have no quarrel with each other, do we?"

SILENT SONATA

"So you called up a trusting teenager who thinks the world of you and lied to him to get what you wanted."

"Lady, you sure love to make everything sound sordid."

"If the shoe fits—"

"Look." He tilted his chin up and cocked his head to one side. "I'll admit I hoped Paul would let me get a look at this mysterious piece of music I'm supposed to have stolen. That's why I gave him that spiel about the notations. I had to do something. I couldn't address your accusations without knowing what I was up against."

His honesty disarmed her. Unfortunately, most of his explanation made perfect sense. If indeed he'd played something that had "lodged in his head," so to speak, he would want to confirm what the piece was before he believed what she had to say.

The only flaw in his logic was that he couldn't have memorized "Endnote" from one hearing. She knew it, and she suspected he knew it. She ought to give him a copy just to prove that fact alone.

Of course, if he were stealing copies, that would be stupid, wouldn't it? But surely a thief wouldn't be sitting here with her discussing the missing "Endnote."

Something wasn't right here.

At her continued silence, he quipped, "Can't blame me for trying," and flashed her an ingratiating smile.

Oh, he sure could use that charm to his benefit. Her stomach did flipflops every time he aimed it in her direction, which irritated her no end. "Mr. Bryce, this is serious. I don't think you realize how serious—"

"Lighten up, lady." His smile abruptly disappeared. Closing his eyes, he rubbed his forehead up from the bridge of his nose, then opened his eyes again to level his gaze on her. "And why don't you call me Devin, since it looks as if you and I are going to be having discussions like this forever."

"I don't want to get personal with—"

"Suzanne."

His use of her first name stopped her short. The way he said it, the syllables rolling off his tongue like harp notes, made her tingle down to her toes.

He continued now that he had her attention. "You and I have already gotten pretty personal, it seems to me." Somber and intent, his eyes were fixed on her face. "You've accused me of being a thief. How much more personal can you get?"

He had a point there, she thought. Blast him, he had a way of making her feel mean-spirited and irrational. Until he'd come along, she'd prided herself on being open-minded and evenhanded. She mustn't overreact to his arrogance. They were both music professionals. They should be able to discuss the situation rationally and agree on how to handle it.

"Okay . . . Devin." She forced a smile. "Let's go over again why you played 'Endnote.' "

The wind died for a second, dropping a lock of her blown-back hair into her face. Before she could brush it away, he lifted his hand and brushed it back for her. She stiffened and opened her mouth to protest the intimate gesture, but he'd already jerked his hand away as if startled by his own action.

He turned his gaze from her to stare into the woods beyond. "I've got a better idea. Let's discuss your reasons for thinking I stole the manuscript." He inhaled deeply. "You say I want to claim it as my own. But I've never composed another piece of music in my life. Why would anyone be interested in one lone piece I might present to the public, especially when it's not in the style I play? Why would I suddenly present an avant-garde piece, knowing no one in the music world would take me seriously?"

"Maybe you have a friend who—"

"Composes avant-garde music?" He brought his gaze back to hers. "Yeah, right. I stole the piece to give to a friend. And now I continue to protest my innocence even though I've been told that at least two other people knew of it before it was discovered missing."

"Six other people."

His harsh laugh rumbled from deep in his chest. "Okay. Six other people. Christ, but I'm a stupid son of a bitch."

His sarcasm stopped her short. When he put it that way, her accusations did sound somewhat ludicrous.

"Are you sure," he continued, "the piece was stolen? Maybe you misfiled it. One missing copy doesn't make a robbery."

A robbery. The mugging! Suddenly Suzanne was reminded of where she'd gotten all her righteous indignation. "And maybe the man who attacked me yesterday to steal a copy was a music lover with a penchant for Ressu."

A look of genuine confusion passed over Devin's face. "What?"

"I was mugged yesterday. My attacker stole my briefcase with the photocopy of 'Endnote,' but didn't touch my purse. It was obvious to me what he was after."

She couldn't miss the very real astonishment on his face, nor the hint of horror that lingered in his eyes. Why should *he* be frightened? she wondered, feeling goose bumps rise along her skin.

"Hell, where were you when this happened?" His gaze dropped to scan her body, the concern on his face bringing his thick brows together in a deep frown. "Were you hurt? Did he use a weapon? Christ, I can't believe—"

"No, I wasn't hurt." His obvious, rather intense concern took her aback. "There wasn't a weapon or anything. I was walking on the University of Chicago campus to a planning meeting for the festival concert. The man . . . or woman, I don't know which, rode up beside me on a motorbike and snatched my briefcase. It was over before I knew it."

Her words didn't seem to reassure him much. He jumped up to pace before her with his hands thrust in his jean pockets. "Hell, lady, you've got to be careful in this city, even on a university campus." He stopped directly in front of her. "Are you sure the mugger was after 'Endnote'?"

"Of course I'm sure. A purse snatcher would have taken my purse. First the original, now the copy." Her mouth tightened. "On top of that, you've been trying to sneak a copy from Paul after playing a substantial portion of it publicly. If you were in my place, what would you think?"

He stared off into the trees behind her, his brow knit. "I'd think someone wants to corner the market on 'Endnote' manuscripts."

She couldn't believe he was being so frank, but she was more than willing to take advantage of his candor to find out what was going on. "Now you know why I'm so intent on determining your interest in this."

He nodded, though he still seemed preoccupied. "Yeah," was all he said.

"Well?"

His gaze swung back to her. "I've already explained it to you. A piece of music I'd heard once before popped into my head during last Sunday's recital. It distracted me enough that I played it unthinkingly. When I . . . er . . . realized what I was doing, I stopped and left the stage." He gave her a thin-lipped smile. "It's kind of hard to recover from something like that on stage."

" 'Endnote' is a complex piece, not the kind of thing one picks up from a single hearing. You *must* know the piece from somewhere."

"You're right—I must. If I played 'Endnote' last Sunday, then I got it somehow, obviously from Ressu himself. I sure as hell didn't get it by stealing the original manuscript. Do you really think I would have had you mugged to get a copy? I've already established that I have no use for it."

She stared at him, no longer certain what to believe. "The original will be worth a lot of money in a few years."

He chuckled and shook his head. "Yeah. We both know I need the money. Have you any idea what I get for each appearance, not to mention master classes, overseas tours—"

"I'm well aware of your standing in the music community," she bit out.

"I could tell. Your respect for my 'standing' is what's made you so slow to accuse me, I suppose."

The way he emphasized the word *slow* made her jerk her gaze from his, an unwarranted guilt flooding her.

"Oh, and let's not forget the copy stolen from you yesterday. If I'd stolen the original so I could sell it, what would I want with someone else's transcribed or duplicate copies? They'd be of absolutely no value to me."

Good Lord, but he was making sense. Nonetheless, his story had the same holes in it as before. Her other theories whirled through her head as she tried to figure out why he would have played "Endnote" and where he would have gotten a copy.

Suddenly her face brightened. "You still might know the person who stole the piece. Maybe you're covering up for them."

"Oh, for Chrisake." He speared his long fingers through his hair and stared down at her, eyes alive with frustration. "I'm not doing a very good job of covering up, am I, if I played the supposedly stolen piece in public?"

She jumped to her feet, as frustrated and confused as he was. "I don't know." She crossed her arms over her chest as she faced him. "I don't know what's going on or why you're so stubborn about this or why someone wants my copies. It makes no sense to me either. But the festival concert is coming up, and it's my responsibility to make sure it runs smoothly. I don't want any manuscripts turning up before the official unveiling, possibly marked and distorted. And your playing of it the other night—with a new passage—makes me wonder if one is already circulating."

His expression softened. "You should stop worrying about what happened at the recital and start thinking about why someone wants copies of 'Endnote' badly enough to steal them."

"I don't know," she repeated in a whisper, her stomach a battleground. All of it had her thoroughly confused. It didn't help that Devin Bryce was not at all what she'd expected. Nor was his concerned, gentle tone of voice making it any easier for her to think of him as a thief. "I simply don't know."

They stood silently, she a turmoil of emotion and he the very picture of exasperation. He shoved his hands into his pockets, watching her with a mixture of wariness and the faintest hint of sympathy in his startling blue eyes.

Finally he broke the silence. "Maybe Ressu had an enemy, someone who wants to destroy his reputation even now. How better to strike back at a dead man than to ruin a festival performance designed to honor him?"

His words yanked her out of her silent confused state. "Valentin had no enemies. Everyone loved him. No one would have ever—"

"Everyone has enemies, Suzanne."

The thought of someone hating Valentin enough to want to wreck the festival concert struck her as too outlandish to be believed. Why, Valentin had always been a gentle man, considerate of everyone. Of course he'd been passionate about his art, but no one could fault him for that.

"I can't believe anyone would want to destroy Valentin's reputation that way," she insisted. "Valentin never hurt a soul. Who would want to do such a thing?"

"You tell me."

"No one, that's who. Valentin contributed to the community by lecturing at the University of Chicago, he helped support his fellow Romanians even though he was born in America, he lavished attention on his wife and son—"

"Paul might argue with you on that one."

She flinched, feeling wretchedly exposed to Devin. He saw them all too astutely, easily grasping the way they interacted. How had he managed to insinuate himself into their private affairs?

But she knew how. She'd given him the entry by approaching him after his recital. He was merely taking advantage of it.

Suddenly she only wanted to be rid of him with his cynicism about avant-garde and his cavalier disrespect for Valentin's abilities. And his perceptive gaze. She hated the way he looked at her now, with a touch of pity beneath the mask of dispassionate interest.

She ducked her head to avoid that heart-wrenching pity. "You know nothing about any of it. Who—whoever took these manuscripts has other motives, like greed and personal gain." Her control was slipping, but she couldn't seem to regain it. "It—it can't be anything like you're suggesting. You may have hated Valentin's music, but everyone else recognized his genius. They respected and loved him. All of them!"

With a swish of her skirt, she whirled away from him, but he caught her arm. "Hold on a minute! Don't get so upset about it. Hell, I know you were close to the guy, but that doesn't mean you have to believe he was a saint!"

Jerking her arm free, she stood with her back to him, her body shaking. She stared unseeingly at the trees around them and swallowed convulsively as she tried to regain her calm.

"Look," he said more gently, "I understand what it's like to admire someone, to want to emulate them, only to have them die before you're ready for it." He sucked in his breath sharply, then continued in a deep, emotion-filled voice, "And I understand the need to defend a dead person's reputation. You try to protect them even though they're no longer around to care."

He placed his hand lightly on her shoulder. She didn't pull away. With so many feelings tumbling about inside her destroying her emotional equilibrium, she could hardly reject such a small gesture of comfort.

"But you don't have to stand up for him anymore. You've done enough with this festival concert. No one alive or dead could ask more of you. You probably should try to find out what's going on with these thefts, but don't take it so personally. Let the cops handle it."

She pivoted slowly to face him, disbelief written in every line of her face. "Oh, really? Does that mean I should tell the police my suspicions about you?" Her voice lowered in threat. "Aren't you afraid of what I might tell them?"

He met her gaze steadily. "I've got nothing to hide. If I tell the cops Ressu played the piece for me, they'll believe me. Cops think all musicians are a little flaky anyway. The robberies are something concrete, but your theories about me . . . well, I don't think they'd take them too seriously."

His gaze locked with hers. The air between them vibrated with silent meaning. She thought she could see uncertainty hovering behind the interest and the sympathetic smile. In her bones, she believed he was tied into the robberies of "Endnote."

But perhaps not in the way she thought. If he'd stolen the manuscript or associated with the thief, he was staying amazingly, and unnecessarily, involved with her and Valentin's family. He should be stonewalling her, hiding behind his position and connections. Instead, he seemed as interested in discovering what had happened as she was.

And almost sympathetic toward her. It was the sympathy in his voice that broke down her defenses. "I won't mention you to the police. Not yet anyway."

Did she imagine it, or had relief flickered in his gaze? If so, his low chuckle dispelled it. "Gee, thanks. It's generous of you not to make a fool of yourself for my benefit."

She sat down on the bench, a grudging smile hovering on her lips. "You know, when you're like this, I can almost believe Valentin and you really were friends. The two of you have the same sense of humor."

"But of course I'm not as talented as he was, right?" he

said flippantly as he sat down beside her, a little closer than before.

"Fishing for a compliment?"

He cocked his head with a certain insolence. "Yeah, why not?" The barest suggestion of vulnerability glinted in his eyes. "You slaughtered me in your review. I mean, the least you can do is tell me whether or not you enjoyed some tiny aspect of my otherwise 'egotistical,' contemptuous performance."

Her eyes twinkled at his sarcasm. "Oh, the poor boy's ego is starving these days."

"You're not kidding."

"Okay. You win. I admit I enjoyed many aspects of your performance." With utmost sincerity, she added, "You're very talented, far more so than I'd expected."

"So. The lady is not only intelligent, but perceptive," he said with that unshakable, cocky grin. Then the grin slowly faded into a very different kind of smile. "The lady is also far more likable than *I* expected. Except for that last review, which sounded pretty angry, your reviews usually make you sound kind of stiff and formal—"

"Tight-assed."

"Yeah, I guess I would have called it that . . . before I met you. Now I know it's just . . . careful."

"Careful?"

He edged even closer, his now-serious gaze riveted on her face. "Yeah, careful, safe. You seem to find it safer to live in an ordered world. That way everything fits into a neat pattern. The careful person doesn't operate outside established standards. The careful person lives life by the numbers."

"You make me sound boring." Angry color flooded her face.

"I didn't mean to," he said in a rush, then looked thoughtful. "There's a kind of beauty in order and rules. I'm a musician, so I should know. Music is nothing but order and pattern. But—" He paused, as if choosing his words. "But music is also emotion. The rules are the skeleton, but emotion . . . passion . . . puts the meat on its bones. Truly great musicians aren't only technically expert, but also passionately involved."

She'd heard all of this before, and her intellectual, analytical mind even accepted it, but it was the personal implications she found herself reacting to. "I suppose you've decided I'm not passionately involved in my work." She dropped her gaze to her lap, smoothing out her skirt self-consciously.

"I didn't say that. On paper, you do seem to edit out the passion. But sometimes when you talk . . . especially about Ressu's work . . . it's there, in your eyes, in your voice." His own voice had gone all low and husky. He stretched his arm out on the top of the bench behind her shoulder. He didn't touch her, but she was still intensely aware of his arm centimeters away from her hair.

He leaned toward her, half turning on the bench to face her. "But you seem to be afraid of the passion. You only let it out in dribs and drabs, because it doesn't fit into your careful life. It isn't neat and tidy."

"Passion causes problems," she cut in, adding to herself, *and it's undependable.* She stared off down the pathway, irritated at his intrusion into her psyche. And his more disturbing intrusion into her space. Still, she couldn't move away.

She sucked in a deep breath. "It's fine for someone like you to talk about emotion and passion and letting everything simply happen. No one depends on you. You can make your own rules and not worry how they affect other people. I can't. I have responsibilities, obligations. If that makes me seem stiff, then so be it. I'd rather be stiff than selfish and inconsiderate."

"But are those your only choices? Is the world that rigid? Who knows, maybe your stiffness comes from trying to uphold too many standards and operate by too many rules.

You and I both know that rules aren't always appropriate. Some things don't operate by rules."

She leveled her gaze on him, crossing her arms defensively over her chest. "Like your playing 'Endnote' at the recital?"

A muscle worked in his jaw as he glanced away from her. "Yeah. Trust you to get right to the heart of the matter."

Something about the frustrated expression on his face touched a chord in her. "You like to break the rules, don't you?" she asked with quick understanding. "While I'm busy living up to high standards, you're busy tilting the standards on their sides."

He must have heard the gentle note in her voice, for as he turned his vivid eyes on her once more, his expression softened. "That's me, all right. A rebel." But he smiled.

Raw heat suffused her, quite out of the blue. Something in the upward tilt of his lips and the way the wind ruffled his hair made him seem even more rakish and attractive than before.

He seemed to notice her reaction, for his mouth tautened and his eyes grew unusually smoky as they drifted down to her mouth. "Tell me something while we're talking about high standards." He lowered his voice to a gruff murmur. "What are your standards for the men in your life?"

Her blood began to pound in her ears. The slow, steady drumbeat increased as he leaned a little closer. "Wh-what do you mean?"

"Like boyfriends. Do you have a boyfriend?"

The world seemed suddenly to shift around her, to become an alien landscape fraught with unseen dangers. She wanted to look away from the unwavering interest in his gaze. But she couldn't. She tried to make her voice sound cool and casual. "Not at the moment, if you must know."

"I must know. Because I'm pretty sure I'm about to break one of your rules."

"Oh? And what rule might that be?" Unconsciously she wet her lips with the tip of her tongue.

His eyes followed the movement, hungry, dark, devouring. "The rule that says I shouldn't kiss you."

Shock held her motionless, shock and the tiniest shiver of anticipation. She couldn't respond, couldn't look away, move, or even say anything.

His hand slid onto her shoulder and beneath the soft weight of her hair to curve itself around her neck. At the feather caress of his fingers along the fine hairs at the nape of her neck, her mouth formed a silent "Oh."

Then he leaned forward and lowered his head to hers.

Their lips met, barely touching. The sensation of gentleness so overpowered her she closed her eyes. He increased the pressure until he was truly kissing her, as a man who desires a woman kisses. His lips rubbed hers apart, and his tongue slid along the ridge of her teeth.

Unexpectedly desire bolted through her, and she didn't know what to do. The last man who'd kissed her had been a sober physics graduate student who'd turned into a groping octopus once he'd entered her apartment.

The memory was strong and distasteful enough to make her pull back a fraction, but Devin's fingers on her neck tightened, urging her closer as his mouth closed over hers again, warm and inviting.

I shouldn't be doing this, she thought. *He's manipulating me . . . he's trying to make me forget what happened at the recital . . . I must take charge here . . . I've got to stop . . . this . . . mad . . .*

He lifted his other hand to run one finger over the silky skin of her throat, and her thinning thread of restraint snapped.

He knew it. And like the opportunist he was, he took advantage of it to deepen the kiss. His tongue delved into her mouth as his hands intertwined behind her neck and his thumbs dipped seductively into the hollows behind her ears.

Under the onslaught of his ravaging kiss, her blood, her skin, her very essence grew heated. He sparked the kind of warmth in her that no lake wind could chill. Mindlessly she moved her hands forward to clutch the open edges of his jacket.

In response he shifted his body until his thigh and hers pressed against each other. He dropped his hand to her waist and drew her closer in a possessive gesture ancient as sin. Her heart beat like a runaway metronome in perfect harmony with the bold forays of his tongue.

His lips left hers and moved lower to press against her flushed cheek, her uptilted chin, her trembling throat framed by her sweater's jewel neckline.

"Devin," she whispered, "don't . . ." Her breath caught in her throat as he seized her mouth once more, teasing, tormenting, coaxing her into melting. With a moan of resignation, she slid one hand beneath his jacket to mold the hard muscle of his chest, and he groaned deep in his throat in response.

The kiss seemed to go on forever. The wind blew around them . . . a voice or two trickled through the trees to where they sat . . . she noticed none of it. For possibly the first time in her life, Suzanne was bowing to an impulse, and she realized as she dragged her hand down his rock-hard chest and over to rest on his waist that she liked it, liked the stabbing thrusts of his tongue, the way he toyed with hers before sucking it back into his mouth.

A twig suddenly snapped loudly nearby, followed by a rustling of leaves, as if someone were running away. It startled them both. Suzanne jerked back from Devin first, reminded of yesterday's mugging in a place much safer than Olive Park.

Her breath still came quickly, as did his, and her hands clutched his jacket tensely. Both looked around, searching the little clearing where they sat. But whoever had been there . . . if anyone had been . . . was gone.

A faint smile formed on her face as she turned her gaze

back to Devin. "This isn't the best place for this sort of thing—" she began, but the words died in her throat as she caught the way he looked at her now.

Desire had faded completely from his face. Instead, he looked tormented, his eyes splintered ice. As if in a trance, he glanced down to where his hand clutched her waist. He withdrew both hands, then rubbed one absently with the other before rising to his feet and half turning away from her.

He ran his fingers through his hair, over and over, his breath a series of quick gasps. She could see his profile as he struggled for control, the lines of his face twisted as if he felt some deep pain. He refused to look at her.

Embarrassment overwhelmed her, and a terrible sadness at his obvious rejection. What had happened? What had she done?

"I'm sorry," he said at last. "I had no right to . . . to do that."

The impersonal coolness behind his words made her want to cry. "Rebels don't apologize for breaking the rules," she whispered, unable to filter the hurt out of her voice.

If it affected him, he didn't show it. "Some rules should never be broken, even by rebels."

Those should be her words, not his, she thought as a desperate panic swelled in her throat. Did he think he could unleash this passionate emotion in her, then shut it off like a water faucet?

"I see I'm not the only one who has trouble letting things happen." Her wounded feelings sharpened her tone.

As if he hadn't even heard her, he said in a strained voice, "If you need any help with this problem concerning the 'Endnote' copies, let me know. I'll do what I can." He breathed deeply. "Maybe I can ask around to see if anyone else has heard about a copy circulating."

"That would be useful." She fought, unsuccessfully, to keep an even tone.

So that was it, she thought. He'd come, he'd conquered, and now he planned to waltz off, secure in the knowledge that she wouldn't harass him any longer. Let him think that, she told herself in hurt anger. She wasn't finished with him yet.

"Do you need a ride somewhere?" he asked, still not looking at her as he bent and picked up his satchel.

"No," she choked out, then added, her voice slightly more steady, "no. I think I'll sit here a moment alone."

He glanced over at her then, his expression veiled. But his eyes glittered like uncut sapphires. "All right then. I'll call you in a couple of days to see how it's going." Then his mouth softened the barest fraction. She thought his eyes dropped to her lips, but she wasn't sure, because he turned from her then, his body rigid. "Be careful." The words sounded more threatening than cautionary.

Then without so much as another glance her way, he left.

8

♪

When the phone rang, the Turk was in the middle of a cold shower, his gaunt, nutmeg-hued body shaking from the chill. Normally he took long hot showers. Bathing was one of his favorite pastimes now that he'd made his home in this heathen land. He sometimes felt the need to wash the stink of foreigners off his skin.

But this cold shower was another matter indeed. He welcomed the excuse to get out, although he took his time sliding from behind the shower curtain and reaching for a towel.

The phone was already on the seventh ring by the time he reached it. Nonetheless he paused to flip on the recorder and the tracer before he lifted the receiver.

"H'lo?" he grumbled as he propped the phone between his ear and his shoulder so he could wrap the towel around his waist.

"Where have you been?"

He recognized the voice instantly. It was the person he knew only as "Frankie." He didn't know if Frankie was a man or a woman, native or foreign, young or old, because Frankie always spoke in a whisper to mask gender, accent, and age.

The Turk glanced over at the briefcase he'd casually slung onto his desk. It lay open, papers spilling out of it. "I obtained what you wanted. That's all you paid me for. After that, my time belonged to me. I went out to drink with friends."

"You stupid imbecile!" Frankie hissed. "Yes, you obtained what I wanted, but you drew attention to yourself and put her on the alert! Idiot! You should have sneaked the manuscript away from her, not stolen it in broad daylight! This is a disaster, a complete disaster!"

The Turk's sharp dark eyes flickered over the tracing machine. It had produced a number, not that it would be of much help. Frankie always called from a pay phone. "It is not easy to steal something unobtrusively. I followed the woman from her house. It took a long time to make certain she was alone. And with campus police roaming the grounds and white phones . . . I couldn't risk anyone seeing me on the campus. They are very strict about intruders at that university. I did my best."

"It was not good enough! You should have found some way to slip it from her secretly, like you did at her house. She still is not certain if that copy was stolen."

"Listen to me, Frankie. I cannot—how do you say it?—read your mind. You said steal the manuscript. I stole the manuscript. You must give more explicit instructions when you want more than a simple theft performed." He paused a beat. "Or you can hire someone else who can read your mind."

But of course, Frankie would not hire anyone else. First of all, the Turk had come to Frankie very highly recommended. Secondly, the Turk had dealt with Frankie many times over the last year, and had never disappointed his employer. Also, Frankie claimed to like the Turk's foreign roots. Now Frankie trusted no one else with his peculiar jobs.

The Turk had gained that trust with careful work. He always did as he was told. He never asked too high a sum for his services, although he knew enough to price himself into the market. And he never double-crossed an employer once he'd agreed to a job, no matter how much more the employer's competitors or enemies offered.

The Turk was sure Frankie knew all this. It was why he might rant and rave, but he would always come back to the Turk. At the moment, however, Frankie was being irritatingly silent.

The Turk shifted the receiver to his other ear. "When do I receive the remainder of my pay?"

"You bungled it. I am not giving you any more."

A slow smile curved his lips. He'd thought something like this might happen. Frankie paid very well when pleased with the results, but withheld pay if not completely satisfied.

This time the Turk had prepared himself. "A hasty decision, my friend, but one I think you will change when you hear what I have to say. I followed your woman again today."

"Oh? And who gave you permission to do that?"

"I chose to do it. That is enough. She met with a man."

"So?"

"So they were discussing your 'Endnote.'" He looked over at the surveillance equipment piled on his spartan bed, the highly acute microphone, which could pick up the smallest sound from a distance, and the microrecorder.

The long pause on the other end told him his statement had made the desired impact.

"I have a tape," the Turk continued. "I trust it will prove interesting to you."

"Who was the man?" came the terse whisper across the line.

"Ah. You will know that when you purchase the tape."

The Turk remembered the way the woman had whispered the name "Devin" with such passion that the Turk had left his post several yards away to approach the couple and more closely observe what was occurring.

The sight of a handsome, dark-haired man and the golden-haired beauty intertwined in such perfect, erotic surroundings had left him with a powerful erection.

I've been too long without a woman, he thought as his erection returned now. Too bad he had been so caught up in what he was seeing that he'd stepped on that twig and broken their embrace.

Frankie's sigh brought the Turk back to the present.

"How do I know this tape will be worth it to me?" Frankie asked.

"You know it will." Frankie could never resist such an offering, the Turk thought. "Surveillance is my specialty, as you well know. Have I ever disappointed you in that area before?"

There was a pause, during which the Turk casually braced the receiver between his head and shoulder and took up his bottle of lemon-scent cologne from his bureau.

At last Frankie whispered, "All right. You will find the remainder of your pay, plus a handsome addition, in the usual place. You will leave the tape there. If the tape is not left . . ."

The Turk smiled as he took the cap off the imported bottle of scent. He and Frankie might have a sometimes thorny business arrangement, but they knew how to deal

SILENT SONATA

with each other. "The tape will be left. What about the briefcase? Do you want it also?"

"No. Only the manuscript. Leave the manuscript with the tape. But dispose of the briefcase." A pause ensued. "Do you have access to an incinerator?"

The Turk splashed some scent into his hands, then patted it over his angular face as he thought. "Yes, I believe so."

"Burn it then."

Briefly he toyed with the idea of keeping the briefcase and its contents for himself. It was a nice briefcase. He smiled. And the beret had the woman's smell on it.

He shook his head woefully. It was against his strict personal code to go against Frankie's wishes. He hadn't gotten where he was by biting the hand that fed him.

"It will be done?" Frankie asked.

"It will be done."

"Good. After that, I have another job for you. We will discuss it once you have handed me the tape and the manuscript."

"You wish me to steal more of these copies of this musical piece?"

"No, it is much too late for that. But there are other ways of accomplishing my purpose. The job I have for you is somewhat distasteful, but I believe you will find it has its rewards."

With those enigmatic words, Frankie hung up.

Ion Goma and Lydia Chelminscu sat at either end of his dining room table. The sun had long ago risen like a cherry-cheeked child over the calm waters of the lake, heralding a glorious, sunny day, but neither paid much attention to the brilliant sunlight surrounding them.

"I tell you, Mariela isn't going to change her mind," Ion Goma grumbled, drawing in the smoke from his pipe. "I spent an hour on the phone last night, trying to convince her. Nothing I said persuaded her. She still believes the festival concert should be cancelled. Ah, God preserve me from the foolishness of women."

Lydia's patient, intimidating stare lingered over him.

Ion sighed. The last thing he needed was to alienate his one ally, although he regretted she was female. "I don't mean you, of course. You have good sense. You listen to logic, and don't follow the irrational paths Mariela and Suzanne strike off on."

Lydia sighed, planting her elbows on the table and folding her hands together. "Perhaps Mariela isn't being so irrational after all. Perhaps it is best. With all this craziness about Valentin's final piece, it may be foolish of us all to continue."

"Don't say that! We still have a copy. The piece can still be performed. It is a shame we must allow that little tramp Cindy to do it, but Mariela seems determined to use her." His expression grew haughty. "This is another example of what I mean. If Mariela hadn't been following some foolish sentimental notion, she would have taken my advice on who should play Ressu's music."

"It hardly matters who plays the pieces, Ion." Lydia's gaze was distant. "And I'm beginning to believe the festival concert should not occur either."

He'd wondered when this would happen, how long it would take the Romanian government to withdraw. He didn't bother to hide his sneer. "That's because you now know who Valentin really was. I should have realized you and your people would eventually uncover the truth, though I'd hoped it would happen *after* the concert, not before. If you hadn't learned who he really was, you would not be saying these things!"

Anger flared up briefly in her cold eyes. "That has nothing to do with it!"

"It has everything to do with it, doesn't it?" He wanted to put her on the alert, to force her to defend her pride. "You and your compatriots rushed to sponsor a concert for an eminent Romanian who all believed had been raised in

America by his exiled Romanian parents. But you lost your enthusiasm, didn't you, when you discovered he was actually Cornel Ceauşescu, a defector and the nephew of a man hated by every Romanian alive."

Lydia's lips thinned, and she reacted as she always did when reminded of Valentin's real identity. She withdrew into herself, working her bony hands nervously and lapsing into a silent meditation of the situation at hand. Ion couldn't blame her. He himself had recoiled when he'd first learned the truth two years ago after seeing a familiar face in a relative's photo album.

Ion thought back to that day, when he'd visited his cousin, a new immigrant to America, and they'd looked through childhood photographs. Ion had been stunned to find Valentin Ressu's face among those in a picture of his cousin's academy classmates. But the name hadn't been Ressu. It had been Ceauşescu.

Ion had stored away his newfound knowledge in a little safe in his mind. He'd never told Valentin he knew. Instead, he'd saved it for the time when he could use it to his advantage. He was still waiting for that time to come. Valentin would probably have been aghast if he'd realized that Ion knew his secret, for they'd only been acquaintances.

No wonder Valentin had changed his name, Ion thought as he took a drag on his pipe, savoring the rich tobacco. No wonder Valentin had pretended to be a native American. Until Ceauşescu's execution in 1989, the tyrant had slated for assassination all defectors who'd crossed him, no matter what country they fled to. Certainly he would have done so with a relative who'd dared to humiliate him by leaving.

Through various sources Ion had learned that in Romania, Cornel Ceauşescu alias Valentin Ressu was believed to have drowned at the age of twenty-four. There was no way of ascertaining if that had been the official story given out by Ceauşescu's lackeys or if Valentin had staged his own death before he fled to the West.

Ion wondered if Lydia would know, but did not ask. She was edgy enough as it was. After all, the Romanian government at present had its hands full trying to convince its people that it was not simply a new Communist regime in disguise. It didn't need the image problems that supporting Ceauşescu's nephew would produce.

"Do you think it's possible Mariela has just now learned the truth about her husband's past?" Lydia said, breaking her long silence. "Perhaps that is why she wishes to cancel the festival concert."

Ion shook his head. "I don't see how Mariela could have been married to Valentin Ressu and not know everything. Granted, Valentin kept his secret very close. None of his friends know it, to my knowledge. But surely he would have told his wife."

"Perhaps. But men cannot be trusted to tell anyone the truth." Lydia's shoulders slumped and a faraway look entered her eyes. "Men lie even to their wives."

Ion didn't take the comment personally. He shrugged. "If you are correct, then it will shock Mariela to learn of all the lies."

Lydia's face grew taut in alarm. "You are not thinking of telling her, are you?"

"I might. If she doesn't know the truth, then hearing of the heavy burden Valentin shouldered might shame her into continuing with the festival concert."

"And if she does know, then what will you have accomplished? She'll hate and fear you once she realizes others know her husband's secret. A fiery love for Romania still burns within Mariela. She will not want you to shame her before her people."

Ion's voice hardened. "Fear can be a powerful weapon. She won't dare to act against my wishes if she knows I hold such a secret."

Lydia eyed him keenly for a moment. "And what would your wishes be?"

"To have the festival concert continue at all costs." He

fingered the bowl of his pipe thoughtfully. "Although I admit I also wish it to have a different pianist . . . and a different committee chairman at the helm."

"What's wrong with Suzanne?" Lydia asked, her eyes narrowing.

He tapped his pipe on the table as a sneer formed on his lips. "What's not wrong? She can't even keep her hands on the most important sonata of them all. Worse yet, she's an American who can never hope to understand the importance of this concert to Romanians. Leave it in her hands, and she will botch the entire thing."

"For a man who has lived in America most of his life, you are oddly nationalistic," Lydia observed wryly.

Ion nodded, ignoring the sarcasm implicit in her statement. "I am a Romanian first. My parents made sure of that. It galls me to see this entire business being run by three foolish women, two of whom are non–Romanians—the haughty Miss Winslow and the incompetent Cindy Stephens. I admit it. I'd do almost anything to see those two removed from the festival concert."

Lydia eyed him skeptically. "Even if it meant the festival could not go on?"

"Bah. Don't be absurd. If those two were removed, it could only improve matters. As long as your government, the Romanian Society, and Amarcorp continue to support us, and Mariela backs the festival concert, we do not need those two. I already know of a talented Romanian pianist who would be more than willing to oblige us. And as for Suzanne . . . why do you think Mariela wishes to cancel? Because of Suzanne's bungling with the copy of the last piece."

"Suzanne was robbed," Lydia said sharply.

"So she says. She probably lost the piece herself, and doesn't want to admit it."

Lydia eyed him with curiosity. "Or maybe someone who hates her would like us all to believe that. Maybe someone who hates her would have her attacked to make her look incompetent."

He raised his eyes from his pipe and met her questioning gaze, but refused to respond to her implicit accusation. He didn't want to encourage her suspicions.

"What if my government withdraws its support?" she asked quietly.

A smile tipped his lips up around his pipe's mouthpiece. He pulled out the pipe. "And defeat your political purpose? I thought your government is building a new image. It wants the world to see that Romania has as much interest in the subversive music of its countrymen as the next newly liberated Eastern bloc country. If you withdraw, you will look bad."

"If we stay, and you cause havoc or reveal Ressu's secret," Lydia said in a deadpan voice, "it will make us look worse."

He bit deeply into the pipe stem. "Withdraw if you wish. We will make it without you. But the festival concert will go on, I promise you that."

"Fine." She rose to her feet. "I had decided to recommend to my superiors that we withdraw our support. Our conversation today has only strengthened that decision. I will not have my people cast our lot with a man who would create chaos in an organization by eliminating two perfectly competent members simply because they were not Romanian."

The anger that had only simmered in him before now boiled to the surface. "Go ahead! Make your recommendation! I wager your superiors will side with me in this. They are men, after all. They will see the logic of supporting me."

She paused to fix him with an insolent glare. "You may be right. They are men, as you say. And men cannot be trusted. But it doesn't change my decision."

With that, she grabbed her coat and stormed out of his apartment.

He watched her go, his temper raging. What did she know about such things? Not as much as she thought, that was certain. Such arrogance from a woman was unseemly. Lydia had been too long in America. She was starting to remind him of his ex-wife, the bitch. His ex-wife too had sought to tell him what to do, to order him around.

He scowled. Despite his wife's Romanian roots, she'd eventually turned into another tough, liberated American woman who thought she could do everything without a man's help, a woman like Suzanne Winslow. It was women like Suzanne who corrupted women like his wife and Lydia by encouraging them to enter professions once reserved for men—in business, medicine, and yes, academia.

But at least Lydia is a Romanian, he thought, hoping she wouldn't do as she said. She wouldn't be able to convince the Romanian government to pull out solely on the strength of her dislike of his methods, but if she told them about the thefts and Mariela's desire to cancel, she might persuade them.

He couldn't let that happen. He thought a moment, wondering if there were a way to prevent it. He hadn't been successful in convincing Mariela. She was too concerned about the theft from Suzanne's house and the mugging.

Everything centered around Suzanne. He thought a moment, drawing deeply on his pipe. Perhaps there was a way to remove Suzanne from the picture, so she could no longer alarm Mariela with her mishandling of the "Endnote" piece.

A slow smile lit his face. He picked up the phone and dialed, then waited while the phone rang twice. "Amarcorp Industries," a secretary's brisk voice answered.

"This is Ion Goma of the Romanian Society. I would like to speak to Mr. Wilder, if I may."

"Why, hello, Mr. Goma," said the voice, now much warmer. "Let me see if Mr. Wilder's available to take your call."

He settled back in his chair to wait.

9

♪

The phone rang and Suzanne bolted up in bed, her heart racing. It took her a second to realize where she was and fight back the terror that overwhelmed her. She'd lain down for only a short nap, but she'd had a nightmare—not a full-scripted dream, but snatches of images that were horrifyingly real. Memories had mixed with fantastic unreality. She'd seen Valentin in his coffin at his funeral, but he was clutching a copy of "Endnote." Then the man on the motorcycle was following her with a gun in his hands . . . except his face became Devin's and the gun became a satchel that spilled sheet music everywhere. She slid on the music and began disappearing into a black night with Devin's laughter ringing in her ears. . . .

She shook her head, fighting off the lingering grip of the nightmare. The phone kept ringing. After the fourth ring, the machine clicked on, but when she heard Mariela's voice sounding frantic, she picked up the receiver. The machine clicked off.

"I'm here, Mariela," Suzanne said. "Is something wrong?"

"I don't know what to do," the woman's voice came all in a rush, a frantic edge to it. "I've received a copy of that terrible letter they sent to you. You have seen it, no?"

No. Suzanne hadn't checked her mail yet that day. "Hold on," she grumbled into the phone, then took the cordless handset with her as she went to check her mailbox. "I haven't seen any letter but I'm looking. Who're 'they'?"

"Amarcorp."

Amarcorp. The festival sponsor. Suzanne's hands trembled as she found a letter with Amarcorp's letterhead on the return address, ripped the envelope open, and took out a letter.

As she unfolded the sheet of paper, she noticed it was addressed to her with carbon copies sent to everyone on the committee. Quickly, she scanned the words:

> It has come to our attention that two copies of Mr. Ressu's final work have disappeared while in your care. This situation causes us some concern. As I am sure you realize, the success of the festival concert rests on its appeal as the world premiere of Mr. Ressu's last piece. Thus, if you cannot resolve the problems regarding the security of the Ressu manuscript, we will have to recommend to Mrs. Ressu your removal from the position of committee chairman. Otherwise, we will be forced to withdraw our support from the festival concert.

It was signed by a Mr. Wilder, no doubt some CEO with a perverse concern for security.

Anger exploded through her as she crumpled the paper. This couldn't be happening. For Pete's sake, who'd told Amarcorp about the mugging?

Everyone at the meeting had known about it. But of those, she could think of only one person who might want to see her step down as committee chair—Ion Goma with his nationalistic zeal and chauvinist ideas.

Blast the man!

"Now we will *have* to cancel," Mariela's voice came over the line, sounding almost relieved. "If Amarcorp withdraws its funding at this late date, we cannot continue with the concert. Without them we cannot pay for the rental of Mandel Hall and the Steinway or print flyers or advertise in the papers—"

"Amarcorp isn't our only sponsor."

"It is the primary one."

Suzanne fought for control of her tone. "You seem as

determined as ever to cancel the concert. I thought you said you'd think about not canceling."

"I have thought of nothing else."

Why was it that every time Mariela spoke of the festival concert these days, she spoke with quiet sadness? "What happened, Mariela? Something has upset you and made you want to end this. And don't try to tell me it has anything to do with the thefts. Two weeks ago you would have fought anyone who tried to cancel the concert."

There was a long silence on the other end.

"Mariela?"

"I—I cannot explain to you why I wish it ended. It is a private matter."

"Is it because you're angry with Valentin for making me literary executor? I mean, I didn't think it would bother you, but—"

"No! No, of course not." She took a deep breath, then continued more gently. "You are like a daughter to me, Suzanne. Valentin wrote his will three years ago, and I insisted that he make you executor."

Suzanne swallowed. She hadn't known that.

"It has nothing to do with you." Mariela paused. Her heavy sigh came over the line. "That's not entirely true. I do worry for your safety with all these thefts. I would rather cancel the concert than have you harmed."

Suzanne gazed down at the crumpled letter in her hand, fighting a sudden wave of nausea. All her plans, all her work . . . evaporating before her eyes. Her voice barely above a whisper, she said, "And what if I do as Amarcorp says? What if I step down? What if I end my involvement with the concert?" It hurt her throat just to say the words. "If I bow out, then you won't have to worry about my safety and Amarcorp's fears will be quieted."

"Amarcorp! Pah! We both know why they are concerned. Ion Goma has no doubt run to them with stories about you. He's made no secret of his dissatisfaction with your heading the committee. I will not give him the pleasure of seeing you step down. You belong at the helm, no matter what he says to Amarcorp."

The vehemence in Mariela's voice startled Suzanne. "Does that mean you *do* want to go on with the concert?"

"Oh, I do not know," Mariela said with anguish. Then she hesitated, as if gathering herself together. "I am so confused. I have . . . learned many things about my husband to upset me these last few days. I do not know what I want."

Suzanne's curiosity was definitely roused. "What kind of things?"

Mariela's voice grew distant. "Nothing. Little things. I should not have mentioned it. I am making much of nothing, no doubt. Perhaps you are right. Perhaps we should continue with the concert. Perhaps I am being foolish. But I worry about these thefts. And even if we continue with the concert, what will we do about Amarcorp?"

"Let me deal with that. I'm sure I can find another sponsor in a pinch. Ion Goma's got another thing coming if he thinks dirty tactics like this will work."

Mariela kept silent for a moment, then said, "And what about this Devin Bryce? Why is he interested in my husband's music? Why does he want a copy of 'Endnote'?"

The abrupt change of subject took Suzanne by surprise. Then an image of Devin filled her mind. None of this had happened until after Devin Bryce had played "Endnote." Well, almost none of it. The original manuscript had been stolen before the recital. But the mugging, Mariela's sudden desire to cancel the festival concert, and now this letter from Amarcorp had occurred after Devin had gotten involved.

"I don't know what he has to do with any of it," Suzanne said, not certain if she should tell Mariela about Devin's crazy tale. "But I'm trying to find out." She thought a moment. "He told me he knew Valentin fairly well, but I take it you've never heard of Bryce or met him?"

"I have no idea. Valentin introduced me to so many people, so many musicians. I could never keep all of their names in my head. I may have met him or heard his name mentioned. Who knows?"

"But if one of Valentin's friends had come to your house often, you would have known him, right?"

"Valentin had many visitors I knew nothing about."

There it was again, that impenetrable sadness. Suzanne itched to question Mariela further, but she knew the woman well enough to know she could be stubborn about preserving her privacy. Unfortunately, her stubbornness wasn't helping Suzanne figure out if Devin Bryce had known Valentin well enough to hear him play "Endnote."

Suddenly an idea struck her. She did know one person who might be able to tell her more about Devin Bryce. A smile flitted across her face. Oh, yes. She might be able to get to the bottom of this after all.

"I have to go," she told Mariela. "I have an appointment." *Sort of,* she thought. "But don't worry about all of this, okay? I'll talk to Amarcorp and I'll find out what's going on with Bryce. It'll be okay. I promise. I'll call you as soon as I have more definitive answers."

"All right. But I still don't know what I want to do—"

"It's okay," Suzanne said gently. "I'll abide by your decision about the concert. You keep thinking about what you want to do." She paused. "Just remember, Valentin's music should be more than just his. It belongs to the world."

Mariela gave a bitter laugh. "Unfortunately, I know that better than anyone." After that cryptic comment, she hung up.

Suzanne sat staring at the receiver a moment, then shook her head. She had no idea what might have put Mariela in such a state, but she felt sure the highly emotional woman had simply heard some trumped-up rumor or something about Valentin. Surely in time Mariela would see the falsity of such stories.

Suzanne shrugged, hoping one day she'd hear the whole

SILENT SONATA

answer to the mystery. In the meantime, however, she at least could get to the bottom of one mystery.

Why Devin Bryce had played "Endnote."

Bloomsday Pub looked different in daylight, Suzanne thought. For one thing, it was half empty. For another, the spring sun streaming through the windows gave it a homey, comfortable appearance entirely out of character for a bar.

She looked at her watch. Maggie's shift began in a few minutes, or so the bar owner had told her. Suzanne fidgeted on the stool, eager to talk to the one woman who might shed some light on the mysterious pianist.

As she stared unseeingly at the bottles ranged behind the bar, she thought back to her crazy encounter with Devin in Olive Park and how he'd tried to convince her of the irrationality of her accusations. Unwillingly she also remembered how that encounter had ended. Devin had dealt her ego a killing blow with his kiss, first shattering her restraints and then apparently despising her for letting him shatter them.

The pain of rejection surged in her again, but she fought the anger it roused in her. She must stay rational and not go off half-cocked just because some man had shared a kiss with her, then had thrown her aside like a toy he was finished playing with. Nor could she allow her hurt feelings to make her accuse him falsely. She thought of the letter from Amarcorp. She wasn't accusing him . . . not yet. But it was prudent to find out more about him, wasn't it? If she discovered he'd been a great friend of Valentin's, then fine, she'd drop everything and stay away from him. Most definitely stay away from him.

But if he were lying . . . well, she had to explore the possibility, didn't she? Someone was behind all these attempts to sabotage the festival. She had to find out who. And if Devin could lead her to the culprit . . . great.

"Hey, sweetie. Patrick tells me you were lookin' for me."

The lilting voice at her side startled Suzanne out of her depressing ruminations.

She turned to Maggie with a wan smile. "Hello again." Suzanne was pleased to note that Maggie wore a friendly expression.

"After Devin tore out of here last week like a bat out o' hell," Maggie continued, settling her rounded hips on the barstool next to Suzanne, "I thought I might see you again."

"I beg your pardon?"

"Oh, he hardly ever brings a woman in here, and then no more than once. The ones he does bring aren't the kind to rile him up like that. Busty, easygoing types, if you know what I mean."

Suzanne nodded, wide-eyed, trying not to take offense at the insinuation that she was far from "busty." She could hardly imagine Devin dating "busty, easygoing" women anyway. Then again, she wasn't at all certain what type of woman he *would* like.

Maggie went on. "So when Devin brings in a woman with some class, and then takes her up to his special room and has a rip-roaring good argument with her . . . let's just say, I think there's hope for him yet."

The wheels turned quickly in Suzanne's mind. She'd intended to ask Maggie a few questions about Devin and his friends, hoping the talkative woman would say something, anything, about Devin's involvement with Ressu. But Maggie obviously thought Suzanne and Devin were having a relationship. What's more, Maggie clearly approved.

Suzanne could set Maggie straight. . . . Or, she thought abruptly, she could use the situation to her advantage.

Don't stoop to his level, she cautioned herself. Then she thought, *Why not? He sneaked around, questioning Paul behind my back. Why not try his tactics?*

Why not? Because she wasn't a devious person. She

prided herself on her straightforward approach to problems, her willingness to be truthful with people.

Yet one look at Maggie's amiable expression told her that truth wouldn't get Suzanne nearly as far in this instance as lies would.

Before Suzanne could let her scruples overtake her, she blurted out, "Yes, well, you know Devin. He has a temper."

There. The farce was established.

Maggie nodded amicably. "He doesn't blow up often. But when he does, he can be a real bear. Though it wasn't like him the other night to put his hand—" She broke off and gave Suzanne a sidelong glance. "Oh, that's right. I don't think he wanted you to know about it."

Suzanne gave her an exaggerated expression of wounded feelings. "Devin never tells me anything."

Maggie searched her face, amusement glinting in her eyes. Then she shook her head and laughed. "Now ain't that a pitiful expression. Geez, you're as bad as he is with those hangdog looks."

Suzanne couldn't hold back a grin. "Okay, you caught me. Now tell me what happened to his hand?"

"He put it through a window upstairs, in that room you two was in the other night. And don't ask me why, because I don't know. He sailed in from that recital and stormed up there to smash things for a while."

"I'm sure the owner appreciated that." Suzanne's heart raced as she tried to make sense of Devin's anger after the recital.

"Oh, Patrick didn't care, believe you me. Devin's never done anything like that before. We can overlook a few lapses." A mysterious expression crossed Maggie's face. She searched Suzanne's face for a moment. "I suppose you and I should have a little chat about our friend Devin. If you give me a second, I'll check with Patrick and see if he minds if you and I sit somewhere private and have a cup of java while we flap our jaws."

"I don't want to get you in trouble with your boss," Suzanne protested as Maggie slipped off the stool.

"No problem." Maggie winked. "Patrick's my husband. He won't care as long as I don't take too long." She glanced around the room. "It's not busy now anyway." She sauntered off, disappearing into a door behind the bar.

When Maggie returned, she led Suzanne to a comfortable corner. Then she placed two mugs of steaming coffee on the table pressed up against the window.

As they settled into their seats, Suzanne remained silent, waiting for Maggie to start things off. To her chagrin, Maggie decided to grill her first.

I should have expected this, she told herself. It made sense that Maggie would want to know more about her. But it did turn the whole encounter into a sort of perverse version of the father asking the potential son-in-law what his intentions were.

With a sigh, she answered Maggie's questions, telling Maggie about being a musicologist at the University of Chicago and glossing over how she and Devin had met. When Maggie asked about her family background, Suzanne remained reticent at first, but something about the rosy-cheeked barmaid broke down her defenses enough so she could briefly explain about her father, her three stepfathers, and her mother. At least in this she could stick to the truth, she thought wryly.

"Look, Maggie," Suzanne interrupted when the conversation got to be a little too personal, "you know more about me now than Devin probably does. So could I ask a few questions about him?"

Maggie's bemused grin told her the woman had only been waiting for Suzanne to balk, trying to see how much she could get out of her. Fleetingly, Suzanne wondered who was trying to pump whom for information.

"All right, then," Maggie said, "I've been rude enough, haven't I? So talk to me. Why'd you come all the way down here to discuss Devin?"

Suzanne drew in a deep breath. "It's just that . . . well, sometimes Devin says and does things I don't understand. He doesn't talk about himself much and . . . I—I think if I knew more, I could deal with him better."

"Makes sense." Maggie shrugged, but shot her a searching glance.

Avoiding Maggie's eyes, Suzanne took a long sip of coffee, then said, "For example, Devin doesn't seem to have any friends. He told me once he had a friend named Valentin Ressu, but I've never met the man." She breathed deeply and lied again, "And the only other man he's ever with is Jack."

"Yeah, well, Jack's his manager. As for other friends, I don't know. I've never seen him with anybody but Jack either. This guy . . . what did you say his name was . . . Valentin? Well, I never met any guy named Valentin."

"I think he was . . . uh . . . is . . . another pianist."

Maggie shook her head, her generous lips pursed as she thought a moment. "Nope. Don't guess I ever met him or heard Devin mention him. Come to think of it, Devin doesn't hang around with other musicians much."

That didn't necessarily mean he hadn't known Valentin, Suzanne thought, but it confirmed her suspicions that their relationship hadn't been close. "Why doesn't he have any friends? It shouldn't bother me that he doesn't, but it does. I mean, the friends a man chooses show what kind of man he is."

Maggie leaned forward, clutching the mug in her plump hands with their fingernails painted an outrageous orange. She fixed Suzanne with a concerned gaze. "You got it bad, don't you, sweetie?"

"Wh-what?"

"The hots for Devin."

The blunt statement brought Suzanne up short. With painful clarity, she realized Maggie had voiced what she herself had refused to acknowledge up till now. Suzanne definitely had "the hots" for Devin, although she wanted to believe that was all she felt—a basic, body-to-body sex thing. She stared down into her own mug, unable to craft a believable answer that didn't give her away.

"Oh, you don't have to explain it to me," Maggie added conversationally. "The boy's a hunk. He's got his father's sweet blue eyes and his mama's strong face. And it's not only his looks either. He cares about those he loves, and shows it."

Suzanne mumbled something in agreement.

Maggie watched her intently. "You know, we'd have lost the pub if not for him."

Suzanne's head shot up. "Why?"

"The bank was going to foreclose on us a few years back." Maggie's eyes misted. "The pub had been in the family for years, the loan was nearly paid off, but we'd been havin' a rough time with money and couldn't keep up the payments." Her mouth tightened into a hard line as her gaze wandered over the room. "When the bank threatened to foreclose, Patrick ran around like a chicken with its head cut off, tryin' to find some way to pay the bank. The only man with money he knew was Devin. So Patrick went to Devin, hat in hand, asking for a loan, and Devin gave it to him." She snapped her finger. "Just like that, no questions asked."

Speechless, Suzanne gazed at Maggie in frank surprise.

"We're close to paying it off now," Maggie continued, "and business is doin' good. Patrick thinks Devin walks on water, and I admit I got a soft spot for him myself."

Suzanne's cheeks reddened as she dropped her eyes from Maggie's. Guilt soaked into her, cold and heavy, making her ashamed of what she was doing. Maggie had a generous soul, no doubt about that, and she obviously had good reason to care about Devin. If she ever found out what Suzanne was up to, she'd be devastated.

Suzanne had to force herself to remember Devin's strange performance and his aloof behavior at the park.

Okay, so he was good to his friends. That didn't make him incapable of other forms of treachery.

"Anyway," Maggie went on after taking a sip of coffee, "I think it's time he got something nice in his life."

Suzanne looked up again, wondering if Maggie had decided, based on their limited conversation, that Suzanne would be "nice" for Devin.

Maggie's gaze locked with hers. "Do you love him?"

Of course not, she wanted to cry out, but she couldn't tell Maggie the truth. Oh, why was she so terrible at deception?

She swallowed and opted for an answer as close to honesty as she could get. "I don't know. I feel as if I barely know him. And I certainly don't understand him."

Maggie nodded. She leaned back in her chair and crossed her legs. "I probably shouldn't do this. But I got some Irish blood in me, and I'm a woman besides. I believe in intuition, and down deep I have this feeling about you and Devin. I think you'd understand him real well if you knew more about him, so I'm gonna tell you some things I probably shouldn't."

"I would appreciate that," Suzanne murmured in a strained voice.

Maggie gave her a conspiratorial wink. "Tell you what, sweetie. I won't tell Devin you were here if you don't tell him who told you this, all righty?"

Ignoring the pinpricks of guilt that grew sharper by the minute, Suzanne nodded. This was too good a chance to pass up simply because of a little guilt.

"Good." Maggie gave her the once-over, took another gulp of the cooling coffee, then settled back against the chair as if ready for a long tale. "First thing you should know is Devin's father died when Devin was a boy."

A rush of sympathy filled her. "It sounds as if neither of us was very lucky when it came to fathers," she said softly. "How did Devin's father die?"

Maggie's eyes went all sad inside. "He killed himself, poor fool."

Good Lord, Suzanne thought. *Poor Devin.* Another needle of guilt pricked her, silencing her for a moment. Finally she ventured to ask, "Why?"

Leaning forward, Maggie planted her calloused elbows on the table. She cupped the mug before her, gazing at Suzanne through heavily mascaraed lashes. "Now that's an interesting question."

"You don't know?"

"I know and I don't know. I know what drove him to the point, but I don't know what pushed him beyond it."

"What drove him to the point?"

"First he lost his job. Then the Church excommunicated him. And finally his enemies harassed him and his family until he could bear it no more."

"His enemies?" Suzanne probed, her heart in her throat.

"Yes." Maggie's face hardened. Suddenly she looked very much her age, the lines at the corners of her eyes more clearly marked than before. "Patrick and I come from the same neighborhood Devin grew up in. As late as Devin's younger days, you couldn't move without running into some Irish gang."

"Devin's father was involved with gangsters?" Suzanne asked, a little incredulous. Actually, that might explain a few things—like where Devin could find a mugger to do his bidding.

Maggie looked at her sternly. "No, no, not like you think. But Devin's father Walter had a friend who worked for Jimmy Mahoney. Mahoney's gang was the biggest, the most important. Most of the neighborhood got their living only 'cause of him. Either their sons worked for him or their husbands, or they paid protection to his gang for their businesses. And Walter's friend, God rest his soul, was Mahoney's bookkeeper."

Her eyes dark with remembrance, Maggie hunched over her coffee. "No one really knows what happened—if the bookkeeper crossed Mahoney or if Mahoney got some faulty information about his bookkeeper that made him not trust him. Anyway, Mahoney had a contract taken out on the bookkeeper. We learned that later, after Mahoney's death."

"Where does Devin's father fit in to this?"

Maggie's gaze snapped to Suzanne's as if she'd suddenly remembered she had a listener. "Walter Bryce knew about the contract." She shook her head, her expression shuttered. "No one knows how . . . unless perhaps Devin or his mother Nora know and they're not saying. But Walter knew it almost the day Mahoney put the contract out. He warned his friend, and his friend skipped town."

Suzanne privately wondered if Devin's father hadn't been more connected to the gang than anyone realized, but she kept that speculation to herself. "What happened then?"

A scowl passed over Maggie's face. "Mahoney was infuriated, of course. He raged and tore the neighborhood apart until he found out who'd tipped off his bookkeeper. Then he set out to destroy Walter."

"I thought you said Walter killed himself."

"He did, but only after Mahoney had taken everything away from him."

"I don't understand. Why didn't Mahoney simply kill Walter?"

Maggie shook her head. "I think he was worried about all these people beneath him who were beginning to rebel. First his bookkeeper, then this upstart Walter. He decided to make a big impact, to show the neighborhood who was boss. Some people ain't as scared of dying as they are of living in poverty and disgrace. So Mahoney decided ruining Walter would make a bigger impact, I guess. And he had the right connections to do it. First, Walter's boss at the shop claimed he couldn't give Walter work anymore. Then the Church excommunicated Walter. Then—"

"Wait a minute," Suzanne interrupted. "You said that once before. How could a gangster persuade the Church to excommunicate Walter if Walter wasn't doing anything wrong? Is the Church that corrupt? I mean, I'm not Catholic, so I don't really know, but I can't understand why the Church would take such drastic action simply because a gangster asked them to."

Absently rubbing the lipstick off the edge of her mug, Maggie sighed. "Ah, well, that part's more complicated."

I thought so, Suzanne told herself, then urged Maggie, "Tell me."

Maggie looked uncomfortable all of a sudden. "Devin would tear me into little bits if he knew I'd told you this."

"Come on, Mags." Suzanne deliberately used the same nickname Devin had. "You've come this far. I won't tell him you told me. I promise." That was one promise she thought she could keep.

Maggie's eyes scanned the room as if watching for spies before she leaned as close as she could across the table. "Walter was a bit odd," she said in a half whisper.

"How so?"

Again Maggie looked both ways in the room. "You're gonna think this sounds nutso, but it's true, I swear it. Walter could see the future. He predicted stuff for people, using Tarot cards. He knew things no one could know. He saw things. I think that's why he knew about Mahoney's contract on the bookkeeper."

Laughter bubbled up into Suzanne's throat. She had to fight to contain it. For this, she'd had to lie to get the truth out of Maggie—this ridiculous assortment of superstitions?

Maggie glanced furtively around once again.

"It's okay, Maggie, I promise," Suzanne coaxed, trying to keep the humor out of her voice. "No one cares nowadays if you think Walter Bryce fooled with Tarot cards."

Maggie gave her a sheepish grin. "Patrick does. He says they're cards of the Devil. He'll be mad as hell if he knows I've been telling you all this. He liked Devin's father, but he didn't like the way he spent his off-hours." Her brow drew into a frown. "The Church didn't either. All Mahoney had to do was tattle to the priest about Walter's activities, and Walter was thrown out on his ear without a hearing. After that, he was pretty much ostracized, even by people who'd come to him for his readings. It killed him to be cut off like that—it just killed him."

Sympathy for the Bryce family welled up in Suzanne. These days, no one would care that a man did some fortune-telling in his time off. They might whisper behind his back and say he was eccentric, but they'd mostly live and let live. This was especially true in Bridgeport, which had such a wide mix of cultures, it couldn't afford to be clannish or suspicious of foreign ideas. But in the mid-sixties, the neighborhood had still been tightly knit, clannish, and suspicious of anything they didn't understand.

If this man Mahoney really had been the unspoken leader of the community, who would have crossed him or come to the defense of a strange bird like Walter Bryce?

"After that, it was only a matter of time," Maggie continued in a mournful whisper. "Sometimes the Bryces would wake up to find messages written in blood in the yard or a strange Irish charm hanging from the trees, left by Mahoney's men to frighten them. They were cut off from everyone, and Walter most of all. I think he got it into his head that if he weren't around, everything would be all right again for Devin and Nora."

"Why didn't he simply take the family away somewhere?"

Maggie smiled. "I can tell you didn't grow up poor in Bridgeport. When your whole life has been one tiny spot on the earth, when you're an unskilled laborer like he was without money or position, it looks hopeless. Oh, Nora had family in California. She tried to get him to move out there, but they didn't have the money for such a big move, and he wouldn't go anyway. He wanted to find some way to pay Mahoney back. I think . . . I think he went a little crazy toward the end. He roamed the streets, shouting about how evil Mahoney was."

"How old was Devin then?" Suzanne whispered, the story wrenching her insides.

"Seven. So young." Maggie gave a ragged sigh. "One day after the cops picked a raving Walter up and brought him home, shaming him before his wife and son, he snapped. Nora took Devin out with her to the grocery, I think to get away from Walter's insane shouts. When they came home . . ." Maggie shook her head, her eyes filling with tears. "Devin ran ahead like little boys do. He found Walter first, in the living room. Walter had put a gun in his mouth and—"

"Oh, dear Lord," Suzanne whispered, unable to hear the rest, but able to imagine it in more detail than she wanted. A seven-year-old Devin came in to find his father. . . . There would have been blood everywhere, his own father's blood. She couldn't even stand to think of it. How had Devin stood it? How had he grown up even remotely sane?

She ached for that small boy, a deep, sharp pain that made it difficult for her to breathe. No wonder he didn't talk about his family to the press, no wonder he was so reticent about his past. It wasn't the kind of past anyone would want to discuss. No doubt he wanted to avoid the pain of reliving it, of having the sordid details repeated for the millions of readers.

Suddenly she felt small and cheap. No, she hadn't dug into his past to print it for the world to see, but that knowledge didn't make her feel any better. She'd still been uncovering an old story best left covered. And the worst irony of all was that she'd learned very little that got her closer to uncovering the reason for Devin's involvement with the missing copies of "Endnote."

Maggie had lapsed into a reflective silence, her eyes haunted with memories of the past. She spoke at last. "We've all lived with guilt since that day. Not long after Walter's death, the cops put Mahoney away for tax evasion. He died in prison. And our neighborhood felt unclean for their part in it. Oh, everybody did what they could to repair the damage. Walter's old boss offered Nora a position, and even gave Devin a little money for sweeping up the shop after school. One of the priests gave Devin free piano lessons to continue the ones the boy had started taking at the age of six. Still, it was never enough . . . never will be enough."

She fixed Suzanne with a bleary-eyed gaze. "Devin still lives with the memory of that day. You can see it in his eyes sometimes when he plays the piano. None of us can wipe away that sorrow."

She stared at Suzanne a long time. After a moment, the sadness cleared from her face and she sat up straight, wiping the mist from her eyes and smearing her mascara. Then she ventured a faint smile. "Such a terrible story I've told you. But it helps you understand, don't it?"

Suzanne nodded mutely, so ashamed of the deception she'd pulled on Maggie that she couldn't speak.

Maggie patted her hand, misinterpreting her silence. "Yes, it's a sad story. But you see now why I want him to find a good woman who can blot the pain out of his eyes. I can tell by the way your heart shines in your face you'll be good for him."

Suzanne couldn't bear any more. She had to get away, before Maggie started planning their engagement and asking about wedding plans. It had been a terrible idea to come here. The thousand tiny pinpricks of shame had grown to knives, stabbing her with regret and guilt.

"I—I can't stay. I have to go," she whispered to Maggie as she stood.

Maggie looked alarmed as she clutched at Suzanne's arm, long fingernails digging into the skin. "I didn't mean to upset you, sweetie. Please don't go."

Suzanne closed her eyes, forcing herself to breathe evenly, deeply. She mustn't make Maggie suspicious. Maggie must never know what Suzanne had done. Never. Suzanne mustn't heap that pain and guilt on Maggie.

"I have to go," she repeated softly, forcing herself to

meet Maggie's concerned gaze. She lied, groping for the only plausible story that would hold any weight with Maggie. "I—I promised Devin I'd meet him this afternoon, and I'm already late. I don't want him to suspect where I've been."

Maggie nodded. "Neither do I. You won't tell him who told you all this, will you?"

"No. No, of course not." After her pulse had settled into a semblance of normality, she smiled wanly and patted Maggie's hand. "Thank you for telling me. It means so much to me to know."

Then she gently pulled her arm from Maggie's grasp and headed for the door. It was true, she thought sadly, it did mean a lot to her. The more she knew about Devin, the more she understood why she'd been attracted to him from the minute she'd seen him. Because he knew the true meaning of suffering.

Now she knew why he'd spoken with such understanding of losing loved ones. But his loss had been far more tragic, far more destructive than hers. At least Valentin had left her with good memories, with a fine legacy in his music. Devin's father had left him nothing but bitter memories.

She saw his arrogance in a new light now. Unlike her mother, whom Suzanne had been comparing him with over and over, Devin's temperamental nature came from surviving pain. After what he'd gone through, what did other people's petty concerns matter to him?

No, that wasn't quite true. Until he'd withdrawn from her in the park, he'd shown a great deal of compassion and sympathy for her petty concerns. He'd understood, as no one else had, what her loss had cost her.

But he'd also put it in its proper perspective. The festival concert wasn't worth meddling in people's lives, and certainly not in his. Or Maggie's. Suzanne clutched her purse tightly against her chest and prayed that Maggie would never tell Devin of their conversation.

Then she made a decision. Devin was right. It was time

to let the police handle it. And time to put aside her suspicions about Devin. Okay, so Devin hadn't known Ressu, and he'd lied to her. Maybe he'd had valid reasons, she told herself.

And if he didn't?

It doesn't matter, she thought. *Let the police root out the truth.*

She couldn't bear to pursue Devin any more. Somewhere in the middle of her conversation with Maggie, she'd lost the heart for it.

10
♪

Three days had passed, and Devin still couldn't wipe the memory of his last encounter with Suzanne from his mind. Odd flashes of her disturbed his thoughts when he least expected it, like the image of her with her skirt blown between her legs by the wind as she stood accusing him of despicable crimes. She hadn't even noticed the way the wool molded her shapely thighs. But he had.

Then there was the way she'd vacillated between believing his half-truths and protesting the lack of logic in them. Or the way she'd watched him leave, hurt feelings and confusion written on her beautiful face.

He gritted his teeth. Hell, he'd really lost it that day, he thought as he gathered his strength and thrust the weight bar upward. Beethoven's "Funeral March" thundered from the stereo in his lengthy bedroom, suiting his somber mood.

What had come over him in Olive Park? He'd let down

his defenses, allowed her to get under his skin. He'd even encouraged it by sympathizing with her. What kind of insanity had possessed him to open up like that, to comfort her . . . to kiss her?

With a groan he closed his eyes, letting the bar drop back down as he savored the memory of that kiss, of a soft mouth yielding beneath his . . . a slender hand sliding over his chest . . . a delicate throat scented with perfume.

No wonder Adam and Eve had lost it in the Garden of Eden. All he'd had to do was be plunked down in the middle of a park in spring with a sexy woman, and next thing he knew he was kissing her passionately. There was something to this business of spring fever. He'd had it bad three days ago.

He opened his eyes and pushed up against the weight bar again, relishing the strain on his pectorals. At this point, self-inflicted pain seemed the only answer for overcoming his wayward sexual urges.

What had happened in the park had been more than a sexual urge, unfortunately, and he knew it. It had been the breaking down of walls, for both of them. For one brief moment, they'd connected, and on more than one level.

It was all very fine for her to break down her walls, he thought as he lowered the bar. Except for her suspicions of him, she had no reason not to.

But he had too many reasons to count, and he regretted that day immensely. Bad enough he'd lost control and done what he'd been fantasizing about ever since he'd met her. Even worse was knowing he couldn't have her . . . despite the kiss, despite her response. While she'd been kissing him, she might have temporarily forgotten what lay between them, but he hadn't.

She was a curious, skeptical, educated woman, who'd keep digging at the truth until she exposed his secret to the world. And he couldn't risk that, not when so much rode on his keeping it hidden . . . his career, his mother's support, Jack's livelihood. No, much as he hated it, Suzanne was off limits.

His fingers curled into fists around the bar. Well, she couldn't have any doubts about that now. He'd sent her the message loud and clear. Giving her the cold shoulder at the end had torn him in two. He hurt to think of it, of the way she'd answered his statements in a small, still voice.

With a growl he forced the bar up again. He wanted to let the relationship take its course so bad he could taste it. And taste her. God, how he could still taste her on his mouth, her skin, alive, warm, and responsive to his touch.

It would have been better never to have met her, never to have come so close.

"Damn it, Ressu, you did this to me, you and your 'Endnote'!" he ground out under his breath as the bar clanked down again.

His muscles too sore to bear any more, he slid off the bench and reached for a towel. As he wiped the sweat from his face and chest, he strode down the hall toward the kitchen in search of juice. Not orange juice, he told himself. Ressu could have his damned watered-down orange juice.

On his way, he passed through the living room and caught sight of the piano. A grimace twisted the corners of his mouth. Unfortunately, Ressu apparently wasn't through meddling with his life and his career.

Devin stared down at the piano he feared touching for the first time in his life. As he stood there, the terror that lay just beneath the surface of his equilibrium threatened to shatter that surface as it swelled upward. It took all his control to keep it submerged. He'd been successful so far, but only because this time he was fighting for more than normalcy. He was fighting to keep his sanity.

These days, every time his fingers neared the keys, Ressu's damned ghostly hands took over and the composer's fragmented emotions scattered Devin's own thoughts. That was why he kept away from the piano, from the powerful force lurking there, waiting to hold him captive.

This possession was so different from the others, he thought, so much more intrusive. He'd always sensed from the snatches of emotion and memory he picked up on when his hands were possessed that it took an enormous effort for the ghost composers to connect with him. That was why the same composer never played through him two days in a row. Sometimes months passed before enough energy could be produced between him and a particular composer to repeat a possession.

It had long been the only thing that kept him sane, for he sometimes went weeks between possessions, and during that time, he played music the way he wanted to.

But Ressu . . . hell, the ghost was making a profession out of this. The draw he exerted on Devin was eerily unnatural. What an understatement, Devin admitted. Even now, standing at a distance and just looking at the piano, he could almost feel the heightened pulse and cold sweat of impending possession.

But he knew what would happen if he gave in and sat down to play. Ressu would make him drum out the same piece once more. "Endnote." Devin had tried everything—filling his thoughts with another composer's music, listening to a piece on the stereo right before preparing to play . . . even practicing on another piano. Nothing had worked.

Nothing, not a damned thing. It was as if his entire repertoire were a scratched record, and his hands were the needle stuck in the same groove. Only he couldn't lift the needle to get it past the scratch. Hell, he could hardly wrench his hands from the piano once Ressu had taken them over.

His gaze fell to his traitorous fingers. He wanted to play Tchaikovsky, Schumann, Haydn, damn it! He'd welcome Liszt or Chopin or anybody else possessing his hands right now. Instead, all he got was Ressu over and over and . . .

"Why, for Chrisake, why?" he said aloud to a ghost he couldn't see. "What do you want from me, damn you? Why are you doing this to me?"

And why "Endnote," the piece everyone was interested in? Hell, if Ressu had chosen to do this as some sort of petty revenge for an imagined slight, he'd certainly picked the right piece to screw up Devin's life. "Endnote" was bad news—look at what was happening to the copies of it.

As he remembered what Suzanne had told him about the mugging, a different kind of terror seized him. Wasn't it an odd coincidence that Ressu kept forcing him to pound into the piano the same piece someone else was bent on stealing? Were the two things related? Did Ressu know something about the piece he couldn't reveal except through playing it repeatedly? Or was the composer simply calling attention to his last effort?

Was Ressu stuck in his own ghostly scratched record? That thought struck him numb. This could be a hellish maze he and Ressu were trapped in together, destined always to wander in a horrifying dance, to be linked forever . . .

With an explosive curse, Devin reached for his imaginary cigarettes, then cursed again when his hand patted an empty pocket. Christ, but he was sick of trying to figure out what was going on!

A sense of futility overwhelmed him. As his heartbeat tripped faster and faster, he fought the encroaching despair. What the hell was he going to do about this insane situation? He had to jar them both out of this sick maze, to beat the forces trapping them both in a nightmarish limbo. He had to do something, before this drove him as crazy as Mahoney had driven Dad. But how?

Staring at the closed grand, Devin forced himself to calm down, to think rather than feel. He remembered his mother's words, that his trouble with his gift came because he sought to control it, to restrict it to his agenda.

He began to consider. Maybe Mom had a point. Maybe

it was time he stopped fighting Ressu's ghost and started working with him. What if he did let Ressu play the music as often as the ghost wanted, let the ghost get it out of his system? Maybe—

The shrill ring of the phone broke into his thoughts. It took him a second to focus his attention back on the real world, the one with phones in it, and another second to regain enough presence to pick up the phone.

"Hello," he growled.

"Hey, Devin. I'm down at Bloomsday with Maggie." It was Jack's voice.

For the first time that morning, Devin relaxed, even smiled. Just hearing Jack's voice made him feel less tormented. Bloomsday Pub, eh? A little early in the day for Jack to be drinking, he thought, but hell, the guy deserved a break occasionally.

Then he heard a whispered discussion in the background with Maggie hissing, "You traitor!"

This was more than a social call, he realized. "What's up, Jack?"

More whispering in the background. Jack apparently ignored it on his end. "Maggie here has some stuff to tell you as soon as I can persuade her to do it."

The whisper rose to a low protesting murmur. "I promised I wouldn't tell him, you traitor. Hang up!"

"Jack, what's going on?" Devin asked. The background noise at the pub was distorting some of Maggie's words so he couldn't be certain of what she was saying.

"You gotta tell him," he could hear Jack say.

"I don't have to do anything!" came Maggie's snarling reply.

A scuffle ensued, during which Maggie apparently tried to wrest the receiver away from Jack in order to hang it up. "Hold on," Jack muttered into the phone. Then he said to Maggie, "I'll tell him if you don't. And I might get it all wrong."

Abruptly the sound of scuffling stopped. "Please, Jack,

don't make me break my promise to her," Maggie cried. "I only told you so you'd help me keep them together. I didn't think you'd say anything to Devin. Come on, Jack, don't do this!"

"Goddamn it!" Jack shouted at Maggie, so loud it carried quite well over the line. "The woman's a goddamned reporter, Maggie! Stop defending her!"

Icy fingers of fear stole around Devin's heart as Maggie gasped in the background.

"No, she's not!" Maggie's voice protested. "She's a musicologist. She told me!"

Devin closed his eyes and grasped the receiver nearly tight enough to break it. "Hey, Jack, who are you two talking about?" he growled into the phone, as if he didn't already know.

"Suzanne Winslow. She came to see Maggie yesterday."

Instant anger flared up in Devin. Great. Now the woman was sneaking around behind his back, talking to his friends. "Put Maggie on."

Another discussion ensued on the other end, but eventually there was a slight noise and Maggie came on the line. "H-hello, Devin."

He modulated his tone. "Hey, Mags. What's all the fuss about?"

"Is she . . . is she really a reporter?"

He could hear the guilt in her voice. Damn Suzanne Winslow and her stupid vendetta. She had no right to use Maggie like this. "Not exactly. She . . . er . . . she's the one who wrote the bad review about me, the one you wouldn't read."

"Oh." Long pause. "So she's not your girlfriend."

Devin opened his eyes to stare into his empty apartment, forcing back the fury that welled up in him like a poisonous gas. "Uh, not exactly, no."

"She—she told me she was your girlfriend. Well . . . not quite, but she implied it."

"Did she?"

"Yeah. She said she had the hots for you."

He didn't know whether to laugh or to put his fist through another window. "Did she say why she came to talk to you?"

Maggie sighed. He could almost imagine her hunched over the phone, her eyes watching Jack warily as she clutched the receiver. "She told me she wanted to understand you better, so she needed to know more about you, like who your friends were and . . . and stuff."

The ice around his heart hardened into a shrinking igloo that threatened to freeze it stone-dead. "Did she ask about a guy named Ressu?"

"How did you know that?"

He laughed grimly. "Don't ask."

"Devin?"

"Yeah, Mags?"

"I thought she really was your girlfriend. I mean, you brought her here the other night, and . . . and she . . ." She broke off with a sad sigh. "She lied to me, didn't she?"

Yeah, he thought, the little schemer had lied, all right. He should have never agreed to meet her at his stomping grounds. But at the time he hadn't known the insane accusations she'd make.

He struggled to bank his fury, not wanting to alarm Maggie. "Don't worry about it. You didn't do anything wrong. You thought you were doing me a favor by talking to her. Hell, maybe you were." *Yeah, right,* he thought.

"But . . . but I told her things . . . about you."

He raked his fingers through his hair and stifled a groan as he dropped onto the couch. When he got his hands on Suzanne Winslow . . .

"Like what?" he couldn't help growling.

"I told her about the loan you gave us for the pub and your other girlfriends and . . ." She was stalling for time, and he knew it.

"And about Dad?"

Her silence was his answer. Pain shot through him, liberally laced with anger. How dare Suzanne invade his life this way? Wasn't it bad enough that her stepfather had invaded his hands?

Maggie's words flooded out, full of anguish. "Geez, Devin, I'm so sorry. I feel awful about this. But she seemed so nice. She really seemed like she knew you. She told me about herself—" She broke off with a groan. "Oh, no. Was she lying about that stuff she said about her stepfathers and being a musicologist?"

He sighed. "No. That part's all true."

"But nothing else?"

"Well—"

She groaned again.

He deliberately made his voice sound casual. "Listen, Mags, I don't want you to let this upset you, okay? It's no big deal. Jack's exaggerating a bit when he says she's a reporter. And she and I have been . . . er . . . sort of involved. So you didn't do anything wrong, you hear me?"

"Really?" Maggie said, the faintest hint of hopefulness in her voice.

"Really. Don't worry about it." He chose his words carefully. "But . . . um . . . I'd rather have Suzanne ask me these questions herself, you understand, so if she comes around again—"

"I won't say a word. Honest, I won't. I'm sorry, Devin. I got such a big mouth, you know? But I never talked to the press about you before. You know I haven't. Don't be mad at me. Please."

He smiled to himself despite the pain and rage roiling in his gut. "I could never be mad at you, Mags." He only hoped she believed him. She tended to be awfully sensitive. "Look, I gotta go now. Put Jack back on the line. And don't think about it anymore. Promise?"

"I promise," she murmured, although he feared she'd hash it over in her mind a million times, or worse yet, bother his mother about it. Well, the damage had been done, he thought. It was too late to do anything about it now.

Jack got on the phone. "What is it with this Winslow woman? She got it in for you for some reason? Maggie said you took her here the other night, so what the hell's going on?"

"Everything. Suzanne and I've been having this ongoing argument about my performance the other day. She claims I played a Ressu piece that I wasn't supposed to."

"Come again?"

"It's very complicated, and I'll explain everything soon." Unconsciously, his voice hardened. "But right now, I want to talk to her."

"And you need her phone number."

"No. I need her address."

Jack gave a low whistle. "I don't know about this, Devin. You sound pissed off. I don't know if you should actually talk to her, face to face. You might lose your temper and do something you might regret. You've been doing that a lot lately."

"Get me the address, Jack," Devin ground out.

"Now, big shot, listen to reason—"

"Get me the damned address, or I'll call every musician in town until I find one who knows it. I'm going to get it one way or the other. You going to help me get it or not?"

The silence on the other end of the phone told Devin he'd pushed Jack a little too hard this time.

"Ressu's that avant-garde Romanian composer who died a while back, isn't he?" Jack's voice was strained, as if he were trying to control his temper.

Sucking in his breath, Devin murmured, "Yeah. Look, I'm sorry, Jack. You're right. I've been in the devil of a temper lately. But I've got to talk to her."

"Why does she think you played a Ressu piece?"

Devin shut his eyes and cursed under his breath, debating how much he should say. "Because I did."

To his surprise, Jack didn't ask any more questions. "I'll get you the address," he said softly into the phone.

When Jack hung up, Devin prowled the house like a panther searching for prey. Hell, he'd sure misjudged the situation this time. Suzanne Winslow had a talent for making people lower their guard with her. First him . . . then Maggie.

And don't forget Paul, he reminded himself. The day after Paul had said he'd keep Devin's questions mum, the kid had spilled his guts to Suzanne.

Still, Devin couldn't believe she'd gone to the pub to pump Maggie for info. She really was bent on destroying him, wasn't she? What he'd feared throughout his career was finally coming to pass. Maggie had told Suzanne about Dad, and the talkative waitress had probably hinted that Walter Bryce had been clairvoyant. Suzanne would think that was humorous, if not insane.

What would she do with the information? Chronicle the eccentric performances in his career? Speculate publicly about how he knew the Ressu piece? Would she guess the truth, or come up with a far more disastrous explanation? Worse yet, would she use his admittedly turbulent childhood to prove he had the kind of background that would turn anyone into a criminal?

He slammed one fist into the other. Hell, what was he going to do? He felt poised on the edge of disaster. Was that what she sought now—revenge for his refusal to explain how he knew "Endnote" and why he'd played it? Would Suzanne Winslow bring him down the same way Jimmy Mahoney had brought Dad down?

Unbidden, an image of his father rose to mind, a haunting image of him with a gun crammed in his mouth—what was left of it—and his head a pulp of blood and gore. In the other blood-smeared hand had been a crumpled note with the words, "Forgive me, for I have sinned."

Devin stared sightlessly at the phone, but he saw another day and time, a horror of blood and screaming. Then came the incessant questions. Why hadn't Dad fought harder? Why hadn't he taken his vengeance on Mahoney? Why instead had he chosen to punish his family? For that was essentially what he'd done, whether he'd intended to or not. Not a day went by that Devin didn't remember the sight of his father's blood.

He couldn't forget. He never could, except when he was playing. When his fingers touched the keys, all his pain twisted into beauty, like raw silk spun into cloth. He could forget everything during the gallop of Bach's fugues, the melodic arabesques of Mozart, the trembling glory of Tchaikovsky.

And when a composer's ghostly fingers fused with his, he could even find a kind of peace. That was why he didn't always seek to control his gift. Sometimes it gave as much as it took. He hadn't lied when he'd told his mother he didn't hate it.

Right now, however, he feared it more than he ever had in his life. Mahoney could no longer hurt any of them. He'd died in prison long ago. But Suzanne Winslow . . . she was quite alive and most definitely a force to be reckoned with. And she wanted to take his reason for living away from him, damn her!

"Not this time," he muttered under his breath as the phone rang. His father might not have fought, but he intended to fight with every ounce of his being.

Even if it meant fighting Suzanne Winslow.

11
♪

"I'll be out late, dear," Suzanne's mother was saying as she stood in the doorway to Suzanne's house. "After I stop by the gallery for a bit, I'm going to that party in Arlington Heights. You sure you don't want to go? It should be amusing."

Which means there'll be lots of young, handsome men willing to flatter you, Mother, thought Suzanne unkindly, then hated herself for thinking it. *I'm certainly turning into a bitch these days.*

"No, but thanks," she said aloud from where she sat beside the phone, her nose buried in her personal phone and address book. "I've got more calls to make."

"Still haven't found anyone who'd replace Amarcorp if the company bails out?"

Suzanne glanced up, startled that her mother had even paid attention yesterday when she'd explained the sudden financial problems that had arisen regarding the festival concert.

"No." Suzanne smiled. "But I haven't given up yet."

She turned back to thumbing through her book, but stopped when she realized her mother still hesitated in the doorway. She looked up.

Her mother was watching her, an odd expression on her face. "You seem rather caught up with this festival concert for Valentin."

Suzanne shrugged. "I suppose I am."

"You really miss Valentin, don't you?"

Suzanne gave her a half smile, then nodded.

Her mother's eyes grew troubled. "I . . . I only wish you'd known him better."

What an odd thing to say, Suzanne thought. She knew Valentin as well as anyone except perhaps his wife . . . er . . . wives. Then again, perhaps as his wife, her mother had seen things about him Suzanne hadn't been privileged to see. Her mother's statement reminded Suzanne of her phone conversation with Mariela. . . .

"Why should I have known Valentin better?" Suzanne asked, genuinely curious now. Her hands toyed idly with the book as she watched several emotions pass over her mother's face.

"No reason," her mother finally said. "I'm being reflective for a change, but I'm sure I don't have the faintest idea what I mean." She smiled a false bright smile. "You know me. Sometimes I speak when I don't have a thought in my head."

Then her mother turned and opened the door. As she went out, Bartok strolled in from another room. Just when he looked as if he might make a mad dash for the door, her mother shut it behind her. With a soft cat sigh, Bartok settled himself on the rug.

"You little traitor," she muttered under her breath as she went to the door, shot the dead bolt into its slot, then switched on the outside porch light in case she forgot to do it for Mother later. "One day I'm going to get you for deserting me every time Mother's in the house. You only come around when you think you might get a chance to make a break for it."

Bartok liked few human beings. Suzanne was one of them. Valentin had been another. But with Suzanne's mother . . . well, the cat had an annoying tendency to hide in Suzanne's bedroom as often as possible when she was visiting.

Suzanne sometimes wished she could do the same, particularly when Mother made one of her classic impenetrable statements.

Like the one she made just now, Suzanne thought as she returned to her post at the phone. Mother's ditz facade didn't fool her. Mother definitely had a reason for speaking.

"What do you think she was hinting at?" Suzanne asked Bartok. He was already dozing contentedly on the rug and obviously had nothing to add to the subject.

She shrugged. No point in trying to understand the labyrinth of insinuations and bizarre ideas that represented thought to Mother. It would almost be easier making sense out of James Joyce's *Finnegans Wake,* which at least followed a pattern.

Shaking her head, Suzanne dismissed her mother from her mind. Then one unsuccessful phone call followed another as she sought a sponsor who could replace Amarcorp in a pinch. She got the same answers over and over. Either the company's funds for support of the arts were already tied up elsewhere or they had no budget for such projects in the first place. More than once, she cursed Amarcorp for throwing this monkey wrench in her plans.

It was Goma she ought to be cursing, she told herself, since he was obviously the one who'd set Amarcorp off. She'd love to confront him and tell him how much his antics were costing the festival. But he'd deny everything anyway.

As it neared five P.M., she realized she could do little more today, now that business hours were ending. She could prepare for tomorrow though. She picked up the newspaper lying on her coffee table and began to scour the business section for likely names, highlighting those that looked promising.

She'd worked for about an hour, only stopping to eat a quick bite, when the doorbell rang, startling both her and Bartok, who roused from his nap to eye the door with suspicion.

Suzanne pursed her lips. Who could be visiting her on a weeknight? A student? Not likely. Most students were too intimidated to track down a lecturer at her home. It was probably a salesman or one of those kids who sold candy to raise money for their schools.

The doorbell rang again, twice. Bartok meowed as if in imitation of the annoying bell.

Oh, for Pete's sake, she thought, slamming down the paper and scowling at the door and Bartok in turn.

She strode to the door and peered through the spy hole. "Uh-oh," she muttered.

Devin Bryce stood on her doorstep, illuminated by the single outdoor bulb. He looked almost sinister in the harsh light, his chin with the faintest shadow of beard and his mouth a taut line. A deep frown etched his brow as he glanced away from the door and around the neighborhood.

Prickles of apprehension tingled along her skin. What in creation was Devin doing here? And why? After their conversation in the park and her talk with Maggie at the pub, she'd thought she would never see him again. Should she let him in, or pretend not to be home?

While she debated what to do, he caught sight of her car in the drive, and pounded the door with his fist, apparently deciding that the doorbell didn't work. "Suzanne, I've got to talk to you!" he bellowed.

Better let him in, she thought, *before he brings all my neighbors running.*

She turned the latch on the dead bolt, then opened the door warily, keeping an eye on Bartok in case he tried to bolt. The minute Devin's eyes scanned her, she became conscious that she wore her knockaround sweat pants and shirt. Of course, he wasn't exactly dressed to the nines, but she'd gotten used to seeing him in blue jeans. Besides, he looked good in his casual clothes. She, however, looked like a fashion model reject.

He didn't seem to notice as his eyes pinned her to the spot, turmoil in their depths. "Can I come in?" he asked, though the words sounded more like a command than a request.

"Uh, sure. Of course." She stepped aside to let him pass. Her heart sinking to her stomach, she finger-combed her hair as he crossed the threshold, then dropped her hand quickly when he pivoted to face her. He shut the door while she stood watching, incapable of reacting. Bartok, after looking over the intruder with distinct distaste, wandered off into another room.

Summoning up her hostess instincts, she asked, "Would you like some coffee or juice or—"

He cut her off with "What will it take for you to leave me alone?" The harsh words reverberated around her.

She stared at him, openmouthed. "What? *You're* the one who's shown up on my doorstep without any warning."

He ignored her statement. "After our talk in the park, I was prepared to walk away from this, to let you do whatever the hell you wanted. If you called the cops on me, fine. I had nothing to hide." Pain distorted his features into a hostile mask. "But you couldn't do it that way, could you? You had to talk to Maggie and involve my friends in this . . . this vendetta of yours."

Oh, no, he'd found out. Suzanne sucked in her breath. What could she say? How much did he know? "Wh-what did Maggie tell you?"

"Everything." His eyes fixed her with their accusing, brittle glass gaze. "She told me how you pretended to be my girlfriend. She said you told her you wanted to 'understand me' better." He nodded his head fiercely. "Yeah, you wanted to understand me better all right. You wanted to make sure you could build a case against me."

"No, that's not what—"

"Did you get enough information to spin a convincing story, Ms. Winslow?" The name came out like a curse. " 'Local Pianist with Sordid Past Steals Composition,' " he said as if reading off a headline. " 'After Devin Bryce found his father dead by his own hand, the traumatized youth turned to a life of crime. His talent wasn't enough to block out the memory of his father's brains splattered all over—' "

"Stop it!" she shouted, covering her ears. "Stop it!"

He advanced on her, his expression merciless. "Or maybe you'd like to play up the insanity angle and talk about my father's clairvoyant tendencies. Perhaps it *would* be better to portray me as the son of a raving loon—"

She whirled away from him, wanting only to escape that acid, accusing voice, but Devin caught her arm.

"What's wrong, can't stand to face the heat in person?" he hissed. "Of course not. Asking a person questions to his face means risking that he'd want to keep his secrets to himself. You knew a woman like Maggie would be easier to manipulate than a criminal like me." He was working himself up into a fine rage, and the look in his eyes scared her to her core. "Hell, lady, you're even more resourceful and devious than I gave you credit for! Quizzing me got you nothing, so instead you went behind my back to badger my friends!"

Turning her face slowly up to his, she said nothing, too ravaged by guilt to do so. She stared at him, skin flaming and eyes hurt, the only outward manifestations of the devastation he'd wrought inside her.

"Well?" he finally asked. "No evasive defenses, no justifications to offer on your behalf, Ms. Winslow?"

She pried his fingers from around her arm where he'd been gripping it so tightly it had left red marks. Then she lifted her chin and asked shakily, "Are you quite finished, Devin?"

She deliberately used his first name to remind him that even if he'd forgotten the intimate kiss they'd shared, she hadn't. He seemed to note it, for a brief flicker of awareness lit his eyes. Then he gave her a mock bow. "Of course. Please don't let my rudeness disturb you."

"There's no excuse for what I did." Relishing the startled expression on his face, she continued, "Just as there was no excuse for the phone calls you made to Paul behind *my* back."

He opened his mouth to retort, but she held up her hand. "No. You've already had your chance to, as you put it once, 'disembowel me' with words. Now you're going to give me a chance to speak."

"To explain." He sneered. "As if you could."

"To apologize."

Suspicion lined his features. He backed away from her, settling his hips against the back of the love seat a short distance away. He crossed his arms over his chest. "Okay. Have at it. This should be very interesting."

She wet her dry lips with her tongue, her heart pounding. Why did it matter to her so much that he not condemn her for what she'd done? For Pete's sake, she still hadn't ruled out the possibility that he'd stolen the original "Endnote," although she'd decided to drop the whole matter. If anybody had the right to condemn, it was she, so why did she care what he thought? Let him think what he wanted of her —he'd do so despite what she said.

But she did care, she admitted. She cared a lot. No point in pretending otherwise.

His eyes watched her, wary and smoldering with anger. She couldn't stand the expression on his face, the accusation in his frown.

She drew in a deep breath. "I'm sorry I pretended to be what I wasn't when I went to talk to Maggie. And I'm sorry I hurt you by doing so." She swallowed. "But I'm not sorry I asked her questions or that she told me so much about your past. It did help me understand you, and I didn't lie when I told her I wanted to understand you better." She hastened to add, "But not for the reasons you said."

"So you didn't ask her about Ressu?"

"Of course I did. But you asked Paul about 'Endnote,' pretending you intended to play it. I think we're even on that score."

His expression softened infinitesimally.

A wan smile crossed her lips. "It's simply that I . . . I didn't expect her to tell me the rest. She made all these assumptions about you and me, and . . . I let her, I guess. I didn't realize what a tragic story I'd find. I'm so sorry."

Her eyes dark with sympathy met his gaze. His lean jaw went rigid, and he muttered a low curse as he jerked his head to one side, refusing to meet her gaze.

"Don't you *dare* pity me," he ground out furiously.

Uncertain what to do, she watched his anguished profile.

He released a ragged breath. "You can keep your damned pity. Hell, it's been more than twenty years now. I'd adjusted to what happened. Then you come along, probing into stuff that isn't any of your damned business. Now Maggie feels terrible, and I . . ." He trailed off.

"Oh, Devin, I really am sorry. I didn't think Maggie would tell you. I'd hoped she wouldn't."

"Yeah, I'm sure you did." He sighed. "So what do you plan to do, Ms. Winslow, now that you know my shameful family past?"

Despair rent her at his sarcastic use of her name. He hadn't accepted her explanations, nor her sympathy. He still believed she could be so unfeeling as to use any of what she'd learned against him.

"I'm not going to do anything," she whispered.

His head shot around. He leveled his hot gaze on her. "What do you mean?"

It was hard not to flinch, but somehow she managed to face his gaze squarely. "I mean, obviously I have no evidence to base my accusations on, so although your reasons for . . . playing 'Endnote' remain obscure to me, I think it best that I drop the entire matter. I've already been to the police about the stolen copies, and they're looking into it. I plan to leave it at that and not mention you to them."

For some reason, her words seemed to incense him even more. "You're dropping the whole thing? Just like that? You and I both know you asked Maggie about Ressu. What did she say?"

"She said she'd never heard you mention him, nor had she ever met him. But, of course, that doesn't mean you weren't—"

"His friend or at least a respected colleague. No, it doesn't, and you know it. But lack of evidence isn't why you're dropping this, is it?" He looked haunted, a tortured expression on his face. "You're dropping it because you feel sorry for me, because you feel guilty about tormenting a guy who's already had such a 'hard' life. That's why, isn't it?"

Crossing her arms over her chest, she rubbed them with her hands to dispel the chill trickling through her body like liquid nitrogen. She looked down.

"Isn't it?" he demanded.

The blood rose in her face. "What do you care? I'm not pursuing it. That's all."

"No. That's not all. It will never be all, will it, until we get this straight?"

For a minute, he looked helpless, uncertain. He ran his fingers through his hair in jerky, nervous movements. Suddenly his face cleared as if something had finally occurred to him. His eyes surveyed the room, searching for something, and they fell on her baby grand.

He pushed away from the love seat and went straight for the piano. "You don't believe I've got nothing to do with these missing copies," he said as he reached it. "And I have a funny feeling this business with the missing copies isn't going to end here."

She found that comment curious, even more so because of the regretful tone in which he said it.

He sat down on the piano bench and lifted the piano fall board, exposing the keyboard. Then he half turned to fix her with a defiant gaze. "Since we talked, I've played that piece from the recital again, and I figured out you were right. It was one of Ressu's. I finally remembered exactly when I heard him play it. And you tell me it's 'Endnote', so you must know what you're talking about."

She watched him silently.

"I think it's time I proved I knew Ressu and didn't steal a copy of 'Endnote.' If I play the piece I played at the recital for you, exactly as Ressu played it for me, would that convince you?"

"But you've already played it once . . . you've already obviously memorized the music."

He nodded. "Right." He thought a minute. "Okay, but consider this. If I'd stolen the piece, I'd play it with my own interpretation. But you should be able to recognize if it's done the way Ressu did it, shouldn't you? If I play it the way he would have, won't that prove something?"

"You don't need to do this," she protested, wondering why he suddenly looked a little mad, even obsessed.

"I want to play 'Endnote' for you. Sit down and listen."

The tone of command in his voice shook her. Hugging herself more closely, she rounded the love seat and perched on the front of it. "O-okay."

His eyes moved to the keys before him. Lifting his hands from his lap, he then rubbed them as if seeking to bring life back into them. They did look pale in the dim lamplight of her house. So did his face.

He placed his fingers over the keys. She noticed the sweat forming on his brow and wondered at it, for her house certainly wasn't hot enough to raise a sweat. And he'd insisted on doing this. Why was he so nervous?

With a sudden, startling intensity, his fingers dropped to the keys. At first the notes jolted her. They weren't from "Endnote," that was certain. As poignant beauty shaped the notes into a sweet, plaintive melody, she recognized the notes and melody of another Ressu piece, one with far more emotional significance for her than "Endnote."

Her mouth dropped open and her gaze flew to Devin's face, but he didn't even seem to notice she was there anymore. His brow was twisted, as if the music required some terrible effort on his part, and he concentrated completely on the keyboard.

Bartok suddenly shot into the room, startling her. His hair stood on end, and he hissed at the music coming from the piano.

Fear engulfed her too. Something about the choice of piece, the way Devin played the notes, made the fine hairs on her arms stand on end. There was an uncanny truthfulness in Devin's treatment of the piece. She had the frightening feeling that even Ressu's bust atop the piano was smiling to hear it. In a daze, she rose and walked to the piano, wanting to see his fingerings.

But as she neared the piano, a wave of nostalgia struck her motionless, forcing her to shut her eyes and drink in the astonishing music.

Images flickered in her mind, snatches of her childhood. She saw Valentin tickling the backs of her hands to make her arch them more as she played . . . Valentin scolding her, then ruffling her hair as an afterthought . . . Valentin contorting his face into a fierce Beethoven-like expression to tease her. The memories were bliss and torture.

All her grief, which had been relatively suppressed, now marched starkly through her body, taunting and sneering at her for ever thinking she had dealt with Valentin's death. And merging with the grief was the galling realization that Valentin had played this particular piece for Devin, the piece she'd thought no one would ever hear but herself. Absurdly it hurt to think of Valentin sharing this special piece with an outsider.

She struggled to subdue such a petty emotion, but before she'd even mastered her feelings, Devin was playing the final phrase. Her breath caught in her throat as the last lilting notes sounded across the room, then hung in the air, audible reminders of a different time.

As he had at the concert, Devin jerked his hands back from the keyboard the moment he'd finished. If he felt horror this time, he masked it, but she did sense his discomfort. At least Bartok had stopped hissing, although he stalked the room, on guard for the next assault from the piano.

Devin was apparently finished, however. He turned to her, his mouth opening to speak, but when he caught sight of her standing a few feet from him with her body shaking, he closed his mouth without a word.

She felt compelled to say something, although she couldn't meet his gaze. Tears welled in her eyes, but she willed them not to fall. Like the sky during an electrical storm, her body felt highly charged . . . with grief, pain, fear . . . even an intense longing to be a little girl again watching the great Ressu at work.

She spoke haltingly, barely able to rein in her emotions enough to speak. "You've . . . certainly proved . . . you knew Valentin."

The barest hint of surprise flickered in his gaze. "You recognized the piece," he stated flatly.

"Of course I recognized it. And you knew I would. I . . . I simply can't believe he played it for you. 'Girl-flowers' was my private composition, a child's air, nothing more. Valentin wrote it for me when he first married Mother." She paused, trying to force breath through a throat already tight with the bittersweet pain of remembering. "I think he meant it to ease my shyness. I loved it. So . . . so he played it for me often."

Rubbing a tear out of her eye, she went on. "But of course, you probably know that, since you know the piece. I'm sure Valentin told you."

She didn't even see him move through the blur of her tears, but in moments he'd risen and taken her by the arm to lead her to the love seat. Next thing she knew they were sitting there beside each other.

Devin's hands trembled as he clasped her hands tightly. "I'm sorry, Suzanne. I didn't mean to hurt you, but I had to make you listen. It's important, probably even more than you realize."

"I know you must think I'm crazy to mourn him this way.

He wasn't even my real father. . . ." She couldn't look at him. "Valentin's death was perfectly natural, even if it was untimely. It was nothing like your father's—"

"Shhh, shhh. Loss isn't measurable. No one can say my pain's worse than yours. Obviously Ressu meant a lot to you. I could argue that my loss should have been easier because I'd had less years with Dad than you had with Ressu. But that would be dumb. Grief is grief. It comes and goes without rhyme or reason. It never disappears, although, believe me, time does make it bearable."

His arm slid around her shoulder, and she leaned automatically against him, closing her eyes and breathing in the spicy scent of cologne. Somehow it comforted her to think he'd actually stopped to put on cologne before he'd come charging over here ready to tear her to pieces.

Suddenly something furry swept along her legs. She opened her eyes and looked down to see Bartok whisking by before jumping up in Devin's lap, purring for all he was worth.

"Friendly cat," Devin murmured.

"Not usually." Why was Bartok acting so oddly? When Devin had first walked in, the cat had avoided him. Then again, maybe Bartok had sensed who Devin was from his playing, and Bartok *had* liked listening to the CD of Devin playing Tchaikovsky.

"Actually, Bartok's a fan of yours," she managed to say with a hint of humor in her voice.

"Really?" Devin looked at her with raised eyebrows as he set Bartok on the ground. The cat settled himself on the floor at their feet and went to sleep.

"Yes. Valentin would have a fit if he knew. He gave me Bartok for my—"

She stopped short as she realized she'd spoken of Valentin as if he weren't dead at all. A sudden chill sent a shiver through her.

Devin's hands tightened on hers. "Want to talk about it?"

She gazed unseeingly ahead. "What? Valentin?"
"Yeah."
She thought a moment. Did she want to talk about the things she'd bottled up inside . . . the way it hurt not to be able to talk over her book with Valentin . . . the jolt she got every time one of Valentin's former students mentioned his name in a class . . . the fact that she felt abandoned at the beginning of her career without him there to give her fatherly advice?

No, she suddenly realized, she didn't want to talk about it and not because it hurt. She didn't want to discuss Valentin, because . . . because after hearing "Girlflowers" played as only he could have played it, she found she felt less troubled. Like a doctor lancing a boil, Devin's playing had cut into her soul and sucked some of the poisonous grief from her, giving her the first relief from it she'd had in a long time.

"I think we've talked enough about the past," she said, looking up into his face, "don't you?"

"Yeah." He lifted his hand to brush back her hair from her eyes, then allowed his hand to settle on her shoulder.

His tenderness brought all her guilt from before welling up in her again. "Devin, I do want to apologize for misleading Maggie. It was a stupid, inconsiderate thing to do and—"

He pressed his finger against her lips. "It's forgotten. As you said, we've talked enough about the past."

Then his expression altered and something about it warned her he had other things to discuss. "I take that back. I do want to ask you one question about the past . . . if you'd let me."

"What's that?" Her attention had shifted to watching the way his eyebrows came together when he was serious.

His gaze flicked to the bust on the piano, then back to her. He jerked his head toward the bust. "That's him, isn't it? It's a pretty good likeness."

She nodded, wondering what this was leading to.

"I guess that means he and you were pretty close, since you've got that bust on your piano." He looked a little uncomfortable.

"We were close, yes. But you knew that."

His eyes met hers as he blurted out, "Were you and Ressu lovers?"

The question stunned her at first. She ought to have been outraged, but the hesitance in his voice and the fear that glimmered behind his eyes as he anticipated her answer kept her from being angry.

"No," she told him quite firmly. "No, I didn't feel about him that way." She tried to remember Ressu as a physical body instead of as her friend, and suddenly the very idea struck her as funny. Had Devin actually thought . . . had she been so starry-eyed about Valentin around Devin that . . .

She chuckled aloud. "No, definitely not. For Pete's sake, Devin, he was . . . what . . . at least twice my age when he died, and happily married besides. He also was *not* a good-looking man, in case you hadn't noticed."

"And that's important?"

"No." She stared down at her lap. Devin was, on the other hand, a very good-looking man. She didn't want him to think that was the only reason she was attracted to him. "But Valentin didn't do anything for me in terms of sexual attraction. You know what I mean. Besides, I always thought of him as a father. He really was my father in many respects. I could never have been attracted to Valentin that way."

"Are you attracted to me that way?"

Her eyes met his as she fought the urge to smile. How could one of the most enticing men she'd ever met not see how insanely drawn to him she was? He was actually looking at her as if he doubted what her answer would be.

"Maybe," she couldn't resist saying with a certain amount of coyness.

His whole body responded to that reply. He relaxed his

jaw, and his eyes took on a different, entirely sensual expression. He lifted a hand to stroke her cheek. "Maggie says you have the hots for me. Is that true or were you just saying that to get her to tell you things?"

Suzanne flushed but wouldn't look away. "I didn't exactly say that. She drew that conclusion on her own."

"So you lied about that."

She couldn't believe they were discussing her attraction to him. It embarrassed her to no end. "No . . . well . . . not exactly . . ."

"Come on, Suzanne. Answer the question. Do you have the hots for me?"

"It wouldn't be very wise of me to answer that, would it? Last time I . . . um . . . demonstrated what I thought about you, you acted as if I were a leper afterward."

"That won't happen again." He ran his thumb along her lips.

His face darkened with passion, sending all thought right out of her head and her apprehension racing after it. In its place, desire reigned, hot, sweet, demanding. "Why not?" she managed to ask shakily.

"Because last time I was afraid of what you might find out about my past if I let you get too close. This time you already know all my secrets."

He lowered his head to plant a kiss on the top of her head. The light touch sent delightful shivers through her. She closed her eyes and murmured in a breathy voice, "Really? I know all your secrets?"

Now he moved his lips lower to her temple where he set a kiss of such feathery softness, she barely felt its impact on her skin. "All the ones that count," he rasped.

Then his mouth covered hers, blotting out the lingering vestiges of her concern about Valentin and "Endnote." There was simply Devin with those deft fingers of his stroking her arms and hands while he teased her with light kisses, dipping his tongue in her waiting mouth almost playfully.

The playfulness made her ache from unsatisfied yearnings more than a possessive kiss might have. She twined her arms around his neck, urging him closer. He responded by shifting her onto his lap and leaning back into the corner of the love seat so that one of his thighs lay against the back of the love seat. Her bottom easily fit in the juncture between his legs, and he settled her there, his hands moving to cup her face so he could kiss her more and more deeply.

A series of warm, delectable kisses followed, each bolder than the last, until they were both frantic with wanting a deeper intimacy. He skimmed his hands over her back, her arms, her sides, and she did the same. She slid her hands inside his rough denim jacket, and he sighed deep in his throat, plunging his tongue with accelerating rhythm into the warm willingness of her mouth.

At that moment, she forgot who and where she was. Nothing mattered but their linked mouths, their roving hands . . . the uncontrolled passion rousing up within her, like a bear that had been too long in hibernation.

Suddenly he broke away from her mouth, his eyes alight with wanting, his lips curved in a smile. "So, Ms. Winslow, answer my question. Do you have the hots for me?"

The husky timbre of his voice seeped into her senses like rich perfume. She grinned. "Fishing for compliments again, Mr. Bryce?"

He nipped at her lower lip. "Answer the question, lady, or I'll have to take more drastic measures to find out."

That's when it hit her. They were going to make love. Now. Tonight. She knew it as surely as she knew she wanted to. Tonight there'd be no broken-off, flirting play, unless he did the breaking off. Tonight she'd forget about Ressu and "Endnote" to explore the strange connection between her and Devin.

And she'd do it because she wanted it so badly, it made her body thirst simply thinking of it. She wanted him with a fierceness she'd felt only for her work. She wanted to taste every inch of him, to feel those skilled fingers explore other parts of her, to join with him.

He lowered his mouth to her ear and ran his tongue around the outer rim before whispering, "Answer me, Suzanne."

She arched her neck back as he trailed his tongue over her earlobe and down the slender column of her neck. He did wonderful things to her with only the tip of his tongue, making her heart trip faster.

"Oh, yes. Definitely. I have the hots for you," she breathed.

"Good," he murmured against the hollow of her throat. "Because I've gotta tell you, lady, since the day we met I've been burning up inside wanting you. If I don't have you, they'll have to cart my ashes away in the morning."

"Wouldn't want that," she managed to say thickly as his hands worked their way under the sweatshirt to her bare waist. This was the point at which she'd become hesitant in her few previous sexual encounters. It wasn't that the intimacy bothered her. But once a man got this close, she started getting paranoid about her body.

Yet with Devin she felt languidly unconcerned, as if she could trust him with the knowledge of what lay beneath her clothes without fearing he'd share that knowledge with his buddies.

He doesn't have any buddies, that's why, she reminded herself before he slid capable hands up her ribs, drowning all coherent thought in the pure pleasure of physical sensation.

His capable hands wandered higher, up the inside of her sweatshirt toward her breasts, which were bare, since they were on the smallish size and she never felt the need to wear a bra when she was knocking around the house.

When his hands discovered her secret, he chuckled. "You're full of surprises. I see your obsession with rules doesn't extend to your underwear."

"Devin!" she protested weakly, but he ignored the protest, obviously enjoying the unexpected delight of caressing her bare skin. Then before she could even react, he'd lifted her sweatshirt to free her breasts.

The berry-tinged tips pebbled under his dark gaze, but he didn't hesitate long enough to allow her to feel embarrassment. He shifted their bodies until he could easily bend down and suck one nipple into his mouth, his hand pressing up under the breast's pert, soft weight to make it more accessible.

With a sharp cry, she gripped his shoulders and closed her eyes, bending back as his mouth, so hot, so ravenous, taunted her. He took his time tonguing the sensitive skin, rousing such acute sensations of pleasure in her that she thought she'd float right up into heaven if he didn't stop.

When the critics had said he looked like a devil and played like an angel, she thought, they little knew it depended on what instrument he played. Only a devil could play a woman with such skill or raise such sinfully delicious urgings in her.

She'd begun to go all warm and silky inside when he abruptly halted his motions to lay his head in the hollow between her breasts. "Suzanne," he said in a choked voice.

"Y-yes?"

"What do you want from me? If this is going nowhere, you'd better tell me before I lose my mind completely."

She opened her eyes, then focused on the dark head at her breast. She automatically buried her fingers in the glorious thick mane of hair, feeling his body stiffen against her as she did so. He lifted his face to hers.

A flame of awareness sizzled between them. Pain, joy, desire . . . his face held a full spectrum of emotions. They rainbowed inside her too, blended so thoroughly she couldn't separate the individual hues. All she knew was she wanted him. And, heaven help her, he apparently wanted her just as much.

She couldn't, wouldn't deny him. In a voice of surprising

calm, she said words she'd never said to another man before. "Will you stay the night?"

The shock registering in his crystalline eyes told her she'd caught him off guard. Then a fierce smile transformed his face into the face of a predator. "Only if I don't have to sleep on this damned love seat. Contrary to what you'd expect, love seats weren't made for making love."

Her throat went dry at his bluntness, but she'd made this choice almost from the moment she'd met him, and she wasn't the kind of woman to back away from a challenge. With a trembling smile, she disentangled herself from him and stood beside the love seat, stretching out her hand to his as her shirt slipped down to cover her once more.

"I have a bed," was all she said, matching his bluntness with her own.

He grinned, then clasped her hand and rose to his feet. As he enfolded her in a tight embrace, his sweet, provoking mouth settling over hers, she knew with certainty she'd never regret meeting this particular challenge.

12
♪

It's too late, Devin thought as he followed Suzanne into the darkened hall, his hand clasping hers. He'd told her they must stop before he lost his mind completely. Yeah, right. He'd already lost his mind, his body, his heart, and whatever other parts of himself weren't tied down. Apparently that included all of them. He'd put himself totally in her hands. And here he was, grinning like an idiot.

This is nuts, he told himself. *I'm trotting right down the road to hell and loving every step of it.*

He had Ressu to thank for this. Good old Ressu. Until now, Devin had hated him, but after Ressu took over his hands to play that delicate little piece that made Suzanne believe him, he found himself warming to the guy.

Granted, Ressu must have had his reasons. Devin didn't have the faintest idea what they were, unless it was to make Suzanne like Devin. He grinned. Hey, maybe the whole thing was just an elaborate matchmaking scheme from the beyond.

If so, it was working pretty well. And to think he'd come here intending to give her a piece of his mind! A trace of his earlier anger briefly assailed him, spoiling his pleasure. He thrust it from him. Suzanne felt bad now about involving Maggie. Besides, did it matter what she'd done? They'd both sneaked around behind each other's back. If anyone had acted unforgivably, it had been he. He'd played what she considered to be stolen music. He'd kissed her, then treated her badly.

He smiled. Not anymore. She wasn't out to destroy him, so he could let bygones be bygones. To hell with all his control, his fears. What had it brought him but misery? For once in his life, he deserved a little happiness.

Only the smallest twinge of guilt disturbed his thoughts. He *had* lied about his relationship to Ressu. Maybe Ressu had wanted him to—Devin didn't know whether he had or not—but Suzanne would hate him for lying if she ever found out. He thrust the guilt back into the recesses of his mind. He wouldn't ever let her find out.

No, he wanted to get to know Suzanne, which he couldn't do if "Endnote" stood between them. And despite all his reluctance in the past to get close to a woman, he found he wanted to do it this time. Hell, who knew what might happen even if she did find out about his gift? She might actually accept it.

What if she couldn't? He forced the thought from his

mind, refusing to think about it when her sexy body was ahead of him gliding along the narrow, darkened hall.

Then they reached the open door to what was apparently her bedroom, and he shook his head in disbelief. She really was going to do it. Thank God he wasn't the only one who wanted to press this to its most satisfying conclusion.

But when she turned to face him with the slightest hesitation in her expression, he held his breath.

"I hope you don't think I'm a tramp—" she began.

He jerked her to him and cut off whatever she was about to say with a ravenous kiss. Only when her body turned to putty under his fingers did he draw back. "And I hope you don't think I'm a thoughtless seducer, because I sure as hell don't think you're a tramp."

Then he was walking her backward through the entrance, his mouth devouring hers, his hands clutching her against his waist so tightly that their every step pushed the hard bulge in his jeans against the vee of her thighs. The exquisite ache of desire had tautened his every muscle, and he thought he'd die if he couldn't finish what they'd begun.

Her scent, Chanel No. 5, seeped into his nose and lungs, so that even with his eyes closed, he knew exactly whom he was caressing. Not that he wouldn't have known. Who else had lips sweet as candied apples, but far more lethal? Or velvety skin in every soft secret place designed to drive a man mad?

She drew back from him to whisper, "We're here." He opened his eyes to discover they were in her bedroom. Pulling away from him, she flipped a switch that turned on the room's two lamps. She stood there motionless, waiting. Her cat—she'd called it Bartok—sauntered in behind them, surveying Devin as thoroughly as Devin was surveying Suzanne.

Devin's body still throbbed from unfulfilled desire, but he forced himself to clamp down on his feelings. He wanted this first time with her to be special, so he had to get some control. As he struggled for supremacy over his hormones, he appraised her bedroom, a slow smile rising to his lips.

Only Suzanne could have a room so neat and devoid of frills. But it wasn't the scholar's room he'd expected either. Somehow she'd managed to make it thoroughly modern, but feminine. The furniture was Scandinavian-style, all blond woods. The bedspread on the double bed had bold stripes and geometric designs, but in some light-green-and-beige color. The curtains matched, of course, as did the large nubby-looking rug covering half the wood floor.

It was the kind of room an interior decorator would have loved. He should have known Suzanne would never have a haphazard collection of furniture like the stuff in his apartment.

It suited her, all of it. The room gave off a kind of warm glow and soft femininity without being cloying. And it was, of course, scrupulously clean.

Automatically, he knelt down to untie his shoes.

She laughed. "What are you doing?"

"What does it look like? I'm taking off my shoes. I'm not worried you won't respect me in the morning, but I *am* worried you won't forgive me for dirtying your rug."

When she remained silent, he twisted his head up to look at her. She'd crossed her arms over her chest. He could tell by the expression on her face, he'd hurt her feelings.

"Hey, I'm sorry, honey. Guess I'll have to watch my mouth better around you. Sometimes I say what I think, and everybody else be damned." He straightened and walked to her side. "Hell, I'll leave them on if it'll make you feel better."

She ventured a smile. "No, no . . . I'm being silly. But I—I don't want you to think I'm so uptight I can't stand a little dirt on my rug."

"It wouldn't bother me if you did hate dirt on the rug." He reached out and drew her to him. "My mother's the same way. Gets on my case all the time about tracking mud in. I'm used to it."

"But—"

He cut her off with a kiss. Time to get her off her insecurities, before she started having second thoughts.

He was the one who should be having second thoughts. Was he actually standing here undermining all the years of self-control, of keeping himself aloof from intriguing women?

Yeah, he was, he admitted wryly, savoring the taste of her on his lips. And he didn't give a damn. His hands slipped down to cup her sweet little butt, and her resulting moan built his tension to an unbearable peak.

Sliding his hands beneath her sweatshirt, he lifted it and worked it over her head in a couple of quick movements. Her hands were pulling on his jacket before he'd even finished.

Now she really was making him crazy, he thought as she yanked at the sleeves, trying to get the jacket off him and in the process rubbing her soft breasts against his jersey. With a growl, he tore off the jacket, then his jersey, until they both stood there topless.

Her face was flushed, either with pleasure or embarrassment—he couldn't tell which—but she planted her hands on his chest and gazed up at him with wondering eyes.

"Are all pianists this . . . this well-developed?" she asked, gliding her hands over his muscles, then rubbing her palms in circles over them as if testing their strength.

Her expression would have suited a wide-eyed teenage girl more than her. It made him want to strut like a peacock. No wonder musclemen were such jerks. Much more treatment like this, and his head would inflate to a monstrous size. All those hours bench-pressing had finally paid off, he thought, a grin forming on his face. Never again would he curse that machine.

He lifted his hands to her hair, allowing the rumpled, satiny strands to scatter over his fingers. "Are all musicologists this damned sexy?"

Her smile of delight caught him unawares. It almost hurt

SILENT SONATA

—this trusting innocence of hers. He forced the guilt back down. Hell, for once in his life, he deserved to have a woman smile at him like that, and he was selfish enough to grab at the chance, even if he'd gotten it by lying about his supposed friendship with her stepfather.

Eager to forget, needing to forget, he caught her head in his hands and planted a possessive kiss on her lips. As she gave herself up to the kiss, he trailed his hands downward over her neck and shoulders to her breasts. He paused there to revel in the sheer pleasure of filling his hands with her warm flesh.

She groaned, and then moved to undo his belt buckle. He continued to caress her breasts as she worked loose his belt, then the button and zipper of his jeans. Only when she tried to slide the jeans past his hips did he pause in his touching of her to kick off his shoes, then yank off his pants and briefs.

"Ahh," he murmured as he pressed her to him, letting her feel the urgent rigidity of his body, of his very acute arousal. His mouth covered hers, no longer playful, but hungry, demanding, intense. He trailed both hands down beneath the band of her sweat pants and slid the pants down past her hips. Her lips clung to his as she shimmied the pants down her slender legs until they lay on the floor in a crumpled heap.

He drew back to look at her, then sucked in his breath. She wore practical cotton panties, of course, the kind you could find in any discount store. Yet they looked sexy as lace and silk on her, for they were so thin he could glimpse the hair beneath the cloth.

He slipped his finger under the edge that encased one of her thighs, then ran his finger along until he reached the place between her legs.

The dampness there undid him.

A moan sounded deep in his throat as he picked her up in his arms and strode to the bed. Once there, he laid her on the bedspread. Bartok hopped up onto the bed beside her.

Devin frowned. "No cats in the bed, buddy," Devin murmured as he scooped the cat up and strode to the door. Bartok struggled free before Devin even reached the doorway and jumped down, then sauntered off down the hall with a dignified air. Devin shut the door behind the cat as Suzanne let out a muffled giggle.

He turned back to her and approached the bed, a grin on his face. "Sorry, but I gotta draw the line somewhere."

She gave him a trusting smile.

Why did she have to look at him like that, he thought, with her face open as a flower to the sun? It reminded him he hadn't quite come clean with her, nor ever intended to.

When he hesitated with one knee already resting on the bed, her expression grew clouded and she asked in a husky, uncertain voice, "Something wrong?"

His gaze traveled over her body, starting with her honey-gold hair splashed across the meadow-green coverlet and moving downward over every inch of her creamy skin. She sat up, her hand reaching for the edge of the coverlet, but he caught her hand.

Hell, he would have her . . . he must have her. Otherwise the fragile thread between them might break, and he suddenly knew he couldn't bear that.

"Nothing's wrong that making love to you won't cure." Without pausing to reconsider, he lowered himself to cover her body with his.

As soon as he sealed his mouth to hers, she apparently forgot any objections she might have had. Her body arched up as she clasped his arms, pressing her belly and thighs against him until he thought he'd go mad.

In truth, Suzanne too thought she'd go mad. She'd never experienced this feverish desire to have all of a man, to want his body over her, around her, in her.

She wanted to touch him, to memorize the rough contours of his body, so different from hers. Sliding her hands down his muscled back, she cupped his taut buttocks. His groan of response made her heart race with the sheer pleasure of sensual power.

Quickly he stripped her underwear from her and tossed the scrap of cotton to the floor. Their bodies came together again, skin to skin with nothing between them.

She should be embarrassed and timid, she told herself, yet for the first time, she felt nothing but pride in her body. Of course, it helped that he kept murmuring compliments in her ear, breathing endearments that made her pulse beat a heavenly cadence.

"Your skin's so silky," he said as he ran his hands over her arms, then pressed a kiss into the crook of her elbow.

She shivered with delight. He slid one hand between their bodies to cradle her most intimate place. More than willing to be at the mercy of his talented hands, she curved up to receive them as he fondled her skillfully. His fingers plumbed her depths, darting rhythmically with the finesse only a keyboard player could manage.

Light consumed her, light and energy and an unadulterated hunger so powerful she ached with need.

"Ah, honey," he breathed into her ear, "you're so wet. Looks like I was wrong. You're as uncontrolled as I am."

"I have a great teacher, that's all," she gasped as he sent wonderful sensations scattering off into all parts of her body. "Devin, Devin . . ." she cried out, wanting more, needing all of him.

His hot hardness lay trapped between their bodies, the sleek, warm flesh a blatant reminder of what he had to offer. Without pausing to think, she reached to touch him as he was touching her. He growled and buried his face in her hair.

"You trying to ruin me?" he quipped, then stiffened as her hand closed around him. " 'Cause you're doing a good job of it, honey."

Thrilling to his words, she smiled and turned her head toward him, then ran her tongue along the edge of his rock-hard jaw. When at the same time she stroked the warm weight in her hand, he moaned deep in his throat.

"That's enough," he grumbled, then rose up and slid into her without warning, eliciting a gasp from her.

He felt heavenly inside her. No doubt about it, she thought, there was something to be said for losing all control.

"Much better," he said as he began to move, withdrawing and thrusting, gently at first, then with more insistent motions.

She shifted to accommodate him more completely, and he growled and nipped at her shoulder.

"You're making me crazy," he murmured, then thrust deep into her to prove the truth of it.

"Crazy . . . mmmm," she whispered as pleasure built in her at each stroke. The whisper turned into a low moan when he drove hard into her, giving her such intense sensations of delight that she clutched his back to bring him into her more tightly.

After that, conscious thought took second place to physical sensation, to the sheer joy of relinquishing control to her urges. Whenever he made a movement that pleased her and brought from her a soft whimper of response, he repeated the motion until after a few minutes he was anticipating her desires so thoroughly she began to think he could read her mind, or at least read her body.

Sweet whispering touches filled her senses. His body was thunder and clouds all at once, driving but gentle, powerful but dreamy. True to his profession, he offered her the music of the skies, and she soared up into it with eager mind, eager body.

Then at last the multihued sensations of desire rocked her body—fierce, brilliant, delightful. She dug her nails into his shoulders and cried out as she felt carried over the top of a cliff into pure white, exultant space.

"Oh, Christ, Suzanne," he murmured against her neck, then found his own release, filling her with his hot seed.

He collapsed on top of her, and she held on to him as aftershocks of pleasure vibrated through her body, and through his next to hers. So delicious, she thought. She'd never dreamed it could be so delicious.

After they lay there panting a moment in comfortable silence, he rolled off her. Then he pulled her on top of him to lie cradled against his chest. "I don't want to let go of you yet, but I don't want to crush you to death either," he muttered in explanation.

Their legs were entwined. With her ear to his chest, she could hear his racing heart. She planted a soft kiss into the hair lightly sprinkled over his chest. She relished the feel of his solid mass beneath her, the tangible evidence of his strength.

He stroked her back, then rested his hand on her hip. "I always knew it would be like that between us."

"Mmmm." Now that it was over, she felt a strange urge to keep silent. She didn't know why. Maybe she was afraid if they started talking, he'd turn cold and pull away as he had when he'd kissed her in the park. Only this time it would hurt a whole lot more, because she'd allowed herself to trust him, utterly and completely.

But he wouldn't leave her this time, would he, she told herself. This time he offered her both warmth and protection, companionship and security. Pouring over her like nectar was an acute sense of well-being so profound it cocooned her. He'd once accused her of wanting only to be safe. Perhaps he'd been right. But paradoxically, in relinquishing her body recklessly to him, she'd found a kind of safe haven, a place of such sweet, lambent joy that she wanted only to burrow into it and luxuriate.

"So what happens now?" Devin whispered as his fingers played with her hair, stretching it out in tangled webs across her shoulders and back.

"That's up to you." She turned her head up to look at him and rested her chin on his chest. His eyes held a tropical warmth, brilliant and inviting in their opaque blueness.

"As I recall, the original invitation included staying the night."

She gave him a delighted smile. "It did, didn't it?"

"Does that mean we sleep now, or do you have any more plans to separate me from my sanity?"

"Who knows?" She wriggled against him playfully until his eyes darkened. "I say we go with the flow."

"Paul says you don't know how to do that." A mischievous glint lit Devin's eyes.

Her startled gaze met his. "You talked to Paul about me . . . about how I'd be if . . . about this?"

He grinned. "You'll never know, will you?"

She pursed her lips quite deliberately. She rubbed her fingers along one flat male nipple, then teased it with her mouth until he groaned.

She lifted her head in triumph. "Well, did you?"

"Nah," he muttered in a decidedly strained voice. "But he *did* say you didn't know how to go with the flow."

She snuggled against his shoulder and traced the edge of his ear with her tongue. "And what do you say, maestro?"

"I say Paul doesn't know a damned thing about you." He shifted her body to his side, then turned to trail his fingers down her belly, inching lower and lower with each word. "And I plan to keep him in the dark on the subject. Him and all the other men who don't know a damned thing about you."

He stroked between her legs, and she gasped sharply, then ground up against his hand with a murmur of delight. To her surprise, he was hard again and pressing against her thigh.

"Let's go with the flow," he whispered. "If you're up to it, Little Miss Priss."

Her eyes widened seconds before he covered his body with hers once more, blotting out her surprise at his use of her childhood nickname.

"Yes, let's go with the flow," she echoed, then gave herself up to the marvelous music of desire.

13

♪

Suzanne woke abruptly out of the middle of a deep sleep. Something was wrong. She couldn't put her finger on what it was, but something had awakened her.

She lay there a moment, her heart beating fast as she tried to isolate the source of her unease. The room was engulfed in blackness except for the luminous dial on her bedside clock, which read 3:00 A.M.

She shifted, and a slight soreness between her thighs brought everything flooding back . . . Devin touching her, making love to her, falling asleep beside her. He'd been gentle and sweet . . . and fierce and demanding. A smile brightened her face. So this was how it felt to let go completely.

Languidly, she rolled to her side and reached for him, but found only Bartok, who lay beside her, purring in his sleep. She sat up quickly in bed, her heart pounding.

Surely Devin hadn't left. Then she heard faint sounds of movement coming from another part of the house. Devin. It had to be.

That must have been what woke me, she thought as she slid out of bed, careful not to wake Bartok. She switched on a small lamp. Sure enough, Devin's shirt and shoes lay scattered on the floor. Hunting for her robe, she moved quickly around the room.

Odd that the noise would have awakened her, she thought. Usually, she wasn't a light sleeper, particularly when Mother was staying—

"Oh, no," she muttered to herself as she jerked her robe on, "I forgot about Mother."

That was what had set off her internal alarm bells. How could she have forgotten Mother might be home any minute, if she wasn't home already? Mother would have a field day if she found Devin Bryce running around the house half dressed in the middle of the night.

Not that Mother would disapprove, Suzanne thought as she fumbled with the tie belt to her robe. A grim smile crossed her face. No, Mother would be delighted, but she'd probably make a fool of herself trying to assess how serious Devin was about her daughter.

That thought made Suzanne hasten down the hall. Fortunately, Mother's door was open and the room still dark and empty. But she had to locate Devin before Mother came home and stumbled on him rummaging around.

"Devin," Suzanne called out as she moved through the living room past the piano. He wasn't there.

Then she noticed the light shining from beneath her study door. She opened the door. "Devin, my mother—" she began as she caught sight of him standing in the middle of the room.

The words died on her lips, however, as he lifted his face to hers. He was holding a piece of Valentin's transcribed music in one hand and her notes for it in the other.

And he looked like a boy with his hand caught in the cookie jar.

"What are you doing in here?" she demanded, distrust constricting the muscles of her throat.

He raised one eyebrow at her accusing tone. "Looking for copies of 'Endnote'," he said in a deadpan voice.

She paled.

He stepped toward her with a worried expression. "Hell, Suzanne, it's just a joke. What happened to your sense of humor?"

She looked more closely at the piece of music he held. It wasn't 'Endnote,' but some minor sonata that had been published some time ago. A wave of relief went through her.

"I couldn't sleep," he continued, his tone defensive, "so I thought I'd . . . you know . . . kind of look around. I ended up in here. I hope you don't mind—"

"No, no." She felt very silly. "I'm sorry, I've been a little edgy ever since the mugging."

And for a moment there, she added to herself, *I forgot I could trust you.*

She could, couldn't she? Last night had proved that, hadn't it? Her eyes met his, searching for the guilt she'd thought she'd seen earlier, but if it lay in the depths of that enigmatic gaze, he hid it well.

She'd probably imagined it. Or else it had been the very normal reaction of someone who'd been caught looking through someone else's things.

What was more, looking at him reminded her of everything that had happened the night before. Wearing only his blue jeans—no shirt, no shoes—he looked sexier than any male model. His feet were planted wide on the carpet, and the concern in his expression made her heart turn flipflops.

"I didn't mean to wake you," he apologized. "I tend to be a late-to-bed, late-to-rise kind of guy, thanks to all my concertizing. I usually don't get to sleep until late, so I have trouble sleeping if I go to bed earlier than normal."

Now she felt even more like a paranoid, irrational fool who saw thieves behind every corner. "I understand. It's no problem. Really."

He regarded her quietly for a moment, then handed the papers to her. "Here. I saw them lying on the desk and took a look. I tried not to mess up anything."

She took the pages without a word.

"So." He shoved his hands in his jean pockets. "That's one of Ressu's pieces, isn't it?"

"Yes."

"What's the other stuff, notes or something for your book?" he asked in a tone of polite interest.

"You might say that." She stared down at the papers.

"What's all the chicken scratch at the top for, if you don't mind telling me?"

She looked up at him, but he seemed merely curious. *I really am getting paranoid,* she told herself. Besides, why not tell him? He'd demonstrated repeatedly that he had no interest in avant-garde. It wasn't as if he'd run out and publish his own book on the subject.

"Look"—he broke into her thoughts as she hesitated—"I didn't mean to pry. Forget I mentioned it, okay?"

That decided her. "No, no. I want you to know. It's just that it's the key part of my thesis." She flashed him a modest smile. "It's my big discovery. And to tell the truth, I haven't told a soul about it."

"I see." He gave her a smile that was encouraging but not probing as he ran one hand through his unruly hair.

Desire stirred in her belly once more, and her eyes drifted downward of their own accord. The man sure looked great wearing nothing but blue jeans.

She dragged her thoughts back to the papers in her hand. How could she give him her body, but not her trust? She spoke in measured tones. "The chicken scratch, as you call it, is Morse code."

"No kidding." He edged closer and peered over her shoulder at the sheet of paper. "Morse code, huh? Never met anyone who took notes in Morse code. You must be awfully determined to keep your big discovery a secret."

"No, you don't understand. The Morse code *is* my big discovery. You see, Valentin worked Morse code into his sonatas." She paused to let that sink in.

His eyes narrowed. "Did Ressu tell you about this or something?"

"No. I discovered the pattern myself after he died."

Devin's expression mirrored extreme skepticism. "Let me get this straight. You picked out notes in Ressu's work that could be interpreted as Morse code, and now you're convinced he put them in there on purpose?"

"Wait a minute, maestro, before you start telling me how

silly it is." She leveled a haughty gaze on him. "I have proof Valentin did it on purpose. When I was cataloging Valentin's papers and manuscripts, I found his code notations on one of his manuscripts with the corresponding words written above them."

His eyes widened. "Really?"

"Yes, really." She laid the piece of Ressu music down on her desk and smoothed it out. "When I studied the coded words, I found they corresponded to actual notes in the music. First, each piece had a musical theme signaling the beginning of the Morse code message, the same theme in every sonata.

"Then," she continued, "buried in the music that followed was one note that represented the Morse code message, usually an F-sharp or an A. Every time that particular note appeared, it represented another symbol in the Morse code message. Half notes were dashes and quarter notes were dots. At the end the signal musical theme would reappear, telling the listener the message had ended." She hummed the theme for him. "Clearly, he wanted the messages to be heard and understood, so he chose a theme even a simpleton would recognize after a few times." As she finished, she glanced up at Devin to gauge his reaction.

He still looked as if he thought she might be deranged. "He did this with all his pieces or just the one you came across?"

"In all the sonatas of the Sonata Cycle." Her voice grew more excited as she warmed to her subject. "Once I found the signal theme, I had no trouble laying out the notes and finding the messages."

His fingers traced the notes of the piece on the desk until he found the theme she'd hummed. "What are the messages like?"

"They're quirky, but nice. One of the lines for this piece reads, 'A soul-fed heart grows as swift as light travels.' Sometimes they're almost lyrics, like one in the fourth sonata that says, 'When time has slept its longest sleep, tomorrow's day will be night's leap.' Pretty nifty, huh?"

"Yeah, nifty." He seemed distracted, his brow knitted in thought.

She could understand why he would have trouble believing her. Sometimes, as she'd sorted the notes of each sonata into recognizable groups that spelled letters in Morse code, she'd questioned her own thesis. But she'd always found a pattern, always. Besides, she'd remembered how Valentin had enjoyed explaining coding systems to her when she was a child, and that had given her thesis some validity.

How like Valentin, she thought, to make his work accessible on more than one level. She couldn't wait until her book was published and her interpretation revealed to the music community. Once they saw his genius, his work might gain the appreciation it deserved.

"Why do you think he did it?" Devin asked, bringing her out of her thoughts. "Did he actually think the average listener would get it?"

"I don't know. I doubt it. He used to say he was doing for music what James Joyce did for literature in *Finnegans Wake*. You know how Joyce used *reign* but meant *rain* and *rein* all at the same time, giving a layered effect to language? Well, I think Valentin tried to achieve the same kind of layered effect by adding words *in* his music instead of *to* his music as lyricists do."

Devin stared thoughtfully at the piece of music. "I don't guess it's such a strange idea. Musical rebus—using the names of notes to spell out something in a musical theme—has been around for centuries, and this isn't that different."

"Yes, but no one uses Morse code, do they? I think that's original."

He nodded. "It's original, all right." He paused, then toyed with the sheets of paper before asking nonchalantly,

"And what about 'Endnote'? Did he follow the pattern there, too?"

"Of course. It's the final piece in the Sonata Cycle. He had to follow it throughout all the sonatas."

"What's the message in 'Endnote'?"

She looked up at him, eyes sparkling with mischief. "Among others, 'Listen, listen to what I have to tell you.' As you might imagine, I found it amusing that you chose to play that particular passage in concert."

His eyes narrowed. "Yeah, amusing." He thought a moment. "But didn't you tell me I played a different version of 'Endnote' at the recital?"

She thought back, staring absently at the piece of music on the desk. "You did. You added a phrase I didn't recognize." Her eyes met his. "I'd forgotten. Why did you do that?"

For a second, she thought he wouldn't answer. He looked disturbed and distinctly uncomfortable. Then his face cleared. "Ressu played it for me that way. He must have . . . must have added the phrase to it . . . er . . . right before he died."

"He must have!" Her voice rose in her excitement. This was an important development she couldn't ignore. "Devin, you've got to play it for me with the additions. I want to hear it."

His smile suddenly seemed a little too tight, too forced. "Right. Sure. Whenever you want. You want me to play it now?"

The sound of the front door opening and shutting brought them both up short.

"What the hell—" he exclaimed.

Suzanne groaned. Oh, no, she'd forgotten . . . again. "It's my mother."

The surprise on his face was almost comical. "You live with your mother?"

"No. She's visiting."

As he muttered a string of curses under his breath, she

was already scanning her office frantically as if expecting some door to suddenly appear that she could whisk him through. "Devin . . . I can't let her see you here."

But it was too late. She heard her mother in the hall and before Suzanne could even switch off the light in the office, her mother's voice rang out.

"Zanny? What are you doing up so late? You never—"

Her mother's flow of words shut off abruptly as she entered the room and found Suzanne and Devin standing there. An amazing series of emotions passed over her face—shock, recognition, wariness, and finally a distinct pleasure. The pleasure raised Suzanne's defenses more than anything.

"I see you have a visitor," her mother said smoothly, one hand reaching up unconsciously to brush a lock of hair into place. "Well, aren't you going to introduce us, Zanny?"

Devin's initial expression of alarm slowly changed to faint amusement. "Yes, *Zanny,* aren't you going to introduce us?" His eyes twinkled mischievously.

Blast him, she thought. It was so like him to find the whole situation amusing.

Mother turned a peremptory gaze her way. Mother's white sequined dress, which sparkled in the office's bright lights, made her look like some ice queen commanding her subjects, though admittedly a queen of the stout Viking variety.

Suzanne choked back a hot retort. "Mother . . . Devin Bryce. Devin . . . my mother, Felicia Winslow."

Devin took her mother's proffered hand and shook it. When her mother flashed him a winning smile in return, a grin formed on his face.

"Of course, I didn't *need* an introduction to know who you were." Her mother's voice dripped with warmth. "I've been enjoying your talented playing for years."

"Thank you."

The humorous gleam in Devin's eyes made Suzanne want to hit him for standing there so smugly, shirtless and barefooted and so obviously come from her bed. No telling what Mother was thinking.

Suzanne decided she'd better get rid of Devin before Mother chose to tell them both exactly what she was thinking. "Devin was just leaving."

Mother gave her a haughty glance. "Zanny, I am not a complete idiot. And although I did at least marry the men I slept with, I'm not a prude either. Mr. Bryce is welcome to stay if he wishes. You need not throw him out on my account."

If it had been possible at that moment to spontaneously combust from embarrassment, only ashes would have marked where Suzanne stood. Her face turned a hundred shades of red as she fought the urge to turn tail and run. She couldn't look at Devin, and she certainly couldn't look at her mother.

Her mother seemed completely oblivious to her embarrassment. She turned to Devin with a smile. "I was about to make myself a cup of hot spice tea. Why don't you join me, Mr. Bryce? It's not often I have the chance to chat with a famous pianist and—"

"Mother, don't be absurd," Suzanne snapped. "You were married to a famous composer and you had plenty of chances to chat with famous pianists."

"I'd love some tea, Mrs. Winslow," Devin broke in, ignoring Suzanne's comment. "And please call me Devin. All my friends do."

Suzanne shot him a murderous glance, but he winked and smirked at her, making her want to throttle him on the spot.

"I shall, thank you," her mother said with a smile. "And do ignore my daughter's bad manners. She always worries I'll say something to embarrass her, but you know how it is with children. They're always ashamed of their parents."

"Oh, I'm sure that's not the case with Suzanne . . . er . . . Zanny," Devin said smoothly. "She must be very proud of you and your work. I can't imagine her being ashamed of such a talented mother."

Boy, was he charming the toes off of Mother, Suzanne thought, and having a couple of laughs to boot. She was going to kill him later. Most definitely. She'd take that denim jacket of his and strangle him with it . . . simply wrap the long sleeve around his neck and pull until she wiped that insolent smirk right off his lips. . . .

Her mother placed a hand on Suzanne's arm, drawing her attention from Devin. "Will you join us for tea, dear?"

I'd rather be buried alive, Suzanne thought. But what choice did she have? She didn't dare leave Devin alone with her mother to talk about her. Against her better judgment, she gave her mother a curt nod.

Then her mother's gaze trailed down over Suzanne's flimsy robe, which wasn't held entirely closed by her cloth belt. "I'll understand if you wish to put on some clothes first."

This time Suzanne fiercely fought the blush threatening to stain her cheeks. For Pete's sake, she wasn't a child anymore. Why was she letting Mother get to her like this?

"Yeah, I guess I should do that, too," Devin said, his tone surprisingly gentle.

She glanced up in surprise to find him looking at her with sympathy. At least he wasn't laughing at her anymore, she thought. The tenderness in his eyes warmed her, diminishing some of her awkward feelings.

"No, you're fine as you are," her mother said and took Devin's arm. "Believe me, I've seen enough men's hairy chests not to be shocked by the sight of one more." She made a shooing gesture at Suzanne. "Go on now, Zanny, and get dressed. We'll meet you in the kitchen."

Suzanne would have protested, but knew it would be fruitless. Her mother would simply continue to make not-so-subtle digs about Suzanne's state of undress until Suzanne lost her temper and made a fool of herself in front of Devin.

SILENT SONATA

So Suzanne merely muttered, "Be back in a minute," and fled down the hall to her bedroom. Frantically she searched for the clothes she'd been wearing earlier, then pulled them on with lightning speed, spurred on by the dreadful thought of Devin and Mother having a cozy chat about her.

Sure enough, as soon as she entered the kitchen, she overheard her mother saying, "One time when she was only seven, I went to put in her drawer some ribbons I'd bought her. When I opened the drawer, she screamed, 'Don't put them there!' As it turned out, she'd organized all the ribbons precisely, and she didn't want me to mess them up. Can you believe that? Zanny has always been the most fastidious child."

Suzanne groaned. *Oh, boy, not the ribbon story,* she thought.

Devin looked up to see her standing there and a cocky grin crossed his face. "Your mother's been telling me all about your childhood, Zanny."

Odd how when he used her nickname, it came out sounding sexy. She fought the desire drifting up in her belly, a desire only intensified by the sight of him so happily ensconced in her house. He looked so cursedly comfortable sitting there in her kitchen with his chair propped back on two legs and his hands shoved into his blue jean pockets. He fit, too, as if the kitchen had been built for him to sit in.

Suzanne padded over to sit at the table next to him. "Yes, well, Mother always tells only one side of the ribbon story. My reason for organizing the ribbons wasn't an insane fastidiousness. I'd made a design with them and was waiting until Valentin got home to show it to him. I screamed because I didn't want her to mess up my design before he could see it."

"I still say it was a rather extreme reaction," her mother interjected as she shot Devin a knowing glance from her stance by the stove.

"I was seven years old." Suzanne scooted her chair under the table. "Most seven-year-olds are prone to extreme reactions."

Especially a seven-year-old who'd been handed a new stepfather only a few months before, she thought. When Valentin had first married her mother, Suzanne had been terrified of the big bear of a man. She would have done almost anything to make him like her, mainly because she didn't think she could survive his disliking her. Funny how her perception of him had changed through the years.

"Anyway," her mother said, taking the steaming kettle off the burner and pouring boiling water into each of three waiting mugs, "Valentin didn't call you Miss Priss for nothing."

Suzanne went rigid and opened her mouth to retort. Then she felt a hand on her knee. She turned her gaze to Devin in time to see him mouth the words, "I'm sorry."

She laid her hand over his and squeezed. At least he understood how difficult this was for her. Their eyes locked, and she read in his gaze the reassurance that nothing her mother could say about her would affect his own opinion.

Then his eyes darkened a shade. His hand glided higher up her thigh, and she sucked in her breath. For Pete's sake, all he had to do was stroke her and she turned soft as melting butter.

"So, Devin, where are you from originally?" her mother asked as she stirred instant spice tea powder into the mugs.

The hand withdrew, but Devin's eyes remained on Suzanne, intense and burning. "I'm a local boy. I was born and bred right here in Chicago."

"Oh? What part of Chicago?"

"Please, Mother, don't pry," Suzanne put in as Devin stiffened ever so slightly. Any stories her mother might tell about Suzanne would be infinitely preferable to the third degree she could give Devin about his past.

"It's okay." Devin turned his gaze to her mother. "I'm from Bridgeport, Mrs. Winslow."

"Now, now, my name is Felicia. None of that 'Mrs. Winslow' nonsense or you'll make me feel old."

Devin grinned. "Oh, but . . . er . . . Felicia, you couldn't be a day over forty, if that."

Her mother gave a tinkling laugh as she placed a cinnamon stick in each cup and the cups on a tray, then brought the tray to the table. "You're an incorrigible flatterer. You know good and well I'd have to be at least fifty to be Zanny's mother."

"Fifty!" Devin exclaimed with mock surprise as he took a mug from her. "Hell, I never would have guessed."

Suzanne bit down on the giggle that rose in her throat. Mother was right—he was thoroughly incorrigible. And he knew exactly how to manipulate Mother. It was almost funny to see Mother flutter around like a teenager in response to his compliments.

About that time Bartok wandered into the room, apparently awakened by the noise. He looked as if he were headed straight for Devin, a cat grin on his face. Then he caught sight of Mother and made a sharp U-turn, back to Suzanne's room.

Her mother gestured toward the hall as the last bit of Bartok's tail swished down it. "My daughter's cat doesn't like me," she said conversationally.

"You're kidding me," Devin said. "The cat isn't much of a judge of character, is he?"

"Don't push your luck, Devin," her mother warned, but playfully. "Even *I* tire of flattery after a while."

He grinned over the top of his mug, then removed the cinnamon stick and laid it on the table before taking a sip of the steaming tea. "Mmm. Delicious." His eyes sparkled as he continued to give her mother that audacious grin.

Suzanne found herself relaxing. "That's it. Keep on Mother's good side," she said with a wink at Devin. "Mother's one of your most loyal fans anyway, and you don't dare offend her. She'll never go to another of your concerts if you aren't nice to her."

Devin laughed and her mother glanced at her in mock reproach. Suzanne grinned back shamelessly, then drank some of her own hot tea.

"Speaking of concerts," her mother remarked, "I was very disappointed in your recital last Sunday."

Suzanne's grin disappeared. She shot Devin an apologetic look. His smile too had faded, replaced by an expression of wariness.

Her mother continued. "What was all that nonsense you played in the middle of the Chopin? One minute it was lovely and the next minute the most horrendous noise was coming from the piano—"

"Mother!" Suzanne protested. "It's not polite to attack a guest's performance—"

"I don't always agree with Zanny's reviews," her mother went on, ignoring her daughter's protests, "but for once she was right on the money. That garbage you played would have sent even a stupid cat like Bartok howling from the hall."

Suzanne bristled. "That was Valentin's music," she declared defensively before Devin could say anything. "It wasn't garbage."

"Valentin's music?" Her mother glanced at Devin. "Really?"

"Afraid so." Devin's expression was unreadable, his eyes alert and almost fearful as he set the mug down carefully.

Suzanne's mother burst out laughing. "Oh, that's rich, that's too rich! You played Valentin's music in a recital? Oh, the irony of it. How enormously funny!" She laughed again, sending cold trickles of apprehension down Suzanne's spine.

Her hands grew cold despite the warmth of the mug she held clutched in them. Devin no longer looked relaxed. He toyed with the cinnamon stick almost as if it were a cigarette, then lifted it to his mouth. He'd actually gotten so far as to suck it before he jerked it out with a grimace and tossed it on the table. Then he crossed his arms over his chest in a defensive gesture that set off little warnings throughout her body.

"What's so ironic about Devin playing Valentin's music?" Suzanne asked her mother with an anxious frown.

Her mother turned to her. "Oh, it's just that I talked to Valentin a few months before he died. We got on the subject of Devin quite by accident, because Valentin had heard through community gossip that Devin had been engaged to play at Orchestra Hall on the date Valentin had hoped to play."

Suzanne suddenly didn't think she wanted to hear any more, but Devin didn't change the subject. He sat there with that shuttered expression on his face, making her heart plummet to her toes, and she couldn't find the words to stop her mother either.

"Valentin was livid," her mother went on. "He railed against the Allied Arts Series for ignoring his genius in favor of a man he said was—and I quote—'a no-talent exhibitionist who'd hoodwinked the public.'" She turned to Devin. "No offense, but my ex-husband hated your guts. Personally, I think he was so jealous of your success, he couldn't see straight. How ironic that you played his music on the very date he'd wanted to perform it himself! Dear Lord, he probably turned over in his grave a few hundred times hearing you do it."

Anger at Devin's betrayal threatened to rise up in her throat and choke Suzanne. She thrust the mug of tea away from her, feeling sick. If Devin hadn't looked so blasted guilty, she might still have wondered if Mother was mistaken in her assessment of Devin's relationship with Valentin.

No, Mother wasn't mistaken. Mother might have little discretion and even less tact, but whatever she blurted out tended to be the truth. It had been one of the things that had destroyed her marriages—her tendency to say exactly what she thought or knew to be true to whomever she wanted, without an ounce of concern for that person's feelings.

Mother wasn't lying. But Devin was. She watched his gaze settle on hers, a hesitant vulnerability in its depths, and she knew instantly she was right.

Nausea built up from the pit of her stomach. She should have known. She'd never thought it rang true that he would have been even an acquaintance of Valentin's, but she'd ignored her instincts. He'd played "Girlflowers" for her, and that had broken down all her resistance. How had he found out about the song? she wondered.

Paul popped into her head. That's how Devin had known. Devin must have wangled the music out of Paul some way. Her head ached. That made no sense. Paul wouldn't have done such a thing, would he have?

But it also made no sense that Valentin would rail against Devin to Mother, then turn around and play his latest work for him.

Look at that face, she told herself as she watched Devin. *He lied. You can see it in his eyes. And he knows he's been found out.*

There was a plea in that face, a subtle plea for understanding. Boy, did he know how to manipulate her, she thought, jerking her gaze from his. So much for letting go completely. This was what she got for not controlling her emotions.

And her sexual urges. She'd let her blasted hormones set her on a course to disaster. She should have clamped down on her foolish desires, she told herself. How stupid could she be?

"So tell me, Devin, why on earth would you have played Valentin's music?" her mother was saying. "It's absolutely wretched stuff."

It was more than Suzanne could endure. "Mother, I need to speak with Devin a moment. Alone."

Her mother's eyes widened and for the first time she

seemed to notice the tense atmosphere in the room. She looked from Devin's stony face to her daughter's stricken one. "I didn't mean to insult him, Zanny. You know how Valentin felt about Devin. Everyone knows. It was bound to be common knowledge since they were both based in the same city—"

"It has nothing to do with what you said," Suzanne interrupted, her fingers tightening into fists under the table. She mustn't lose control now, not in front of Mother. She had to be strong, firm, even though her heart was splintering into a million tiny shards. She forced her voice to sound normal. "I simply need to have a word with Devin, okay?"

Devin didn't even protest. He stood up, looking like a man headed to his own execution.

"Suzanne Denise Winslow—" her mother protested.

"Excuse us a moment," Suzanne murmured as she too rose and walked from the room.

He followed her down the hall—she could hear his muffled steps behind her—but she refused to slow her pace enough to walk beside him.

As soon as she cleared the door to her room, she whirled on him. Without a word, he entered and shut the door behind him.

"I'm going to ask you one question, Devin, and this time you'd better not lie. Do you hear me?" Her eyes searched his face. "Tell me, did Valentin ever play 'Endnote' for you?"

For a long moment he stared at her, his mouth implacable. "Not exactly—"

"I want a straight yes or no answer."

"I can't give you a straight yes or no answer. It's kind of hard to explain—"

"That means you can't explain it without making yourself look bad." She glared at him. "Okay, if you won't answer that question, then tell me this. Were you and Valentin friends?"

He hesitated, a multitude of emotions playing over his

face. Finally, he said quietly, "No. We met once at a party. That was all."

She hugged herself tightly. She'd expected the answer, but it still hurt. Good Lord, how it hurt!

"How . . . how did you know about 'Girlflowers'?" she went on, despite the despair and resentment threatening to rust out her iron will.

He looked blank.

"The piece you played last night, the one Valentin wrote for me."

He paused, as if trying to figure out what to say. His eyes looked bleak, but still he seemed to search for words.

"Never mind," she said through gritted teeth. "I'd rather not hear another of your bizarre excuses that make no sense." She remembered him rummaging through her office, looking at her notes. She'd been right to be suspicious. But she'd let him hoodwink her. "You must think I'm such a fool, to believe every strange story you come up with to explain your position, when the truth is obvious."

His eyebrows arched upward. "It is?"

"Yes. You—you have clearly been digging into our lives to get the information you need for your dirty little game. You talked to Paul, you got into my house and into my study. . . ." She trailed off, only to explode again. "I don't know what you're up to, but I don't want any part of it!" She faced him with defiance. "Listen to me! I want no part of it! Why don't you leave us alone—me, Paul, Valentin—" She broke off with a sob.

"Ressu's dead, Suzanne."

"Yes, yes! But he and his work still deserve to be treated with respect! They don't deserve to be part of your sick plans—"

"You are so damned obsessed with him!" Fury flared in his face as he took a step toward her. "He was human, he had flaws. You've got him up on some pedestal . . . you're practically worshipping the son of a bitch. He was just a man, damn it. He's not worth throwing away what we have!"

"What exactly do we have?" she asked in a tortured voice. Her throat felt swollen and raw with suppressed sobs. She wanted to curl up in a corner somewhere and hide from the world. "It . . . it can't be much if you can lie to me without an ounce of regard for my . . . my feelings. You deliberately lied to me. You knew what I thought, but you let me go on thinking it so you could cover up whatever it is you're doing with 'Endnote.' Maybe even so you could get me into bed—"

"Christ, how can you believe that?" he raged. "You'd think after what we just shared that you'd know what kind of man I am." He took another step toward her, reaching for her this time, but she backed away from his outstretched hand.

His frown deepened to a scowl. He rubbed the bridge of his nose, frustration clearly written on his face. "Okay, I blew it. I misled you, I admit it. But there were reasons for what I led you to believe. It's just that . . . hell, I don't know if you're quite ready to hear them."

The uncertainty, the reluctance in his voice, shattered her control. "You're right! I'm not ready to hear them, not if they're more insane tales, more blasted lies!" Not even bothering to hide the anguish in her face, she bent down and gathered up his shirt, jacket, shoes, and socks. Then she straightened and thrust them at him. "Get out, Devin! Now!"

He took the bundle from her, his eyes bleak. "Listen to me. I know it looks bad—as if I've been trying to deceive you all along—but it's not as bad as you think—"

"Oh? I thought I could trust you. I thought you cared about me. Instead, I find you were using me for some strange, nefarious purpose."

"It wasn't a nefarious purpose—"

"Do you think it matters what your reasons were? You

held me in your arms and lied to me. I can't forgive you for that."

"Please, Suzanne." His desperate expression seemed chiseled in a face of marble. "I need you. Give me some time. Don't just shut me out."

Unable to bear the plea, she whirled away from him and said in a voice barely above a whisper, "I'm going into my study now, and I'm going to lock the door. When I come out, you'd better be out of this house, Devin, or . . . or I'll call the police."

His voice behind her sounded cold as frozen metal. "Go ahead. You're going to call them anyway to arrest me for my 'strange, nefarious' crime."

She turned back to face him, hurt and angry. "Tonight may have meant nothing to you, but it meant something to me. All I want now is for you to leave me alone. I don't care about 'Endnote.' I don't care how you knew Valentin. Go on with your secret plans, whatever they are, but leave me out of it and get out of my house!"

"Okay, okay, I'm going," he ground out as set down the bundle of clothes, picked his shirt out of the jumble, and began to put it on. "Hell, I was crazy to think this would work. You're too obsessed with your logic and your rules to trust me based on something as unpredictable as the way you feel. But damn it, Suzanne, I didn't intend any of this to hurt you. If you ever take a chance on trusting your feelings, you'll realize that. Maybe then you'll be ready to hear what I have to say."

She strode past him, headed for the door and the hall that led to her study.

He caught her arm as she brushed past him. "Don't kid yourself, Suzanne. I'm going, but that doesn't mean I'll be gone from your life. The kind of passion unleashed between us tonight doesn't disappear simply because you rationalize it away."

He lowered his head until his mouth nearly touched her ear. As she stood there, unable to move, his voice thrummed, low and anguished. "I'll haunt you awake or asleep, until you see me in every dream, hear me in every voice, feel me in your blood. You'll not easily rid yourself of me, of the feelings you have for me."

The determined assurance in his voice sent a thrill through her for which she hated herself. So did his touch. She fought the insidious desire.

"Thanks to your lies, any feelings I had for you are dead," she managed to whisper through a throat clogged with pain.

"Are they?" He laughed harshly, then yanked her up against him before she even knew what was happening. Holding her head still between his hands, he crushed his mouth down on hers in a kiss so hard it bruised her lips.

When he drew back, her breath came in quick gasps and her eyes were wide. She felt paralyzed by the maelstrom of emotion he'd called up in her with just that one kiss.

He searched her face with dark glowering eyes, satisfied at what he saw there. "Maybe not as dead as you thought, eh, honey?" he said mockingly.

Recoiling as if she'd been slapped, she jerked away from him. Then clutching to herself the ragged remains of her dignity, she fled down the hall to her study.

14

♪

As Devin sped away from Suzanne's house with wheels squealing, the barest brightening of the sky signaled dawn's approach. He paid scant attention to it or to his driving.

He was too angry to notice anything . . . angry at himself, at Ressu, even at his dead father for unwittingly bequeathing the second sight to him. And most of all, he was angry at Suzanne.

Oh, sure, she had every right to be pissed at him, he told himself. Yeah, he'd lied to her. He'd be the first to admit it. But what alternatives had he been given?

You could have told her the truth last night after Ressu played "Girlflowers," his conscience reminded him.

He snorted. *Right. She would have decided I was nuts, and where would I be then?*

You wouldn't be driving down the street with the pieces of your broken heart rattling around inside you.

He slammed the accelerator to the floor. *Don't be absurd,* he told his conscience. *My heart's definitely intact, especially after the scene Suzanne and I just played in her bedroom.*

Hell, he and Suzanne had made love once. Okay, a couple of times, he corrected. So what? He'd found out that for all her supposed logical thinking, she was an irrational hothead waiting for any excuse to thrust him out of her life, which he should have realized all along. But it didn't have to affect him. He'd made a mistake in judgment, chosen the wrong woman to get involved with. It happened to people all the time.

With a groan, he clenched the wheel until his knuckles whitened. Who was he kidding? This wasn't the same as when his cheerleader girlfriend had broken up with him in high school or when he'd decided to stop calling the last woman he'd dated.

This was Suzanne, the woman who could make him feel like a million bucks, who accused him of fishing for compliments in the same breath she gave them to him. And now she hated him.

Christ, but it hurt! And it was his fault, all his fault!

He'd sure made a mess of things, he thought with despair. He should have told her the truth before they made love. Even if she'd rejected him after hearing it, he would have been able to save himself from getting too involved.

Now he was in so deep he'd never dig himself out of this. He shook his head, the hurt making his stomach bunch into knots. This was why he'd never let himself care for a woman deeply before. It was bound to end in disaster every time. He'd known better than this, he told himself furiously. He'd damned well known better!

Instead he'd given her the weapon to hit him with. A profound sense of futility made his breath quicken. As he exited the freeway, he cursed Felicia Winslow for spilling the beans. If not for her, everything would have been fine. After he'd bluffed his way through Suzanne's catching him in her study, where he'd been snooping around hoping to find clues to why Ressu was tormenting him, he'd really thought he was home free.

Then Felicia Winslow had opened her mouth. Hell, he could have gone a long time without telling Suzanne the truth about his connection to Ressu. After all, it would have been the only way to continue the relationship, he reassured himself. What woman in her right mind would believe a story as outrageous as his?

One who cares about you, his conscience whispered.

That thought sent regret arrowing into his heart. He clutched the wheel now, staring at the road with blind numbness.

What if she *had* believed him? What if she'd turned out to be the kind of woman he'd always wanted—caring, considerate, and willing to accept his strange gift?

Sucking in his breath, he fought the waves of despair threatening to engulf him. Had he thrown away his only chance at happiness? Had he misjudged the situation totally?

His mother's words came to mind—*One of these days, dear, you're going to have to trust someone.* Could this have been the day?

With a cry of anger, he willed the pain into a remote part

of his mind. He couldn't go on speculating about the impossible like this. He'd blown it big-time, and no amount of rationalizing could change that.

But there must be a way to repair the damage, he protested. He couldn't let her simply walk away. If she knew the truth, maybe she'd give him a chance. Problem was, how could he get her to listen?

Play Ressu again, he thought wryly. *At least last night while she was listening to "Girlflowers," she believed me. Yeah, that's what I need—for Ressu to do more of his apparent matchmaking.*

Or was it matchmaking?

The question stunned him. It shifted his concentration from Suzanne to that afternoon's bizarre possession. Why *had* Ressu deliberately switched modus operandi and played "Girlflowers" when he should have been playing "Endnote"?

His brow knitted in thought. Clearly, Ressu had wanted to establish his identity for Suzanne in a dramatic way, and he'd certainly succeeded. Hell, even the cat had recognized the ghost's entrance! Despite being caught up in the midst of the possession, Devin had been conscious of the cat's hissing.

Of course, Suzanne had been oblivious to Ressu's ghost, even though she'd certainly reacted strongly to the piece. Had Ressu wanted her to feel his presence? Had he been trying to communicate with her directly somehow? Devin's eyes narrowed. After all, Ressu *had* chosen to play "Endnote" at the only recital of Devin's that Suzanne had ever attended. Why? Was that a sort of communication too?

Of course, Ressu could have done his little performance at the recital out of spite. If what Felicia Winslow had said was true, Ressu had wanted that date for himself. It would certainly explain why Ressu's ghost had tormented him constantly.

Devin shook his head as he pulled into the parking lot of

his apartment building. No, there was more to it than that. He sensed it. For example, Ressu had changed "Endnote" when he'd played it through Devin. According to Suzanne, there'd been an added passage. She'd known it because of that stupid—

He stopped short. Morse code. Hell, in the argument with Suzanne, he'd forgotten all about their discussion about Ressu's use of Morse code. How could he have forgotten that? The minute she'd told him about it he'd wondered if the messages had anything to do with Ressu's playing "Endnote."

He parked, then sat there, amazed. Of course! Ressu was trying to pass some message on to Suzanne! That's why the damned guy kept playing the piece over and over through Devin, and that's why he'd added a passage! He had something new to say, and the Morse code would allow him to say it in a way only Suzanne would understand.

Trouble was, she wasn't listening. Devin closed his eyes as the awesome responsibility of what Ressu had entrusted him with engulfed him. Given the incredible rate at which Ressu had been possessing him and the difficulty ghosts normally seemed to have in taking Devin over, this message must be tremendously important. Devin had almost assumed that the frantic nature of the possessions had been because Ressu died recently, but now he wasn't so sure.

Perhaps Ressu's message was too important to wait. Perhaps the ghost was willing to sacrifice his "ghost health," if there was such a thing, to gift Devin with his precious message.

Now, come on, Devin told himself as he got out of his car and strode toward his apartment building. *You're jumping to an awful lot of conclusions here.*

For all he knew, Ressu was simply concerned about Suzanne's adjustment to his death and was trying to comfort her from beyond the grave. That was why he'd played "Girlflowers" instead of "Endnote" for Suzanne. Yeah,

Devin told himself, the whole thing could be as simple as that.

Devin entered the lobby, swerving to avoid the motorbike parked directly in front of the door. When he reached the elevator, he pressed the button, watching with increasing impatience as the elevator took its time coming down.

No, he thought. There had to be more to it. There was a kind of desperation about the way Ressu kept possessing his hands. Besides, if the ghost had simply wanted to comfort Suzanne, he certainly wouldn't have played "Endnote" every time Devin had sat down at the piano alone. No, Ressu had embedded an important message in "Endnote," and now it was up to Devin to find out what it was.

Devin groaned at the same time the elevator doors finally opened. He got on, his stomach twisting again into a million knots.

Hell, Ressu, why me? he thought as the elevator inched upward. *It's bad enough you got me linked up with Suzanne who's determined to destroy me after giving me a glimpse of heaven. Now you want me to play hero and pass on your urgent message. Why can't you just leave me the hell alone?*

Unfortunately, Devin knew the answer to that. There was no one else. Who else allowed dead musicians an outlet for their frustrations?

That's me, Devin thought bitterly, *safety valve to the phantoms. It's me or nothing.*

The elevator door slid open, and he walked out into the hall headed toward his apartment. He reached for the doorknob, then froze. A sudden uncanny fear that someone stood on the other side of his door assailed him. He put his key in the lock and turned it, surprised to find that the door was indeed locked.

He paused. Okay, so maybe he was overreacting. Maybe he was letting all this spooky stuff about Ressu get to him. Then again . . .

He turned the knob and pushed the door open an inch. The faintest scent of lemony clean wafted from inside.

SILENT SONATA

Not in my *messy apartment,* he thought. Then without even stopping to think, he squatted and rolled forward, shoving the door open before him as he did so.

Something swished through the air above his head, barely missing him. Devin twisted around into a crouch, his eyes scanning the room for some weapon.

But his assailant had regained his balance with lightning speed, and now came at Devin with what looked like a police nightstick. Devin rolled to the right, but not fast enough. The guy brought the stick down on his ribs . . . hard.

He moaned and stumbled to his feet. Then all his street-fighting instincts from his Bridgeport childhood surfaced as he lunged for the wiry, masked man who now seemed intent on getting away.

Devin was the larger of the two men, and as his full weight hit the other guy, they both went crashing to the floor. The man still clutched the nightstick in one hand, but it was his fist that he slammed into Devin's bruised ribs. Devin grunted, then quickly retaliated, smashing his own fist into the man's face repeatedly.

Not the hand! Devin could almost hear Jack saying. He rolled off the man, again searching for some weapon, but his assailant was stronger than he expected. The man had risen as Devin turned his back. Then with a foreign-sounding oath, the man swung the nightstick down on his head.

Devin dropped to his knees, pain exploding in his head. He fought to stand, to ward off the next blow. When none came, he twisted, just in time to see his assailant scurry through the doorway.

"Hey!" Devin yelled as he caught a glimpse of spotless white tennis shoes and dark hair. Stumbling to his feet, he weaved toward the doorway, still holding his head. He reached the door in time to see the guy disappear through the exit door to the stairs.

It took him precious seconds to decide what to do. The elevator had already gone, so that wasn't an option—it took too long to come up. He tried to run for the stairs, but the pounding in his head slowed him. After his slow descent down the first few flights, he heard echoing steps far below and began to acknowledge he wasn't going to catch this guy.

Sure enough, when he reached the lobby, his assailant had disappeared, although Devin heard the sound of an engine roaring to life right outside. By the time he ran through the front doors, the only sign of the burglar was white smoke lingering in the air from what must have been the motorbike Devin had seen as he came in.

"Damn it, you bastard!" he shouted, gingerly rubbing the bruise knotting up on the back of his head. If the guy had a motorbike, he'd be long gone and damned hard to trace, since a motorbike could race down the skinniest alleyway inaccessible to a car. Devin would never find him now.

Frustrated and angry, Devin stalked to the pay phone in the lobby and called the cops, who promised to send someone as soon as possible.

Knowing it would be some time before they arrived—after all, this was only a burglary and a minor assault—he took the elevator back up to his apartment. Rage seethed within him. What a morning this had been! First, he'd gotten kicked out of Suzanne's house, then he'd been half beaten by a masked burglar!

He wondered if the guy had done any damage to his apartment. In the struggle, Devin hadn't exactly had time to look around, but the man couldn't have taken much, thanks to Devin's surprising him in the act.

By the time Devin reached his apartment, he'd reduced his rage to a low simmer. At least the guy hadn't walked out with his stereo. Then again, he thought, how would a guy on a motorbike have hauled off a stereo anyway, even if he hadn't been caught in the act?

That thought took hold of him as he walked in through the doorway to his apartment to discover that his apartment seemed little affected by the burglar's presence, except for the area where they'd fought. He looked around in disbelief. Not a single damned thing had been touched, and certainly nothing seemed missing. He went quickly to his hidden safe, but it was still locked and when he opened it, he found everything intact.

He released a sigh of relief. Apparently he'd surprised the burglar before the man could take anything or even look around much. Thank God for small favors.

Although his entire body ached from his struggle with the burglar, Devin felt slightly reassured to know that the guy hadn't gotten away with much. He walked to the couch and plopped down in the middle to wait for the cops. That was when he saw it. It was a small thing, a tiny, metal toollike object no bigger than three inches long, lying on the floor beneath the edge of his coffee table.

But it certainly hadn't been there before, so it had to have been left by the burglar. What was it? A tool for opening safes? No, that was ridiculous. He didn't know much about breaking and entering, but he figured safecrackers were pretty sophisticated these days. They probably used some fancy electronic doohickey for doing that kind of work.

He started to pick up the tool, then stopped when he remembered it might be useful to the cops in getting fingerprints. He stared at it a moment, then looked upward to the edge of the coffee table. The phone sat right above it.

An uneasiness came over him that wouldn't be dispelled. He distinctly remembered setting the phone on the couch before leaving the apartment.

But now it was sitting on the coffee table with a mysterious tool lying right under it. Hell, maybe he'd been watching too many detective movies lately, but it looked an awful lot to him as if someone had been fooling with his phone.

He shook his head at his foolish assumption. Nonetheless, he had a sudden urge to flee his apartment. Coming on the heels of Suzanne's strange revelations about Ressu's

Morse code messages and those thefts of "Endnote," this was a bit too weird for him.

Could someone actually have tampered with his phone, maybe even bugged it? A cold sweat broke out on his skin.

That's crazy, he told himself. *Why would anyone bug my apartment?*

Why indeed, he thought as he remembered the obsession everyone seemed to have with "Endnote" copies and the fact that he'd played the damned piece in front of God and everyone. A cold, sick fear suddenly assailed him. In a flash of memory, he heard Suzanne telling him about the guy who'd mugged her. Her assailant had been on a motorbike.

"Ah, hell!" Devin muttered aloud, his blood roaring in his ears.

"Endnote." That damned piece of music again.

Only with a great deal of effort did he resist the temptation to lift the phone and hurl it across the room. Fingerprints. He had to remember the cops could get fingerprints.

The thought of the cops helped him fight down the surge of panic rising in him like some subterranean monster. The cops were on their way, thank God. He looked around, wondering if any other bugs could have been planted. *You've been watching too many movies,* he told himself. Besides, the cops would get rid of any others or at least assure him there were none. Then everything would be back to normal.

Yeah, right. There was still some maniac out there trying to steal copies of "Endnote." If a message were really buried within the piece, that maniac was apparently aware of it and was willing to go to great lengths to keep it secret.

If the cops *did* find bugs in his apartment, that also meant the maniac was out there watching him, too, and all because he'd played the damned thing. Or could it be because of something else . . . his strange abilities . . . his past . . . his—

An iron net of fear dropped over his heart, squeezing,

destroying. His childhood filled his memory . . . flashes of veiled warnings by gang members . . . threatening talismans hung from the tree in the front yard . . . Dad's blood soaking into Mom's best "for company" chair.

He clenched his hands, willing the memories to disappear and with them the fear. He couldn't let fear wrap him in its icy ropes as it had Father. He had to stay strong, alert, and capable of confronting the enemy if necessary.

This Ressu business wasn't any different from the attack Mahoney had made on his family all those years ago. That battle had also been fought in the shadows of uncertainty and innuendo. Dad had let the sly forces of slander and treachery destroy him. Devin mustn't succumb to the same insidious tactics by becoming paranoid.

But the mysterious assailants weren't after only him, he reminded himself. A different kind of fear gripped him now, one far more paralyzing. If someone was after "Endnote" copies, Suzanne could be in far more danger than he was.

"Ressu, what have you gotten us both into?" Devin cried out, his voice twisted and tortured as it echoed in the silence of his apartment.

Out of the stillness came the faintest whish of a slip of a sound. The wind blowing outside? Some ghostly answer? Or was he just hearing things? Hell, this whole thing was making him doubt his sanity.

"That's enough, I've had it!" he gritted out, jumping to his feet and edging around the couch.

No more conjectures about all this. It was time to find out what Ressu had put in that damned piece. Time to sit down at the keyboard once and for all and let Ressu's ghost play to his heart's content.

Once Devin made that decision, his mind started racing. Yeah, that was what he had to do. Play the damned thing as many times as necessary. He had a tape recorder he used for recording bits of his own practice sessions. If he could get the mysterious "new version" of "Endnote" on tape, he might be able to decipher the message obviously hidden there. Then he could get the message to Suzanne.

Okay, so right now the woman wouldn't let him within a mile of her. It didn't matter. Once he'd recorded and decoded Ressu's message, he'd find a way to make her listen. Hopefully, it wouldn't take him long to figure it out.

Thank God Suzanne had explained to him last night how Ressu's Morse code messages worked. He ran over it again in his mind, satisfied that he remembered the musical theme she'd pointed out and the note she'd said was the message note. Hell, he already had part of the piece deciphered. What was it she'd told him? Part of the message in "Endnote" was "Listen, listen to what I have to say."

"Hey, Ressu!" he shouted into the eerie stillness of his apartment. "I hope you're here, and I sure as hell hope you're ready to put out! Because it's show time, buddy!"

And Devin was finally ready to listen.

15

♪

When Suzanne left the house, she thought a brisk walk over to the University of Chicago campus would do her good. She could clear her head, escape Mother's questions about what had gone on with Devin, and get her mind off her meeting with Amarcorp's CEO tonight, who would decide the festival's fate. Besides, she'd promised to take Cindy a copy of "Endnote."

Stupid, stupid, stupid, she thought now as she patted for the fiftieth time the place where a sealed manila envelope

SILENT SONATA

containing the thin sheaf of music lay nestled between her zipped-up jacket and her blouse.

As she strode under the chestnut trees, she scarcely noticed the scarlet flash of cardinals among the branches or the monarch butterflies floating from violet to rose. Instead her heart was pounding, her palms sweaty, and she'd spent the entire walk peeking back to see if anyone was following her. She was supposed to look nonchalant, but she probably looked more like a character from a bad spy movie. All she needed was a trench coat to complete the effect, she told herself peevishly.

True, she'd done everything she could to make her exit from the house appear typical. No one could possibly know what she was doing. She hadn't told Mother why she was leaving or called Cindy at the dorm to say she was coming. So she ought to be safe.

"Ought to be" wasn't much comfort, however, in light of the fact that someone had stolen the last copy of "Endnote" she'd walked over to the university. What if the assailant got more violent this time?

Now you're getting paranoid, she told herself.

Then she drew herself up stiffly. For Pete's sake, she had a right to be paranoid after all that had happened. She'd been mugged. Now someone was systematically trying to destroy her festival plans. And last night she'd been betrayed by a man she'd foolishly thought she could trust.

Pain sliced deep through her, reminding her why she'd really left the house—to get away from thoughts of Devin, the only man who'd ever turned her world upside down.

But that was fruitless, wasn't it? She couldn't help thinking of him. His curse had been working, just as he'd known it would. He haunted her thoughts every moment, until she wondered how many weeks, months, years, it would take to expunge him from her.

It had been only a few hours since they'd gone from whispering endearments to flinging accusations. Worst of all, the accusations made her doubt the endearments that had come before. She'd bared her heart to him, and what had she gotten for it?

So much for "going with the flow," she thought as the hollow feeling in the pit of her stomach intensified. Her torment increased in proportion to her memories—of intense looks, whispery kisses, languid caresses. Her breath caught in her throat. It had been such heaven to be held by him, to experience real passion in his arms.

So how could one man have been so gentle and so deceitful at the same time?

You didn't give him much of a chance to explain, a tiny voice whispered within her. *It might not have been as bad as you thought.*

She steeled herself against the weak impulses making her think such a thought. For Pete's sake, she'd found him rummaging through her papers! It almost surprised her he hadn't broken into her safe and stolen her copies of "Endnote"!

Come on, Suzanne, you're exaggerating, that same little voice said.

Well, maybe. But Devin had admitted he'd lied. It wasn't as if she'd accused him of something he hadn't done. Even if he hadn't stolen anything out of her office, it was obvious the man was up to no good.

Of course, he wouldn't need to steal a copy of "Endnote" anyway. He obviously already had one—he'd played it at the recital. Now that she knew he'd lied about his friendship with Valentin, she was back to her original thesis about how he'd known "Endnote."

But if he had a copy, why did he ask Paul for one? the insidious voice whispered.

The questions struck her as important, but she couldn't deal with them. "I don't know," she muttered to herself. Right now she didn't know anything. None of it made any sense—the lies he'd told were jumbled up with his apparent sincerity in other things he'd said.

And the passion they'd shared cast everything in a different light, so she no longer knew what was believable and what wasn't, when he'd been lying and when he'd been telling the truth.

You've got to stop obsessing about this, she told herself as she neared Cindy's dorm building. *It doesn't do any good to think about it, and you certainly don't need that complication in your life with everything else that's going on. Devin Bryce is no longer a part of your life—no seeing him, talking to him, or even thinking about him. Got that?*

Sure. Piece of cake. A simple task of tearing out her heart by the roots, so she wouldn't, couldn't feel anymore.

A heavy sigh escaped her lips. It was no use. The lonely, harsh, unyielding emotions banging holes in her insides wouldn't be put to rest with a few admonishing words. No, time would have to do that for her. If only she could make it hurry up, she thought as she entered Cindy's dorm building and climbed the stairs to the second floor.

Then she forcibly thrust thoughts of Devin from her mind for the moment to concentrate on her task at hand. Stopping in the second-floor hallway, she reoriented herself. She'd been here once or twice before, often enough to know where Cindy's room was. With any luck, Cindy would be in her room. If not, perhaps Cindy's roommate would let Suzanne in to stash "Endnote" somewhere.

Suzanne couldn't wait to get rid of the manuscript burning a hole in her jacket. Let Cindy deal with keeping the copy hidden.

Suzanne stopped in front of Cindy's room, relieved to have gotten there without incident. She settled her beret more firmly on her head, then raised her hand to knock, but a low moan coming from inside stopped her.

Her eyes widened. For a second, she thought Cindy or her roommate might be hurt. Suzanne put her hand on the doorknob, fully intending to burst into the room.

Then a giggle from inside made her change her mind. Feeling a little guilty, she hesitated there, listening, uncertain whether to knock or come back later or wait outside for a few more minutes.

She heard a young female voice inside ask with husky seductiveness, "How do you like it? Is it sexy or what?"

The voice was Cindy's, she realized, no doubt about it. There was also no doubt about what was going on behind the door. Suzanne's skin flamed as a long silence ensued. Turning from the door, she started to walk away.

Then she heard an awkward male voice reply, "It sure is. But you'd be sexy no matter *what* you were wearing." The voice deepened, recovering from its shock. "Now come here and let me take it off of you."

She knew the voice instantly. Paul. Oh, for crying out loud. Paul and Cindy. How long had this been going on?

A strange wave of protectiveness welled up within her. Paul was only eighteen, and Cindy was about to graduate. Okay, so that wasn't a big difference in age, but he certainly wasn't in Cindy's league. The older girl had the looks to bring any man on campus to his knees. Why was she hanging around with Paul, who unfortunately was a little homely?

Possibilities swarmed through Suzanne's head, most of them awful. *She's using him,* Suzanne thought instantly, then chastened herself. *Don't jump to conclusions. Paul can be a real sweetheart when he wants to be.*

A soft murmuring from the other side of the door reminded her that Paul was being a real sweetheart right now. For an instant last night flashed through her mind. She closed her eyes in torment, fighting the warm desire rising in her belly.

And that was how Cindy's roommate found her, standing there like a guilty voyeur outside the door.

"Hey, you here to see Cindy?" the roommate asked breezily as she fitted her key in the lock, oblivious to the faint sounds coming from within the room.

"Uh . . . uh . . ." Suzanne had lost all capacity for

speech, too busy dealing with her embarrassment at being caught listening at the door.

Cindy's roommate didn't seem to notice. "I think she's here," she was saying as she thrust open the door. "But if she isn't, you're welcome to come in and wait—" The roommate broke off when she caught sight of the two naked bodies sprawled on the bed.

Suzanne and the roommate stood transfixed at the sight as the two inhabitants of the bed stopped their activity to gape at whoever had dared to interrupt. Surprisingly, Cindy's face showed agitation rather than embarrassment. But Paul's expression mirrored Suzanne's as he turned scarlet from his hairline to the tips of his toes and everything . . . *everything* . . . in between.

Suzanne thought she'd drop through the floor if she didn't get out of there quickly. Lowering her eyes, she babbled, "Hi, Paul, Cindy. Just came by to give Cindy the copy of 'Endnote' she asked for."

Then she swiftly unzipped her jacket and whisked out the manila envelope. Still keeping her eyes averted, she dropped the envelope on the nearest flat surface, and muttered, "See you later."

Without another word she fled.

"I can't believe I did that," she mumbled to herself as she made a beeline for the stairs, wondering what the three undergraduates must have thought of her. Which would they consider worse—her leaving the manuscript and talking to them as if nothing had happened? Or her embarrassment at seeing Cindy and Paul coupling right there before her eyes?

Probably the latter, considering the nonchalant attitude most of her students had toward sex. Cindy, Paul, and Cindy's roommate were probably at this very minute discussing how she was a "typical, uptight professor," but she didn't care. If it meant she was a prude, so be it, but she definitely wasn't used to barging in on people while they were . . . well . . . doing it.

Suddenly she heard a voice call her name behind her. She was tempted to ignore it and keep going, but she didn't. With an aggrieved sigh, she stopped and turned, chagrined to see Paul running down the hall after her, buttoning his shirt as he came.

At least he's got his pants on now, she thought wryly.

As he neared, his face reddened again, but he quickly gained control of his emotions. "Suzanne, I want to explain—"

She shook her head to stop him, not wanting to hear a complete litany of his relationship with Cindy, not at the moment anyway. "There's no need. What you do in your private life is your own business. I—I'm terribly sorry I came in while you and Cindy were . . . oh, blast it, you know what I mean."

He thrust the hair out of his face, allowing her to see the sheepish grin forming on his lips. "Yeah, I know. Uh . . . don't worry about it. I know it was kind of embarrassing, but—"

"Let's stop talking about it, okay?" Her face reddened again. "Look, I did what I came to do, so I'm going home now." She managed a weak grin. "Then I'm going to shut myself up in the house for about a week until I can stop blushing."

He smiled. "I guess it was a shock, huh?"

"To say the least," she muttered, turning to go.

He detained her with one hand. "Suzanne?"

She sighed and turned to face him. "What?"

"Are you . . . are you going to tell Mother?"

The question took her completely by surprise. She looked at him incredulously. "About what? Finding you in bed with a girl . . . er . . . woman?"

"No, no." The words rushed out. "But . . . well, if Mother knows about Cindy and me . . ."

Suzanne was beginning to get an inkling of the source of his agitation. "Yes?"

He stared down at his feet, hanging his head a little as he

used to when he was a boy. He tucked his hair behind his ears and sighed. "It was *my* idea that Mother choose Cindy as pianist for the festival. I went on and on about how Father thought Cindy was such a great student and stuff like that until she agreed with me. But if she thinks I did it just because Cindy and I—"

"Did you?" Suzanne asked quietly, but she knew the answer. She'd taught enough freshmen boys to know that hormones were an incredibly powerful force in an eighteen-year-old male, second only to the hunger for pizza, or for that matter, any food that came in sufficiently huge quantities.

"Well . . . not exactly . . . I mean, Cindy's talented, you know? She's got a lot of ability. And Father did like her playing . . . at least, I *think* he did."

Suzanne couldn't help it. After all that had happened in the last few days, Paul's last statement struck her as funny. A hysterical giggle rose in her throat, which turned into full-throated laughter that wouldn't stop.

Paul looked angry, then alarmed. "Suzanne! What's got into you?"

She shook her head and gasped out between bursts of laughter, "I . . . I don't know . . . oh, Paul . . . you *think* Valentin liked her playing?" She forced herself to calm down, aware that Paul found her laughter very insulting. It took an effort, but after a few moments, she got her hysterical hilarity partially under control.

She shook her head, fighting down another wild giggle. "We chose Cindy to play because you . . . you had the hots for her?" She paused for breath. "For Pete's sake, Paul, couldn't you find another way to show your affection?"

The stony expression on his face sobered her up the remainder of the way. He thrust his chest out and planted his hands on his hips, looking for all the world like his father had looked when he was angry. "She's a good pianist, and you know it."

"Well, yes, but—"

"You're just prejudiced against her because she's not only talented, but popular and sexy, too. You think the only women who have any brains and ability are stiff-faced, prudish professors like you! You're jealous, that's all!"

The accusation hit Suzanne like a blow to the chest, and it brought the same kind of physical pain. She wanted to defend herself, to taunt him by saying that Devin Bryce had found her sexy, Devin Bryce, one of the most talented pianists in America. Then she reminded herself that Devin Bryce had also lied to her about a lot of things. Her sexiness might have been one of them.

Paul continued to stand there, cocky and arrogant, convinced of the soundness of his argument. She knew he was wrong—boy, how she knew it—but she also knew arguing with him wasn't the best thing to do right now, not when he had that stubborn look on his face. All he'd do was hurt her more if she tried to defend herself, and she couldn't bear any more pain at the moment.

Still, Paul reminded her of Devin right now, and she felt an insane urge to hit him in the stomach as hard as she could, to make him hurt as she was hurting. Or better yet, to point out to him that Cindy's involvement with him was undoubtedly motivated by self-interest.

No, she told herself, *I can't be that cruel, even if it is probably true.*

Instead, she'd better get away and nurse her wounds in private before she struck out and said something she'd regret later. She whirled on her heel and stalked off down the stairs, trying to maintain her dignity, not caring that he would view her retreat as a victory.

She could hear him stumbling down the steps after her.

"Suzanne, wait!" he called out.

She increased her speed, the anger building in her like a volcanic flood.

"Are you going to tell Mother?" he shouted from the stairs.

Shaking her head, she kept going. She didn't know how he'd interpret that, and she didn't care. She had to get out of there.

Would she tell Mariela? she thought to herself as she half ran through the dorm doors and onto the sidewalk. Probably not. Mariela was still wavering in her decision to cancel the festival concert, and hearing about Cindy and Paul certainly wouldn't persuade her not to cancel.

Besides, Cindy probably was the best pianist for the job anyway. With the funding problems the festival was having at the moment, it would have been hard to find a big-name pianist to play the pieces who wouldn't also charge an arm and a leg.

Still, it galled Suzanne that Cindy had manipulated Paul in order to get what she wanted. And Paul in turn had manipulated Suzanne. Suzanne winced. First Devin. Then Paul. *And let's not forget dear Mr. Goma,* she told herself cynically, *another man out to sabotage my life. It's enough to turn a woman into a man-hater.*

She shook her head, walking briskly toward her house. She couldn't make this mess disappear simply by assigning blame. No, she'd have to work her way through it. If she could detach herself emotionally from it all, review it logically and analytically, and somehow find the thread of sense running through the incidents . . .

Her stomach roiled at the thought of sorting out the past few days into neat little groupings of three. Then the truth hit her with startling clarity, jolting her from her planning: she couldn't disengage anymore. No matter how she tried, she couldn't rationalize the emotions away. They lay inside her, powerful and heart-wrenching lumps of raw pain.

Tears welled in her eyes. *Oh, blast it,* she told herself, *I'm not going to start blubbering like a baby, am I?*

She needed someone right now, and there was no one to help her through this. Valentin was dead, and she had no one else. Except Mother. Although it was absurd, she had this crazy desire to talk to Mother, to unburden herself and try to gain comfort from the woman who surely knew more about emotion than anyone.

The more she thought about it, the more she clasped the idea to her like a lifeline. Yes, Mother would understand, wouldn't she? Suzanne glanced at her watch. Mother wouldn't have left for the gallery yet.

She thought a moment. Mother would understand the feelings, but the question was, would she care? Suzanne didn't know if she was ready to bare herself to her mother and risk having her make light of the torment in Suzanne's soul. Then again, had Suzanne ever really tried to establish an emotional connection with her mother? She'd always feared being rejected or having her pain made light of by her sharp-witted, cynical mother.

Still, what if she'd been mistaken about the woman who'd raised her? What if all it took was for Suzanne to take that one step forward, to risk the possible rejection?

The possibility took hold of her as she hurried toward her house. After all, her life already lay in a shambles around her. What did she have to lose?

Her heart raced as she neared her house. Maybe it was time to take a chance. She took the steps two at a time and swung open the door, which her mother always kept unlocked.

Maybe if she simply . . .

The thought fled her mind as she stepped inside, for her mother sat gingerly on the edge of the love seat, and across from her was seated Lydia Chelminscu.

Suzanne stopped short in the doorway, staring. It took her a moment to leash her feelings and don her public persona once again.

What on earth was the Romanian woman doing here?

Aloud she said, "Lydia! How nice to see you."

Lydia rose to her feet. "I hope you don't mind me visiting you like this. I needed to speak with you about some matters concerning the festival concert."

"No problem." Actually Suzanne wished Lydia had chosen a better time. Suzanne had a sneaking suspicion she knew why Lydia was there. No doubt Ion's poison had spread further. For Pete's sake, this was a mess. Too bad Lydia hadn't waited until after Suzanne's appointment with the head of Amarcorp. At least then Suzanne would have had something to tell her.

Suzanne's mother stood up as well. "I'll leave you two alone then. I have to get ready to go to the gallery anyway." She straightened her dress surreptitiously, then smiled, a little coldly even for her. "Suzanne, I only need to give you a few messages. Could I speak with you in the kitchen a moment?"

"Of course." Suzanne turned to Lydia, flashing her a reassuring smile. "I'll be with you in a second. Make yourself at home."

Her mother whisked out of the room, and Suzanne followed her.

As soon as they cleared the kitchen door, her mother shut it with a mysterious look. "Who *is* that woman?"

"She's one of the members of the festival concert planning committee. Why?"

"I found her wandering around outside, poking in the bushes and muttering to herself. I think she's a little . . . you know"—she paused to make a circular motion next to her ear—"loony. She scared the wits out of me when I caught sight of her outside the window."

Suzanne shivered, her eyes narrowing. "That *is* strange. I wonder what that was all about."

"I don't know, but I'd keep an eye on her if I were you," her mother admonished with dramatic emphasis, raising both eyebrows knowingly.

Look at us, Suzanne thought suddenly. *Mother and I are as jumpy and suspicious as two old maids with a gigolo.*

Resisting the urge to smile, Suzanne tried to look serious. "Yes, yes, I'll keep an eye on her, Mother. Thanks for the warning. Now I'd better get out there before she does any more snooping."

Her mother nodded, a concerned expression on her face. Suzanne's urge to smile faded, and a lump formed in her throat. This was her mother, after all, the woman who'd given birth to her. Yes, Mother had a lot of irritating characteristics, and Lord knew she could drive most people nuts. Sometimes Suzanne even wondered if Felicia Winslow wasn't a little loony herself.

Still . . .

Bowing to an impulse, Suzanne gave her mother a quick hug and whispered in her ear, "I love you."

For a moment, her mother looked startled. Her mouth gaped open, and she stared at her daughter as if seeing her for the first time. Her lower lip began to tremble. Then she lifted her hand to whisk a lock of hair back from Suzanne's forehead.

For a moment, a chord of understanding was struck between them, and Suzanne glimpsed a hint of what her mother must have been like when she was a young, hopeful sculptor, looking at the world through idealistic eyes.

Then her mother drew her devil-may-care, woman-of-the-world cloak about her again and dropped her hand. "You're a good girl, Zanny," she said in an oddly strained tone. Then she pushed her daughter out of the kitchen. "Now go get that madwoman out of our . . . I mean, your . . . house before I leave, so I won't worry about what she's doing in here while I'm gone!"

Suzanne strolled back into the living room, a faint smile on her face. Maybe there was a tiny place in Mother's heart for her after all, she thought. Perhaps the time had come in her life to find out.

But first she had to deal with Lydia. She made her smile brighter as she rounded the love seat and sat down.

"I'm sorry. Mother had a number of messages to pass on to me that she felt couldn't wait."

Lydia nodded, her eyes flickering briefly. "Your mother probably thought I was a little mad."

Suzanne's hands tensed in her lap. Surely the woman

hadn't listened in on their conversation? The thought sent chills through her. "What do you mean?"

With a shrug, Lydia cocked her head to one side and studied Suzanne. "She saw me examining the bushes outside your house. I think she thought I was a burglar."

"Ah, yes," Suzanne remarked uneasily. "Well, she did happen to mention that."

Lydia nodded. "I thought she might. I suppose I *am* a trifle crazy. All of us who lived in Romania under Ceauşescu are that way. We see microphones everywhere. We worry about who is lurking under the windows." She gave a tentative smile, although the eyes behind that smile were calculating. "I find myself checking rooms always to see where a microphone or a camera could be hidden. Ceauşescu was insane about surveillance." She shook her head, her expression darkening in remembrance. "Did you know that Ceauşescu had microphones installed in nearly *every* room in the entire country?"

Suzanne nodded. She'd heard Ion Goma talking about it once.

"Reams and reams of paper were produced daily," Lydia continued, "printouts of conversations. We all knew that other ears heard our every word. It was like living in the world's largest one-room apartment." She shook her head mournfully, her gaze fixed on some distant point beyond Suzanne's vision. "Never any privacy."

She snapped her attention back to Suzanne as a wan smile crossed her face. "So we are all paranoid, and I most of all, for I was part of a dissident group seeking to free Romania from the tyrant. I spent most of my days in house arrest."

Suzanne hadn't known that. She gazed at Lydia with concern. "It must have been difficult."

Suddenly looking uncomfortable, Lydia nodded. Then she drew in a deep breath. "Ah, but now those days are past us. We are free."

Suzanne got the impression that Lydia was saying the

opposite of what she really thought. In truth, Suzanne knew the Romanians were still debating whether or not the new government represented substantial, healing change. Its leaders, after all, had been Communists once, although they'd opposed Ceauşescu.

Abruptly Lydia fixed Suzanne with an intent gaze. "Which brings me to why I have come to speak with you. Ion Goma has expressed his concern to me about these robberies. He is, like me, paranoid."

Suzanne stiffened. "Yes, I know. He wants me to step down as coordinator of the festival concert."

Lydia leaned forward, bracing her elbows on her thighs and cupping her hands together. Her eyes probed Suzanne's face. "Do you wish to do as Ion asks?"

"No, of course not." Suzanne shook her head violently. "This is my project. I have to do this."

For a moment, Lydia remained silent, her hands lying calmly in her lap. Then she sighed. "I thought you would say that. Don't misunderstand me. I believe you are the best person for the job. Ion Goma is a hothead. He could never run a project of this magnitude on his own. Mariela knows it, and so do I. Unfortunately . . ." She trailed off, looking away.

"What?" Suzanne demanded as she detected a hint of foreboding in Lydia's voice. "Tell me what you've come to say, Lydia."

Lydia sat back, smoothing her skirts as she did so. At that moment, Suzanne's mother breezed in the room. "I'm leaving now, Zanny. I don't know when I'll be home."

Suzanne looked up. The faintest smile of affection graced her mother's face. Her mother's gaze moved to Lydia, then back to Suzanne and there was a hint of concern in her eyes. Then she sniffed and left the house.

As soon as the door shut behind Suzanne's mother, Lydia lifted a cool, distant gaze to meet Suzanne's. "My government has expressed concern about the way the festival concert is being run. They have requested that I withdraw their support, financial and otherwise."

"But they'll change their minds if I step down, right?" Suzanne put in bitterly.

"No, no," Lydia hastened to say. Then she made an equivocal gesture with her hand. "All right, yes, perhaps they would, but only because that would restore Amarcorp's faith in the project. My government does not like trouble, you understand? They want everything to move smoothly."

"It *will* move smoothly, don't worry. I have a meeting with Amarcorp tonight. It will all work out, you'll see. But I'm not stepping down. If I have to mount this festival concert by myself, I will. You have to talk to them, Lydia. You have to explain I can take care of it."

For the briefest moment, Suzanne thought she glimpsed terror behind Lydia's polite, government-official expression. But it was gone so fast Suzanne wasn't certain if she'd seen it at all.

"I know you will organize it beautifully. I have told my government so. But they insist on withdrawing support. I am sorry. There is nothing I can do about it."

"But Lydia, the things that have happened have been so minor. I don't understand why it should concern the Romanian government."

Lydia nodded. "You are right. They are minor." She looked away from Suzanne, an expression of discomfort crossing her face.

That's when Suzanne knew there was something else, some other reason for the Romanian government's pulling out. "Tell me the truth. Why are they really withdrawing?"

Lydia looked startled. Then her face stiffened. She hesitated a moment, then leaned forward again to whisper, "I cannot tell you."

"Why not?" Suzanne said in her normal voice, which elicited a furious glare from Lydia.

"It is . . . dangerous to tell you. Now you tell me something. Why are you so concerned with this concert that you will ignore these . . . these incidents that are happening to ruin it?"

"That ought to be clear to everyone! Valentin was my mentor, my friend! I think he deserves a fine tribute, don't you? And what do you mean by *dangerous*?"

Lydia shrugged. "There are things about Valentin Ressu that you do not know. I cannot tell you what they are, but you must trust me when I say you don't want to know."

Suzanne's mother had hinted at much the same thing only the day before, but Suzanne didn't enjoy hearing it any more now than she had then. She glared at Lydia resentfully.

A cold deadness entered Lydia's eyes, frightening in its hollowness. "You should end your involvement with this concert immediately. You are . . . dabbling in matters of enormous import. You must get out while you can."

Suzanne's eyes narrowed. "This has to do with 'Endnote,' doesn't it? You know who's behind the thefts of 'Endnote.' "

Lydia lowered her voice to an angry whisper. "If you have any copies of that wretched piece, you should throw them out! You must listen to me. You put yourself in grave danger by persisting with this festival concert!"

The desperation behind Lydia's words told Suzanne quite effectively that she'd stumbled onto some government secret of frightening importance. "Why? Tell me all of it, Lydia, and I'll cancel the concert myself."

Lydia shook her head, her expression becoming wary all of a sudden. She'd said too much, and she knew it. Still, she lowered her voice and leaned forward to say, "You should look closer to home for the person behind the thefts. There is . . . ah . . . a certain individual who would go to great lengths to force you down as committee chairman. Perhaps even to stage a few . . . ah . . . robberies to make you look bad. You understand?"

Suzanne's eyes narrowed. Only one person wanted her out. "Are you talking about Ion Goma?"

Lydia's expression didn't change. "This person, whoever it is, could be very dangerous. And he . . . or she will not stop until you are out of it. Even if it takes hurting you physically. Now do you understand why you must abandon the project?"

"I'm not giving this up, no matter what idiocy Ion Goma tries. But if you have evidence that he's at fault, then perhaps I can have the police—"

"No!" For a brief moment, fear flared in Lydia's eyes. "No. I have no proof. Of anything. Only suspicions. But do you wish to continue with this madness until you do have proof? And you are perhaps lying dead somewhere?"

Suzanne shuddered. "I'm sorry, Lydia. Perhaps you're right about Ion, but I think you're exaggerating."

"Fine. But you cannot say I did not warn you."

"But, Lydia—"

The woman stood abruptly, then turned and pointed an oddly well-manicured finger at Suzanne. "You don't know what you are dealing with." She lowered the finger. Reaching down to pick up her light coat, which she'd apparently been sitting on all this time, she shook her head. "You simply do not understand. Well then, go on with your foolishness. My government will not support it."

Then Lydia donned her coat quickly, smoothing the rumpled twill. And without another word to Suzanne, she whisked out the door, slamming it behind her.

Suzanne sat there stunned for a moment, shocked into silence by Lydia's vehemence. For Pete's sake, could Lydia really believe Ion would try to kill her? Oh, sure, the man had a temper, but murder? Simply because she wasn't Romanian?

Or did Lydia have another reason for warning Suzanne that she wasn't revealing? And what about that crack that Suzanne didn't know everything about Valentin? Good Lord, all these people with secrets. Devin and Lydia were poking around inside and outside her house. People were warning her off the festival concert right and left. And copies of "Endnote" were disappearing.

She shook her head, her throat tightening. Maybe Lydia was right. Maybe it was time to rethink this whole scheme of hers.

Then she caught sight of the piano with Ressu's bust, and tears stung her eyes. She remembered a few moments ago, when she'd told Mother she loved her and Mother hadn't been able to say it in return. Valentin had said it and often. He'd meant it, too. Even Paul had to admit that while he hadn't always gotten along with his father, Valentin had never denied him genuine affection.

And genuine affection seemed to be a rare commodity these days, Suzanne thought with sorrow, remembering the way Devin had touched her even as he told her lies.

She clutched her stomach and bent over, tears beginning to flow. "Tell me what to do, Valentin. I want to repay you for everything you gave me. But it's getting harder and harder all the time."

Then she dropped her head into her lap and sobbed.

16

♪

Devin exited the Dan Ryan Expressway, grateful he'd missed rush hour traffic. He rubbed his eyes with one hand, fighting to stay awake. How much sleep had he gotten in the last few days? Two hours? Three? Yeah, three at most.

A weak smile crossed his face. Ah, but he'd managed to transcribe Ressu's message, and that was all that mattered.

Well . . . except getting it to Suzanne. Transcribing the message had been a breeze compared to that. He'd called and left numerous messages on her answering machine. Reluctant to say anything about "Endnote" on the phone for fear her phone might also be bugged, he'd merely asked her to call and said it was urgent.

Apparently, she didn't believe him. She'd ignored every message. Then he'd gone to her house, but she'd refused to answer the door, although Bartok had meowed at him from the other side. Finally, he'd resorted to the ultimate devious means and had left a message on the machine for Felicia Winslow instead.

Thank God Felicia Winslow apparently still liked him despite the other night's fiasco, he thought. That had made it easy to coax out of her Suzanne's schedule for the day. Felicia hadn't been able to tell him the room or building number—he'd had to call the university's music department to get that.

But he'd gotten it.

He glanced quickly at his watch. It was 10:10 A.M. Good, he wouldn't miss Suzanne's class. He shook his head as he came up East Fifty-fifth Street. Getting her to listen might be tricky, but now that he knew the message, it was essential.

He patted his pocket to reassure himself the transcribed message was still there. But he didn't need the written words to remember Ressu's message: *"Listen, listen to what I have to tell you. Love yields death if altars kill men.* Radu. Radu." Those four lines seemed all of a piece. They didn't make much sense, but he figured the first two were enigmatic lines of the kind Suzanne had described, and "Radu" was some important Romanian word Ressu had stuck at the end.

As far as Devin was concerned, the real message came a few bars later. *"Destroy all copies of 'Endnote,' "* it said. The meaning of the other lines might have been impenetrable, but there was no mistaking what Ressu meant in the last one. Ressu was pretty explicit for a dead man. No doubt this was the new passage, which Ressu had inserted during Devin's first recital and which Suzanne had never heard before then.

Still, Ressu's message didn't offer any explanation of why the manuscript should be destroyed, and that irritated Devin. Couldn't the composer have added a few words to clarify? Hell, Suzanne would look at Devin as if he were stark raving mad when he showed her this. She already thought he was suspicious as hell. What would she think when he told her the ghost of her dead mentor wanted her to destroy the copies of his last work?

Maybe Devin should tell her about the "electronic monitoring devices" the police had found in his apartment. For a moment the familiar creeping terror came over him. He hadn't told the cops his theories about why the bugs were there, but he had some definite theories. Someone was awfully interested in tracking down all the copies of "Endnote."

He stared at the bruises on his hand from where he'd pummeled his assailant. No wonder Ressu wanted it destroyed. Apparently half the underworld wanted a copy of the thing, although Devin hadn't yet figured out why. The old guy must know something the rest of them didn't. Now all Devin had to do was get Suzanne to listen to Ressu's message and destroy every existing copy.

Yeah, right. With a sigh, Devin pulled into the parking lot next to the University of Chicago Hospitals on the edge of campus. He glanced at his watch again: 10:20 A.M. Suzanne's mother had said her class ended at 11:00 A.M. He'd better hustle.

And hustle he did, despite the soreness he still felt in his ribs. It took him only ten minutes to find Suzanne's class in Goodspeed Hall. He stood outside the classroom, wondering what to do. Accost her when she came outside? Go in and get her?

He peeked into the room through a window in the door.

SILENT SONATA

To his relief, the class was relatively small. At least he wouldn't lose her in a rush of students exiting the room. As he scanned the room, he caught sight of her standing at the front with her back to the class, filling notes in on the blank musical staff painted on the chalkboard and gesturing as she spoke.

Hell, the woman looked good enough to eat. As usual, she wore her jaunty beret perched on her head, but her hair cascaded out from beneath it like a flow of gold. Her blouse looked impeccable, modest but attractive. And every time she stretched up to place a note on the top line, her straight skirt cupped her bottom slightly.

He muttered a curse as his loins tightened. Didn't she have any idea what a fetching picture she made like that? Quickly he glanced around the room at the male students. Most were busy scribbling, but he caught sight of one tapping his pencil and smiling as he watched Professor Winslow's cute little behind.

Devin wanted to throttle him. Instead, Devin eased the door open and took a seat at the back of the room, next to the lecherous undergraduate.

"Hey, aren't you supposed to be taking notes or something instead of gawking at your teacher?" Devin muttered to the student while trying to fit his lanky body comfortably into the ridiculously small student desk.

"Hey, who the hell are you?" the student snapped, giving him a quick once-over. "That teacher's got a nice ass, or hadn't you noticed? I'll stare at it if I want."

Devin clenched one fist under the desk top. "Uh-huh. Well, I'll mention to Professor Winslow the full extent of your interest in anatomy when she and I have dinner this evening."

It was petty, maybe, but effective. The kid looked him over again, glancing from him to Suzanne and back. Then with a shrug he bent his head and starting scribbling.

Devin's self-indulgent smile lasted only a second, however, before Suzanne turned around, and her eyes met his.

The minute their gazes locked, he forgot about the undergraduate and Suzanne's skirt and even the transcribed message from Ressu tucked into his shirt pocket.

He forgot everything except how much he wanted to erase the hurt expression now crossing her face. She too hadn't been sleeping well, as evidenced by the faint pallor to her skin and the hint of dark circles under her eyes. Bleak pain tightening her lips, she flinched from his gaze, as if the force of it on her was too much to bear.

Then she seemed to pull herself together, to acknowledge the roomful of waiting students. She continued lecturing for a few minutes, her discomfort only slightly evident in the self-conscious way she spoke.

Suddenly she halted her lecture. A slow smile creased her mouth with a hint of cynical humor. "Some of you may have noticed that we have a guest with us today."

Devin instinctively cringed. Several pairs of eyes surveyed the room until they settled on the one suspicious character who didn't fit. He ignored the whispers of interest and watched Suzanne, wondering what she was up to now.

Her smile broadened. "The pianists among you may recognize Mr. Devin Bryce from his concert photos. I know you'll be familiar with his excellent playing."

The whispers grew louder then. He tried not to feel like a zoo animal on display.

"The rest of you have probably heard of him from the papers, so I'm sure you're all aware of his reputation for brilliance."

She didn't have to say it with such sarcasm, Devin thought, stiffening in the uncomfortable chair.

"Since he's decided to grace us with his presence today" —she continued to address the class, darting an occasional smug glance his way—"I think it would be wonderful if he'd agree to speak to us about the hardships and rewards of being a famous concert pianist. What do you think?"

Devin groaned as the class let out a chorus of approval.

SILENT SONATA

Trust Suzanne to come up with this ingenious way of humiliating him publicly, he thought. She definitely had her heart set on getting back at him for lying to her. Well, at least she hadn't thrown him out of the classroom.

"Mr. Bryce?" she asked from the front of the room, a note of challenge evident in her voice.

No way in hell was he going to resist *that*. He untangled himself from the cramped desk and stood. "Sure. Why not?" Deliberately he flashed her his most charming grin.

To his complete surprise, she colored. Ah, so she wasn't as immune to him as she pretended. The thought comforted him as he made his way up the narrow aisle.

"Thank you so much, Mr. Bryce." Heavy irony coated her words. She held out the chalk to him as he reached the front. "I know my students will enjoy hearing anything you have to say. It will also give me the opportunity to go back to my office and grade the papers they've been begging me to finish."

Another loud murmur of approval came from the class, but he scarcely heard it. So that was her game, eh? Disappear while she had him trapped at the front of the classroom? He shook his head. The woman didn't know whom she was dealing with, did she?

He took the chalk from her, making certain their fingers touched as he did so. She jerked her hand back from him as if it had been burned. The taunting smile vanished from her face. In her eyes shone resentment, distress, and a definite urge to strangle him.

Well, he could deal with that. Later. "Thank you, Professor Winslow, but I'd hoped you'd stay to hear me speak."

"I'm sorry, but I can't." She turned to leave. He could tell from her stiff spine that she was using every ounce of control to keep from tearing into him.

"Suit yourself." Feigning nonchalance, he turned to the class. In a loud voice, he announced, "I know your professor wants me to speak on life as a famous pianist, but I'd rather discuss a new discovery that's been made about Valentin Ressu's work. How many of you know how Morse code works?"

The students shrugged and cast glances at each other, but out of the corner of his eye, Devin saw Suzanne stop short on her way out the door. She turned slowly and fixed him with a wrathful gaze guaranteed to fry him on the spot.

"I suppose most of you are at least familiar with Valentin Ressu's compositions," he continued now that he had her attention. "After all, I understand he was composer-in-residence here for a while."

Several students nodded, trying to look knowledgeable.

"Excuse me," came Suzanne's hollow-sounding voice from the door. "Mr. Bryce, before you continue with your intriguing topic, could I have a word with you?"

He bit back a grin. "Of course." He gave the class a broad wink. "This will only take a minute. Teacher wants me in the hall."

To a chorus of chuckles, he strode from the room, shutting the door behind him.

"How dare you!" she snapped the second the door was shut. "You have no right—"

"I had to talk to you. I couldn't think of any other way to get your attention. You wouldn't answer my calls, and you wouldn't open the door to me when I came by yesterday. What else was I supposed to do?"

"You were supposed to leave me alone! I didn't answer your calls because I didn't wish to see you!"

He'd never felt so lonely in his life. Even her stance was defensive. She held her arms crossed over her chest and stood separate and apart, as if an invisible and very thick wall stood between them.

It shattered him to see her as closed today as she'd been open two nights ago. "Okay, shut me out of your life. Try to forget everything that happened between us." His voice lowered to a husky whisper. "Go on, do it. Blot out of your mind the night we made love." Her expression grew even more stony, but he went on relentlessly. "But at least listen to me for five minutes."

She shook her head wordlessly, then pivoted and began to walk away.

"You know that new passage you claimed I'd added to 'Endnote'?" he called down the hall after her.

She paused a moment. Slowly she turned to stare at him. She didn't speak, but he could see the spark of interest in her eyes.

"There *was* a new passage," he continued. "And after you showed me the Morse code stuff, I worked out what it said."

"Where did you get this new version?" Her words were clipped and harsh, reminding him that she didn't trust him one bit.

He sucked in his breath. Must he explain all that here? Now? Was there some way he could get her to listen to the message first and then his explanation about how he got it?

No. Suzanne wouldn't listen to him until she knew everything, and this might be his only chance to get her alone again. But hell, they were standing in the middle of a public hall, with a bunch of curious students only a few steps away, for Chrisake!

As he stood there, uncertain what to do, a voice echoed from behind him, calling Suzanne's name.

Suzanne's gaze shifted as Devin half turned to see what was going on. An elderly woman and a short, burly man in uniform were coming up the hall, anxious looks on their faces.

"There she is!" cried the woman to the man, gesturing down the hall to Suzanne.

Suzanne apparently recognized the woman. "What is it, Phoebe?"

Devin remembered that Phoebe was the name of the secretary he'd spoken to that morning.

"Oh, dear. You won't believe what's happened!" Phoebe began babbling as she and the man reached Devin and

Suzanne. "It's . . . it's simply dreadful! First you and then Cindy! I can't believe it! On *this* campus! I never thought I'd see the day—"

Suzanne turned her questioning gaze to the uniformed man, who apparently was a campus policeman. "What on earth has happened?"

"You're acquainted with Cindy Stephens, aren't you, professor?" the man asked.

Suzanne frowned. "Yes, of course. She's the pianist for the Ressu festival concert I'm spearheading."

"Well, looks like somebody don't like her too much. There's been another mugging, like the one they done on you. Only . . ." His jaw clenched, making him look like a fierce bulldog.

"Only what?" Suzanne's hands had fallen limply at her sides, and her mouth was drawn tight with concern.

Devin moved to stand beside her, then placed his hand on her back reassuringly. She didn't seem to notice, though she unconsciously moved closer to him.

"Well," the burly man went on, his eyes lowering from hers. He looked extremely uncomfortable. "Looks as if her attacker knocked her out, then took a hammer or something and . . . well, he must have hit the fingers of her right hand with it. Broke 'em all in several places."

A choked gasp left Suzanne's lips. "Oh, dear Lord, Cindy," Suzanne whispered, closing her eyes. "Her fingers, her poor fingers . . ."

Remembering the nightstick he'd been hit with a few days ago, Devin cringed. The muscles in his hands instinctively tightened, as if to protect themselves from this terrible evil that deigned to take away a pianist's ability to play.

"Not Cindy, not Cindy," Suzanne kept repeating, her cheeks pale as death. "I—I should have known something like this would happen. It's all my fault. I—I should have listened to Lydia. . . . I should have listened to her!"

Suzanne's words brought Devin up short.

Apparently they had the same effect on the campus officer, whose eyes narrowed instantly. "Excuse me, Professor. Who's Lydia?" He reached into his pocket and flipped out a notepad.

Suzanne stared at the officer, her eyes wide and frightened. "She's . . . she's a member of the festival concert planning committee. She was concerned about me because of the mugging, and she . . . she seemed to think that . . . that I should call the concert off or at least destroy the copies of 'Endnote.'"

Sheer black terror clutched at Devin. This Lydia had tried to warn Suzanne about "Endnote," too? he thought with a shudder. What the hell was the significance of that piece of music anyway?

"'Endnote'?" the officer asked.

"'Endnote' was the manuscript the mugger stole from me." Suzanne's mouth grew taut. "Do you know if Cindy had a copy of 'Endnote' on her?"

"Don't know," the officer muttered.

"Cindy was going to play 'Endnote' at the festival?" Devin interrupted. He couldn't put that nightstick out of his mind. The officer's eyes grew more alert as he watched Suzanne for the answer to that question.

Suzanne's eyes met Devin's. "Yes. She was to play all the sonatas."

"Christ," Devin muttered under his breath.

The officer scribbled something in his notepad. "Looks as if somebody didn't want her playing the piano anywhere."

Suzanne flinched at his comment, drawing her arms around her stomach and letting out a low moan.

"Honey, do you even know if Cindy had a copy of 'Endnote'?" Devin asked.

"Hey, buddy, I'm asking the questions here," the officer broke in indignantly. "Who are you anyway?"

"I'm Professor Winslow's boyfriend." When Suzanne didn't dispute the statement, Devin felt relieved.

She seemed too distracted to dispute much of anything.

"Suzanne," he repeated, ignoring the officer's disgruntled expression. "Did Cindy have a copy of 'Endnote'?"

Suzanne stared away from him, her chin trembling. "Yes. I gave her one yesterday."

"Great." Devin let out a string of curses as he ran his fingers through his hair in agitation. Hell, Ressu certainly had a good reason for saying, "Destroy 'Endnote.'" The manuscript was lethal.

"I should never have . . . I shouldn't have—" She broke off with a shudder, then began shaking uncontrollably.

Devin took her in his arms. "You didn't know. It wasn't your fault."

Actually, it was his fault if it was anyone's, he thought. If he'd only told Suzanne about Ressu and the ghosts earlier, she might have gotten Ressu's message soon enough to prevent this.

Suzanne was now crying in his arms, silent sobs making her body shake as a slow flood of tears dampened his shirt. He stood there holding her, knowing he could do nothing to help and blaming himself for letting it come to this. Christ, what a mess he'd made of everything!

By this time, the students in the classroom had come out to see what all the ruckus was about. Phoebe, who'd been standing there wringing her hands, quickly took charge. She dismissed the students, fielding their questions admirably.

One or two stared at Suzanne as she stood shivering in Devin's arms, her head buried against his chest and sobs coming from her throat. But Phoebe shooed them away, and managed after a few minutes to clear the students out of the hall by promising to fill all of them in later about what had happened.

After the hall had emptied, the officer turned his attention to questioning Suzanne again. "Professor Winslow?" His tone was gruff, but oddly gentle. "I need to ask you a few more questions. We need to figure out what persons involved with this 'Endnote' piece seemed suspicious to you."

Suzanne shuddered and drew herself tight against Devin's body. For a moment, she lingered there, not speaking a word. Then she pulled back from him, wiping her eyes as she did so. Slowly she lifted her gaze to Devin's. Confusion and fear both were written on her face. There was even a hint of accusation in her expression.

Did she think he'd had something to do with this? he wondered. Hell, did she really think he could break a woman's fingers?

Maybe not, he told himself, but she still didn't know everything, and he was the one uncertain quantity in this equation. No wonder she couldn't exactly trust him. After all, her earlier question had demonstrated she still wasn't certain if he was a thief. And he'd said nothing yet to set her straight.

He waited for her to mention her suspicions to the officer. For a long moment, he held his breath, never flinching from her questioning gaze. It took all his power to resist the urge to gather her up into his arms again and make her forget what stood between them.

But apparently some small part of her trusted him yet, for she turned from Devin to tell the officer, "The only ones who knew about 'Endnote' were the festival concert committee members—Ion Goma, Lydia Chelminscu, Roger Kelly here at the university, Mariela and Paul Ressu, and Cindy, of course."

Every muscle in Devin's body went limp with relief. The officer glanced from her to Devin curiously. Then he nodded, jotting down each of the names. "Okay, I'll consider all of them as potential suspects, except Cindy, that is. But this Lydia Chelminscu, the one who warned you. I want to know more about her. Do you think she was involved with this?"

Suzanne shook her head. "I don't think so. She seemed frightened of whoever was, though."

"Do you think she knew who it was?"

Suzanne looked at the officer, an uncomfortable expression on her face as she thought a moment. "Actually, she made some insinuations, but she didn't come right out and accuse anyone."

"Who did she think it was?"

Sucking in her breath, Suzanne glanced up at Devin, then back to the officer. "She implied it could be Ion Goma. Last night I had a talk with a corporation who sponsored us. Now they're not too happy with him. That would give him ample reason to come after me, but I don't know why he'd try to hurt Cindy."

"Maybe this Lydia woman was casting suspicion on this Ion to draw attention away from herself."

"Maybe. But if she were planning something like this herself, surely she wouldn't have warned me the way she did, would she?"

"You never know," the officer said with a shrug. "You could be right. But we'll have to question her anyway. And this Ion Goma. You'll need to tell me how to get in touch with them both. And the others, too, of course. Well, except for Professor Kelly."

"Of course." Quickly, Suzanne reached into her purse and pulled out a small address book. After searching a second, she gave the officer several phone numbers. Then she answered a few more questions with sharp, terse answers.

As Suzanne spoke, Devin made a decision. She might put up a fuss, and she might still be unsure of him, but he wasn't letting her out of his sight until he told her everything and made her understand that she absolutely must heed Ressu's warnings.

"Where did they take Cindy?" he heard Suzanne ask the officer after they'd finished with the questions.

The officer flipped his pad back into his pocket. "She's over at the hospital. They're setting the bones in her hand and checking her head out for a concussion. The attacker couldn't have hit her head too hard—she came out of it pretty fast, or so she says."

"I can see her, can't I?"

The officer shrugged. "Don't see why not. I gotta go back and file a report, then talk to the city cops. I'll keep in touch. You're gonna be around, huh?"

"Yes."

In silence, she watched the officer leave, hugging herself tightly. It made something twist inside him to see her so distraught.

"I don't think you should go over there yet," Devin said, breaking the silence.

Suzanne turned to gaze up at him, a startled expression on her face as if she'd forgotten he was there. "Why not?"

"You don't know what that guy was after or if he's coming back."

"I don't care. Cindy's sitting there with a broken hand thanks to my giving her a copy of 'Endnote.' I have to be there for her." She fixed him with a penetrating stare. "You don't have to come, though."

There was no mistaking the mistrust lurking in that stare. Although her instincts made her turn to him for comfort, her rational side still doubted him. A lot.

But that didn't change a thing. He stepped closer. "You're not getting rid of me this time, Suzanne. If you insist on visiting this pianist, it's fine by me. I'll be glad to go with you. After that, however, you and I are going to sit down and discuss what we didn't talk about the other night. Whether you're ready for the truth or not, you're going to hear what I have to say. And you're going to listen. You *have* to listen."

Her eyes grew wide as saucers and her lower lip trembled. She didn't argue, but tightened her arms once more over her chest protectively. "Okay. But I must see Cindy first."

Much as he wanted to spill the beans to Suzanne right there in Goodspeed Hall, he figured he'd better wait until they could be somewhere private. No telling how she'd react.

Besides, seeing Cindy might jolt her into listening to what he had to say.

He nodded tersely. "Then let's get it over with."

Without another word, Suzanne turned and strode off toward the elevator, not even turning to see if he followed.

This is going to be hard, Devin thought as he walked after her. He'd never told anyone the truth, and he hardly knew how to begin. Yet if ever there'd been a reason to describe his "gift" to someone, it was now. He doubted Suzanne would listen to the rest of his tale if he refused to explain how he knew "Endnote."

He grew tense as they came down in the elevator. Already he was worrying about who might be lurking on campus to harm Suzanne.

No, this had all gone on long enough, he thought. Time to tell her everything once and for all.

He only hoped he'd survive the telling.

The Turk's hands shook as he unpacked his knapsack. He took out the nightstick that lay topmost. He stared at it, his heart pumping furiously.

Frankie hadn't told him the girl would be so pretty, that her skin would be the soft white of alabaster, or that her hand would be so small, so delicate, so fine.

Her hair had shone in the sunlight, like a beacon drawing him to her. His hands had acted on their own, raising the nightstick, then striking down with enough force to knock her out.

He'd half expected her to defend herself like the cursed man whose apartment he'd bugged. That had been a more satisfactory experience, even if the Turk *had* been seen, which wasn't what Frankie had wanted. Still, the Turk always relished knocking around a rich foreigner. Too bad he couldn't have done more damage, but he'd been afraid the noise might bring someone running.

SILENT SONATA

Why hadn't he enjoyed hurting the girl? She was a rich foreigner too. Perhaps it had bothered him because she hadn't been knocked out by his first blow, so that when he'd begun on her hand, she'd screamed. Or perhaps because the screams had turned to begging and pitiful sobs.

Distasteful. He hadn't expected it, but pounding her hand to crush the bones had been distasteful.

He closed his eyes, then opened them again with a curse. America was making him soft. Yes, the girl had been beautiful. In another time and place, he might have wanted to avail himself of such beauty. Yes, she had entreated him not to hurt her. Still, did any of that matter?

Unfortunately, it did. Maiming a young woman had not been to his liking. He'd been offered such crude jobs before and refused them, preferring jobs that required less visibility and more skill. Even at home in Turkey he would not have performed such a task.

A smile twisted his face. At home. It would have been different in Turkey. No one would have asked him to maim —they would have asked him to cut off the girl's hand completely. He should not be quibbling so over this task. Being asked to simply maim was not so awful. After all, the young woman with strawberry hair had been dressed in wealthy clothing. She was rich, and riches compensate for a great deal of physical pain.

Ah, yes, he thought as he contemplated the money Frankie would be paying. Riches could compensate for a lot of things, like performing distasteful tasks.

He laid the nightstick carefully on the table. At least this time Frankie should be pleased. After the Turk had erred so terribly in his surveillance of the apartment of the man named Devin, Frankie had railed at him for half an hour on the phone.

The Turk winced. Frankie wasn't happy at all these days. The other woman—the one at the park—was on her guard, and now so was the man.

But Frankie should be pleased after today's work.

Briefly, an image flashed into the Turk's mind of a hand twisted, the broken bones pressing through the flesh in places.

He swallowed hard, then shook his head. No, the pretty young woman with the strawberry hair wouldn't be playing the piano again anytime soon. And that should make Frankie very happy.

17

♪

It took Suzanne and Devin little time to discover that Cindy had been admitted to the hospital for observation because of the possibility of concussion.

Now acute awareness of the man standing beside her in the elevator made Suzanne more and more jittery as they neared Cindy's floor.

His presence threw her into confusion. She couldn't deny she'd been absurdly pleased to have him turn up at her lecture. Nor could she deny she was glad to have him stand beside her now. Today she'd take comfort from almost any quarter. Between Lydia's warnings and the horrible maiming of Cindy, she felt frightened, angry, hurt . . . and very vulnerable.

But she didn't know how she could handle another discussion with him about "Endnote." Not now. Not today. She needed time to assimilate all that had happened, to examine her feelings for him, which were apparently still as strong as ever.

She must escape that somehow. Later they could talk. But right now . . .

SILENT SONATA

A small sigh escaped her lips, barely audible. Nonetheless, he heard it.

"You sure you want to do this?" he murmured as the elevator moved up.

She swallowed. "Of course I want to do it."

"Suzanne, the officer didn't say how badly she'd been beaten. It might be—"

"I want to be there," she clipped out.

They'd reached Cindy's floor by that time. They left the elevator and began to walk past the lounge area there. Suzanne stayed Devin's hand, a sudden idea taking hold in her mind.

"I think you should wait here." There must be another exit off this floor, she thought, perhaps a stairwell on the other end or another elevator. She could use one of them to slip away once her visit was done.

He scowled. "Why?" His face was all angles and shadows in the harsh light, and she found herself wanting to reach up and stroke his unshaven cheek.

She resisted the urge as she met his fierce gaze. "Cindy doesn't know you. It might upset her to have a stranger around when she's . . . she's not herself."

Devin's eyes formed two suspicious slits in his stony face. She wondered if he could read everything she thought. Sometimes she almost believed he could.

After observing her a moment, he nodded curtly. Then he strolled into the lounge. She could see him through the glass window settle his lanky form into an armchair and cross his arms over his chest.

Relief flowed through her as she went up the hall. With any luck, she could deal with Cindy and be out of here before Devin knew she'd gone.

As she turned the corner into another hall, however, she began to hear shouting at the farthest end. Then a shrill scream echoed along the passage, followed by a voice shrieking, "Out! Out! I don't want you here!"

Suzanne recognized Cindy's voice immediately and

rushed in the direction of the noise, noting that the nurses on the floor were too occupied with other patients to deal with the commotion.

It took her only seconds to find Cindy's room. The young woman was sitting up in the narrow hospital bed, waving her good arm as if to ward off evil spirits. Paul stood beside her, trying to put his arm around her to soothe her as she continued to shriek that she wanted him out.

Cindy's eyes were wide, their centers dilating as she shouted. One side of her head was bandaged, making her look somehow off-center, like a woman-creature—half beauty, half beast. But even the half-beauty part was snarling, baring her teeth at the intruders who'd dared to disturb her in her lair.

Suzanne stood dumbstruck by the transformation until Paul noticed her behind him.

"Suzanne!" he cried. "God, I'm so glad you're here! Cindy's hysterical! I don't know what to do! You think I should get a doctor? Do you think when that bastard hit her on the head it hurt something in her brain?"

His frantic questions seemed to affect Cindy more than his attempts to calm her down had. She immediately stopped shrieking, fixing them both with a shrewd gaze. "I am *not* hysterical." She took great gulps of air, obviously trying to gain control of herself. "There's nothing wrong with me, except my hand is broken into bits, and I'll never play the piano again!"

She held up her splinted hand, uttering a sharp cry as she did so. Gingerly she laid it back down in her lap.

"Are you hurting?" Suzanne asked quickly. "Have they given you anything for the pain?"

"Oh, yeah, they pumped some drugs into me. For all the good it did."

Suzanne stepped closer. "Do you want me to get a nurse and have her increase the dosage?"

Cindy looked up from contemplating her hand. "No! I don't want anything from you, do you hear me? I want you gone! This instant!" She nodded her head at Paul, refusing to look at him. "And take him with you!"

Paul's hurt expression, coupled with Cindy's obvious look of distress, made Suzanne change her mind about talking with Cindy right now. Feeling protective of Paul, Suzanne put a gentle hand on his shoulder. "Come on. Cindy's had a traumatic experience. Why don't we come back when she's feeling better?"

"Don't come back," Cindy gritted out. "I want nothing more to do with any of you nutcases! And Paul, you tell that crazy bitch mother of yours I'm going to kill her when I leave here! You tell her that, okay?"

Paul stiffened under Suzanne's hand. "What's Mother got to do with this?"

"Don't be such an ass, Paul!" Cindy retorted. "She did this to me, don't you see? She ruined me . . . I'll never be able to play . . . never!" Her voice broke on that word, and tears started to course down her face. "She's destroyed my career! Your stupid mother destroyed my life!"

By now Paul's face had drained of color, making him look like a lost little boy.

Suzanne fought the urge to upbraid Cindy. After all, the younger woman had every reason to be hysterical. Instead Suzanne said in a soothing voice, "Calm down, Cindy. You're upset over what happened. That's understandable, but don't say things you'll regret later."

Suzanne tightened her hand on Paul's shoulder.

But he seemed unaware of the comfort she offered. "Why . . . why would you think Mother did this?" he asked Cindy, his voice quavering.

Suzanne didn't give Cindy a chance to answer. "Your mother didn't do this. Cindy's just upset."

Cindy snorted. "I'm upset all right! With Mariela." She fixed Suzanne with a wild stare. "And with you too. You had to set her off, didn't you? I suppose you told her about Paul and me."

"No, of course not!" Suzanne recoiled at Cindy's shocking statement. "That was none of my business!"

"You're absolutely right! But it's never stopped you from meddling before, has it? Trying to get me out of the festival . . . trying to malign me . . . well, you got what you wanted, didn't you? I'm out now, that's for sure!"

Suzanne sucked in her breath, fighting the surge of anger welling up in her belly. She had to remember Cindy wasn't quite herself at the moment. "Cindy—"

"Don't talk to me! All you say is lies anyway, and they won't change anything. So leave! Now!"

Suzanne wanted to leave, but she couldn't. She had to know one thing to ease her conscience. "When . . . when that man attacked you, did you have that copy of 'Endnote' on you, the one I gave you yesterday?"

Cindy tossed her head back and the free half of her hair flew wildly as she gave Suzanne a malicious glance. "No. And if you're implying this has anything to do with your mugging a few days ago, don't bother. I'm not that stupid. This has nothing to do with 'Endnote,' and you and I both know it!"

"Are you sure you didn't—"

"No! Mariela did this, and it had nothing to do with that theft of 'Endnote'!" Cindy's eyes narrowed. "Did you try to fool the police into thinking they were related? Did Mariela put you up to that so she could cover her ass? Well, it won't work. I've already told the police about the whole lot of you! They'll make sure all you vipers get what you deserve! Especially Mariela!"

Suzanne tensed. This was more than simple hysteria. Cindy clearly had some insane idea about why she'd been attacked. But where had she gotten such an idea? And why blame Mariela?

Cindy's words had roused Paul from his hurt silence. "What do you mean, you told the police?" He jerked away from Suzanne's hand to stride up to Cindy's bed, looming over her with his face dead white. "Damn it, Cindy, what the shit do you mean? There's nothing to tell! You better not have fed them a bunch of lies about Mother or I swear I'll—"

"What'll you do, mama's boy?" Cindy shrieked. "Break my other hand?"

Paul's face flooded with color. "Why are you being such a bitch about this? Mother had nothing to do with this, and you know it!"

"You can say what you want, but your dear mother set out to destroy me, and she succeeded!" Cindy's face twisted into an ugly mask as she said the words.

Paul clenched his hands at his side. "Shit, you're loony tunes! Why would Mother do something like this? Because she found out about me and you? You really think that would make Mother break your fingers? Don't be ridiculous!" He snorted. "She isn't strong enough to do it herself, and she's not going to hire some criminal to do it. Besides, if she wanted you out, all she had to do was announce she didn't want you to perform, and that would have been the end of it. Or she could have cancelled the festival concert."

"She *tried* to cancel the concert, remember?" Cindy said, a cruel slant to her mouth. "Obviously, when Suzanne wouldn't let her, she resorted to more drastic measures!"

Shaking with anger, Paul leaned on the bed and stared Cindy down. "You've lost your fucking mind! I should have listened to Mother and Suzanne when they told me you weren't their first choice for pianist. You don't deserve to play Father's music, that's for sure!"

Suzanne shifted her feet uncomfortably at Paul's words, but Cindy's eyes turned cold as frozen air. A sneer formed on her lips. "Your *father* thought I deserved to play it. That's why your mother doesn't want me involved. She's jealous as hell."

An icy tremor shook Suzanne. Something in Cindy's face warned her they were treading dangerous waters. "Paul, I think we should leave—"

"No!" he exploded. "I want to hear what the lying bitch

has to say!" He fixed Cindy with a baleful glare. "Why would my mother be jealous of you? Because you were Father's student?"

A look of triumph lit Cindy's eyes. "Oh, come on, Paul. You're not that much of an idiot, are you?" Her words dripped honey though her gaze would have frozen boiling water. "Do you think your father was blind? Look at me. I'm younger than your mother and a lot prettier. And I know all about music. I also knew what made your father tick. You think he wanted to spend his time with a woman who thinks a staff is a walking stick? Who couldn't possibly appreciate his genius? Of course not!"

She was smirking now. A wave of nausea hit Suzanne. Surely, Valentin wouldn't have lowered himself to . . . to . . .

"We were lovers, Paul. Lovers," Cindy taunted him, answering Suzanne's question.

Paul staggered back from the bed, an incredulous expression on his face.

With a gloating smile that marred rather than enhanced the beauty of her face, Cindy continued to torment him, heedless of his horror. "Do you really think I ever gave a shit about you? After making love to your father, I could never regard you as anything but half decent in bed."

"That's enough!" Suzanne ordered as Paul reeled away, pain etched in every line of his young face.

But Cindy wouldn't stop. "The only reason I ever let you touch me was because you reminded me vaguely of your father. And because you could make sure I played his music in the festival. I wanted to be there when the world saw Valentin's genius. I wanted to be the one to give him fame. Your mother couldn't give him fame, but *I* could. *I* could have made people remember him forever." Her expression changed, growing embittered. "And your mother knew it. That's why she did this to me."

A sob escaped the girl's throat, but Suzanne couldn't summon up sympathy for her. Suzanne had been right about her character all along, although it provided small comfort to know it. Suzanne too had wanted to bring Valentin fame, but not at the cost of other people's dignity and happiness. The thought of Valentin making love to this grasping, heartless creature . . . it made her stomach churn.

Paul looked as ill as Suzanne felt. "You're lying," he cried, his slender shoulders shaking. "It's all lies!"

"You think so? Ask your mother about that. She knows the truth. She found out a few days ago." Her eyes brightened with the fury of bitterness. "Didn't you wonder why she wanted to cancel the festival concert all of a sudden? Well, that's why. She found out about me and your father."

Unfortunately, what Cindy said made sense. It explained why Cindy had taken up with Paul, and it certainly seemed to explain why Mariela had wanted to cancel the festival concert.

Suzanne shook her head. She didn't want to believe it. Yet the seeds of doubt had been planted in her breast, and she couldn't seem to root them out.

What had Mother said? "I only wish you could have known him better." Had Mother known about Valentin's affair? Suzanne wondered now. Then she paled. Had there been others that Mother had never spoken of?

Of course, Valentin had apparently been seeing Mariela while still married to Mother, but Suzanne had always felt that was different. Now she wondered if it really was. Could a man who'd cheated on his wife once, no matter how tyrannical his wife, be trusted not to cheat again?

Paul seemed to sort through the same questions. His eyes were vacant and staring. He kept opening his mouth to speak, then closing it as Cindy looked on, momentarily forgetting her shattered fingers as she basked in her moment of triumph.

"When everyone pressured Mariela to continue with the festival," Cindy went on gleefully, "she must have decided to confront me. She showed up yesterday after you left my dorm room and told me she'd never let me play in the festival. Ask her if you don't believe me. Ask her!"

Paul shrank back from the bed, from the twisted expression on Cindy's face. Suzanne clutched at him, her own horror momentarily lessened by her concern for him. She wrapped her arms around him, holding him close as she'd done when he was a child.

Cindy's expression turned grim. "I warned Mariela if she tried to kick me out of the concert, I'd tell everyone about Valentin and me. Everyone! I guess she didn't think I'd do it. Or maybe she thought her brutal tactics would scare me into silence."

Cindy's hollow laugh echoed in the room. "Well, guess what. I don't scare easily. You can tell your mother to go to hell. And you can warn her I told the police about her. They'll put her away for this." Her torment distorted her face as she looked down at her bandaged hand, cradling it as a mother cradles a child. "They'll put that bitch away," she said with undisguised venom.

The last statement elicited a moan of anguish from Paul. He wheeled from Suzanne in a rage, and it took all her strength to hold him back from Cindy.

The hurt and anger etched in his face drove Suzanne over the edge. She still reeled from the knowledge of Valentin's duplicity toward his family, but she wasn't about to let this bitter young woman destroy both Paul and Mariela.

She gripped Paul's arms and stared at Cindy over his head, her eyes blazing. "You're pathetic, Cindy, you know that? That 'bitch' has more class, more style, more beauty than you could have in a million years. You know as well as I do that Mariela wouldn't stoop to something like this!"

Cindy glared at her. "Mariela is—"

"Shut up! You've been sitting here spouting poison for the last five minutes. Now it's my turn to talk." Suzanne paused, then went on with more firmness in her voice, "I think you're the one who's jealous, Cindy. You're jealous because you know you only held Valentin with your prowess in bed. In the end, he stayed with his wife, didn't he?"

Cindy looked as if she wanted to throw something, but at least Suzanne's words had gotten Paul to stop struggling.

"I didn't see your name mentioned in Valentin's will," Suzanne went on relentlessly. "He didn't make any deathbed confessions to Mariela. No, he kept his tawdry little affair with you a secret, because you were nothing more than a body to him. And he wasn't about to jeopardize his marriage for the sake of a manipulative schemer like you. He had more sense than that."

"You liar! You stupid liar!" Cindy began screaming, rage contorting the smooth lines of her face. "Valentin was in love with me!"

"My father could never have loved you!" Paul shouted back.

The two began a shouting match, venting their rage on each other. Suzanne watched them both helplessly, fighting to restrain Paul and wondering if she'd made a mistake in taking on the obviously distraught Cindy.

Suddenly the door opened behind her. She thought it might be a nurse responding to the raised voices, but as she turned, she heard Devin's voice, cool and calm above the shouting. "What's going on, Suzanne?"

"Oh, thank heaven you're here, Devin," she said in a rush, so glad to see him she had to restrain herself from running into his arms. "Paul is trying to kill Cindy."

It was nearly the truth, she thought. Her entire body seemed engaged with trying to keep Paul from lunging at the girl. At least Cindy hadn't jumped from the bed and tried to strangle Paul.

"Paul—is this Ressu's son?" Devin asked as he grasped Paul's shoulders with enough force to hold him back.

She nodded.

"That's enough!" he commanded Paul firmly. "Come on, stop it!"

For a moment, Paul blindly fought the hands that held

him. But as Devin's voice penetrated the thick fog of his anger, he went slack.

He twisted his head around to look at the man who held him.

"Devin Bryce?" he asked as Suzanne's words of greeting apparently registered.

"Yeah. It's me. You finished shouting at the lady?"

Paul glanced back at the bed, his face suffusing with anger once again. "What lady?"

"Listen to me, you little shit—" Cindy began, then broke off suddenly. The heart-shaped lips thinned into a line as she surveyed Devin for several minutes.

She glanced at Suzanne and Paul, then back at Devin. "Devin Bryce, huh? What are you doing here?" Her eyes narrowed. "Wait a minute. Paul said something about you at the festival meeting. Something about you hearing Valentin play 'Endnote.'" Her expression grew more agitated. "Are you supposed to be taking my place at the festival? Is that what you're doing here?"

Devin stiffened and opened his mouth to speak. But Paul cut him off. "Yes, yes!" he hissed wildly, glancing back at his idol. "That's why you're here, huh, Devin?" Paul turned to sneer at Cindy, who'd gone pale. "See? We already have a replacement for you. We don't need you, Cindy! And no matter what you claim, my father didn't need you either! Father loved Mother, not you!"

"Stop it!" Suzanne commanded, clasping Paul's arm and pulling at it.

But it was too late. Paul had set Cindy off again. "What is this?" Cindy's face contorted with rage. "Are you all in cahoots together? Did you have my hand destroyed so you could bring in Devin Bryce? God, I'll have you *all* arrested!"

"Come on, Paul," Suzanne said under her breath, jerking the teenager back with more force than she'd intended.

For Pete's sake, the last thing they needed was Cindy to add another innocent person to her list of guilty culprits.

SILENT SONATA

Devin grabbed Paul's other arm, then helped Suzanne as she began dragging the struggling boy toward the door.

"You just try arresting us!" Paul was shouting now. "Just try it, you bitch!"

"I will, don't worry!" The cry followed them out the door and down the hall as a nurse ran past them, finally responding to the noise. Another nurse tried to tell them to "get the boy out of here."

Devin and Suzanne nodded as they increased their pace. Between the two of them, they finally got Paul down the hall far enough so he couldn't hear Cindy's muffled taunts.

Paul's shouting voice petered out as he slowly became aware of the people in the hallway staring at him. After a moment he went limp, and Suzanne and Devin released him. He lunged forward, as if intending to return to the room, but Devin caught him around the waist.

"That's enough, tiger," Devin muttered as he restrained the irate teenager. "The best way to deal with a hysterical woman is to leave her the hell alone."

Precisely how you dealt with me the other night, Suzanne thought wryly, but kept her thoughts to herself.

"But she'll have my mother in jail! I've gotta keep her from getting my mother arrested! I've gotta talk to her!"

"Devin's right. It's too late for that," Suzanne put in. "Don't worry. The police know hysteria when they see it. They'll question your mother, she'll give them an airtight alibi, and they'll dismiss Cindy's ravings as nonsense."

Paul stopped struggling, but turned an anguished gaze on Suzanne. "What if they don't? What if . . . what if . . . Mother really had something to do with it?"

Suzanne forced a reassuring smile to her face. "Surely you don't believe your mother would crush a girl's hand, Paul."

Paul pushed Devin away. Devin released him once again, but kept a wary eye on him. Paul shoved his hands in his pockets. "I don't know." He shook his head mournfully. "Mother used to say if she ever caught Father with another woman, she'd cut off his . . . his . . . well . . . you know what. She seemed pretty serious. So if she knew about Father and Cindy . . ."

Devin's face had remained impassive as he heard for the first time what all the shouting had been about. Now he interjected for Paul's benefit, "Yeah, well, women think they're serious when they say stuff like that. That doesn't mean they are."

"Listen to Devin," Suzanne said, the faintest edge to her voice. "The man knows women well."

That got her a raised eyebrow from Devin, but Paul seemed oblivious to the double meanings behind the interchange. His eyes turned bleak and bitter. "Too bad I don't." He hung his head. "I—I guess you both think I'm dumb for having been taken in by Cindy like that. I mean, she used to tell me what a handsome guy I was." He managed a self-mocking laugh. "I guess I should have known right then she was a liar."

Devin answered before she could even think of anything to say. "Believe me, we all get our heads turned now and then. When a girl who looks like Cindy starts inflating your ego, it's easy to convince yourself she's telling the truth. Eventually you learn to consider the source before you listen to flattery. Sometimes the people who love you the most are the ones willing to risk hurting you by telling you the honest truth."

Paul screwed his face up in thought as he pondered what Devin had said. "Consider the source, huh? Does that mean Cindy could also have been lying about Mother?"

"At least give your mother the benefit of the doubt," Devin murmured and Suzanne echoed his statement.

Privately, Suzanne had trouble accepting Mariela as a woman who'd stop at nothing for vengeance, but how well did she know Valentin's wife? Could anybody know how a woman would react who'd discovered that her husband had been cheating on her?

Of course, Mariela's husband was dead now. Didn't that make a difference?

Belatedly, Suzanne reacted to Cindy's declaration, her gut twisting at the thought of Cindy and Valentin together. Hard to believe Valentin had taken such wretched secrets with him to his grave. She'd never guessed he could do this to Mariela, sweet, gentle Mariela.

And she certainly didn't know if the image she had of Mariela could be trusted.

So what on earth was she to tell Paul about his mother? She wanted to comfort him, but over the last few days, she'd discovered that a number of people in her life had lied to her. How could she possibly sort out for him what was lies and what wasn't?

"Well, either way, I want to talk to Mother," Paul said at last, stiffening his shoulders. He refused to meet Suzanne's gaze. "I've got to warn her about what Cindy's up to. And —and I want to know the truth about Father."

Suzanne stared at him, affection warming her heart. Today he had his hair tied back in a ponytail, which oddly enough made him look younger rather than older. Never had she cared so much for this lonely boy who'd been like a brother to her. And never had she felt so utterly unable to help him through a crisis.

"Are you sure you want to do that right now?" Suzanne asked. "You've had a big shock. Maybe you should let it settle—"

"I'm not a kid anymore, Suzanne." Paul lifted pain-filled eyes to her. "Don't you see? I have to find out what Mother did, so I can help protect her if she had something to do with this." He drew himself up straighter. "Father let her down. I'm not going to."

A surge of pride in him made Suzanne fight back tears. He certainly wasn't a kid anymore, not after this afternoon. Any illusions he'd had about his father had been shattered. It must be devastating to lose a girlfriend to one's dead father.

"Do you want me to go with you?" She added hastily, when his face clouded with anger, "Not because I think you're incapable of handling it, mind you. But I don't want you to feel you're all alone."

A ghost of a smile played over his face. "Thanks, but I'd rather go by myself, you know?"

As he turned and walked down the hall, she realized she was the one feeling alone and left out. The family was already beginning to close ranks against outsiders, and no matter how much she'd wanted to be part of Ressu's cozy family, she'd always been an outsider.

Devin was staring at her now, his eyes filled with sympathy. Suddenly she wanted nothing more than to lay her head against his chest, to feel him comfort her. She almost didn't care anymore what his ulterior motives were. He'd stayed with her through a traumatic time. She had to believe his concern was at least partly genuine.

As if on cue, he drew her into his arms, cradling her head in the curve of his neck. "I'm sorry, honey. I know all this has been hard for you."

A subtle, tangy scent of male cologne invaded her senses, bringing her almost as much comfort as did his soothing touch. It felt so wonderful to let him hold her. She must have been insane to want to sneak away from this.

Or to have forgotten how good it could be.

"Come on," he whispered. "Let's get out of here. You've had enough crap for one day."

Wordlessly, she nodded and let him lead her to the elevator and then out of the hospital.

"Where are we going?" she asked after a while as they passed through the automatic doors into the parking lot, headed the opposite direction from where they'd come in.

"I'm taking you home with me." Almost as an afterthought, he stopped short and turned her face up to his. "Okay?" His eyes reflected uncertainty. And perhaps pain as well.

"Okay," she managed to get out.

She might regret this later. But the thought of going home to an empty house . . . and the bust of Valentin staring from her piano . . . was more than she could endure.

She'd take her chances with Devin.

18
♪

Suzanne and Devin said little as they drove to his apartment. Suzanne didn't want to speak of Valentin at the moment, yet he filled her mind. Valentin and Cindy. How could a sensitive, intuitive man like Valentin have felt anything at all for a shallow, grasping creature like Cindy?

Stop being so harsh on Cindy, she told herself. *Cindy's behavior today was perfectly justified. She saw her career destroyed by some nut with a hammer.*

The beginnings of terror skittered down Suzanne's spine. That nut with a hammer still ran loose out there somewhere. Why should he stop with Cindy?

"Devin?" she asked tentatively.

"Yes?"

"Why would anyone smash a girl's fingers like that?"

The corners of his mouth hardened as he clenched the wheel until his knuckles whitened. "I don't know. I hoped *you* could tell me."

A shuddering sigh escaped her lips. She stared ahead, only dimly conscious of the road-eating speed of his car or the brilliant, midafternoon sunlight glinting off the other cars around them. It was a pleasant spring day. And she hardly noticed.

"I take it you don't think Mariela did it?" he asked when she remained silent. "From what I gathered of the conversation back there, Cindy had been . . . er . . . involved with Ressu. I suppose knowing her husband was unfaithful could drive a woman to act crazy."

Suzanne's mouth tightened. "Some women, maybe. But not Mariela. Mariela's a gentle person—"

"Who threatened to cut off her husband's 'you know what' if she caught him with another woman."

A faint smile crossed Suzanne's face. "Yes, well, as you pointed out, saying it is one thing. Doing it is quite another."

"All the same—"

"No," Suzanne broke in, her voice sobering. "Mariela's not the type. She would have been more subtle about it. She'd have been too frightened of getting caught to do something so blatantly violent."

A long pause ensued.

"Then I guess it has something to do with the stolen copy of 'Endnote,'" Devin said at last.

"Probably." She held her breath, wondering if he'd say more.

"And your mugging and the man breaking into my apartment and—"

"What?" The dazzling sunshine suddenly seemed to mock her with its promise of happiness. "Someone broke into your apartment?"

He shot her a quick glance, then turned his eyes back to the road. "Yeah. When I left your house the other day, I surprised this guy lurking around in my apartment. He got out of there before I could catch him."

"Good Lord, did he hurt you?" Her stomach knotted at the thought.

He shrugged. "Not too much. He got in a couple of blows to my ribs, before I punched him."

"That's awful," she whispered, glancing at his shirt, wondering if they'd taped him up. She couldn't help her next words. "How badly did he hurt you? I mean, he didn't break your ribs or anything, did he?"

"Such concern from the woman who wanted me to leave her alone."

She ignored his caustic comment. "Devin, please. How bad were you hurt?"

"A few bruises, that's all. Damned guy was in too much of a hurry to get away, so he didn't hang around to beat me to a pulp."

"What was he after?"

"You're not going to believe this, but he was planting bugs in my apartment."

"Bugs? Do you mean what I think you mean?"

"Yeah. Bugs. Electronic monitoring devices. After he left, I couldn't find anything missing, but I found this suspicious-looking tool by the phone, so I called the police. After they got a look at the tool the guy left behind, they did what they called a 'sweep.' They passed this instrument over the house, and it went off every time they found one."

So much for the pleasant spring day, she thought. Now a sinister presence seemed to lurk behind every flowering bush, every budding tree.

His face drawn, Devin pulled into a parking lot outside an apartment building.

She fought to keep her cool. "How many did they find?"

"Five. They told me the man who hid them was an expert and probably would have gotten away with it if I hadn't stumbled onto him doing it."

She shuddered, drawing her arms tightly around her body. "Wh-why would anyone bug your apartment, Devin?"

He parked the car, then shut the engine off, staring up at the building as he did so. In a toneless voice, he said, "I played 'Endnote' at the recital, remember? I guess they want to know where I've put my copy."

Avoiding her eyes, he got out of the car and slammed the

door. Quickly she did the same before he could even come around to her side.

She rounded the car to head him off at the back. "Why didn't you tell me?"

He strode off in the direction of the building. She had to hurry to catch up with him. She yanked at his arm, forcing him to stop. "Why didn't you call and tell me?"

Glittering a solemn crystalline blue, his eyes met hers. "I've been trying to reach you since it happened, remember? You wouldn't return my calls or open the door to me."

"Oh."

Yes, of course. He *had* been trying to reach her, but her pride had prevented her from talking to him. She suddenly felt very small.

He turned and strode forward once more. She followed, feeling as if someone were squeezing her heart in a vise. Part of her wanted to apologize, but for what? For not liking the fact that he'd lied to her? For still being uncertain of how much she could trust him?

So they went up in the elevator in silence, standing apart, afraid to touch or to restore the tentative connection forged between them when they'd made love and throughout the day's wrenching events. Never had she felt so alone.

"Here it is," he murmured as they reached his floor. They left the elevator, still silent, and walked to his apartment together.

As they stood at the door, a sudden self-consciousness assailed her as she remembered the last time they'd been alone together. He opened the door and entered, but she hesitated on the threshold.

He turned to stare at her, his expression harsh, unyielding. "Do you want to know the truth about me and Ressu or not?"

He threw out the words almost as a taunt, daring her to turn coward and run. After all the "truths" she'd learned about Valentin today, she was tempted to do just that.

But where could she run to? Despite her successful meeting with Amarcorp, who'd agreed to continue sponsoring the festival concert, the concert plans were still a mess, now that Cindy's hands had been smashed. All her drive to write a tribute to Valentin's genius seemed somewhat silly at the moment. And even her mother promised only a slight refuge from the outside world.

No matter how hard she ran, she could never get away from the questions, the secrets, the curiosity about why "Endnote" had spawned this flurry of reaction.

Nor would she be able to escape the man before her now, whose expression of hurt bravado and carefully banked desire was imprinted on her memory forever. He was watching her with hooded eyes, with legs spread and thumbs hooked in his jeans pockets defensively. He dared her to explore his secrets, dared her to take a chance for once.

She took the dare. Stepping inside the apartment, she shut the door behind her and met his questioning gaze.

"What now?" she asked from where she stood, heart pounding.

His gaze lingered on her face. It probed deep, striving to penetrate her flimsy defenses. Then with a shrug he peeled off his jacket and tossed it on the nearby couch. "I don't know. You want some lunch or something?"

Trust a man to try to solve a problem by filling his stomach, she thought. Her body recoiled from the very thought of food. "No, thanks."

"Okay. Something to drink then? I don't have any ginger ale, but I've got ice water."

She sighed. He was stalling, and she knew it. "Yes, okay. Anything's fine."

"Make yourself at home," he threw out as he turned and disappeared through a door that apparently led to the kitchen.

It was awfully warm in his apartment, she thought as she opened the top few buttons of her prim, starched blouse and removed her beret, tossing it on a nearby chair. Still nervous, she remained standing near the door and glanced around the room. His place didn't even remotely resemble hers, that was certain. Aside from the warmer temperature and the unabashed scent of male habitation in the air, it was cluttered beyond belief.

Sheet music lay strewn everywhere. Empty cans were scattered on every flat surface, and a towel was draped over one arm of a nearby chair.

Not that the clutter detracted much from the decorating effect, she thought wryly. The well-crafted but worn and old-fashioned furniture was of several styles and periods, thrown together as slaves to function without a thought for appearance. The massive, long couch looked incongruous next to the slender legs of the coffee table, but no doubt the couch was one of few that would accommodate Devin's height if he chose to lie on it. Judging by the homey-looking afghan adorning one end and the cushions piled up at the other, he did that often. And the coffee table's slender legs gave him more room to stuff music, programs, coffee mugs, and so forth, underneath.

"It's a mess," he stated casually as he returned, a glass of water in one hand and a beer in the other. "I'm no housekeeper, but I don't like anybody else fooling with my stuff, so it only gets a good cleaning once in a while."

She tried to be charitable. "I'm sure the burglar and the police sweep had something to do with the messiness."

He grinned. "Nope. All me, I'm afraid. The only thing the burglar left behind was a few electronic monitoring devices." He quirked one eyebrow up. "And he wasn't messy at all about hiding those."

A chilling tremor shook her. How violated Devin must have felt to find that a stranger had roamed his apartment freely. Kind of tough for a man who didn't "like anybody else fooling with my stuff."

It must have felt the same as having a stranger attack you on a presumably safe college campus.

Terror gripped her soul anew. "Devin?" She lifted her eyes hesitantly to his.

He moved a step closer. "Yeah?"

"I'm scared out of my mind." The words were little more than a whisper.

His eyes widened, and a muscle worked in his jaw. Slowly he set down the drinks, then approached and gathered her in his arms. "I know," he whispered as he cradled her head under his chin. "I know, Zanny."

His use of her nickname warmed her. As did his incredibly gentle touch. He stroked her back with soothing movements so tender, she could hardly believe a man made them.

"I'm not feeling too brave myself these days," he added. "That's why we've got to talk about this thing."

She shook her head violently. "Not yet," she mumbled into his shirt. It wasn't entirely the attacks that had her scared. It was her fear of what Devin might tell her, of the mysterious answers he had in store for her. "Hold me for a minute first."

His arms tightened around her. "You don't have to ask twice."

His chin pressed into her scalp. Then it shifted and his lips were against her hair.

A different kind of tremor went through her this time. How could she possibly have forgotten the way he made her feel? Sweet, warm sensations were already stealing over her body, and all he'd done was hold her.

His breath became more ragged, ruffling her hair in short, hot puffs. He rubbed his hands more slowly up and down her back now, with an almost sensuous thoroughness that both comforted and excited her.

Later she wasn't certain when the more volatile excitement overtook the comfort. Maybe it was when she angled her head up to press a grateful kiss into the hollow of his neck. Or maybe when he responded by nuzzling her forehead, planting his own kiss at her temple where the blood already quickened.

But before either of them could think about it, she'd lifted her face until her mouth hovered a scant inch from his. And she'd waited, eyes wide and breath held, only partly conscious of the invitation she offered.

She saw desire flare up in his eyes only seconds before he pushed her up against the door, sealing his mouth to hers with a hunger born of suppressed passion and laying waste to any meager resistance she might have dredged up. She buried her fingers in his hair with a little whimper of release. Good Lord, how she'd missed him.

He tore his lips away to murmur, "I'm sorry. I couldn't help it. I—"

She shut him up quickly with a hard kiss. A moan of resignation echoed deep in his throat. His blatant, blistering ardor seared them both as he planted his hands on the door and trapped her between them, his body flush against hers. With increasing urgency, his tongue stabbed into her mouth and tangled with hers restlessly.

Then his mouth wandered to her closed eyelids before following the half-moon curve of her cheek over to her ear, where he teased the tender lobe with half-fierce nips.

"I've missed you." His hot breath warmed more than her ear. He ran the tip of his tongue around the shell, and she gasped, clutching at his waist to pull him closer.

With an almost frenzied eagerness, she groped under his shirt, wanting to touch his bare skin, to reassure herself he was real and not some sweet spirit she'd conjured up. Her sigh whispered between them as she spread her fingers through the matted hair on his chest and ran her hands over the bulge of taut muscle beneath the rapidly warming skin. She found one hardened male nipple and rubbed the stiff nub under her thumb.

He swore under his breath, instantly wedging his knee between her legs until the hot core of her rested against his firmly muscled thigh. Then he slid his hands down to clasp her waist, jerking her hard against him until her own thighs gripped his upper thigh as she sought relief for the burning ache in her lower regions. His knee against the door made it easy for her to rub her bottom along his leg, her tight skirt rucking up around her own slender legs.

Sucking in his breath, he ran a questing hand up one of her exposed thighs, his magical fingers burning her through the thin hose. His fingers explored further under her skirt as his other hand stroked her throat, moving lower and lower into the vee of her blouse. He thrust one finger beneath the edge of her bra to touch the nipple, and she gasped, arching back against the door and digging her fingers into his shoulders as she closed her eyes.

Quickly he worked loose the buttons of her blouse while his other hand slipped between her legs, sliding her skirt further up until it bunched high on her hips. He caressed the skin of her inner thighs through the pantyhose with one hand as he opened her blouse with the other, pushing the edges apart and cupping her breast. She moaned low and deep when he pressed the pad of his thumb against the nipple and began to rub it in a circle through the thin lace of her bra.

His hands held her open and exposed at her two most sensitive points, like a butterfly pinned to a board. He did not kiss her, preferring to concentrate on stroking, fingering, kneading her intimately.

She could hear his breath coming in sharp gasps, feel the heat of his gaze on her half-clad, vulnerable body. She kept her eyes shut, not bearing to meet that soul-searching look. He kept her prisoner to her desire, driving all thought from her mind. When he shifted her on his thigh, widening her legs to allow his hand greater freedom, she groaned loudly and her eyes flew open.

He stopped his movements, although he didn't remove his hands from her body. He was staring into her face with a tormented expression, his dark eyebrows lowered.

"Christ, I want you," he stated fearfully as if the simple statement of fact would make her turn tail and run.

Little did he know there wasn't a thing on earth that could make her run from him right now. Past events, his previous lies, and all the doubts both had engendered now disintegrated to nothing when compared to her violent longing to be intimate with him once again.

Nothing remained, but him. And her.

She touched his face in wonder. As a sculptor smooths clay, she smoothed out the frown lines that wrinkled his brow. "I want you, too."

His eyes closed and he sucked in his breath as she moved her fingers to caress his cheek, then trailed them down his neck and over his chest and firm belly until she reached his jeans. She worked loose the button at the top. He stood motionless, silent, as she unzipped his jeans and slid her hand inside.

Only when she captured in her questing fingers the silky hard shaft trapped there did he seem freed to act. With a low curse, he lowered his knee so she slid down his thigh. He slid his hands behind her hips to unzip her skirt as she worked his pants down over his lean hips.

After that, the two of them stripped each other with a frantic desperation lacking in their first lovemaking, as if afraid something might happen to tear them apart before they could join their bodies.

A pool of clothes formed quickly at their feet until they both stood naked, their bodies straining together. Their hands moved everywhere, memorizing the contours of each other's body.

He wrapped his hand in her hair, holding her head back for an almost brutal kiss, and she reveled in his roughness, arching her body up to meet his other hand, which now tangled with the triangle of hair between her legs.

He finally broke free long enough to mutter, "Come on," then pulled her to the couch. He sat down on the edge and tugged her down to sit on his lap with her back to his chest.

She tried to squirm around to face him, but his hands held her in place.

"Devin," she moaned, aching with the need to link her body with his.

"Shhh." He propped his chin on her shoulder after brushing her hair aside.

She could feel his gaze aimed downward at her naked body seated on his thighs. Like sunlight through a magnifying glass it seared her.

"I want to look at you," he whispered. "Okay?"

The thought of his eyes traveling over her body when it lay so open, so exposed, sent a tremor of anticipation down her spine even as it made her blush. Nonetheless, she swallowed and whispered, "Okay."

Slowly he slid his hands around her waist and up to cup her breasts, lifting them for his perusal. Then he kissed her ear as his fingers began to caress her, teasing the berry-brown nipples with delicate strokes.

"Do you like that?" he murmured, his breath hot against her ear.

"Yes," came her breathy, shameless answer. "Oh, yes."

As he continued his sensuous movements, her head fell back against his shoulder, and her eyes closed. He stroked her for what seemed an endless amount of time, making desire unfurl in her belly like a waking rose.

When she groaned softly, he moved his hands to her thighs, spreading them wide apart. The touch of his cool fingers against her skin there jolted her out of her lassitude. Her eyes shot open as she jerked her legs closed reflexively.

"Don't," he murmured. "There's nothing to be ashamed of, Zanny. All I see is beauty, your beauty. Try to see your body through my eyes."

She shook her head, embarrassed. She didn't want this openness, this vulnerability. She wanted him to make love to her fast and hard, so she couldn't think about the mistake she might be making in letting him get close. His erection grew beneath her legs, pressing into her soft buttocks. The thought of giving in to that hardness, to him, suddenly terrified her.

He'd used her desires against her before. What was to stop him from doing it again?

As if he read her thoughts, he slid his finger between her tightly clenched legs, and she groaned as sensations shot through her. She clutched at his forearms with her hands, her fingers digging into the rigid muscles. He pried her fingers loose, then lifted them back behind her head and his.

"Hold on to my neck," he commanded in a husky whisper, then released her hands. She did as he said, conscious that it opened her even more to him, lengthening her body into one long, erotic expanse of sensitive skin.

She felt the insistent press of his hardness trapped beneath and between her legs. It grew harder as he ran his fingers down her body, over the smooth muscles that tightened each time he touched her.

Once more his hand dropped between her still clenched legs. "Trust me, honey," he rumbled, squeezing his finger between her thighs until he found the place he sought. Then he rubbed against one delicate petal with increasing pressure until she thought she'd go mad. "Let go of your fear, and trust me. I won't hurt you. I swear it. Start by opening your body, and the rest will follow."

His voice lulled her. He nuzzled her neck, nipping at her earlobe as one hand splayed itself over her breast, all fire and heat now as he circled the nipple with his thumb. The finger on his other hand still played between her legs, coaxing and tempting her until her legs fell apart, wanting more of the delicious pleasure he offered.

"That's it," he whispered. Quickly his hand at her breast moved down to hold her thigh aside once more, exposing the soft curls between her legs. Then he took advantage of his access to plunge that maddening finger deep inside her.

How could she think at all when he caressed and teased

her like the virtuoso that he was? He knew exactly where to press, to stroke, to rub. His fingers grew slick from her body's wetness, but still he delved and fondled.

Her embarrassment fled, along with her sense of vulnerability as pleasure rose up in her throat, hot and sweet. His fingers plucked at the very apex of her most secret place, and she writhed against them, wanting more, needing more.

She tried once again to turn toward him, but he held her firmly in place. "Not yet, honey, not yet," he murmured, though his own breathing sounded labored.

"Devin, please . . ." she begged.

"It's yours, honey, if you'll reach up and take it," he whispered against her throat.

She ceased begging when he began a rhythmic stroking too erotic to be believed. Moans erupted from deep within her throat. It was torture . . . it was bliss . . . it was all any sane woman could want . . . and then some.

He made her feel like the first roaring waves of ocean surging toward a nameless promise of reward. Boneless, liquid, her body ebbed and flowed higher and higher toward the moon like the tide drawn upward in its time. She thought she'd never reach it, then she feared she would, and the all-encompassing pleasure would end.

Suddenly one mighty swell thrust her above the clouds. A choked cry escaped her lips as she burst into the wide expanse of space, a sky exploding with stars and light and sweetness until at last she felt one with the brilliant moon.

Never had she experienced anything like it in her life. For the first time, being vulnerable and exposed meant being free.

"Devin, Devin, oh, Lord, Devin . . ." she couldn't stop saying over and over as she drifted slowly back down to earth, still awash with moonrays of pleasure.

His hands soothed her skin, his fingers rubbing lightly over her thighs as if to bring her back gently.

As her cries slowly died, he groaned and shifted her on

his lap. He was still hard. She could feel him, full and heavy beneath her thighs. Suddenly she realized he'd purposely brought her to the peak of fulfillment without taking his own pleasure.

She shifted her body so that she sat across his legs, and this time he let her. Then she looked up into his face. His expression of tight control confirmed her suspicions. His upper lip shimmered with the sweat of his exertions, and his eyes shone starkly with unspent passion.

As he gazed at her, her heart turned flipflops. His face, with its tentative uncertainty, told her everything. This had been his apology, his way of making up for his lies, for hurting her after they'd made love the first time.

All of a sudden, it wasn't enough to have him give her pleasure, apology or no. No matter what he'd done, what he'd said, she wanted him to experience the same ecstasy she had, to find in her body the same fulfillment he'd given her.

Lifting her body to straddle him, she pressed him back against the couch until she sat astride him where he lay.

"Zanny, you don't have to—" he began, the words strained.

She placed a finger over his mouth. "I want to. I definitely want to." Then she replaced the finger with her lips, feeling the violent shudder pass through his body as her breasts were crushed against his chest.

Before he could protest again, she drew back and in one sudden motion impaled herself on him. With a cry, he clutched at her waist as his entire body arced up into her. She gazed at the sight before her. His eyes were shut, his face drawn in an agony of wanting. She ran her hands over his chest, over the sleek, straining muscles. His heat brought forth the scent of cologne, inciting and enticing her.

For a moment she relished the power he'd given her. She tested it, wanting to see how far it extended.

"Open your eyes," she ordered.

SILENT SONATA

He did. They were two glittering crystals in the dark torment of his face. Yet he said not a word as he watched, waited. A thrill of pleasure skittered through her at the force of his gaze on her, and her excitement mounted.

"Touch me," she said.

He did. His hands covered her breasts with almost frenzied movements, caressing them roughly until she cried out, but not in pain. In response, he grew more erect inside her, making her mouth go dry.

"Tell me again that you want me," she whispered hoarsely.

He did, though not in exact words. "Hell, Zanny, I can't take much more of this," he groaned as he dug his fingers into her ribs.

Now he was the vulnerable one . . . he was at her mercy. But she'd had enough of torturing him, though he'd purposely offered her the chance to do so.

"You don't have to." She lifted her hips and came down.

He moaned and bucked against her, driving himself deeper still. Her heart hammered in her chest, keeping time to the rhythm they set with their bodies. With a triumphant gasp, she fused her power to his until they were meeting and separating, meeting and separating in perfect cadence, their bodies straining together to reach the heights.

She no longer knew who rode whom, for he thrust up against her with a power not the least bit subdued by the weight of her body on top of him. Glorying in the ride, she let him take her once more into the rarefied atmosphere of that higher world.

The shimmering sky was hers again, only this time she didn't soar alone. This time, they both were caught up in the draw of the moon, the sweetest thrumming pull of the ages, until at last their joined cries split the air and he spilled himself inside her.

She collapsed atop him, spent and satisfied, her face resting in the hollow beneath his collarbone, her ear against his heart. His heart beat crazily at first, slowing very gradually to a steady pulse. Body to body, heat to heat, they lay there sinking back into normalcy, into the complications of the real world.

After a moment passed, during which Suzanne reveled in the warm feel of his body against hers, he twined her hair around his fingers, then lifted a handful to his lips and kissed it.

"Honey," he rumbled, "I wish we could lie here together for about two more hours . . . or days."

She buried her face in his chest, a tightness in the back of her throat. Oh, if only they could. But they both knew they couldn't. She could tell by the regret tingeing his words that the time had come, the time they'd both been putting off. And he at least didn't want to put it off anymore.

He cupped her chin in his hand, then raised it until her eyes met his. His eyes searched hers, a hint of uncertainty flickering in their depths. "Will you trust me now?" he asked, unsmiling, intent.

What could she say? That she couldn't bear to do otherwise after what had just passed between them? That if she didn't throw herself into his hands completely, she'd wither away into nothing? It would be true.

Still, she merely whispered, "Yes."

He remained silent for so long she wondered if he'd heard her.

At last he sighed. "Okay. Then let's talk."

19
♪

They sat side by side on the couch. Devin could tell from the way Suzanne gripped his hand that she was afraid. He couldn't blame her. What he had to tell her would upset her neat image of the world, no matter what she did with the knowledge.

Her body was a tense, rigid stalk swallowed up by the ample fabric of his only bathrobe. He understood her wish to be somewhat dressed for their discussion. No doubt after all the revelations she'd had today, she wanted the slight armor of clothing when she faced any new surprises.

He'd obliged her by pulling on his briefs and blue jeans, the minimum of respectability. Now he held her hand tight in his, afraid to look at her.

"First," he began, "I want to remind you about the additional passage of 'Endnote' I played at the recital. Just as you thought, Ressu had—" He stopped and corrected himself, "*I* had played a later version." He glanced at her, then fixed his eyes once more on the wall across from them. "This morning at the university you didn't give me the chance to tell you what the message was. Well, I think you'll want to know now."

The message lay folded in his free hand, burning into his palm. Now he handed it to her, watching as she released his hand to take it.

She held the folded sheet between two fingers as if it were glass, her uncertainty showing in the way she glanced from the paper to him and then back. Finally, she unfolded it and read.

When she reached the final line, the blood drained from

her face. "Y-you're sure this is what the Morse code portion of the new passage said?"

"I'm *not* completely sure, no. I'm not as familiar with his technique as you obviously are. But I worked it out several times, and it always came out this way. To be absolutely certain, however, you'll have to hear me play the music and then work it out yourself."

She folded the paper again carefully, a frown creasing her brow. Then she lifted her eyes to his. "Why do you have to play it for me? Why can't you simply give me the version you have?"

He steeled himself. "Because I didn't lie when I told you I didn't have a copy of it. I did learn it from hearing Ressu play it."

She crossed her arms, exasperated. "We've been over this before, Devin. I know you weren't a friend of Valentin's."

"No, I wasn't Ressu's friend. But I heard him play 'Endnote' nonetheless."

"And when was this supposed to have occurred?" she snapped, obviously disappointed that he was apparently sticking to his old story.

He sucked in his breath. Now for the part she'd never believe. "A few weeks ago. At my recital. That wasn't me playing 'Endnote.' It was Ressu's ghost playing it through me."

Complete silence filled the room. After an unbearably long time, he turned to look at her. She was staring at him with widened eyes. "Did you say 'ghost'?"

"Ghost. Spirit. Phantom. Whatever you want to call it."

She flinched at his flippant tone. "You're joking."

"No," he said in as earnest a voice as he could muster. "No, I'm afraid I'm not."

"You expect me to believe—"

A hollow laugh escaped his lips. "No. I don't expect you to believe me. If you did, I'd probably think you were more flaky than I seem. But I'm telling the truth. As I told you before, the truth is very hard to swallow."

She shook her head in confusion, then pulled the bathrobe more tightly about her and glanced furtively around the room, as if expecting demons to jump out from behind his furniture. Her eyes were huge in her face. He could tell that for one moment she actually considered his explanation.

Then her reason apparently reasserted itself, and her eyes narrowed, anger thinning her lips. "*This* is the best story you could come up with? That Valentin possessed you or something? For Pete's sake, Devin, why on earth *should* I swallow such an insane tale?"

"Remember how I told you that bits and pieces of music pop into my mind when I'm playing?" He drew in a sharp breath. "Well, that was the only way I could think of to describe what really happens—the ghosts of dead composers sometimes take over my hands during a concert and play whatever the hell they feel like playing."

Her mouth dropped open. "What?"

Christ, it sounded so silly when he put it into words. No wonder she couldn't accept it. But she had to accept it.

He tried another tack. "I'm sure you've heard about my eccentric concerts, the ones where I deviate from the program. Well . . . I don't have any choice in the matter generally. If . . . if Chopin is in the mood to play a piece of his, he kind of butts in as I'm preparing to play another piece . . . and well . . . he plays what he wants."

She was shaking her head, regarding him with the same kind of fear and revulsion generally reserved for snakes.

"It's true," he went on more desperately. "Hell, Suzanne, would I make something like this up?"

"I don't know. Would you?"

"No, damn it! You've got to believe me. I've had this . . . this gift . . . this curse ever since I was a boy. Mom thinks I inherited it from Dad. He had second sight." He added in a rush, "I'm sure Maggie hinted at something like that to you."

His statement gave her pause, but only for a moment. "Yes," she said, her words dripping with sarcasm, "but she didn't tell me about *your* marvelous talent."

His voice hardened. "That's because she didn't know. No one knows but Mom. I haven't dared to tell anyone before now for fear of what it would do to my career. I preferred to let them believe I was just eccentric, a rebel . . . arrogant."

She shook her head, her mouth drawn tight. "Oh, you're arrogant, all right." Her eyes looked like two bleak caves in her white face. "Y-you tell me this crazy story, fully expecting me to believe it because you say it's true."

He'd tried to prepare himself for her disbelief, but now that he was witnessing it, pain swelled in his gut and tore at his heart. Her look of scorn cut him deeper than he would have ever imagined.

It didn't matter, he told himself. He had to convince her. For her own sake.

He tamped down his hurt and grabbed her hands. "I wouldn't have ever told you, but I had to. Don't you see? Ressu is trying to tell you something from the grave, damn it, and the bastard has chosen me to give you the message. I didn't want this. I didn't want to tell anyone, but your damned Ressu gave me no choice! He hasn't let me play anything but 'Endnote' since the night of the recital, and he's not going to stop playing it until you get the message!"

He was getting through to her. He could tell from the growing horror in her gaze. But she sure as hell didn't want to believe him nor want him to try to convince her. He could tell that too.

She shook her head wildly, refusing to look at him. Jerking her hands away, she rose to her feet, her eyes blazing down at him. "Ghosts, huh? Valentin's ghost, for Pete's sake?"

"Suzanne, calm down—"

"Calm down?" she practically screamed. "You tell me that Valentin's ghost has been possessing you, and you want me to calm down?"

"It's not quite like that—"

"Oh? Then how is it?"

He opened his mouth, but she cut him off.

"No, no, don't tell me how it is." She drew back from him, her expression hurt, confused. And afraid. "No, show me."

"What do you mean?"

"You know what I mean. Come on, I want to witness this strange phenomenon. I want to see you play 'Endnote' now! I want to see this . . . this possession of yours!"

Seeing is believing, huh? he thought as he stood, too. Too bad it didn't work that way.

"I'll play it all you want," he bit out, "but it's not going to prove a damned thing. It's not something you can witness or my audiences would have witnessed it long before now."

"That's very convenient for you, isn't it? Sure makes it easy to support your bizarre tale. Well, I don't care. I want to see you play. If Valentin 'possesses' your hands, *I'll* know, believe me! If anyone would be able to tell, I would!"

"Really? You didn't know the day I played 'Girlflowers,' did you?" he threw out.

She paled. He could see the thoughts racing through her head, see the uncertainty in her eyes, and then the stark fear. "Are you saying that's how you knew . . . how you could play—"

"Yeah. Come on, Suzanne, you said yourself I couldn't possibly have known 'Girlflowers' unless Ressu had played it for me. And we both know Ressu hated my guts. So how did I know 'Girlflowers'? Tell me that?"

She was shaking now. "I—I don't know. I—" She broke off, her eyes accusing him. "If he hated you, why in heaven's name would he . . . I mean . . . his ghost—"

She broke off with a sob. "Good Lord, I'm starting to sound like you now."

"If you're asking why a man who hated me would play his music through me, then I think the answer's pretty obvious. He didn't have many choices, did he? There aren't a lot of talented musicians around who are capable of being temporarily possessed by the dead."

The stark description in his words seemed to stun her more than anything that had gone before. She shook her head, over and over, violently, as she clutched her arms.

"It's a lie," she whispered, though her voice seemed to catch on the word. "It's another one of your odd tricks to get me to trust you. It's . . . I . . ."

"Now you know why I didn't want to tell you," he said gently, moving toward her.

She backed away. "Don't touch me!" Then she glanced wildly around the room until her gaze rested on his concert grand. Returning her gaze to him, she pointed at the instrument. "I want to hear you play 'Endnote,' Devin. Now! And you better be convincing, you hear me? Or I'm going to walk out of this apartment and go straight to the police and tell them you stole 'Endnote' and . . . and . . ."

"And smashed Cindy's hand, right, because I thought she had the remaining copy?"

She let out a choked cry, tearing her gaze from his. "Just p-play it," she whispered.

He took in her shuddering figure, looking so slender and alone as she stood barefoot in the center of his apartment. Could this be the same woman who'd sat astride him, making love to him like some warrior goddess?

Yeah, he thought wearily. It was also the same woman who alphabetized her books and analyzed music. Stuff like ghosts didn't exactly fit into her scheme of things.

"Play it, blast you!" she repeated in a more determined voice.

The challenge in her eyes decided him. "No problem!"

He strode to the piano. "I'm sure your friend Valentin will be only too happy to oblige you."

Actually, Devin wasn't at all sure of that. If all this time Ressu had simply been trying to revenge himself on a man he despised, he certainly had his chance to finish Devin off now.

Devin didn't want to believe Suzanne would carry out her threat about going to the cops, but he daren't believe otherwise either. She was obviously upset, and as he'd told Paul earlier, a smart man didn't argue with a hysterical woman.

He sat down on the piano bench, trying to keep his hands from trembling. Suzanne still stood in front of the couch, her hands clenched at her sides, and her face the color of chalk.

Fear clutched at Devin. So much was riding on this. She had to believe him . . . she had to! He tried to summon up the first few bars of Ressu's piece in his mind, in case the composer failed him.

Then without warning, he felt it—the cold sweats, the racing blood, the surge of power that lifted his hands from his knees and cast them down on the piano.

The music began.

He would have thought by now that Ressu's possession would feel as familiar as an old winter coat. But it didn't. Ressu's ghost had more power than any of the others, probably because he'd died so recently, and that power always hit Devin with a roaring, hellish thunder that wiped everything from his mind but the music.

Now that power swelled his blood as the keys danced. His heart pumped madly, his fingers pounding the keys with ruthless savagery. As usual, shortly into the piece, the ghostly hands became visible, then attached themselves and melted into his own hands.

Tonight the ghostly hands seemed to have more substance than usual, to be almost opaque, but Devin was too caught up in the playing to wonder why.

Then it came to the point in the possession where parts of the spirit's vague memories flitted through his mind. His mouth went dry as images filled his head, more concrete than usual. He saw Suzanne as a little girl, all pink ribbons and lace, Suzanne as a teenager, holding a valentine and crying, Suzanne inside of what looked like a coffin . . .

"No-o-o!" he shouted, using all the force in him to wrench his hands from the piano.

His cry seemed to echo in the apartment as he whirled on the bench, seeking her face to blot out the image of death.

She'd come up to stand beside him. Her eyes were staring down at the keys unseeing, her mouth agape. "Valentin . . ." she whispered.

Then she crumpled to the floor.

Suzanne awakened very slowly, not certain what had happened or where she was. Her head buzzed loudly, but as she grew more alert, the buzzing subsided to a dull hum.

What felt like someone's knees were digging into her back, and her head seemed to be resting in someone's lap. But the rest of her was on the cold, hard floor. She could feel the boards against her bare ankles.

"Come on, honey," whispered a gruff, anguished voice above her. "Don't do this to me, Zanny. You've got to wake up."

Devin, she realized with a start.

"Wh-what happened?" she managed to croak out.

Relief tinged his tone as he answered, "You fainted."

His hands stroked her arms, flooding her with warmth. They were such warm hands, such big . . . gentle . . .

Hands . . . Hands! Her eyes shot open as she remembered.

"Valentin," she said through dry lips.

Devin's face came into focus above her, his mouth grim as fear flared in his eyes. "No. It's me. Devin."

"I—I know. But I saw . . ." She broke off, her eyes

searching his face, then finished in a whisper, "I saw Valentin's hands."

Devin turned ashen. He clutched her arm, his fingers digging into the skin. "You saw them?"

"Well . . . I saw something that looked like Valentin's hands, hovering over yours . . . actually . . . more like stuck to yours."

He squeezed her arm so tightly, she thought he'd break it. His eyes stared blankly at her.

"Devin," she whispered, "you're hurting me."

At first what she said didn't seem to register. Then the blank look left his face, and he swore under his breath, releasing her arm.

"Hell, I'm sorry. I wasn't thinking. It's . . . it's just that no one's ever seen the hands before. No one but me."

An insidious fear disturbed the surface of her existence. All the things he'd told her before she'd fainted passed through her mind . . . the message he'd claimed that Valentin wished to give her . . . his story of Valentin's ghost's possessing him . . . his explanation for how he knew "Endnote."

And then the ghostly, frightening hands . . .

With a choked cry, she tried to sit up. He wouldn't let her, instead shifting her body to cradle her head in his arms.

"It's okay, honey, calm down. There's nothing to be afraid of."

"No?" She twisted her head to face him, her throat raw and tight. "You tell me that Valentin's ghost is wandering the earth t-trying to get a message to me from the grave, and I'm not supposed to be afraid?"

A faint smile touched his lips. "When you put it that way, I guess it's pretty understandable."

You're not kidding, she thought. Her heart pounded in her ears, and her stomach felt queasy. She turned her face, resting it against his thigh, her eyelids shut tight against a world that had suddenly tilted upside down.

"Suzanne?" he asked brokenly after a moment.

She groaned, not wanting to hear any more about ghosts and possessions and desperate messages.

"I've got to know," he continued. "Does this . . . does this mean you believe me?"

A long sigh racked her body. She rubbed her cheek against his thigh, reassured by its solidity. "I don't know. I don't want to believe you. But I . . . I can't ignore what I saw with my own eyes."

His hand stroked her cheek, feathering down to her chin. She opened her eyes to gaze up at him. What she saw there pierced her to the heart. His eyes glimmered bleakly like those of a hurt little boy who longed for acceptance. She could tell he wanted her to believe him with an intensity that was almost frightening.

But how could she believe him? she asked herself. The whole idea was insane.

Then again, as Devin himself had pointed out, why on earth would he make up such a story? It certainly wouldn't benefit him to tell her this bizarre tale if he didn't believe it to be true. As he'd said, telling the wrong person could ruin his career.

Still, his believing it didn't make it true. He could be deluded . . . maybe he *had* heard Valentin play the pieces sometime . . . maybe . . .

She stopped short. If he was crazy, then so was she, for having seen those ghostly hands.

Besides, bizarre as his tale was, it explained so many things she'd not understood before . . . how he'd known "Girlflowers" . . . why he'd exploded when she'd found out the truth about his childhood . . . why he'd been so evasive from the beginning.

Out of nowhere, a snatch of Shakespeare from her college days popped into her mind: *There are more things in heaven and earth, Horatio, / Than are dreamt of in your philosophy.*

Hamlet. Her mouth twisted in a wry smile. Now she

could understand why the poor prince had vacillated when his father's ghost told him tales. Accepting those other "things in heaven and earth" was no mean feat.

She stared at Devin, then lowered her gaze to his hands, the ones she'd seen taken over by Valentin's. Yes, *taken over,* she told herself determinedly. She couldn't deny what she'd seen simply because it didn't fit anything she'd ever experienced.

Devin had accepted that other reality. He'd accepted it, and acted on his belief, knowing that no one in their right mind would believe what he had to say. He'd kept his secret close in his heart until she'd come along. Until Valentin had invaded his life.

She swallowed hard. "Wh-when did all this start?" she couldn't resist asking. Slowly she sat up beside him, her body shifting into place with reluctance. She took his hands in hers, stroking them thoughtfully. "When did you start . . . uh . . . having ghosts show up at your concerts to perform?"

His fingers tightened on hers. He released his breath all at once, as if he'd been holding it for some time. "When I was six." His voice was strained. "The very first piano lesson I had."

Entwining her fingers with his, she forced a smile to her lips. "What happened?"

He stared at her with wide, distrustful eyes, a bleak harshness carved in the lines of his face. "Why do you want to know?"

"Because I want to understand."

"You think I'm crazy, don't you, that I'm hallucinating or something?"

There was no mistaking the fear in that voice. Even now he protected his secret from a world that could never accept or understand it.

"No. Or if you are, then the insanity is catching. I know what I saw, Devin. If you're hallucinating, then so am I."

He gazed at her, uncertain.

She gave an exasperated sigh. "Okay, if you won't tell me what happened back then, at least explain to me what I saw today."

"Ressu's hands."

"Yes, I know that. But how does it work? Do you . . . you call him up or something? Is there some . . . some special preparation you have to do or—"

She broke off at his harsh laugh.

"I'm not a warlock or a medium or anything like that, Suzanne. Hell, I wish I *could* call him up, him and all the others. If I had the power to make them come and go at will, I'd make their visits a little more convenient."

She thought that over a moment. "So they pounce on you when you least expect it?"

He gazed at her silently, as if weighing how much he should tell her. After a moment, he seemed to make up his mind. "Yeah, sort of. I usually have a lot of physical sensations right before it happens—quickened pulse, cold sweats. Then—" He shrugged. "Then I start playing something I hadn't prepared to play. Usually Chopin, Beethoven, or Liszt, but mostly Chopin. And sometimes others."

He regarded her warily, waiting to see what she'd do with his confession.

She weighed her words. "It must be terribly unnerving," she ventured at last.

The harsh laugh sounded again. "Yeah. Unnerving and scary as hell. I've gotten used to it some, but it still takes me by surprise every time."

"What . . . what goes through your mind when it's happening?"

For some reason, her question seemed to disturb him profoundly. He hesitated a long time before answering it. "Mostly all I think about is the music. Then toward the end, I see bits and pieces of what the ghost must be thinking . . . memories . . . stuff like that."

That was interesting, she thought. "What do you see when Valentin takes you over?"

SILENT SONATA

He paled, refusing to meet her eyes. "Today I saw his memories of you. As a little girl. And then as a teenager."

She had a funny feeling he was leaving out something, but she didn't think she should press him about it. "As a teenager?" she asked instead.

"Yeah." A smile tipped the edges of his mouth.

"How did I look?"

He raised one eyebrow. "Decided to take a page from my book and fish for compliments?"

She blushed.

With a chuckle, he said, "You looked great, as always. But you didn't seem too happy. You were holding a valentine and crying."

The specificity of his statement startled her. She sifted back through her memories. One thrust itself into the forefront, giving her an eerie tug on her insides.

Only with an effort could she shake off the spooky feeling. "That must have been the time my boyfriend ended our relationship by sending me a . . . a valentine breaking it gently to me."

"How thoughtful of him," Devin muttered gruffly, but he wasn't smiling.

"He was a jerk."

"I'll say."

They both remained silent a moment. Then her curiosity got the better of her. "Do you see images of the past even for Chopin?"

"Sometimes. Little vignettes of his life. I could probably tell the historians more about Chopin than is written in all his biographies put together."

Her eyes lit up. "Really? But . . . but that's great! Think about the books you could write."

"Listing what for sources? Am I supposed to say I got the stuff straight from the horse's mouth?" His smile turned grim again. "No, the knowledge I gain isn't of much use. But it's amusing." He paused, raising one eyebrow.

"And it helped me with you, didn't it? I mean, that's how I knew about Ressu and his watered-down orange juice."

The spooky feeling returned. She'd forgotten about his statement at their first meeting. She'd never dreamed then how bizarre his source of information would prove to be.

"You see," he continued, "after the possession's all over, a little bit of the composer's personality lingers with me—mostly surface stuff like preferences for food and hobbies." He sighed and glanced mournfully toward the kitchen. "Ever since your friend has taken up residence, I've been drinking a ton of watered-down orange juice. And until now, I didn't even *like* orange juice."

She couldn't miss the resentment buried in his voice. "How can you stand it? If you're always having these composers take you over, how can you even function?"

He shrugged. "Ressu is atypical, believe me. My impression with all the others has been that it takes a lot of effort for the . . . er . . . ghosts to connect with me, so it doesn't happen often, every few weeks or so at most. Then I play a piece no one expected, and the audience applauds my eccentricity." His mocking smile barely disguised his pain. "The ghosts know better than to screw everything up by playing when I'm with an orchestra or by interrupting a piece." He paused to amend, "Well, most of them. Ressu seems to have a mind of his own. He couldn't even wait for me to finish a piece before he barged in."

That sounded like Valentin, all right, she thought with a smile. "Valentin can . . . could be a little impatient at times," she quipped, eyes sparkling.

Her light tone seemed to relax him. The corners of his mouth tilted slightly up. "Tell me about it. Ever since the recital, he won't let me play anything but 'Endnote.' I couldn't figure out why . . . until you told me about the Morse code."

His words reminded her of that terrible night, the things she'd said, the things she'd accused him of. Well, he *had* lied to her, she told herself, but he'd certainly had good reason to.

"I'm sorry I didn't listen to you the other night," she said softly.

He raised their linked hands to his lips and kissed each of her fingers. "I don't blame you for being pissed. I should have told you before, but I was afraid—"

"I wouldn't believe you," she finished. She went on, self-mockery in her tone, "Gee, I wonder why you were afraid of that? Because I'd accused you of being a thief? Because I'd gone around behind your back to ask Maggie questions?"

"Yeah." He drew himself up with his typical cocky arrogance. "You were getting to be a pain in the ass, weren't you?" He grinned.

Then his grin faded as his eyes went all smoldering and intense. "I wish I'd told you everything sooner." He looked away. "It's just that I've spent so many years hiding it all . . . that I didn't know quite what to do with you."

"So you made love to me instead."

He swung his gaze back to hers, the lines around his mouth creasing grimly. "Do you regret it now that you know why I misled you? Now that . . . now that . . . you know what a freak I am?"

Pure astonishment held her silent a moment. Had he been so afraid then . . . so afraid she'd reject him for his strange powers? "You're no freak," she whispered. "You're different, and I certainly don't hold that against you. I seem to recall you telling me that not everything operates by rules. Well, you should listen to your own words."

An achingly poignant expression of wonder filled his face. "It doesn't bother you, does it? That I have this weird ability." He said it as if he couldn't quite believe it.

She forced a smile. "I may be tight-assed, but I can be flexible, especially when it comes to musicians. You're talking to a woman who likes avant-garde, remember? I get my thrills from listening to the music of people who wedge paper clips, among other things, between the strings of a piano to make them sound funny. What's a few ghost composers compared to that?"

He stared at her speechless, then jerked her up against him, winding his arms around her tightly. "Oh, Zanny, Zanny. I should have told you the first day I saw you." He nuzzled her, then sprinkled kisses over her hair. "You don't know the hell I've been through these past few days, worrying that you'd never agree to see me again. When you wouldn't even open the door to me . . ."

She hugged him close, relishing the strength in his arms. "I wasn't exactly having a wonderful time," she whispered against his shoulder. "You were right. You haunted me. I couldn't get you out of my mind."

"After I got over being pissed, I realized how much I'd lost." He drew back, leveling an earnest gaze on her. "You got to me. No one's ever gotten to me like that before. I wanted every part of you so badly, it made my soul cry. I still do."

It was the first time he'd ever hinted he wanted more than simply a casual affair, that he felt something deeper for her than mere sexual attraction. And the intensity of his statement, the yearning behind it threw her into confusion.

She didn't know if she was ready for this, for him. She didn't know how she felt. Her life had been turned upside down over the last few weeks, and she no longer knew what she wanted.

"It's okay," he murmured. "You don't have to say anything. We've got plenty of time, honey."

She read the understanding in his eyes and relaxed. Somehow she knew he would never push her or try to manipulate her feelings the way her mother always had. He would wait until she was ready, until she could deal with her volatile emotions.

Raising her hand to stroke his face, she said, "Thank you. As I told Paul, you understand women very well."

He raised one eyebrow. "Is that why until today you were ready to scalp me at a moment's notice?"

"I had good reason most of the time, don't you think?" she said dryly. "You were rather evasive every time we discussed 'Endnote.' "

At the mention of Valentin's piece, Devin's face fell. He sighed. "That damned piece of music. I suppose we have to deal with it now."

"What do you mean?" she asked.

He clasped her hands and stared down at them, as if looking for the answer to life's riddles in her palms. "Your buddy Ressu has gone to a hell of a lot of trouble to get his message to you, honey. He's played with my life and career and possibly yours, too. And he's fought whatever demons they have to fight on the other side to make a connection with me." He lifted his eyes to her. "Obviously, he thinks the message is worth his effort. So I suggest you . . . we . . . listen to it."

"The message being, 'Destroy "Endnote." ' "

"Yeah. I know it goes against your grain to do it, but hell, look at the trouble the damned thing has caused. You got attacked, my apartment was bugged, and a talented pianist's fingers were smashed. Not to mention that this Lydia woman has apparently been warning you about the danger of keeping the thing around. I think you should do what Ressu says and destroy the damned manuscript."

She drew her hands from his and stood, her back to him as she gazed at the chaos of his apartment and then through the windows to the afternoon sky. Instinctively she withdrew into herself, crossing her arms over her chest.

"I know you're right, Devin. I *know* you are. But . . . but it hurts so much to do it. This is a significant work of art, a masterpiece. If I destroy it, what will it do to Ressu's reputation? I'm . . . I'm literary executor of his estate, the caretaker of his genius, if you will. It's hard for me simply to eliminate this piece for all time."

"He wrote other pieces."

"I know. But this is the end piece, don't you see? It finishes the Sonata Cycle, it makes everything else have meaning."

"Yeah, well, it'll finish something else if you're not careful," he rasped as he too stood to his feet. "Like your life, for example."

The very real possibility behind his words made her flinch. She shuddered, drawing her arms more tightly around her chest. "So you think I'm personally in danger?"

A long pause ensued. Finally, Devin muttered a low curse. "I didn't want to tell you this, but I think I'd better. Those images I saw of you today when I was playing . . . there was one more. The one that made me cry out and wrench my hands from the piano. I didn't want to mention it earlier, but . . ."

He paused.

"What did you see?" she whispered.

"You in a coffin."

"Oh, good Lord," she cried out, turning to face him, her heart chilling within her breast.

"I don't think it's anything but a warning," he went on hastily. "Ressu was trying to scare me into seeing what could happen if you continued with this. And guess what, honey. He succeeded. He scared me shitless."

Well, at least Devin wasn't alone in that. Everything that had happened in the last few hours had thrown her into a state of constant terror. Only Devin kept her from becoming completely unhinged. Much more of this . . .

No, she had no choice. "There won't be any more of this."

"What?"

She stared at him. "It's over. That's it. The end. You've convinced me. Valentin wants 'Endnote' destroyed. So I guess I'll destroy it."

The relief on his face was unmistakable. "Good."

"I only hope it's not too late to stop this madness."

"It won't be," he said through gritted teeth. "Because

SILENT SONATA

you're going to be very vocal about your intentions to everyone who knew about the piece."

"The festival concert planning committee," he said dully. "Oh, Ion Goma's going to have a field day with this. All his opinions about me will be confirmed at last."

Her gaze drifted to the piano. So it was over, was it? She fought to ignore the dull thud of pain in her chest. A lifetime's work to be truncated. And for what? They didn't even know.

And it didn't affect only Ressu's work. There was her book as well. Did this mean she had to scrap it? Would it make a difference if she couldn't talk about "Endnote"? Of course it would. It would always make a difference.

"Suzanne, honey?" Devin said, moving up behind her and putting his hands on her shoulders.

"Yes?"

"You need to do it as soon as possible."

He was right of course. She hated it, but he was right. A lump stuck in her throat, making it difficult for her to speak, so she nodded instead.

"I'm sorry, honey. I really am."

She shook her head, placing one of her hands over his. "It's okay. You've probably suffered more from all this than I have. Maybe now Valentin will leave you alone."

His hand tightened on her shoulder. "Hell, I hope so." A moment of silence passed. "Isn't there some way I can help? I feel like the prophet of doom sending a disciple out to sow discontent. I don't imagine this committee of yours will take kindly to the news that you're scuttling the premiere of 'Endnote.'"

Some would, some wouldn't, she thought. Actually, Lydia, Mariela, and maybe even Paul would probably be relieved, and Cindy couldn't play the piece now anyway. The only one who'd protest would be Ion and possibly the university.

"Could I . . ." he began, then trailed off. She twisted

her head to look up in his face. He still felt so uncertain with her, she could tell.

"What?" She planted a kiss on the broad back of one of his hands.

That seemed to decide him. "Could I go with you?"

At an earlier time she would have been suspicious of his request, but now she recognized it for what it was—a desire to stay close. After all that had passed between them, she could understand his fear that once she left, she might change her mind about him.

"I'd like that," she said softly.

To her pleasure, his eyes lit up. "Where to then?"

She thought a moment. "Mariela's. Before I start destroying copies of 'Endnote,' I ought to get her permission. And I'm going to have to come up with some logical explanation for why I want to do it."

Right now, she couldn't think of what to tell Valentin's widow. Then remembering Cindy's astonishing confession that afternoon and the fact that Paul had gone to talk to Mariela about it, Suzanne drew in her breath sharply. No doubt about it. This would not be easy.

20
♫

Mariela lived in Hyde Park not far from Suzanne. As Suzanne and Devin exited the freeway, bound for the Ressu house, Suzanne's palms grew clammy. She stared out at the late-afternoon sun glinting off the windows of the stately homes on Woodlawn Avenue. How on earth was she going to explain to Mariela why copies of Ressu's "Endnote" had to be destroyed? Mariela would think she'd lost her mind.

Suzanne wiped her palms on her rumpled skirt and sighed. Devin glanced over at her. "It'll be okay, honey."

But she noticed he couldn't quite disguise his own nervousness. His hands fidgeted on the wheel, then he patted his pocket. Finding nothing there, he swore.

"I could sure use a cigarette about now," he muttered, half to himself.

She eyed him with surprise. "You smoke?"

"Not anymore. But I haven't yet figured out a way to get rid of my desire for it." He flashed her a sudden grin. "It's like trying to stop thinking about a particularly intriguing woman."

His hand slid to cup her knee, searing her where he touched her, as he turned his gaze from the road to give her a consuming look. The car veered slightly to the right, narrowly missing a parked car.

"If you don't keep your eyes in your head and your hands on the wheel," she protested, "you won't have a cigarette *or* an intriguing woman, because the woman will be lying dead in a smoldering wreck."

"You can be a pain sometimes, you know that?" he retorted, but he grinned as he said it and turned his gaze back to the road. The hand remained resting on her knee, and after a while she took it in hers.

She stared down at the finely molded bones, the fingers that Devin claimed were sometimes taken over by supernatural forces. Even now his astonishing story sounded incredibly farfetched. Yet she believed it. What choice did she have? She'd seen Valentin's hands controlling Devin's, and she couldn't deny the evidence of her eyes. Besides, strange as it seemed, Devin's ghost explanation tied all the loose ends together better than any theory she'd come up with.

She glanced at Devin, noting the self-assured way he maneuvered the car, even with one hand clutched in hers.

She burned to know more about this enigmatic man with the bizarre secret. A million questions tumbled through her mind.

Finally, she worked up the courage to ask the one she'd asked earlier, which he hadn't answered. "How did all this start? With the ghosts, I mean. Will you tell me?"

His hand on hers tightened. "There's not much to tell."

"I see. Ghostly hands appeared over yours one day and you said, 'Hell, I guess I'm possessed. Better learn to live with it.'"

He relaxed his grip, then grinned at her reasonably good approximation of his manner of speech. "Not exactly." He remained silent a moment before drawing in a deep breath. "Okay, you win. Here's the whole, crazy story."

His voice lowered to a toneless rumbling. "When I was six, I saw my first piano. Mom had saved up to buy it, because she thought it would bring some 'culture' into the house." He smiled, remembering. "The instrument seduced me from the minute they delivered it."

"Seduced you?" she said with amusement.

"Yeah. That's the only way I can describe it. I wanted to touch it, stroke it . . . make it sing—"

"*Seduce* is the word, all right." The tiniest bit of sarcasm overlay her words.

He raised one eyebrow. "You jealous of a piano?" His eyes glittered with amusement as he shot her a quick glance.

"No. I know what all you musicians are like, remember? Sex and music, sex and music . . . that's all you're interested in."

"And food," he added with a straight face.

She took in his large frame, which was tightly squeezed in the seat of his Ferrari, despite his putting the seat back as far as it could go. "Right. Food."

"Anyway, I hassled Mom to get me lessons, and she was tickled pink to do it. I guess she figured her plan to put some culture in the family was already starting to pay off.

SILENT SONATA

So she arranged for the lessons and took me to the piano teacher's house that first time.

"The teacher's wife sent me to the parlor to wait while she fetched her husband so he could talk to Mom. I went into the parlor where I found the piano. I sat down at it, curious to see if it looked like ours. As I sat there, a man walked into the room."

Caught up in the story, Suzanne stared at Devin and wondered at the sudden crystalline quality of his eyes.

"He was youngish," Devin continued, "with hair longer than that of most adults I knew. He fixed me with a stern gaze and said, 'We've been waiting for you a long time.' He confused me. I thought he was saying Mom and I were late for the lesson. I stammered out an apology, but he waved it away.

"'A talent lies deep within you,' he told me in halting English. 'A talent . . . and a gift. I will free the talent and make it blossom. In return, my friends and I wish to make use of your gift. We wander here in this place, and we can sing no more. But with you . . . we can sing again.'"

Devin paused, his eyes misting. "It all sounded like gibberish to me. I sat there wondering how I'd persuade Mom to find me a new teacher since this guy was obviously bonkers.

"But then the man left, and an older man of about sixty came in, telling me he was going to be my teacher." Devin paused, a wry smile on his face. "I asked him who the younger man was, and he told me there was no younger man."

A chill struck Suzanne clear through to the marrow. "Who was he, then?"

The edges of Devin's mouth tipped up in a sad smile. "I found his picture in a book years later. Chopin. It was Frédéric Chopin."

Her hand began to tremble in his. He stroked it reassuringly.

"I never saw another one of them like that," he continued. "I guess they . . . they needed to send a visible spirit to prepare me and it probably took them years to work up to it. After that, all I saw were their hands."

"You mean, you've been seeing these . . . these hands since you were six?"

"Yeah, whenever the maestros decide to . . . er . . . take over."

"D-didn't it frighten you as a child?" She studied his hand as he spoke of things that would have terrified her as a little girl.

He shrugged. "You know, it's funny. It didn't. Not at first. I thought it was some natural side effect of playing the piano. I mean, I found the piano so fascinating, it made perfect sense to my six-year-old mind that the instrument would have a mystical power." His voice hardened. "But I got over being comfortable with it the first time I mentioned the hands and my teacher looked at me like I was insane."

Sucking his breath in, he stared ahead a long time in silence, then released it in a bitter sigh. "And once the rumors started circulating about Dad . . . I learned not to mention the 'ghostly hands' to anyone. Except, of course, my parents."

No wonder he'd not wanted her to learn about his father's strange abilities. How hard had it been all these years to keep his own secret, to hide his real self? "You've never told anyone else?"

"Not even Jack, although I'm sure he suspects I'm not your average, temperamental pianist. We just don't discuss it."

But he'd discussed it with her. He'd risked everything to tell her the truth about himself, so she'd listen to Valentin's message. She interlaced her fingers with his and squeezed them tight.

"You must have been scared to death when Valentin played 'Endnote' and then I popped up out of nowhere accusing you of stealing it."

A wry smile twisted his lips. " 'Scared to death' doesn't quite describe it. When you lit into me at the pub . . . hell, I didn't know what to think. I felt sure my gift had taken a destructive turn. But you want to know what was worst of all?"

Overwhelmed by an odd sense of guilt, she wanted to say, "No," and drop the subject. But he had the right to air his feelings after keeping them bottled up so long, so instead she remained silent.

By this time they'd reached Mariela's house. He parked the car, turned off the ignition, then shifted in his seat so he was facing her.

"The worst thing," he continued in a husky voice, "was that here you were, blazing in with both guns, looking for a way to destroy my career forever, and for about half the night, all I could think of was how much I wanted you. Not just sexually. I wanted to get to know you, to talk to you about music and life and . . . and everything."

He managed a smile. "Until then, I'd viewed my gift as something of a nuisance, a real pain in the ass. Nonetheless, the ghosts gave me joy, even comfort sometimes when they took me over. So even though I resented it, I'd learned to live with it. But after I met you . . ." He paused, his expression dark, wistful, intent. "That was the first time I thoroughly hated my gift."

His confession, said with blatant earnestness, thrilled her to her core. So did the look he was giving her, full of passion and promise. "And now?" she got out through a tight, dry throat.

Lifting his hand to her cheek, he caressed it briefly. "Now I thank God Ressu chose me to pass on his message."

She turned her head into his palm, kissing it. Then she whispered, "Me, too."

Triumph shimmered in his face just before he drew her to him and kissed her hard on the lips, threading his fingers through her hair to hold her head still as he plundered her mouth.

After he'd made her knees turn to water and desire spark to life again in her, he drew back, a serious expression on his face. His eyes were intensely warm, two brilliant lights that could sear her soul if they chose. They searched her face for a moment.

Then he murmured, "After we've taken care of this thing with Ressu, will you still . . . see me?"

Surely he hadn't thought her hesitation earlier meant she didn't want to continue the relationship. "Of course," she said fiercely, planting a kiss on his lips to seal the promise. "You've got to understand, Devin, this relationship has happened pretty suddenly for me. I—I'm not used to . . . to feeling these . . . these . . ."

"Unpredictable emotions?" he asked, his eyes twinkling.

"Yes." She smiled. "You said today, we have plenty of time. Do you think we could play it by ear for a while?"

Feigning astonishment, he quipped, "What? No schedule? No little maps or agendas? Just go with the flow and see where it takes us? You sure you can do that?"

Her eyes flashed. "Has anyone ever told you that you can be absolutely insufferable?"

"I keep hearing that a lot lately," he said with a chuckle.

"Yes, well, you deserve it."

He gave her a rakish smile. "Come on, Zanny. Let's get this Ressu thing over with, so we can start going with the flow."

She laughed. "Whatever you say, maestro."

But the first thing Suzanne saw when she got out of the car wiped the smile from her lips. In the drive of Mariela's brick house sat Paul's car next to Mariela's.

She groaned. "Great, Paul's still here. He's probably talking to Mariela about Valentin's affair with Cindy. That's just what we need on top of all this."

"Leave Paul to me." He rounded the car to her side. "If

you don't want him involved, I'm sure I can persuade him to give you and Mariela some privacy."

"Oh, wonderful. You'll carry him off somewhere to compare notes about my eccentricities."

Devin's eyes twinkled suddenly. "I wonder if he knows the ribbon story," he mused aloud as he walked beside her up the sidewalk.

She rolled her eyes, and he laughed.

It took some time for Mariela to respond to the doorbell. When at last she opened the door, she looked a wreck. Her eyes loomed huge against the delicate bones of her face. Skin pale as moonlight was drawn tight around her pursed lips, and her hands fluttered on the doorknob.

As she caught sight of Suzanne standing there, her face flooded with relief. "Heaven be thanked, you received my message. Come in, come in."

What message? Suzanne thought. But of course if Mariela had tried to reach her earlier, she would have been unsuccessful.

They entered the house, and Suzanne introduced Devin. Mariela acknowledged his presence with a brief nod, but she was clearly too distracted to pay much attention to who he was, or to be concerned about his presence. She took Suzanne's arm and led her through the foyer toward the living room as Devin followed behind.

The buzzing of angry discussion filtered into the foyer. Mariela's lips tightened as a curse suddenly exploded from the living room. Suzanne recognized Paul's voice at once.

Mariela lowered her voice to mutter, "I am so grateful you are here. Ion is making a terrible trouble. He has made Paul very angry."

Suzanne had barely gotten over her surprise that Ion Goma was there when she heard him bellow Mariela's name. Odd that such a small man could have such a big voice, Suzanne thought, wondering what exactly was going on.

As they walked in, Suzanne saw Paul with his fist clutching Ion Goma's shirt and collar as he towered over the smaller man. Paul's jaw was clamped as tight as his fist on Ion's shirt. Ion met his gaze stubbornly, his own hands clenched at his sides.

"Mariela!" Ion boomed again. "Tell this . . . this child to get his hands off me before I drag your family name through the mud simply to teach all of you a lesson!"

"You bastard!" Paul cried, drawing back his other fist.

Mariela rushed to his side and yanked at his arm. "No, no, Paul! Do not do this!" She turned almost frantically to Suzanne. "Make him stop! Please make him stop!"

Suzanne wasn't sure Paul would listen to her any more than his mother, but she took a stab at it anyway. "Come on, Paul. You don't want to upset your mother. She's had enough . . . enough trouble for one day."

Paul jerked his head around, as did Ion. Paul's face showed first relief to see her and Devin standing there in the doorway and then contrition as her words sank in. Slowly he dropped his hand from Ion's shirt and stepped back.

But Ion didn't notice. He was too busy taking in the fact that Suzanne had now entered the picture. The expression on his face was almost comical. His mouth gaped open before he mastered it, twisting it into a sneer of disapproval. Under the influence of a huge scowl, his close-set eyes almost seemed to meld together, giving him the appearance of a furious Cyclops.

He only briefly acknowledged Suzanne before he turned his attention to Mariela. "This is between us, Mariela. Do you truly want her to know the truth?"

Mariela flinched at the fury in his face, but she stood her ground. "You have told my son. Nothing else matters. I care not if Suzanne hears."

Tossing his head in the direction of the doorway, Paul gritted out, "Yes, why don't you tell Suzanne, you bastard, unless you're more of a coward than you already seem to be. Go ahead, make your nasty little threats to Suzanne.

It's what you should have done in the first place." He whirled away in disgust, moving to stand isolated in the corner with his hands thrust in his pockets.

Mariela flushed as she watched her son. She turned her attention to Ion, her eyes filling with tears. "Go on. Tell Suzanne what you wish me to do."

Shifting his gaze from Mariela to Suzanne and back, Ion seemed to consider the matter a moment. Then his eyes narrowed, and he told Suzanne venomously, "I think it's time you stepped down from your position on the committee."

Suzanne nearly cried out with relief. Was that what had Mariela and Paul all upset? Good Lord, Suzanne already knew Ion had been trying to oust her. This came as no great surprise.

"Tell her what you plan to do if she does not step down," Mariela prodded Ion timidly.

"It doesn't matter, Mariela—" Suzanne began.

"Yes, it matters, it matters. Very much." Mariela twisted her hands distractedly as she turned back to Ion. "Tell her—" She broke off with a sob, then seemed to gather the strength to plead, "You . . . you . . . tell her what treachery you intend!"

At the word "treachery," Suzanne's legs turned rubbery. Devin's hand lifted automatically to rest in the small of her back, providing her with some reassurance.

Ion muttered a low curse, his lips curling up in a sneer. He glanced at Paul, but Paul was watching him with a fierce anger, his hands twitching in his eagerness to take a swing at the older man. Ion then met Mariela's gaze, but refused to speak.

"Ion has been speaking of Valentin's family in Romania," Mariela remarked shakily, her eyes never leaving the older man's face. "I knew Valentin Ressu was not my husband's real name. I knew he changed it when he defected."

"Defected?" Suzanne asked, all at sea again. Valentin had been a defector?

Mariela nodded, then swallowed. "Yes. Valentin and I were the only ones to know. Or so I thought." She tilted her head in Ion's direction. "That . . . that horrible man found out the truth. Now he says he will tell everyone if I do not force you to leave the committee so he may be chairman."

"What if he does reveal it publicly?" Devin interjected. His comment brought all eyes to him, as if they'd realized for the first time that Suzanne wasn't alone.

Devin looked a little discomfited by the sudden attention, but continued, "Who cares that Ressu, or whatever his name really was, was a defector?"

"He wasn't just any defector," Ion put in, a glint of triumph in his eyes. "Valentin Ressu was a very special defector, one who would be held suspect by his people if his true identity were discovered."

"And why is that?" Suzanne asked, taking courage from Devin's nonchalant attitude. She was tired of learning about Valentin's numerous skeletons in the closet. Everybody seemed to know one or two. Her voice turned bitter. "Was Valentin some escaped war criminal? A former Nazi perhaps?"

"No," Mariela interjected softly, moving back to Suzanne's side. "Valentin may not have been perfect, but he was not a criminal. But his people . . . they will not understand." She paused, then sighed. "Valentin was Nicolae Ceauşescu's nephew."

Suzanne stood there stunned, her eyes riveted on Mariela's face. Mariela's expression proclaimed the truth of her statements, for Mariela was as easy to read as a billboard. But Suzanne still couldn't believe it. Valentin, a Ceausescu? But he'd always told her . . .

Yes, well, he'd lied about quite a few things, hadn't he? she thought bitterly.

"He wasn't involved with his uncle or anything," Paul hastened to add from his spot in the corner of the room. Then his face clouded. "Was he, Mother?"

"No, no, never!" The hurt expression on her face faded as she glanced at Ion. Her eyes turned wintry, and Ion withered under the icy blast of her stare. "Valentin . . . and I always call him Valentin, though his real name is Cornel . . . was a gentle man, very gentle. He left Romania because he would have no part in the wicked tyrant's plans."

Suzanne didn't know whether to be relieved by Mariela's staunch claim or wary. Her image of Valentin had shifted so much in the past few days she no longer knew truth from fiction. Everyone had a different version of his character, and none of the versions matched hers.

"Why do you want Suzanne to step down so badly that you'd blackmail Mariela?"

Devin's sudden question, directed at Ion and coming from behind her, made Suzanne jump.

Ion sneered at Devin. "Who are you? Her bodyguard?"

"This is Devin Bryce," Suzanne put in. She took great pleasure in watching Ion's expression of contempt turn to one of wary respect. "You've probably heard of him. He's an accomplished concert pianist, and he's interested in Ressu's work."

She hoped Devin didn't mind the white lie. At least it fit in with the few things Paul had said to the group about Devin at their last meeting.

As she'd expected, Ion was stunned. "Are you bringing in another pianist to play at the festival?"

Devin asked quickly, "Why would Suzanne bring in another pianist when you have a perfectly talented one already?"

Suzanne immediately caught on to what Devin was trying to do. No one knew about Cindy's hand being crushed except the police and Suzanne, Devin, and Paul. And possibly Mariela. Therefore, if Ion knew of the incident . . .

If he did know, he masked it well. "Talent, hah! That girl's only talent is in the way she wiggles her behind."

Privately, Suzanne agreed with him, but she couldn't

help bristling at the chauvinistic attitude behind his statement. "And obviously your only talent is in slinging mud."

"Indeed," Mariela murmured approvingly beside her. "But you will not sling this mud at my family. You will leave. You will also ask the Romanian Society to withdraw its support from the festival concert. We will not wish your presence on the committee anymore."

The creases in Ion's brow deepened. "You can't mean this, Mariela! I'm your countryman! You'd choose this mouthy girl over me? This . . . this bold chit who keeps losing copies of 'Endnote' and bringing trouble down on the entire operation?"

"Now wait a minute here—" Devin began.

Suzanne halted him. "*Losing* copies, Ion?" She remembered well what Lydia had hinted at—that Ion might have engineered the thefts to make her look bad. Of course, Ion hated Cindy, too. Her eyes widened. "Good Lord, Ion! Did you have anything to do with Cindy's crushed hand?"

Ion stared at her warily. "What are you talking about?" He shook a bony finger at her. "I have not seen Cindy since our last meeting. I stay out of that little tramp's way."

"Well, someone attacked her this morning and smashed her right hand. It wouldn't surprise me at all to hear you were behind it."

He colored. "You scheming bitch! Is this another story you've invented to get Mariela on your side?"

"Ion!" Mariela commanded, shocking everyone by the firmness in her voice. "You will not speak to Suzanne that way in my house. I am on Suzanne's side because she is my friend. I trust her judgment, as did my husband. She does not ask it. I give it freely. I do it because she gave me comfort when others regarded me as the strange foreigner."

Aware that he trod dangerous ground now, Ion waved his hand in a dismissive gesture, trying another tack. "None of that matters when you're talking about the Romanian

SILENT SONATA

blood that flows through your veins. Remember your duty to your country, your heritage!"

His blatant appeal to Mariela's patriotism might have worked before, but not this time. "My country is where my family is. Suzanne has been family for many years. You know this." She regarded him suspiciously. "That is why you try this . . . this . . . what did Mr. Bryce call it? Ah, yes, this blackmail."

"Not very effective blackmail either," Devin put in, "unless, of course, you actually *want* the festival concert cancelled. If you expose Ressu's heritage, then you'll put an end to the concert, that's for sure."

Judging from Ion's stricken expression, either he hadn't thought of that, or he'd fully expected Mariela to buckle under his pressure and give Suzanne the boot. Probably the latter, thought Suzanne. Ion had always expected women to cave in to his demands. Normally he'd have been right about Mariela. But when it came to her family, she could be surprisingly fierce. Now petite, gentle Mariela had Ion looking like a cornered rat.

Without warning, he swung to face Paul. "What about you, Paul? Do you agree with your foolish mother?"

"Of course," Paul said coolly.

"So. You are willing to let the women rule you in this." Ion gave a contemptuous sniff, his eyes lit with cunning. "I give you the chance to escape Miss Winslow's autocratic commands, and you throw it away. You support her even though she has scoffed at your suggestions in the past."

That's not true! Suzanne wanted to cry out, but she kept silent. The insult was for Paul to answer, not her.

Paul had shifted uncomfortably from foot to foot as Ion spoke, but once the older man was finished, he didn't hesitate in answering. He stared straight at Devin as he repeated the words his idol had said to him that morning, " 'Sometimes the people who love you the most are the ones willing to risk hurting you by telling you the honest truth.' Suzanne has never shied from telling me the truth, and neither has Mother. So if they want you out of the festival concert, then I damned well am going to stand behind them!"

That was the last straw for Ion. He shook his fist at all of them. "I'll take Amarcorp with me! You won't have a penny for the festival concert if you cut me out!"

"We will find other monies—" Mariela began.

Suzanne leaned close and murmured, "I thought you were canceling the festival concert."

"I have changed my mind," Mariela whispered back.

Suzanne stifled a groan.

Ion was pacing the floor, his face flushed and his wiry body wound tight as a spring as he shouted, "You will regret this! I will make all of you very, very sorry! And before I am through, you'll come crawling to me for funding! Crawling!"

"Listen to me, you bastard!" Devin exploded beside Suzanne. He stalked to the middle of the room, blocking Ion's path and forcing the shorter man to halt and stare up at him. Devin continued in a low, menacing voice. "I don't know if you had anything to do with smashing that pianist's hand or not. The cops will decide that. And if you have this burning need to discredit Ressu publicly, go right ahead. Knock your lights out." He paused, lowering his head until he and Ion were on eye level. "But if you lay a hand on Suzanne or her friends, I swear I'll have you clapped in jail in no time flat! I've got plenty of pals in high places, believe me, and they all owe me favors. So stay away from Suzanne and the Ressu family! Is that clear?"

Ion wanted to retort so badly, Suzanne could see his neck muscles strain under the force of his anger. His fists clenched at his sides, but he was no fool. Devin made about two of him and was younger besides. The tips of Ion's ears reddened as he stood there, staring up at Devin, refusing to answer.

"Is that clear, you lily-livered bastard?" Devin repeated.

Suzanne wondered suddenly if Devin were deliberately

provoking the man, hoping he *would* strike out so Devin would have an excuse to beat the tar out of him.

If so, Ion was too astute for that. "Out of my way, you big, dumb Mick!"

Now it was Devin's turn to control his temper, and boy, was he having a rough time at it. His eyes were that unearthly, translucent blue that signaled an intensity of emotion, and every bone in his body seemed poised for a fight. Odd, Suzanne thought. After all these years of assimilation, an ethnic slur could still fire an Irishman's blood.

Nonetheless, she couldn't let Devin take on Ion. "Devin, this is my fight, not yours."

It took a few moments for her words to register. For a moment, she thought Devin might explode and level Ion right there. Then he shook himself, a shudder passing through him. A grim smile spread over his face, and he stepped back, sweeping his hand in front of him as if to say, "Go ahead. He's yours."

She stepped forward. "Ion, I've spoken with Mr. Wilder of Amarcorp." Everyone's eyes swung to her in surprise. "I explained to him your feelings about me and pointed out that they were motivated by bigotry and chauvinism. He didn't seem too pleased about that."

Ion stiffened, his eyes ablaze.

"In fact, he was worried his company might suffer more from accusations of discrimination than from any mishandling of the festival concert they were sponsoring. I think he also wondered how wise it was to continue doing business with you when you had so many . . . distasteful ideas. So you see, Mariela is right. It probably would be best for you to exempt yourself from the project. It would save us all a great deal of heartache."

For the first time that day, Ion looked beaten. "You'll regret this," he muttered, this time ineffectually. One look around the room, and he knew he'd lost. His eyes blazed, but he could do nothing. So he cast them all one last contemptuous glance, then stalked from the room.

As soon as the front door slammed behind Ion, Mariela collapsed onto the nearby sofa. "Dear God in heaven," she whispered, burying her face in her hands. "I should never have taken on this . . . this insane tribute. It has been a nightmare from beginning to end."

Suzanne sank onto the sofa beside her and put her arm around her shoulders. "You can end it whenever you like. Just say the word."

Mariela shook her head. "No, no, you have all been right. I owe it to my countrymen to present Valentin's music to the world."

Oh, no, Suzanne thought, *how am I going to talk her out of this?*

She glanced up at Devin, and he shrugged, clearly at a loss. She was on her own with this one. "You don't owe your countrymen anything. Valentin wouldn't have expected it of you. For all we know, he would never have performed 'Endnote' in public himself. He never talked about it. Who knows if he was planning to?"

"Yes, he was," Mariela protested, lifting her head. "Before he died, he arranged a trip to Munich to perform it."

Devin and Suzanne exchanged glances.

"Munich?" Suzanne asked.

"Of course. You know he traveled often to Europe to perform."

"Well, yes, he toured there, that's true. But why Munich for 'Endnote'? By that time, he could have gone to Romania."

Mariela raised her eyebrows with uncharacteristic irony. "Yes. His countrymen would have welcomed the nephew of Ceauşescu with open arms."

With a grimace, Suzanne acknowledged the truth of Mariela's sarcastic statement. Suzanne still wasn't accustomed to thinking of her mentor as Cornel Ceauşescu rather than Valentin Ressu. "But he'd defected. Wouldn't that have made them accept him?"

Mariela shrugged. "We shall never know, shall we? My

SILENT SONATA

husband believed he would not be accepted. Today in Romania, anyone accused of being the friend or family of Ceauşescu is not a respected person. Valentin was a hero to his people because of his concerts. It would have killed him to see their respect turn to hatred because they learned his real name."

"Wait," Suzanne interrupted. "What do you mean, he was a hero because of his concerts?"

A weak wash of late-afternoon light from the window highlighted the frightened expression on Mariela's face for a moment before it passed. She fiddled with her skirt nervously, her eyes on her lap. "I—I don't suppose it hurts to tell you now. He wished to keep it a secret before. But now . . ." She paused, a tentative smile crossing her face. "A few times a year, when Valentin toured Europe, he performed in Munich for Radio Free Europe. It was a way to give to his people, he said."

"Radio Free Europe." Devin sounded thoughtful. "Isn't that the organization that broadcasts freedom messages into Czechoslovakia, Poland, Romania . . . what used to be countries behind the Iron Curtain?"

Mariela nodded.

Suzanne knew of RFE's work in Eastern Europe, as well as other countries around the globe, but she'd had no idea Valentin had ever been involved.

Mariela said with pride, "Many Romanians heard the concerts of Valentin Ressu. Many received hope from the knowledge that one Romanian had succeeded on the outside."

A lump lodged in Suzanne's throat as she clutched Mariela's hands. As Mariela had said earlier, Valentin might not have been perfect, but he was no criminal. In fact, he was something of a hero, and an unacknowledged one at that.

Tears of relief welled in Suzanne's eyes. "I—I wish I'd known," she stammered.

Paul stepped forward from the corner where he'd been

standing, mute and forgotten. "I wish I'd known, too, Mother." His words were tinged with hurt.

Mariela seemed torn between tears and laughter as she looked up into the face of her beloved son. "Oh, my sweet darling. Your father was a very stubborn man sometimes. You know that. He wanted you to love him for himself, not because he was a hero." She sighed, holding out her hands to Paul.

For a moment, he paused with wounded dignity, his hands shoved deep in his pockets. But he couldn't resist an appeal like that from his mother. He took one reluctant step forward, then with a cry, knelt on the floor in front of her, burying his face in her lap.

They sat there, Mariela stroking his hair and whispering words in Romanian as Paul struggled to hold back tears, the sound of his deep gasps only partly muffled by his mother's skirt.

Devin placed his hand on Suzanne's shoulder, and she put her hand over his, squeezing tightly.

"I . . . I was so cruel to him," Paul was saying, "the way I acted . . . the things I said. If I'd only known—"

"Hush, darling." Mariela pushed his hair back from his face. "You did not know. I think your father was afraid to tell you. What he did was so dangerous. Many times before, Ceauşescu sent assassins into Munich to kill important people at RFE. Your father believed we would be safer not to know."

Paul raised his face to look up at her. Confusion filled his expression. And a hint of wounded pride. "What about after everything changed in Romania? After Ceauşescu died?"

Mariela bit her lip and toyed with his shirt, plucking at imaginary lint. "The fear goes slowly, my son. It takes time for it to seep away. Ceauşescu lies dead in the grave, but his ghost still haunts us." She shook her head. "I thought it best not to speak of it at all." She managed a smile. "Besides, it was your father's wish to be remembered for his music, not his work for RFE."

"I still wish you'd told me."

"Yes. I suppose I should have." Mariela's voice softened. "Your father was a very great man. You must remember that always."

Her hands stilled on his hair and she lifted her eyes to look at Suzanne. "I forgot my husband's greatness for a time. When . . . when I found out about Valentin and that . . . that . . . girl, I was so very angry."

Paul rose and slid onto the couch, holding his mother awkwardly in his arms. Suzanne released her to him.

"Cindy was nothing to him, Mother, I know it," Paul whispered. His eyes met Devin's over her head. "Sometimes men are just plain dumb."

Suzanne smiled wryly. Good description for anybody who took up with Cindy Stephens, she thought.

Mariela twisted her hands in her lap. "I—I never knew, never guessed Valentin had . . . er . . . known this girl in that way until a short time ago when someone who did not sign their name sent me a letter he had written to her. I could not doubt it then."

She broke off with a sob, and Paul pulled her tighter. *Women are so funny,* Suzanne thought as Mariela continued to cry. Mariela had obviously lived with the secret of her husband's true identity for years without being bothered by the fact he was nephew to a tyrant who might have him murdered any moment. But find out he was having an affair, and her world was shattered.

Then again, Mariela had every right to be upset. Much as she might say she regretted her earlier anger over Valentin's infidelity, her anger would never completely recede. In that one respect, Valentin had definitely blown it. Hero or not, he'd never had the right to hurt his family like that.

Mariela cried softly for a moment, her slender shoulders shaking. Then she said, in a voice that wavered, "I was wrong to try to cancel the concert simply because of Valentin's . . . Valentin's foolish actions with that girl. But now I will right that wrong." She stared up at Suzanne, a weak smile on her face. "We will have the concert. We will show the world my husband was a hero."

Suzanne grimaced, wondering how on earth she'd ever get Mariela to cancel the festival concert now. Then she stopped. Was it still even necessary? After all, if Ion had been behind all the thefts, he'd been dealt with.

On the other hand, the message Devin had transcribed had said, "Destroy 'Endnote.' " How did that fit in with all of this?

"Mariela, perhaps we should talk about the festival concert—" she began.

Devin interrupted her, his fingers digging into her shoulder. "Yes, that's a good idea, honey. But could we make it another time? I have to be going. I have an appointment with . . . er . . . Jack in an hour. Besides, I'm sure Mariela and Paul would like to be alone for a while."

Suzanne gave Devin a sharp look, wondering why he was being so abrupt. She knew good and well he didn't have an appointment with Jack or anybody else.

Mariela looked at Devin. "Oh, of course. I understand. We've already taken up so much of your time. I'm grateful you were here when Ion . . . made his despicable threats. Thank you." Then she thought a moment and said pensively, "I don't know if we ever talked about why the two of you came by."

Suzanne drew in a deep breath. "We wanted to—"

"—discuss the festival concert," Devin broke in again, to her extreme annoyance. "But we can do that another time, can't we, Suzanne?"

"Of course," she bit out. Once she got Devin in the car, she was going to get to the bottom of this.

She rose from the sofa, as did Mariela and Paul. The Ressus accompanied them into the hall, Paul still with his arm around his mother's shoulders.

They'd gotten as far as the door when Devin suddenly

SILENT SONATA

turned and fixed Mariela with an intent gaze. "Listen, Mrs. Ressu. I've been puzzling over a Romanian word I remember reading in the news. Maybe you could tell me what it means."

"Of course," she said brightly. "What is it?"

"Radu."

Suzanne stifled a groan, wishing he'd asked her instead.

For a moment, Mariela paled, but she recovered quickly. "Well . . . it is a name, a fairly common Romanian name. But if you read about it in the news, then it probably refers to something else." She sucked in her breath. "After a highly placed Romanian security official defected in the seventies, he revealed that *Radu* was a code name for one of Ceauşescu's methods of eliminating dissenters."

His eyes narrowed. "Oh? What exactly was the method?"

At his question, Mariela's discomfort increased. She slid her arm around her son's waist, clutching it as if it were a lifeline. She ran one hand nervously over her brow, then glanced away from Suzanne and Devin for a moment.

"Without their knowing it, Ceauşescu bombarded dissenters he'd brought in for questioning with radiation that almost always caused cancer shortly afterward." An involuntary shudder made her briefly tremble.

Then she fixed Devin with a gaze of such suffering, it was almost palpable. Her voice dropped to a whisper. "Many dissenters died horrible, painful deaths as a result of his wicked tactics. That, I'm afraid, is *Radu.*"

21

♪

"Christ!" Devin muttered under his breath as soon as the door to Mariela's shut behind them. "I think I'm going to be sick."

Never had he dreamed when he'd deciphered Ressu's message that *Radu* could mean something so awful. He wondered how it fit in with the other lyrics in 'Endnote'—"Love yields death if altars kill men." What could that enigmatic line be? A diatribe on religious oppression? But Ceauşescu hadn't been religious.

"Would you mind telling me what that was all about?" Suzanne hissed as he rushed her to the car. "I hope you had a fantastic reason for whisking me away before I could talk to Mariela about the festival and then upsetting her by mentioning *Radu*."

He paused outside the car. "Did you know what *Radu* meant?"

"Yes, of course. Anyone familiar with the events in Romania over the last few years knows about *Radu*."

"Why didn't you tell me that's what Ressu was talking about in 'Endnote'?"

She shrugged. "You didn't ask. I mean, I've known the messages buried in Valentin's pieces so long I don't even think about what they mean anymore. I always assumed *Radu* was his lament for the terrible things that happened in Romania."

"Yeah, well, I think it was more than a lament," he muttered.

He opened the car door and helped her in, then went around to his side and got in. He started the engine and pulled away from the curb impatiently. While they'd been inside, night had fallen and the darkness only served to heighten his unease.

"Would you please explain?" she demanded imperiously.

Suzanne could be a hell of a bossy woman sometimes, he thought. "Mariela's revelations about Radio Free Europe got me thinking, particularly since all this speculation about Ion Goma's part in the thefts didn't explain Ressu's message to you to destroy 'Endnote.'"

"I wondered about that."

"I did more than wonder. While you and Mariela were talking, I started considering a few things."

She twisted in her seat to look at him. "Like what?"

"Like if you'd been mugged because Ion wanted you out of the picture, then why didn't Ressu warn you about Ion instead of telling you to destroy 'Endnote'?"

She looked nonplussed a second. "Hmmm. Maybe Hamlet was right. You can't trust a ghost."

Devin gave her a scathing look. "That's all you can come up with?"

"Give me a break." She sighed, her shoulders slumping. "I've spent all day listening to bizarre revelations about the men in my life. I think I can be allowed a lame joke or two."

Suitably chastened, he reached over and took her hand. "Sorry, you're right. This *has* been a rough day for you, hasn't it? Tell you what. How about if I take you somewhere for dinner? We've spent so much time dissecting the past that neither of us has had a chance to eat."

"I thought you had an appointment," she said archly.

He grimaced. "No, but I had to get you out of there so we could talk about this Ressu thing."

She rolled her eyes. "Okay, so talk."

"Does that mean you'll have dinner with me?"

"If I don't, the grumbling in my stomach will drown out

anything you have to say, so I guess I don't have much choice."

"Nope, you sure don't." With a grin, he turned onto Lake Shore Drive, headed toward the restaurant he had in mind. "Back to Ressu. Let's analyze this carefully. It's time to use a little logic."

"Definitely *my* area," she quipped.

"Yeah, right, your area," he shot back with considerable sarcasm, then ruefully acknowledged to himself that she did have a tendency to analyze everything in minute detail. Her talents could be pretty useful at the moment. He paused, thinking. "Aside from the peculiar message Ressu gave you, what about the microphones in my apartment? Ion didn't seem to even know about me. Why would Ion bug my apartment anyway, and how would that help him oust you from the committee?"

She frowned. "I don't know."

"Okay. Consider this, Zanny. You were the only person to know about the Morse code messages, right?"

"Right."

"Even Mariela didn't know?"

"Not to my knowledge."

His brow furrowed. "I have to wonder . . . why would a musician who's constructed an ingenious system of meaning in his work keep it such a secret?"

"I told you. He admired James Joyce and wanted to do the same thing in music."

"Yes, but I've spent a lot of time chatting with the Joyceans in Bloomsday Pub. If I remember right, James Joyce challenged scholars to figure out *Finnegans Wake*. He didn't give them all the answers, but he admitted there was meaning buried there and urged them to discover it for themselves."

"True." Her eyes lit with eager intensity as she took up the thread he'd begun. "You know, I've often thought it was odd that Valentin would hide his most inventive method from his audience. It never made sense to me. Why not use it to draw people into his concerts? Even if he didn't tell them what the messages were or how they were buried, he could have told them the messages existed."

"Exactly."

Suzanne stared straight ahead at the road unseeingly, her face taut with suppressed energy. "So if he didn't create them for artistic reasons, why were they there?"

He hesitated a moment before answering. "Mariela told us Ressu performed the sonatas for Radio Free Europe. During the years he was performing, Romania was almost totally blocked off to foreigners. It would have been impossible for Ressu to get in anyway, because his uncle would have had him killed or arrested. Nor would Ressu have wanted to risk blowing his new identity by having anyone recognize him. But on the radio, he could be invisible and still get a message across."

Suzanne swung her gaze to him. He could feel it burning into the side of his face.

Her hand convulsed in his. "Valentin could bury messages in his music that no one would ever detect. He could communicate with relatives . . . friends . . . dissenters." Her voice rose, a sudden note of alarm in it. "*Radu!* Oh, good Lord. Maybe he meant it to be a warning."

"Maybe. Who knows? But I suspect those lyrical messages are one more level of code. They sound like simple, poetic lines, but maybe they have another meaning we don't grasp." He paused, weighing his words. "Honey, it's quite possible that that meaning isn't just a freedom message either, or even a warning. After all, your average person wouldn't have known to listen for the Morse code. But if one person in Romania knew the secret, Ressu could have aired the messages for him or her."

She was silent a moment, mulling over what he'd said. They reached a self-park lot downtown, and he pulled in, finding a space quickly. He turned off the ignition, then twisted to face her.

"Honey," he said softly. "Ressu's messages could have

been politically oriented. You know, sending information about defectors or arranging assignations with emissaries from the West. Stuff like that."

Her skin took on a sudden pallor. "Are you saying Valentin was . . . was working for the CIA or something? That he was a spy?"

He shrugged. "Hell, I don't know. But he apparently didn't want many people to know about his activities with Radio Free Europe. Mariela said as much. Her reason for his keeping it a secret before Ceauşescu's execution made sense. But after the execution? I think he did it because he had to, because he'd given an oath to the U.S. government or something. I mean, there was a big stink in the sixties about Radio Free Europe being an arm of the CIA. He wouldn't have wanted to confirm that, would he?"

"This sounds like something out of a cloak-and-dagger movie, Devin. It's crazy."

"Well, it sure would explain the bugs in my apartment. That's the way political guys work, not the way regular criminals or idiots like Goma do."

She shuddered, hugging herself. "Okay. Suppose you're right. What has that got to do with 'Endnote' and Valentin's warning?"

He gazed at her steadily. After a moment, she turned, her eyes locking with his.

"Perhaps Ressu embedded a dangerous message in 'Endnote,' " he said slowly, "one he'd never intended anyone to hear except his audience through Radio Free Europe."

"That makes no sense. He wrote 'Endnote' after the country was opened up to the West. There was no longer any need for covert messages."

"But think about it. As Mariela said, he couldn't return to Romania himself. Maybe he didn't even know who in Romania had been listening and deciphering all those messages. I mean, spy networks work that way, don't they? No one knows who's a good guy and who's not, right?"

"Right," she murmured, her eyes distant. "So he had this message he'd planned to send into Romania . . . using the same methods he had before."

"Yes, and I'd lay odds the second level of message, the message beneath the lines you deciphered, wasn't anything he'd want someone to get their hands on. Maybe he even thought someone might try to prevent its being heard. I don't know. Anyway, he died before he could pass it on."

"Except he had you." The irony in her voice contained no trace of bitterness. Her lips quivered as she stared up at him.

"Yeah." A muscle worked in his jaw as he thought about the situation Ressu must have found himself in. "The guy was in a fix. He'd left you here among the living, and since he couldn't clean house before the Grim Reaper took him, you'd figured out his Morse code messages. Worse yet, you were planning to have his last piece performed for all the world to hear, including, no doubt, a few Romanians with more than a cursory interest in his works. Ressu knew that was a setup for disaster, especially if someone didn't want the message heard."

"So you're saying he worried about me in the grave? And he tried to warn me?"

Devin pounded the steering wheel. "Of course! He wanted to protect you. And he probably risked a lot by having me play 'Endnote' when you were there at my recital." He grimaced. "Then again, the damned bastard probably figured if the bad guys heard it, they'd go after me instead of you. But you'd still get the message. The guy's slick, I'll give him that."

For the first time since they'd begun their discussion, she smiled. An impish light entered her eyes as she placed her hand on his. "He never did like you much, you know."

"That's the understatement of the year." He groaned. A surge of quick anger at Ressu made him grit his teeth. "Apparently your mentor was perfectly willing to sacrifice me so you'd be safe." He added, speaking into the air, "Thanks a lot, buddy."

She eyed him curiously, her smile trembling on her lips. "Do you talk to him often like that?"

He flashed her a sheepish grin. "Ever since he handed me *this* mess, I have. Who knows if he pays any attention."

"Who knows?" she echoed lightly, but he could tell she was starting to get all choked up again. And everything he'd told her no doubt had disturbed her.

He cupped her cheek, stroking his thumb along the upper swell. "Look, this is a lot to handle all at once, especially on an empty stomach. Let's eat, okay? After we get some food in our bellies, we can discuss it some more, and maybe figure out what we're going to do."

A wisp of a smile curved her lips up. "Sounds good, maestro."

They got out of the car and left the lot. He steered her toward Dearborn Street. She glanced up at him curiously. "I thought we were going to stop at a burger joint."

He shook his head, sliding his hand up her back to her shoulder and letting it remain there possessively. "Hell, no. I'd never take a woman I cared about to a burger joint. Not on a first date anyway."

"So where are we going?"

"Printers Row."

She paused on the sidewalk, her face lit with pleasure. "Printers Row? Won't you need reservations or something?"

He clutched his hand to his heart as if he'd been wounded, a mock expression of pain on his face. "Me? Devin Bryce? Have you no faith in my pull around here? If I can't get us a table, then who can?"

As it turned out, Devin couldn't. Nobody could. They discovered the restaurant was closed for remodeling when they came up the street to find the place dark and the doors locked.

He glanced at her ruefully. "So much for my pull."

Obviously struggling to keep her face straight, she said very quietly, "You know, a tight-assed person . . . someone like, say, me . . . would have called ahead instead of making a mad dash to the restaurant."

"Yes, well, a tight-assed person . . . like you, for example . . . would have missed a lot of fun in the process."

"Oh. I didn't realize standing outside of a closed restaurant with an empty stomach was fun."

He stole a glance at her, noting that the edges of her mouth were quivering from the effort to keep from smiling. "You're really going to rub this in, aren't you?" he growled as he tugged her arm to steer her toward the lights of a fast-food place down the street.

She burst into laughter when she saw where he was pulling her. "You bet I am. We tight-assed types don't get too many victories, and I'm going to savor this one for a long time."

It was so good to hear the laughter in her voice, he thought as she continued to chuckle to herself all the way down the street. Hell, he could easily get used to this, to being with a woman who could laugh . . . not only at him, but at herself.

Sure, she had a tendency to overanalyze everything, but once she'd seen Ressu's hands, she'd taken Devin's statements at face value, despite their apparent absurdity. When it came right down to it, Suzanne was loyal to those she cared about, and that loyalty endeared her to him more than anything.

"You know, Miss Priss," he said as they strolled along, "this will be a unique experience for me. Looks as if we'll have our first real date in a burger joint after all. I hope you brought along a hanky to wipe off the seat."

She took a swipe at him with her purse.

He ducked. "Hey! Watch the rough stuff! You might hurt my hands and ruin my career as a big-shot pianist. Then I couldn't afford to take you anywhere at all."

She looked at him askance, her expression shuttered.

Then she stared down at the sidewalk as they walked along. "So tell me something, Mr. Big-shot Pianist."

Her voice sounded casual. Deceptively so, he thought, automatically wary. "Yeah?"

"How do I compare to the other women you've dated? Maggie said you preferred 'busty, easygoing types.'" Suzanne paused, looking down at herself, and made a face. "I don't know about the busty part, and as you keep reminding me, I'm far from easygoing."

He had to resist the urge to chuckle. It never ceased to amaze him she was so unaware of her blatant appeal. Of course, that was what made her so much fun to tease.

He looked over at her, letting his gaze rest meaningfully on her poor maligned breasts. "Yeah, well, we can't do anything about your personality, can we? As for your breasts . . . they do have those operations . . . what are they called? Breast augmentation?"

"Devin!" she cried out, a horrified expression on her face as she stopped short on the sidewalk.

"I'm kidding, I'm kidding!" he protested, throwing up his hands. Then oblivious to the few people who walked by, he brought his hands down to rest on her shoulders. "Hey, if I hadn't liked the package you came in, not to mention the great stuff inside, you think I would have let you put me through all that hell?" He lowered his voice to a husky whisper. "Besides, everyone knows it's not what you've got, but what you do with it. And, honey, you definitely know what to do with what you've got."

Her sudden embarrassment delighted him no end. He drew her up close and planted a quick kiss on her lips, surprised when she jerked him back for another one.

"And you, Mr. Bryce," she whispered seductively, "do have a few . . . er . . . talents of your own to be arrogant about."

His breath caught in his throat. For a woman who'd been reluctant to discuss her feelings for him, she was being awfully open. "You keep that up," he murmured, "and we won't be eating anything tonight. Not food anyway."

"Devin!" she remonstrated, but her protest was half-hearted, and he couldn't help noticing the way she unconsciously licked her lips.

His groin tightened viciously, threatening to completely destroy his equilibrium. Only the sudden loud rumble that came from her stomach kept him from turning around and taking her back to the car where they could have some privacy.

They both laughed as his stomach rumbled too.

"Come on," he muttered, reaching for her arm, and they continued arm in arm down the street until they reached the fast-food place.

After they'd gotten their food, and she'd enjoyed herself commenting on the massive amount he'd ordered, they found a quiet booth in the back. They ate in silence for a moment, both so ravenous they could hardly keep from wolfing down the greasy burgers. Devin noted with satisfaction that even Suzanne had mustard dripping down her fingers and onto the paper wrapper. Of course, he didn't even bother to worry about the crumbs gathering around his own wrapper. He stuffed as many ketchup-drenched fries into his mouth as he could manage, and hoped Suzanne wouldn't turn away in disgust.

She didn't, although he noticed she couldn't resist busing the table when they were through. Only when she came back from the restroom with a wet napkin to wipe it did he tell her she was going too far.

"Come on," he muttered, "leave that alone. You and I have to talk about what we've got to do."

"We?"

"Yeah, we. You're not alone in this, okay?" He rushed on, not allowing her a chance to protest. "It's simple. We've got to destroy every copy of 'Endnote' in sight. Don't think about it, don't try to reason out the messages or anything. Just destroy the damned things, and make it well known we've done so."

She gnawed at her lower lip, avoiding his eyes. "I . . . well . . . I'd wanted to talk to Mariela about it first."

"I know." He tried not to sound annoyed. "And I jerked you out of there before you could. But it's best this way. You don't want to give her a chance to stop you or even to threaten some sort of legal action. Hell, if you have to, you can lie and claim the bad guys finally succeeded in stealing all the copies."

"I suppose."

"Suzanne, there could be someone out there desperate to keep the copies out of circulation, no matter what. Who knows what he or she's capable of?"

"You're right." She nodded, as if trying to convince herself. "But I'd love to be able to figure out what the messages were."

He rose from his cramped seat, reaching out his hand for her. "Yeah, well, unless you want to find yourself entangled in some international intrigue, I suggest you keep your scholarly curiosity to yourself. Come on, let's go to your house. It's time to get this over with. Then you can call your pals at the police station and report a robbery, and we'll try to make sure the story hits the papers. That ought to get the bastards off your back."

She nodded again, absently, as she took his hand and followed him out the door. They'd almost reached the car before she spoke again.

"You know, it probably wouldn't take much to figure the messages out. If we got some expert to look at them—"

"Have you lost your damned mind?" he exploded. "You want to get yourself killed or something?"

"Well, no. But no one needs to know what we're up to. We could keep a copy just for ourselves. . . ."

"No. Absolutely not." They'd found his car by that point, and he unlocked it. Before she could get in, however, he swung her around to face him. "Listen to me, Zanny, and listen good. I watched my father be destroyed by an enemy I was too young to fight. Now you're up against an enemy I'm sure as hell old enough to fight. And if fighting him and keeping you from being destroyed means burning up a bunch of valuable papers, then I'm willing to do it. Are you?"

She stared at him, her eyes wide and luminous in the fluorescent lights of the parking lot. "I guess I am." She managed a smile. "However, I do think you're entirely too happy about this. Are you sure you don't want to destroy the manuscript just so you can get Valentin back for driving you crazy these past few weeks?"

"I'll admit it's a nice side benefit." He grinned, then winced when she punched him.

Despite their attempts at lightening the situation, once they got in the car and headed back to Hyde Park, a pall descended over both of them. Devin realized how hard it must be for her to contemplate destroying the last work of her mentor's masterpiece, but he also knew he couldn't rest until it was done.

Besides, he rationalized, Ressu obviously wanted it destroyed himself. It wasn't as if they were going against the composer's wishes.

A short time later they pulled up in front of Suzanne's house. Devin turned the engine off and looked over at Suzanne.

She was watching the house, a relieved smile on her face. "Thank heavens Mother's not here."

"How do you know?"

"My car's gone. She took it today."

"Come on then." He opened his door. "Let's go."

She sighed. "Okay."

Both remained silent as they approached the house. He couldn't help the sense of dread that stole over him the closer they got. It was probably simply his reaction to Suzanne's depressed silence. But he kept having the funny feeling that someone was watching them.

Of course, maybe somebody was, and it was just as well. The more publicly he and Suzanne destroyed the manuscript, the more successful they'd be at fending off would-be attackers.

Nonetheless, he found his steps slowing as they approached the house. That uneasy feeling wouldn't go away.

She'd climbed up to the stoop and unlocked the door before she realized he wasn't right next to her.

"What is it?" she asked, turning toward him as she opened the door.

"I don't know. I—I don't know."

Bartok peered around the edge of her door, then seeing that no one noticed him, made a mad dash past Devin for the street.

"Bartok, you stupid cat!" Suzanne cried out. "Catch him, catch him, Devin! He'll disappear for good if you don't catch him!"

Without even stopping to think, he sprinted after Bartok, who'd slowed his pace to stroll along the opposite sidewalk. The cat had already made it half a block. Devin crossed the street ahead of him, then caught sight of something glinting among the dark shadows of a tree nearly a block away from Suzanne's house.

Ignoring the cat, he stared more closely. It was a motorbike, shielded from the street lights where it was parked in the shadows. It took him only a second to realize why it looked so familiar. . . .

"Suzanne!" he cried out, whirling back toward the house. She still stood on the stoop, watching him. "Suzanne, come here!"

She took a step down.

Then a blast shook the air as her house exploded before his shocked gaze.

22

♪

Devin stared bleakly at the white-coated doctor standing before him. "What do you mean, she's still unconscious! It's been five hours already. She wasn't hurt that badly. I saw her in the ambulance—she only had a slight bruise on her head!"

"Her house blew up a few feet away from her, Mr. Bryce, and from what you've said, she knocked her head pretty hard against the pavement when the blast threw her back. Judging from her rapid pulse and her pupils, she's suffering from a concussion beneath that small bruise."

"Oh, Christ," he said hoarsely.

"It could be mild. Or there could be intercranial bleeding. All we can do is watch and wait to see if her symptoms improve. Believe me, it's good that she's alive at all. If as you say, a bomb rather than a gas leak caused the explosion, then there's no telling how much of the blast was directed at her."

Devin and the doctor were standing in the waiting room of the hospital's intensive care unit. Jack Warton stood beside Devin, but could offer his friend little comfort. Neither of them had tracked down Felicia Winslow yet. Suzanne's mother had apparently left the gallery to go to a party somewhere. Devin had already contacted Paul and Mariela, telling them to find Felicia.

As the doctor continued to give his opinion of Suzanne's condition, Devin saw in his mind's eye the image of Suzanne lying motionless in the glass-walled room of the unit, her eyes closed, her breathing so shallow he'd barely been able to see the rise and fall of her chest under the sheet. He felt his guts wrench all over again remembering her pale and slender body hooked up to a bunch of tubes and monitors.

He turned back to the doctor, a fierce expression on his face. "I can't believe you people can't do anything to bring her out of this! For Chrisake, are you just going to let her lie there? Aren't you going to operate or something?"

The doctor gave a sigh of exasperation. "Unless we have signs of bleeding, and so far we have none, there's nothing we can operate on, Mr. Bryce."

"You can't let her die!"

Until he'd said the words, he hadn't dared to think about the possibility. But now the thought that she might not survive reared its ugly head, threatening to destroy him.

A kind of frenzied anger poured through his veins, filling his mind, his body, his soul. "Look, you've got to do something! I don't care what you do, I don't care what it costs. If she needs some special equipment or—"

"All we can do is wait."

"Damn it, you bastard, I want you to—"

"Devin." Jack cut him off, grabbing at his elbow and jerking his head to indicate the others in the waiting room. "Come on, guy. You're upset now. Why don't you let the doctor do his job, okay? You're not helping anything standing out here ranting and raving."

Devin scarcely noticed Jack motion the doctor away. He let Jack lead him to an empty hallway outside the waiting room, but he was sick with fury, poisoned by the insane terror in his blood. As Jack watched warily, Devin paced the hall. "You don't understand, Jack, it's all my fault! I should have gotten Ressu's message to her sooner. Maybe we could have stopped this if I had. She'd be sitting here now with me—"

He broke off, his eyes wild and tormented as he ran his hands over his shirtfront, hunting for the cigarette pack that wasn't there. With a curse, he continued, "She'd be smiling and teasing me like she was last night . . . like when she was . . ."

An image flashed into his mind, of Suzanne gloating in front of the closed restaurant, and looking infinitely endearing while she did it. She was the only woman he could ever imagine wanting. He loved her so damned much, it hurt. And he hadn't told her. He'd been so afraid to frighten her away, to push her before she was ready. Christ, he'd never told her!

He groaned and pounded one fist into the other. "She can't die. She can't. I won't let her die, damn it!"

"Give it some time." Jack's voice was unusually gentle. "She'll come out of it on her own once her body has healed."

"But the bastards won't let her heal!"

"The doctors are doing all they can—"

"Not the doctors!" Devin fixed Jack with tormented eyes. "I'm talking about the people who did this to her. Hell, if they'd bomb her house, they'll find a way to get to her in here! Ion Goma came close to threatening her life, and I don't know for sure he wasn't the one who did this. Then there was the guy on the motorcycle . . . and God knows who else. But do you think the damned cops will post a guard? No, not on your life!"

Jack glanced uneasily around the hall, then back at Devin. "What are you talking about? What is all this stuff about Ion Goma—whoever the devil he is—and a guy on a motorcycle and bombs? The cops said it was a gas leak ignited by the stove pilot, plain and simple."

"Yeah, a gas leak. The guy on the motorcycle worked real hard to make it look like an accident, but I know he rigged it to blow. I know it." Devin's tone lowered to a pained, embittered rumbling as he shut his eyes and rubbed one finger up the bridge of his nose. "Trouble is, I can't convince the cops. All they have is my word about the motorcycle, and they couldn't find it or the guy on it. And they claim Ion Goma has an alibi. So much for my connections, huh?"

"You know, you're beginning to sound loony. I think you should get some sleep, big shot. You're a little whacked out right now."

Devin's eyes shot open. He clutched at Jack's arm, his fingers digging deep. "I'm not crazy, Jack. Somebody's been after Suzanne for a long time now. A guy on a motorcycle mugged her once, and then I caught the same guy bugging my apartment. There's police reports on both of those, if you don't believe me. You'd think the reports would convince them, but they think I'm just distraught and seeing things, especially since they didn't find anything but evidence of a gas leak. You've got to believe me, though, Jack. She's still in danger!"

"Okay, okay." Jack shifted from one foot to the other. He reached for a cigarette and started to light it, then took one look at the NO SMOKING sign, and put it away. "So somebody's after Suzanne. You mind telling me why?"

That question brought Devin up short, knocking the wind from him. All these years of keeping his secret . . . all these years of acting a role in front of the man who'd shoved Devin forward whenever he wanted to quit. Had it really come to this? Was it time now to reveal his "other" talents to Jack?

After all, at this point Devin's only hope was to find who was behind all this, to figure out the significance of Ressu's message so he could persuade the cops to help. Then again, how would he ever get them to help when he couldn't explain how he'd gotten the message and whom he'd gotten it from?

"Listen, big shot," Jack said, breaking into his thoughts. "If you want to talk about it, I'm here. I'm not going to force you to tell me anything. But keep in mind you aren't the only one in this town with connections. Remember my stint during the Korean War. I've still got a few old war buddies. And if you're talking about bombs and wiretaps and crap like that, I know some people who might be able to help."

Devin stared at Jack for several intense moments. He'd temporarily forgotten Jack's service record, mainly because they never talked about it much. But Jack was right. If the cops couldn't help, it could be useful to get the aid of Jack's friends, even if they were a little rusty on the draw.

To do it, however, Devin would have to explain about the messages. He'd have to tell Jack everything. He'd have to open up his soul to ridicule and risk losing his manager.

Then again, if Suzanne had taught him anything, it was that a person who cared for you could handle a lot of eccentricity. Hell, if Suzanne, who didn't accept anything outside the realm of logic, could believe him, couldn't Jack?

Jack had never betrayed him, never let him down. Okay, so what if Jack did decide Devin was crazy? At this point, Devin had nothing to lose by enlisting Jack's aid.

And he could lose Suzanne if he didn't.

He ran his fingers through his hair distractedly, glancing at the door leading into the intensive care unit area. He still couldn't believe it. He'd never forget the way his heart plummeted when he saw her thrown off the stoop, her head hitting the pavement with an audible crack. Just looking at her here, terribly frail and quiet, made him feel so much rage, he could hardly stomach it.

And guilt. Hell, Dad's suicide had enraged him, mainly because Dad had consciously chosen death. But Suzanne hadn't consciously chosen anything. Instead she'd been forced into a dangerous situation, partly by Ressu in his foolish attempt to save her, but mostly by Devin himself, who could have stopped everything before it escalated if he'd just trusted her with the truth about his gifts.

Christ, it wasn't fair! If anyone should have taken that blast, it should have been he!

Devin whirled from the door to face his manager. "All right. I need your help bad this time, Jack. I love her and I have to bring her out of this, even if she blames me for everything once it's over."

"If she loves you as much as you apparently love her, I don't think she'll blame you."

"I don't know what she feels for me, to be honest. That was . . . that was kind of unresolved. And then the bomb—" He broke off, his throat tightening before he could go on. "But damn it, I'm not going to let it stay unresolved! I'm going to do something about it! Are you with me?"

"Sure thing."

"Good. Just keep in mind I have a pretty strange story to tell, so you'll have to bear with me."

An odd smile lit Jack's face. "I always do, don't I, big shot? I always do."

It was confusing, this feeling of remote disinterest, Suzanne thought. Her body lay on the bed, inert. But her mind, her essence, no longer seemed centered in her physical body, so still and silent. She had another body now that drifted above her physical body, that watched everything the doctors did to save her, watched Devin fight with them to make them do more.

She felt disoriented, uncertain about why she was here. She'd been this way, detached from her body, from the moment she'd seen her body lying on the sidewalk. Detached—it was the only way she could describe it. Was this what they called an out-of-body experience? And what did it mean?

All she knew was there seemed no connection between the world she was in and the one she was observing. Once, when Devin had picked up her hand, she'd felt a disturbing ripple of something . . . pain, love, desire . . . she couldn't tell.

But it had soon passed, leaving her once again feeling completely out of touch. It didn't help that Devin had left the room. She missed his presence. She ached more when he was gone.

The thought had scarcely entered her mind that she'd like to see Devin again, when to her surprise she began drifting out of the room and into the hall. She could hear every word of his conversation with Jack. Jack had an incredulous expression on his face, but there was also a hint of resignation in the way he kept nodding at some phrase or another that Devin used.

Devin's voice sounded distant to her, yet it still had the power to move her. She stretched out a formless hand to touch him, then drew it back quickly when she realized she could feel nothing.

She listened for a moment to what Devin was telling Jack.

"Look, I know this all sounds insane," Devin was saying as he concluded his explanation, "but it's true."

Jack took out a cigarette and lit it with shaky hands.

"You're not supposed to smoke in here," Devin said.

His voice washed over her spirit like a fragrant, hot bath. Ah, so she could still feel a few things. She only wished she could touch him, but she seemed constrained by something and couldn't.

Jack answered by taking a long draw on the cigarette. "Let 'em throw me out. After a story like that, I gotta have a cigarette or die."

Wearily, Devin rubbed the bridge of his nose up to his forehead in a familiar gesture that tugged at her heart. "Kind of hard to swallow, huh?"

Jack shrugged. "To be honest, I always knew something weird like that was going on, making you play music out of the blue. Remember, nobody knows your style like I do. Whenever you launched into one of those unexpected pieces, you played differently, with a different style."

"Because it wasn't my style. It was somebody else's."

With a shudder, Jack puffed on his cigarette. "Yeah, okay. Somebody else's."

Suzanne wanted to laugh. Why did everyone get the willies at the thought of spirits playing music? She could remember how the idea had even frightened her. Now it seemed eminently sensible. After all, why lose all those generations of talent simply because the bodies housing the talent were dead?

"I considered talking to you about it," Jack was saying to Devin. "But I didn't want you to misunderstand and think I was prying. I mean, with your dad and all . . . Then when you told me on the phone the other day that you played that guy Ressu's music . . ." He trailed off, his hands shaking as he flicked some ashes onto the floor.

Devin nodded. "I know. Suzanne had pretty much the same reaction when she realized Ressu was trying to reach her from the grave. And you and she know me well. But the cops . . ." He glanced off down the hall, his mouth grim. "Now do you understand why I can't tell them everything? Besides, if they're going to help me figure out the messages, I'll need the transcribed music for the other sonatas, but they all went up in the blast."

Not true, Suzanne thought idly. *I put copies in my safe deposit box after I was mugged.* Funny, but satisfaction suffused her spirit body to know that the material for her book hadn't been completely destroyed by the blast.

Devin went on. "And I sure as hell can't figure out what the messages mean without the help of someone experienced in dealing with codes. Worse yet, the piece with the most dangerous message of all only exists because a ghost played it for me. I can't exactly explain that to the cops either."

Suzanne found Devin's frustration strange. It seemed absurd that the whole world should be so ignorant. Didn't they realize how fragile were the barriers between the "real" world and the spirit world? Devin ought to be able to simply march into the police station and tell his story. But he couldn't, and it struck her as peculiar.

SILENT SONATA

This spirit body of hers seemed natural, and it allowed her to do so much.

Except touch Devin. She wanted to touch him, to reassure him that she was fine. But was she? If she couldn't touch anything, was she fine?

She thought of her body and in an instant, she found herself hovering over it, staring at it. It looked so fragile, so pale. She wanted to make it wake up, make it *do* something.

Yet she couldn't. She didn't know how. For a moment, she concentrated on trying to reenter that still form. Slowly her spirit neared it, merged with it.

Then an intense blast of pain stunned her and sent her spiraling into a world of nothingness.

23

♫

When next Suzanne became fully aware of her surroundings, she saw that it must be much later. Devin sat by her bedside, his head in his hands.

She'd been drifting through a haze of pain, unable to control either her real body or her spirit body and frustrated by that inability. Once again she felt an overwhelming urge to touch Devin, but every time she tried to communicate that urge to her fingers, pain blasted her.

How long have I been like this? she wondered.

Two days. The thought that entered her mind wasn't hers. She knew that much instantly. But it took a second for her to realize to whom the thought, the intrusive voice, did belong.

Valentin.

Does this mean I'm dead? she thought.

He seemed to hear her thoughts. His answer appeared in her mind even as she thought her question. *No. Your body has been hurt, but it can heal if you let it. You have to make a choice. You can return to the living, to Devin, or you can come with me.*

She tried to turn her spirit body to see him, but couldn't. *Why can't I see you?*

He answered immediately. *Because you're too alive as yet. The trauma to your physical body has brought you this far, but you can still go back. If you choose.*

I want to go back, she protested, *but it hurts so badly.*

Yes.

His answer frustrated her, but before she could ask more, Valentin spoke again.

Devin loves you. Valentin's thoughts in her head seemed imbued with a kind of intense brilliance, as if the words were fashioned of pure light.

I know. The thought spoke itself out of her mind before she'd even acknowledged it was true. But it was. Even through her strange detachment, she could feel Devin's love like a lambent heat emanating from his earthly body.

When you were fully alive, I tried to protect you as your Devin is trying to do. I tried to warn you about 'Endnote.'

Her curiosity was piqued. *Yes, tell me about 'Endnote.' Why did you want it destroyed?*

You already figured that out.

So you were a spy.

He paused a moment. *In a way. My friends and I smuggled 'subversive' literature and tapes, even birth-control devices, into Romania. My double-coded sonata messages told our counterparts on the other side where to meet someone who'd transfer the goods to the right people.* She felt him almost smile, if there were such a thing among spirits. *I thought I'd buried my messages so cleverly. Apparently, I hadn't buried them cleverly enough for my best pupil.*

I always was too analytical for my own good.

She felt rather than heard his laugh. *Yes. And as your friend Devin so succinctly put it, I found myself in a fix after the heart attack. You were working feverishly to analyze my pieces without knowing what you were getting into. When I first came here, I couldn't rest, knowing the danger you were putting yourself into.*

With the words came a surge of protective energy from Valentin that washed over her in waves.

I'm sorry I caused you so much trouble, she told him.

It wasn't your fault. I left loose ends. Unfortunately, once I was here my options were limited. Devin Bryce seemed my best chance for reaching you through the barriers, but even though he got my message to you, it did no good. Now you're here. And you don't belong here, you know.

Again the wave of affection flooded her, but this time she sensed it was tempered with restraint. He wanted her to go back. She could tell.

And she wanted to go, but it hurt so much every time she tried. It was so much easier to drift in this quiet place. On the horizon of her consciousness shone a brilliant light. She knew she could go to the light if she wanted.

Why don't I belong here? she asked.

Because someone needs you back there. And you need that someone to make you grow. You have much to learn yet. The two of you can help each other.

Devin? I thought you hated him.

The light swam around her. It blinded her with such intense feelings of well-being and peace that it made her spirit feel even more buoyant and joyful than before. Then as quickly as the light had overwhelmed her, it receded.

That is what I feel for Devin now, Valentin's thoughts hummed in her mind. *There's no room in my new world for hatred, for contempt, for jealousy. It's hard even to remember why I hated him so much.*

Now that the light shimmered on the edges of her vision, she was finding it hard to remember why she'd loved Devin so much. This other world absorbed her full attention, making it difficult to concentrate on anything but its beauty.

But she didn't want to let it swallow her up. If she were to return to the world of the living, she'd have to resist the white light threatening to engulf her.

To keep her attention focused away from that brilliant light, she asked Valentin, *How did you become a spy?*

A long silence ensued. Then he began, *After I left Romania at the age of twenty-four . . .*

It had been two days of complete torture for Devin. Suzanne had lapsed into a coma, or so the doctor had told him. A couple of times, he'd thought he'd seen Suzanne's eyelids flutter, but they'd never opened. And as the hours passed, he wondered if he'd ever seen the movement in the first place.

Either he or Felicia Winslow had been at the hospital every moment. They'd gotten to know each other pretty well, sitting in the waiting room. He'd been able to see why Suzanne had become such a logical person. Someone in the family had to take care of the bills and keep affairs in order, and it certainly couldn't have been Felicia. The woman could hardly fill out a form properly, much less keep in mind the hospital's myriad systematic rules for visitors.

But she was strong willed, and she obviously cared enormously for her daughter. As did he. Unfortunately, all their caring wasn't doing a bit of good. There'd been no change.

It had taken a huge effort, but Devin had finally persuaded the doctor to allow him and Felicia to stay with Suzanne longer than the fifteen minutes every few hours that had been allotted to ICU visitors. The doctor seemed to agree that Devin's presence could only help, but Devin knew the doctor had been influenced by more than simply a desire for the patient's well-being.

Devin had made it quite clear that even if the cops refused to treat the explosion as a criminal matter, it could only hurt the hospital to do the same, because if anything happened to Suzanne while she was in its care, he would bring a mammoth suit against the hospital. So Devin and Felicia were allowed to stay with Suzanne in shifts, serving as her only protection, minimal though it was.

This evening Devin sat beside her, tired and discouraged. Felicia was going to relieve him at midnight, but he didn't know if he could last the hour until then.

He picked up Suzanne's hand and stroked her limp fingers, wondering if she could feel him touch her at all. Did she know he sat here at her side, afraid to leave, but hating to watch her languish into silence?

His hand closed around hers. He lifted it to his lips and pressed a kiss against her fingertips, careful to avoid the needle from the IV tube inserted in the back of her hand.

Once again, fear made the bile rise in his throat. She could die. How could he live if she died before he had the chance to tell her how much he needed and wanted her?

"I love you," he whispered for probably the hundredth time. "You can't leave me now, honey. You've got to hang on."

Not even a flicker of movement rewarded him with the knowledge that she heard his words. In truth, the doctors didn't even know if she'd suffered a hearing loss from the blast.

He ran his fingers along the silky skin of her arm, so pale, so lifeless. What if she couldn't hear him? What if she were trapped in a silent world, unable to heed his pleas?

Devin scooted closer to the bed and laid her arm across his lap, careful not to dislodge the IV. There were other ways of communicating, he thought wryly, remembering Ressu and the message that Jack even now worked with his cryptographer friend to decode.

Until a few days ago when he'd been forced to decode the first level of message in "Endnote," he hadn't known

Morse code at all. Now he knew it well. It was easy to figure out the symbols for "Come back. I love you."

Easy to tap it on her arm, he thought as he repeated the dots and dashes over and over until his fingers felt numb from the effort. And so damned hard to watch her continue to lie still, apparently unmoved even by a tactile expression of his love.

Suddenly a nurse stuck her head in the door. "There's a call for you, Mr. Bryce, at the nurses' station."

"I'll be right there." He laid her arm down gently, wondering if there'd ever be a time when its soft lines weren't marred by the harsh reality of that needle lock stuck in her hand.

In moments, he'd reached the phone at the nurses' station down the silent hall from her room. It took him only a second to determine it was Jack with news about the cryptographer.

"Did you get the message deciphered?" Devin growled into the phone.

"Yeah. My buddy says he thinks the first part isn't in code. The 'Listen, listen' is meant to emphasize the importance of the message. As it turns out, the second part's a lot simpler than we'd imagined. The words form an acronym that—"

The phone went dead. At the same time, the hospital suddenly lost power, although it was restored almost immediately by the emergency generators.

"What the hell—" he started to ask the nurse, but she was already halfway down the hall in the opposite direction, going to check on the patients.

He glanced back at Suzanne's room, then cursed when he realized he'd left the curtains closed, blocking his view of the glass-walled room from the station.

Quickly he moved back down the hall toward the room, his mind running over what Jack had said. An acronym. What did that mean—that the real message was the first letter of every word of the fake message?

SILENT SONATA

Damn, what was the message again? "Love yields death if altars kill men." L–Y–D–I–A. His blood ran cold, remembering Suzanne mentioning a woman named Lydia Chelminscu. And "kill men" had to be Chelminscu.

"Oh, Christ," he muttered, swiftly rounding the corner of Suzanne's room, then stopping short when he saw an unfamiliar figure dressed in street clothes reaching for the IV line, a syringe in her other hand.

Without stopping to think, he barreled forward, knocking the figure to the ground. The syringe went skittering across the floor as Devin struggled to subdue the female body squirming beneath him. With a sudden burst of strength, the woman twisted underneath him, turning to face him. Then Devin felt a hard object thrust suddenly against his belly.

"Be still, Mr. Bryce, or I shall be forced to kill you." The voice was cold as sheet ice, the face a cruel mask.

Devin groaned as fear swelled in him, an insidious parasite that threatened to drain him of his strength. Though he'd never met the woman who was now threatening to blow him away, he had a pretty good hunch who she was.

"Hello, Ms. Chelminscu," he said.

Suzanne didn't have to see the gun sandwiched between Lydia and Devin to know it was there. Like so many other things in this strange limbo, she could sense objects without seeing them.

After Ressu had finished telling her everything, he'd warned her Lydia wouldn't give up easily, Suzanne thought. She'd known he spoke the truth, but had protested that she couldn't do anything about it, not in her present condition.

All he'd said was, *If you want it bad enough, you will find a way.*

No sooner had he finished than Devin had begun tapping out the message he'd only spoken before. It made her yearn so badly to touch him, and her spirit surged toward

him in a blur of affection, tenderness, love. But the pain
. . . the pain held her back.

Then Devin had left the room, and Lydia had appeared. Suzanne had seen her enter and had experienced terror when Lydia pulled out a syringe, but the terror only increased when Devin had returned.

Now Devin was in danger. A surge of anger made Suzanne's spirit body quiver at the thought. She had to help him, she had to! She forced herself to think of being back in her body, to think of struggling with the pain, while at the same time she watched Lydia thrust Devin from her with one push of the gun.

Devin rose slowly, as did Lydia. Unfortunately Lydia never moved the gun except to shift its aim from Devin's belly to Suzanne's heart.

Devin blanched, and Suzanne increased her struggle. Death could be peace, she knew that now, but death without Devin . . . she fought toward her body, the pain washing over her in waves, like a thousand bullets peppering her body. Unable to bear it, she shied back and slipped once more into the spirit world.

Someone entered through the open doorway behind Devin. The man on the motorcycle. Suzanne realized who he was even as she saw the spotless white tennis shoes.

Lydia motioned for the man to shut the door.

"They are scurrying about trying to repair the damage to the circuits and the phone lines," the man said in his foreign-sounding voice. "But that won't take long. I could have created a longer diversion, but I thought you'd planned to be in and out by now."

"Mr. Bryce here showed up unexpectedly." Lydia's eyes flickered briefly over Devin. "You're not supposed to be here," she told Devin with matter-of-fact nonchalance. "Didn't anyone tell you visiting hours were over long ago?"

"I didn't come to visit. I came to protect Suzanne from you."

At his fierce words, Suzanne felt despair, for him and for

her. His fear for her and the love that produced it reached for her, drawing her closer, closer. But the pain . . .

Lydia's smile didn't quite reach her eyes. "Indeed."

Suzanne could tell Lydia was nervous and not quite certain what to do with Devin now that he'd fouled up her plans.

"Yeah," Devin answered, a glint of defiance in his fathomless eyes. "I'm not the only one trying to protect her either. My manager knows you're after her. Even now, he's got the cops on their way over here."

That was a surprise to Suzanne.

Apparently, it was a surprise to Lydia as well. "Of course. The 'cops,'" she mimicked sarcastically. "It's evident how they rush to do your bidding." A mocking chuckle escaped her lips. "A rather crude bluff, wouldn't you say, Mr. Bryce? I'm no fool. The police have not even bothered to place a guard outside this room. My comrade here has been monitoring the police lines for the past two days, and all he heard was some talk about the crazy pianist who'd claimed his girlfriend was blown up by a bomb."

Devin's body tautened like a bow preparing to launch its best arrow. "Things have changed though, now that my manager and I have figured out the message in 'Endnote.' I was just on the phone with him, talking about it. He knows the truth. He knows your name is buried in Ressu's Morse code."

Lydia stiffened, the lines of her face tightening to form a fierce mask.

Devin pressed his advantage. "My manager will get the word out if I turn up dead. He'll tell the cops what 'Love yields death if altars kill men' really means." He thought a moment. Then a flicker of realization lightened his eyes. "Yeah, he'll tell them about the woman who 'kills men.' Who kills them with *Radu.*"

"That's enough!" Lydia barked.

"You had something to do with *Radu,* didn't you? That's what this is all about. You don't want Suzanne or me telling your buddies in the new government about your prerevolution activities, about *Radu*."

So you figured it out at last, Suzanne thought.

His shot in the dark paid off. An angry scowl twisted Lydia's face. "You will not tell them anything, you fool, do you hear? You will leave here with me!"

Devin's voice was nonchalant, but Suzanne could see his hands clench into fists at his sides. "Yeah, right. You'll have to kill me first."

Kill me, kill me, kill me. At those words, something snapped in Suzanne. Lydia was going to kill Devin. She would thrust that gun against his ribs and . . .

That thought galvanized her into action as nothing else had. She didn't care about her own body . . . but Devin. Devin couldn't die simply because she couldn't stand the pain. He couldn't!

She no longer gave a thought to what peace lay behind her in Valentin's world. Although the light still emanated around and behind her, beckoning and promising relief, another light drew her back to the world of the living.

She had to save Devin. And save herself so they could be together.

With her decision, agony wracked her. It was an agony of mind as well as an agony of body, for she was refusing the relief of that other world where peace lay, and her spirit knew it.

She didn't care. She forced her spirit to let the pain course over and through her. She suffered through the thousand pangs of grief and lost chances. Her spirit ached with a fierceness she could scarcely bear, but she struggled through the aching. She had to reach Devin, and now she was so close.

Suddenly, everything altered. Her spirit surged, swelled. Then it whispered, thundered, roared toward her body . . . toward Devin . . . toward life. In a trice, her spirit and her body sprang together like two interlocking puzzle pieces snapping into place. She'd done it! She'd fought past the pain and back into her body!

The trouble was, she could no longer view what was happening from her vantage point hovering above everything. Now that she was in her body, she could see nothing of the struggle going on around her.

She wanted to cry out, to move, to leap from the bed and help Devin. But she could scarcely summon the strength to raise her eyelids, much less leap from the bed.

She could feel love, though, more powerfully than she'd ever thought possible. It spread through her limbs, giving her life, making her determined to save Devin.

She had to. Because she loved him. How she loved him!

But her body seemed incapable of helping him. Even as she fought to rouse her limbs, which stung like feet slowly coming awake after falling asleep, she could hear Lydia tell Devin, "I don't need to kill you to get to her. One shot from this gun and she's dead."

"Then the cops will know she didn't simply die in her sleep, won't they?" Suzanne heard a crunching sound on the floor and realized Devin had suddenly crushed the syringe under his foot.

"You fool!"

"If I have to be a fool to protect Suzanne, then so be it."

"You're coming with me," Lydia commanded. Then she paused and her voice shifted direction. "Turk! Smother the girl, and let's be done with it!"

"It's not going to work," Devin went on relentlessly. She could feel his body edge along the bed, moving to shield her. "You'll have to shoot me first, I tell you. And my friends will hunt you down if they find me dead. What good will it do you to silence Suzanne and me about your participation in *Radu* if you're a fugitive?"

Suzanne felt the pain receding, a little at a time, and in its place energy trickled through her limbs, sluggish but there nonetheless. She could wiggle her toes now, not that it helped Devin much. Then she raised her eyelids, just a little, enough to see what was going on.

There they all were, almost frozen before her. None of them paid her any mind, because they were too engrossed in the drama playing itself out among them. Lydia still held the gun, although now Devin stood between her and Suzanne.

The foreign-looking man Lydia had called Turk looked worried. "Frankie . . . uh . . . Lydia . . . we must leave here before someone comes. Leave them both. It is too late. You must concentrate on escape."

"I can't leave them to ruin me." Lydia's hard voice matched the hard lines of her mouth. The gun didn't waver as she fixed Devin with her pitiless gaze. "They both know the truth. If it should come out, I would not be safe. Do you know how many dissidents died because of *Radu,* how many languish now in hospitals in terrible pain? And all because I betrayed my fellow dissidents to that bastard Ceauşescu, betrayed them for a price."

Suzanne couldn't help but note the hint of self-loathing in Lydia's voice.

"Was it worth the price?" Devin goaded. "Even if you get away with killing us, can you live with the guilt?"

A low, harsh laugh left her lips. "I have no choice. It's no longer a matter of guilt or absolution. Now that Ceauşescu is dead, Romanians want to eradicate every reminder of his treachery. You say your friends will hunt me down? They will not find me. But if my countrymen learn of my part in *Radu,* the sons and daughters, even the friends of those Romanians who died and who suffer now, will seek me out no matter where I flee. My life will not be worth a *leu.* So I must kill you both, and hope I can intimidate your friends —if indeed they know the truth—into silence. Without you and Suzanne, no one else will know of the messages. Mariela will cancel the festival concert, and Suzanne's book, which was destroyed in the blast, will never be published."

SILENT SONATA

Suzanne wanted to protest that her book still existed, that Lydia was defeated already. But even if she could speak the words, would it make a difference? At this point, Lydia seemed desperate and not at all inclined to believe anyone's threats.

"I tried to do this without violence," Lydia said almost pleadingly. "I tried to get rid of all the copies, and when that didn't work, I tried to put an end to the festival concert. I even tried to get Mariela to cancel it by letting her know about Ressu's affair. Nothing worked." Her voice hardened. "So now it has come to this. I have no choice."

"Let's make a bargain then," Devin said with sudden calm. "I'll leave with you. I'll even call my friends and tell them I made a mistake. But on one condition. Leave Suzanne alone. You're not risking much by doing that. She may not even live anyway, and if she does, she might not remember anything. I'll go with you. But leave her here."

Lydia seemed to consider that.

A powerful fury engulfed Suzanne. She couldn't just let Lydia take Devin off somewhere and kill him! She had to stop this madness! But how?

Her slitted gaze suddenly fell on the call button that lay clipped to the bed scant inches from her fingertips. It would bring a nurse, someone else to throw a monkey wrench in Lydia's plans. It wasn't much, but it was better than nothing.

Suzanne swallowed, gathering her energy. Only a few inches, she told herself. At first, she couldn't make her fingers work, couldn't make them obey the summons of her mind. She concentrated all her force on her fingertips, imagining them crawling along the sheets, inching toward the call button.

Suddenly they were doing precisely that. It seemed to take enormous effort to move them, yet they slid with jerky slowness along the sheet. Her head pounded, but she ignored the pain. She had to reach the call button . . . she had to!

"All right," Lydia was saying to Devin. "It's a bargain. She lives if you come with me. And to ensure you uphold your end, I'll leave the Turk here with her until we're out of the building."

"Like hell you will," Devin ground out. "He'll just kill her the moment you and I leave."

Suzanne's finger reached the button, and with a burst of energy, she stabbed it, over and over, praying that the buzzer would ring in the nurses' station.

But would anyone be there? Would the nurses be too busy checking on the patients to heed her insistent call?

"You don't have much choice, Mr. Bryce," Lydia was saying. "I'm going to kill you no matter what. You should take advantage of my generous offer and trust me."

"Yeah, right, trust you, a lying murderess."

"I could kill you right now for that." Lydia began to squeeze the trigger, then seemed to think better of it. Her jaw seemed permanently clenched. "But I can wait. Move toward the door, Mr. Bryce. Take my compromise or I'll shoot you and Suzanne dead right here and not worry about the consequences."

He hesitated.

"Move!"

The door to the room suddenly swung open and a nurse appeared in the open doorway. "Mr. Bryce? Did you ring the nurses' station? Is there a prob—"

The nurse broke off as Lydia swung the gun toward her. With a small cry, the nurse panicked, then turned and ran down the hall, calling for help as she went.

All hell broke loose then. The Turk fled the room down the hall in the opposite direction from the nurse, not even bothering to look back. And while Lydia was distracted, Devin's hand snaked out to grip her wrist, bending it with a quick snap that broke it at once.

Howling in pain, Lydia dropped the gun and twisted free of Devin. She tucked her wounded hand under her other arm, then kicked upward without warning, hitting Devin hard in the stomach. As he doubled over with a cry, she darted for the door. He tried to stumble after her, but two police officers were already coming up the outside hall, followed closely by Jack.

It took several moments for the confusion to clear, for the officers to subdue a now-hysterical Lydia and for Jack to reach Devin, who stood clutching his stomach, though his moans were rapidly subsiding.

"What the devil's going on here?" Jack asked as he clasped Devin's arm, helping Devin straighten.

Devin gestured to Lydia, whose struggle against the police was petering out as she recognized the futility of it. "That's Lydia," Devin groaned. "Lydia Chelminscu."

"The Lydia in the message? The one who's been after Suzanne all this time?" Jack took another look back at Lydia then muttered, "Good thing I called the cops and rushed over here the minute the phone went dead, huh?"

"Yeah, good thing." Devin put a hand on Jack's shoulder. "Thanks, Jack. For everything." He managed a wan smile as he watched them lead Lydia away. "I tell you, I could really use a cigarette right now." Still faintly smiling, Devin turned from Jack to the bed to check on Suzanne.

By now she had no trouble keeping her eyes open, and his gaze met hers.

An astonished expression wiped the tentative smile from his face. "Suzanne?" he asked, disbelief in his voice.

Her throat felt dry and raw from days of disuse, but somehow she managed to force a sound through her lips. At first it was only a kind of strangled cough. She cleared her throat and tried again.

The words came out in a whisper. "You . . . shouldn't . . . smoke . . . Devin."

Devin continued to stand there dumbfounded, although his face had begun to register the faintest bit of hope.

Jack simply shook his head and grinned from ear to ear.

"I tell you, Devin, you don't have a thing to worry about. Only a woman in love would come back from the dead to tell you not to smoke."

24

♪

Suzanne opened her eyes to find Devin pacing one corner of the room while her mother sat in the other, sipping coffee and watching Devin with an amused expression.

Suzanne couldn't resist watching him herself a moment. He looked like hell. His hair was more than mussed. It was wild and unruly beyond belief from the many times he'd raked his fingers through it. His familiar blue jeans were rumpled, as was his jersey. And the strings of one of his worn tennis shoes were untied.

She had to smother a laugh, because it hurt too much to laugh. But oh, did it feel good to see him there, to remember how he'd fought for her.

She wished she could have stayed awake the night before to talk to him about all that had happened. But by the time the police left, she'd been too weary to do anything but lapse into a blissful sleep.

"When do I get out of here?" Suzanne managed to croak out now through cracked lips.

At the sound of her voice, her mother shifted her gaze to the bed, and Devin whirled around. Relief flooded both their faces.

"We were beginning to think you'd . . . gone off again," Devin said thickly, scanning her as if to reassure himself that she was indeed awake, alive, and speaking to him.

"I thought no such thing," her mother interrupted. "Zanny's a hardy woman, like her mother. She just needed a little rest."

Suzanne reached for the button to raise the bed, and Devin rushed to her side to help her place the pillows more comfortably behind her back.

She flashed him a grateful smile. "Have you both . . . been here all night?" Her voice still felt rusty, but talking came so much easier now that she'd had her first real night's sleep in three days. She'd discovered that a coma and real sleep were two very different things, and the latter was ten times more refreshing.

"Of course," her mother said. "I don't trust these hospital people. I mean, dear Lord, look at the gown they put you in. You'd think they'd consider how awful it is to recover in a gown as dreadful-looking as that."

Well, Mother hadn't changed, that was certain, Suzanne thought wryly. Mother's own clothing was, as usual, wildly eccentric—a flashy caftan with a Southwestern print. Suzanne wondered in amusement if it had occurred to Mother to bring her a gown. Probably not.

Yet she knew part of her mother's apparent concern with trivialities just now was her way of coping with the far more frightening possibility that her daughter might have died.

Suzanne glanced at Devin, who leaned up against the wall next to the bed, watching them both curiously. She rolled her eyes, and he grinned.

Mother was here. Devin was here. The only one missing was . . . "Bartok!" she exclaimed, remembering the explosion. "Is he okay?"

Her mother laughed. "That dreadful creature who masquerades as a feline? You barely survived a bomb blast, and you're worried about that ridiculous cat?"

Suzanne flashed her mother an indignant look.

"Bartok's fine," Devin assured her. "One of the neighbors found him wandering around the neighborhood and brought him to your mother." He stifled a grin, not too successfully. "And your mother, of course, brought him to me."

"That cat hates me," her mother added haughtily. "Valentin probably had Bartok brainwashed to despise me before he gave the wretched creature to you." Her eyes narrowed. "And speaking of Valentin, Devin tells me my ex-husband was a spy."

Nothing like changing the subject, Suzanne thought with a smile. Odd, but Mother didn't seem to bother her nearly as much anymore.

But she couldn't say the same for Devin, who broke in with, "Felicia, I don't know if Suzanne's up to talking about that right now—"

"It's okay," Suzanne said. "I would like to . . . to talk about it, actually, sort of compare notes. I . . . um . . . I put a few pieces together while I was in . . . I mean, last night."

She exchanged a glance with Devin.

He seemed to understand what she hinted at, for his eyes narrowed. "Oh?"

"Yes." Suzanne turned to her mother. "Don't you remember, Mother, how rabid Valentin would get about Ceauşescu's policies on birth control and . . . and other political matters?"

Her mother fluttered her hand in a dismissive gesture. "That was because he was mortified to be that wretched dictator's nephew."

"You knew?" Suzanne and Devin exclaimed in unison.

"Of course. Valentin was my husband, after all."

Suzanne regarded her mother with a bit more respect. "Did you also know he buried messages in all those sonatas he played over Radio Free Europe?"

"Well, no. He didn't tell me everything, of course."

Suzanne drew in a deep breath. "As it turns out, the messages were meant to tell his friends in Romania where to pick up smuggled materials—literature, tapes, even birth-control devices. He and an independent group of defectors in America had used the method for years, sending in messages right under the noses of Ceauşescu and his Securitate. It was their way of helping—they kept themselves apart from the formal intelligence organizations like the CIA—but they were pretty effective in what they chose to do."

Devin's ears had perked up, but her mother merely looked curious.

"After the revolution," Suzanne continued, "Valentin expected everything to be hunky-dory. That's why he didn't do any more sonatas for a couple of years. There was no need. Then his contact in America came to him with some chilling news. He'd discovered through his sources that one of their counterparts on the other side was a traitor. What's more, the traitor had been responsible during the Ceauşescu regime for setting up meetings of her fellow dissidents at which one of Ceauşescu's men irradiated the dissidents, unbeknownst to them."

Devin looked a little sick. "Lydia."

"Yes, Lydia. Anyway, Valentin and his contact decided that the contact would return to Romania and do whatever he could to bring Lydia to justice. But shortly before the contact was scheduled to depart, he died under mysterious circumstances."

"Lydia," Devin repeated, this time more coldly.

"At first Valentin didn't know what to do. Ceauşescu was dead, and the damage had been done. Should he make sure Lydia was brought to justice? And how? He couldn't return himself, and who would listen to the nephew of Ceauşescu? He didn't know this Lydia personally, nor did he know a single one of the other dissidents who'd listened to his music on the other side. And he certainly couldn't entangle himself with the CIA and their mess. His only choice, as he saw it, was to resort to his old methods to get the message across."

"But of course he died before he could perform the sonata," Devin interjected.

"Yes." Suzanne remained pensive a moment.

"Did Lydia kill Valentin too?" her mother asked.

"I don't think so. She didn't know he knew the truth, and he kept the sonata a great secret. She only got interested after he'd died, when I started making a big deal about Valentin Ressu's last sonata."

She could see a look of "I told you so" on her mother's face. Her mother had been opposed to the festival concert from the very beginning.

But her mother didn't comment aloud on that fact. Instead, she asked, "How did you find all this out? Surely you didn't 'put a few pieces together' on your own? I mean, it sounds almost as if Valentin told you some of this."

Suzanne bit her lip, uncertain what to say. Should she tell her mother about seeing Valentin on the other side?

Devin came to the rescue. "Lydia told me everything last night while Suzanne was coming out of her coma."

Risking a glance at him, Suzanne saw him wink.

"Speaking of Lydia," Suzanne said, eager to lead the conversation into safer waters, "what's going to happen to her?"

"She'll stand trial here for attempted murder, I suspect," Devin answered. "But I'm sure a little birdie has already called the Romanian embassy in Washington to tell them an interesting story about Lydia's activities in Romania. It wouldn't surprise me at all to see her extradited to be tried in Romania for her other crimes."

Her mother looked alarmed. "Devin Bryce! I hope you haven't gotten yourself mixed up in all this mess."

"Moi?" He threw up his hands. "I never get mixed up in political matters. I just mind my own business and play the piano." He winked again at Suzanne. "Kind of like a musicologist I know."

She rolled her eyes at him.

Her mother sniffed and rose abruptly to her feet. "Well,

since Zanny seems to be feeling better, I believe it's time she had visitors."

"What are we?" Devin said in a mock hurt tone. "Chopped liver?"

"I'm talking about some of her other friends, like Mariela and Paul, who've been driving me absolutely insane with questions about Suzanne's condition. They might as well see for themselves she's doing fine." Her mother turned to Suzanne. "If you're up to it, I'll just step out into the waiting room and phone them. . . ."

"Sure, sure. You do that." Suzanne suddenly thought of something she'd been wanting to ask her mother ever since Cindy had made her startling revelation. "Mother?"

Her mother paused in the doorway. "Yes, dear?"

"When you said . . . you wished I'd known Valentin better, were you talking about his tendency to . . . ah . . . have affairs?"

Her mother looked startled a moment, then glanced away. For a moment, an expression of acute vulnerability crossed her face. "Mariela wasn't the first, Suzanne. She was merely the one he left me for."

Suzanne suddenly saw her mother in an entirely different light. "But you let me believe he was so noble and long-suffering all those years when I blamed you for his leaving."

Her mother shrugged. "Well, for all I know, he had affairs to get away from me." She sniffed. "I'm not exactly an easy person to live with."

"To put it mildly," Suzanne couldn't resist muttering.

To her surprise, her mother chuckled. "True. I tend to be self-absorbed. So who's perfect? You wanted to idolize Valentin . . . who was I to burst your little bubble? He was still a hero to his native country, even if he was a skirt chaser."

What was it Devin had said about Valentin after they'd made love the first time? "He was human, he had flaws. He was just a man, damn it."

Suzanne stared at her mother, a surge of affection filling her. "Thanks, Mother, for trying to protect me. For someone who's self-absorbed, you can be pretty unselfish sometimes."

Her mother's eyes misted, and her voice dropped to a whisper. "Thank God you're okay, Zanny. I don't know what I would have done if . . ." She seemed overcome for a moment, tears spilling onto her cheeks. "You're very special to me . . . so special. I don't always tell you, but you are." She gazed deeply into her daughter's eyes. "I do love you, dear. I love you very much."

Never had so few words had so much meaning to Suzanne. Tears welled from her eyes too. "And I love you, Mother." She sniffled. "I—I always have."

Her mother came to her side and hugged her close, squeezing her more tightly than she ever had when Suzanne was a child. After both of them had gained some control over their emotions, her mother whispered, "I'll go call Mariela now, all right?"

Suzanne nodded.

With a smile turning up the edges of her lips, her mother left.

"Your mother's okay," Devin said softly from the corner. "Even if she did nearly sabotage my relationship with you."

Suzanne turned her eyes to Devin, swallowing the lump that seemed permanently stuck in her throat. "Yes, she's okay. But sabotage does seem to be her strong suit sometimes."

He chuckled, his laugh warming her.

"You never answered my question," she added. "When do I get out of here?"

"When I say so." He softened the authoritative statement by smiling.

She patted an empty spot on the bed beside her, and he slid up to sit next to her. Taking her hands in his, he surveyed every inch of her body. "How are you feeling?"

Trust Devin, and not her mother, to ask that question,

she thought wryly. "Like Bartok after a bath. But I think everything's intact." She licked her dry lips, then cleared her throat. "I can move all my muscles, and I suppose they checked before to see if I had any internal bleeding or broken bones."

She lifted one hand to stroke his cheek, and he sucked in a quick breath.

"Christ, Suzanne, you don't know the hell you put me through. If you had died—"

"I almost did," she said without thinking, then hesitated. Should she tell him the whole story? He'd undoubtedly already guessed some of it. And if anyone would understand her bizarre experience on the other side, Devin would understand. It was one of the things that linked them—this knowledge that what people called the real world was only a fragile, transient dream.

He paled. "Believe me, I know too well how close you came to dying."

With a smile, she patted his hand. "No, you really don't. Valentin gave me a choice, you know."

"Valentin?" His eyes bore into hers, sad and almost fearful.

"Yes, he was there, explaining everything to me. The other side is so beautiful, so tranquil and filled with a strange kind of joy." She'd never forget the glimpse she'd had of life after death. It would always be there to give her peace whenever she felt frightened. "Part of me wanted to stay. But I knew I couldn't."

The lines of his face were bleak. "Did he force you to come back?" he whispered, as if fearing to hear the answer.

She smiled. "No. I wanted to come. I couldn't leave you. There's so much left for me to do before I die, and I wanted to do it with you."

The quick, sweet light of joy suffused his face. He drew her up against him, his arm encircling her back as he cradled her head tenderly against his shoulder. "Oh, Zanny,

Zanny . . ." he murmured huskily, rubbing one hand along her upper arm. "God, I love you so much."

She hugged him close. He felt so warm, so dependable, so caring. Valentin had been right. Devin was what she needed to help her grow. "I love you too, maestro," she whispered.

His hand stilled on her arm, but scarcely a second passed before he asked, "Then how would you feel about being married to a maestro?"

The blood rushed through her veins. Could he really be asking her to marry him? She hadn't dared to think about the possibility before, even while she'd been at death's boundary.

Yet it was the next logical step, wasn't it, for two people who loved each other? Joining their hearts, their minds, their souls?

On the other hand, there were so many things they should discuss first—how their careers could fit together when he spent so much of his time touring . . . what they should do about children . . . where they should live—

"I mean, I know I have a few odd characteristics," he broke into her thoughts. "I'm hopelessly disorganized. I've never used a file box, and I'm really bad about restaurant reservations—"

"And you're cocky," she put in with a smile.

"That too." The faint note of humor left his voice. His hand tensed on her shoulder. "Plus, I have this penchant for letting phantoms borrow my hands when I'm performing. . . ."

He trailed off, and she realized that issue more than any had him worried.

"As long as you don't invite them to supper, I think I can put up with that," she whispered.

He stared at her, his eyes filling with hope. "Is that a yes?"

When he looked at her like that, all her fine attempts to analyze the possibilities seemed to vanish into thin air.

Hadn't she learned that sometimes it was better to go with the flow?

"Hey," he murmured against her hair when she hesitated. His voice quavered the barest fraction. "You can't turn me down, you know. My colossal ego wouldn't stand it."

Not to mention her heart, she thought. For Pete's sake, there wasn't another man in the world she could love as much as this one. So what on earth was she waiting for?

"I'll have to do something about that ego once we're married," she managed to get out through a throat choked with joy. "And of course, that apartment of yours will need a complete overhaul. Not to mention—"

A low moan left his throat as he crushed her up against him, melding her mouth to his to shut her up. Long minutes passed, during which he reminded her quite forcibly that his ego wasn't entirely out of proportion to his abilities . . . in a variety of areas.

Then he pulled back, the beginnings of a grin crossing his face as he cupped her chin in his hand. "You can do whatever you want to my apartment, Little Miss Priss. You can catalog my records, synchronize the clocks, and organize the twist ties. I don't give a damn what you do, as long as you stick around for a few decades or so while you're whipping me into shape."

A smile tugged at her lips. "It'll take me at least that long to get you in shape." She lifted her face to his. "But I think I'll enjoy rising to the challenge."

"Not half as much as I will, honey," he muttered as he began to angle his lips over hers once more. "Not nearly half as much."

Epilogue

♪

Mariela stood beside Suzanne in the wings at Mandel Hall, her eyes filling with tears as they watched Devin play the final notes of "Endnote." Once Devin had agreed to play the pieces, the festival had gone on after all, a year and a half later. There'd been no reason to cancel it after Lydia was sent back to Romania to stand trial.

"It is so beautiful, so perfect," Mariela whispered. "If I didn't know otherwise, I would think Valentin himself taught your husband to play his music with such feeling."

Suzanne bit back a laugh. "Yes, well, Devin's talented in his own right. Besides, he had me to help him."

How true that was, she thought, remembering how she'd had to pound into him that playing Valentin's work required an entirely different touch from playing Chopin. Even though it had been Devin's idea to use him as pianist for the festival, he'd grumbled and groused about the music from beginning to end, telling her that once it was over he'd never play another piece of "dissonant, jumbled-up idiocy" like this again.

But looking at him now, she knew that wasn't true. His face wore an expression of perpetual awakening as he danced his fingers over the keys. Whether he admitted it or not, the music stimulated him, and she suspected he'd find himself sticking a little bit of Cage into his repertoire here and there as time went on.

And a little Ressu as well. Now that her book had come out, they'd been inundated with requests for joint performances and lectures in which she discussed Valentin's work and Devin performed the music. They hadn't accepted too many of them—Devin could stand to play only so much Ressu—but the few they'd done together had been great fun after the hard work of putting her book together.

Her book had been a sticky proposition, after all. She had presented only the first level of code, the "lyrics," and hadn't discussed the probable actual meanings of the Morse code messages, mainly because she and Devin both thought the less published about it, the better. Nonetheless, she'd enjoyed explaining the particulars of Valentin's system and trying to come up with interesting interpretations of the "lyrics."

Now it was time to think about her next project. Perhaps she should try something a little less contemporary. Maybe Rachmaninoff. Or even Chopin. He wasn't so bad. And Devin knew the greatest details about the composer's life. . . .

The audience was applauding now, and Devin was taking his bows. Mariela stepped onto the stage to hand him a bouquet of roses, then gestured for Suzanne to come out.

After they'd all made their bows and Mariela had acknowledged God and everybody for their help with mounting the festival, the three of them finally left the stage, only to be swamped by well-wishers—Maggie, Devin's mother, Jack.

"That's the weirdest music I ever heard," Maggie told Devin, "but you played it good."

Then Maggie turned her attention to Suzanne as Jack started talking to Devin. Maggie had long since forgiven Suzanne for deceiving her, particularly since Maggie's matchmaking tactics had worked out after all.

"How's the baby?" she asked, placing her hand on Suzanne's stomach.

Jack overheard her and turned to mutter, "Maggie, for God's sake, Suzanne is only three months along."

"Watch your language, Jack Warton," Devin's mother protested. "They can hear you in the womb, you know."

Then she gave Suzanne a sweet smile. "Never mind the baby. How are *you* feeling, dear?"

Suzanne had grown to love Devin's mother so much. It still amazed her that this frail little woman could have raised such a hardy man.

"I'm fine," Suzanne answered as she gave the older woman a hug.

Devin's arm snaked around her shoulders. "Yeah, and she'll be better when she gets off her feet. Why don't all of you go on to the reception? We'll meet you over there after Suzanne's had a chance to rest a minute."

Then ignoring Suzanne's protests, he maneuvered her through the crowd to his dressing room, responding to comments as he went. He pushed her through the doorway, then shut the door behind them.

"You stood in the wings the entire concert," he said, a concerned frown on his face.

"Of course."

"Suzanne, you're pregnant. You need to stay off your feet. You shouldn't be standing so long—"

"Oh, shut up. I'm just three months along," she said good-naturedly and hugged him. "Besides, I had to guard against unwarranted possessions. Chopin definitely wouldn't have been welcome tonight."

"Well, believe it or not, Ressu didn't make even one appearance. I guess we wore him out last year."

"I'm sure he was at least watching you prove that you're perfectly capable of performing avant-garde music when you want."

"No gloating now," he muttered, stroking her arm. Then he grinned. "I did pretty well, though, didn't I?"

"Fishing for a compliment, Mr. Bryce?"

"Always."

She shook her head. "I swear, I can see your ego still needs a lot of trimming."

He chuckled and began to lower his head to kiss her when someone knocked on the door behind them.

SILENT SONATA

"Don't open it," Devin growled.

"Nonsense. It might be important." Suzanne opened the door a crack to find a stranger standing outside it, nervously twisting the festival program in his hand.

"Mrs. Bryce?" the man asked hesitantly.

Devin looked over her head. "I'm sorry, but my wife is resting right now. She'd be happy to talk to you in a few minutes at the reception."

"Yes, of course," the man murmured and started to turn away.

Something in the man's foreign accent struck Suzanne with a weird feeling. "No, no, that's okay," she hastened to say. "Please. I'd be happy to talk to you."

Devin groaned behind her.

But the man brightened. "I will not take much of your time. I simply wanted to say that I enjoyed your book very much." He said it with an odd gleam in his eye. Then he turned to Devin. "And I enjoyed the performance even more. It has taken me two years to save enough money to make a trip to America. I'm glad I was able to come for the festival. Valentin Ressu's music means a great deal to me. When he was alive, I spent many hours listening to it on the radio, studying it, recording it. My countrymen . . . will always be grateful for his concerts."

Her pulse quickened as a peculiar feeling drummed in her blood. "You listened to Valentin's music on the radio in Romania?"

He looked at her strangely. "Yes. On Radio Free Europe."

Suddenly she knew who this man was, even if he hadn't exactly identified himself. It was as if Valentin himself had told her. Her blood quickened as he met her gaze.

"Did the messages do any good?" she whispered.

The man's eyes widened a fraction before he caught himself. Then he smiled, a soft ghost of a smile. "Sometimes it does one good just to know there is a friend on the other side. Mr. Ressu was a very great man. I would have been extremely honored to meet him."

A lump formed in her throat. "I'm sure Valentin would have been honored to meet you, too."

Something passed between them, a look, a hint of acknowledgment. Then the man gave a little nod, turned, and walked away.

"Was he who I think he was?" Devin asked behind her, his voice quiet, almost awed.

"I believe so. Somebody had to have been taking down those messages and deciphering them."

Devin pressed the door closed, then drew her to him, engulfing her in his arms with a sigh. "You know, I'm beginning to think Ressu wasn't so bad a guy."

She chuckled into his shirt. "Oh, really? Even though he cheated on his wives and practically got us both killed?"

"Yeah, well, that wasn't too great. But I have to give him credit for fighting the good fight. And for one other thing."

"Oh, what's that?"

He clasped her chin, turning her face up to his. "Throwing you into my lap, honey. I can forgive him all the rest as long as I have you."

It was a very long time before they joined the reception.